COWBOY RESURRECTED

BY
ELLE JAMES

First published in Great Britain 2013
by Mills & Boon, an imprint of Harlequin (UK) Limited,
Eton House, 18-24 Paradise Road, Richmond, Surrey TW9 1SR

© Mary Jernigan 2013

ISBN: 978 0 263 90378 2
ebook ISBN: 978 1 472 00752 0

46-1013

Harlequin (UK) policy is to use papers that are natural, renewable and recyclable products and made from wood grown in sustainable forests. The logging and manufacturing processes conform to the legal environmental regulations of the country of origin.

Printed and bound in Spain
by Blackprint CPI, Barcelona

A Golden Heart Award winner for Best Paranormal Romance in 2004, **Elle James** started writing when her sister issued a Y2K challenge to write a romance novel. She has managed a full-time job and raised three wonderful children, and she and her husband even tried their hands at ranching exotic birds (ostriches, emus and rheas) in the Texas Hill Country. Ask her, and she'll tell you what it's like to go toe-to-toe with an angry three-hundred-and-fifty-pound bird! After leaving her successful career in information technology management, Elle is now pursuing her writing full-time. Elle loves to hear from fans. You can contact her at ellejames@earthlink.net or visit her website at www. ellejames.com.

This book is dedicated to my husband, whose love
and support helped clear my schedule to write!

Chapter One

Elena Sophia Carranza gunned the throttle to make it up the steep, rocky slope, doing her best to keep up with Hector. Thank God he'd taken the precious extra time to train her on how to ride a dirt bike in rough terrain. There was no more treacherous landscape than the border crossing between Mexico and the United States leading into the Big Bend National Park.

"You can do this, Señorita Elena, but you must be brave," Hector had insisted when they'd set off on their desperate escape. "Once we leave, we cannot return."

She'd known that from the start. Her ex-fiancé, Antonio, would not stop until he found her. And if he did catch her, there would be the devil to pay.

Squeezing Hector's hand, she'd whispered, "You must call me Sophia from now on. Elena no longer exists."

"Sí," he'd agreed before mounting his bike and taking off.

It was imperative Sophia commit to her goal, or she'd die. Others had risked too much to help her break out of the compound. Hector had risked his life and his future to get her this far. The least she could do was hold up her end by keeping pace with him, not going so slow as to put them both in jeopardy. They had come across the United

States border without being detected thus far. Now all they had to do was find help.

They'd splashed through the Rio Grande at a low-water crossing before dawn and headed into the canyons, zigzagging through the trails, climbing, dropping down into the shadows, heading north as far as they could before Antonio discovered their betrayal and came after them.

No matter what, Sophia couldn't go back. Even if she could withstand another day of physical and mental abuse, she refused to let the tiny life growing inside her suffer the same.

Escape seemed impossible from the far-reaching Mexican Mafia *la Familia Diablos.* As soon as Antonio realized she'd left, he'd send a gang of his *sicarios,* enforcers, to find and return her to Mexico or leave it for the Americans or the vultures to clean up her body.

As far as Sophia was concerned, she'd rather die and take her baby to heaven with her than subject another innocent life to the evil of Antonio Martinez and the drug cartel he called family.

Anna, her only friend in *la Fuerte del Diablo,* the Chihuahuan compound, had compromised her safety and that of her young son to get Sophia out. Sophia couldn't fail. Too many had risked too much.

Deep in the canyons of the far edges of Big Bend National Park, Sophia dared to hope she could evade Antonio and his band of killers long enough to find a place to hide, a place she could live her life in peace and raise her child.

Sophia had been born in Mexico, and her mother was an American citizen, ensuring Sophia had dual citizenship and could speak English fluently. Unfortunately, she no longer had her passport. Antonio had stripped her of identification after he'd lured her away from her family in Monterrey.

Once she found a safe haven, she'd do whatever it took

to reinstate her citizenship and ask for asylum. In exchange, she'd give the Americans any information they wanted on the whereabouts of Antonio's cartel stronghold on the Mexican side of the border. Not that it would do them much good. The Mexican government struggled to control their own citizens. What could the Americans do across the border?

Sophia knew that Antonio had contacts on the American side. High-powered, armed contacts that guaranteed safe passage of his people and products for distribution. Since the death of the former cartel boss, Xavier Salazar, Antonio had taken over, amassing a fortune in the illicit drug trade of cocaine, methamphetamines, heroin and marijuana. His power had grown tenfold, his arrogance exponentially, but he reported to a higher boss, a mysterious man not many of the cartel had actually seen. Rumor had it that he was an American of great influence. True or not, every time he visited, cartel members who'd betrayed *la Familia* were executed.

Sophia's only hope was to get far enough onto American soil and reach Hank Derringer. Anna said he would help her and protect her from Antonio. She'd said Señor Derringer was an honest, good man who had many connections on both sides of the border.

Her motorcycle hit a rock, jerking the handlebar sharply to her left. Sophia's arms ached with the constant struggle to keep the vehicle upright. She slowed, dropping farther behind Hector as they climbed yet another steep trail. They'd been traveling for hours, stopping to rest only once.

Her stomach rumbled, the nausea she'd fought hard to hide from Antonio surfacing, telling her she needed to eat or her body would set off a round of dry heaves that would leave her empty and weak.

When she thought she could take it no more, the beating sound of chopper rotors swept into the canyon, the roar bouncing off the vertical walls.

Adrenaline spiked through her, giving her the strength to continue on.

Ahead, Hector climbed a trail leading to the rim of the canyon.

Sophia shouted, wanting him to wait, seek cover and hide from the approaching aircraft. She feared Antonio had discovered her escape and sent his enforcers to find her and bring her back. He had the firepower and access to aircraft that would enable him to extract her from the canyon. Sophia had seen the airplanes and helicopters near the compound's landing field. Money truly could buy anything.

Hector cleared the top of the trail, then leaped over the edge and out of Sophia's sight. The helicopter pulled up out of the canyon headed straight for Hector.

Sophia prayed the aircraft was the bright green and white of the American border patrol. The setting sun cast the vehicle in shadow. When it moved close enough, Sophia gasped. The helicopter was the dull black of those she'd seen at *la Fuerte del Diablo*. Her daring escape had been discovered.

She skidded to a stop, hiding her bike beneath an overhang of rocks. Her entire body shaking, she killed the engine and waited, the shadows and the encroaching nightfall providing as much cover as she could hope to find until the helicopter moved on.

As the chopper passed over her without slowing, Sophia let out the breath she'd held, then gasped as sounds of gunfire ripped through the air.

Madre de Dios. Hector.

Her foot on the kick start, Sophia fought the urge to race to the top of the canyon rim to help Hector. Nausea held her back, reminding her she wasn't alone. The child inside her womb deserved a chance to live.

Sophia waited fifteen, twenty minutes, maybe more, for the helicopter to rise again into the sky, then realized it must have landed and the crew might be searching for her. She remained hidden for all those agonizing minutes, while the sun melted into the horizon. Storm clouds built to the west, catching the dying rays and staining the sky mauve, magenta, purple and gray.

When the helicopter finally lifted and circled back, Sophia pressed her body and the bike up against the canyon wall, sinking as far back into the darkest shadows as possible. The chopper hovered, moving slowly along the trail they'd just traveled, searching.

For her.

After what seemed like hours but was in fact only minutes, the aircraft moved on, traveling back the way it had come.

The smoky darkness of dusk edged deeper into the canyon, making the trail hard to find. Sophia eased her dirt bike out from the shadow of the overhang. Tired beyond anything she'd ever experienced, she managed to sling a stiff leg over the seat and cranked the engine with a hard kick on the starter. At first, the bike refused to start. On the fifth attempt, the engine growled to life. With a quick glance behind her, she was off, climbing the trail more slowly than she'd like in the limited light from encroaching nightfall.

At the rim of the canyon, her heart sank into her shoes.

The other motorcycle came into view first, lying on its side a couple hundred yards down the steep slope. Ahead on the trail lay the crumpled body of Hector, her ally, her only friend willing to help her out of a deadly situation.

She stopped beside Hector's inert form, dismounted and leaned over the man to check for a pulse.

The blood soaking into the ground told the tale, and the lack of a pulse confirmed it. Hector Garza was dead.

Sophia bent double as a sob rose up her throat. Tears flowed freely down her cheeks, dropping to the dry earth, where they were immediately absorbed in the dust.

Anna had sent Hector to guide her. Hector had been the one to encourage her along the way. He'd arranged to buy the bikes from a cousin in Juárez and had hidden them in a shed behind his brother's house in Paraíso.

The hopelessness of the situation threatened to overwhelm Sophia. The only thought that kept her going was that Anna and Hector would have wanted her to continue on. Sophia brushed away the tears and looked around, not sure which way to go. Instinct told her to head north. With only a compass to guide her, and the few provisions she'd loaded into her backpack, she was on her own. Alone and pregnant.

Afraid the helicopter would return, Sophia removed the rolled blanket tied to the back of Hector's bike and secured it to her backpack. She forced herself to climb back on the bike, the insides of her thighs and her bottom aching from the full day of riding and the strain of remaining seated on the motorcycle across the rough terrain.

She removed the compass from her pocket and clicked the button illuminating the dial. She set her course for north and took off across the desert, the night sky full of stars guiding her. With the threat of rain fast approaching, she increased her speed, refusing to give up when she'd come this far.

Before long, she came across a barbed-wire fence. If she hadn't seen the silhouettes of the fence posts standing straight and tall in a land of short, rounded and oddly shaped cacti, saw palmetto and sagebrush, she would have run right into the razor-sharp barbed wire.

Hector had armed her with wire cutters for just such an occasion. He'd warned her that the wire was stretched taut and not to get too close or, when she cut it, she'd be wrapped in the sharp barbs, unable to extricate herself without grave harm.

Sophia held her arm out as far as she could when she cut through the bottom strand. The wire snapped, retracting into a coil farther down the fence line.

She cut the other two strands and drove her bike through, exhaustion making her movements slow and sluggish. If she didn't find a place to hide soon, she'd drive off a bluff or wreck.

With only the stars and her compass to guide her, Sophia picked her way across the terrain, dodging vegetation not nearly large enough to hide a dirt bike or a woman, but large enough to cause serious damage should she hit it.

After the third near miss with prickly pear cacti, she finally spotted the square silhouette of a small building against the horizon. No lights gleamed from windows and no electricity poles rose up into the night sky, which might indicate life inside.

She aimed her bike for the dark structure, her body sagging over the gas tank, her hand barely able to push the throttle.

As she neared the building, she cut the engine and drifted to a stop, ditched the bike in the dirt and walked the remaining distance. She swung wide to check for inhabitants. Nothing stirred, nothing moved around the exterior. The building had a lean-to on the side and a pipe chimney. The place appeared deserted.

Sophia opened the door and peered inside. With the starlight shining through the doorway, she could see twin bed frames, no more than cots with thin mattresses rolled toward the head. A potbellied stove stood in one corner, and a plank table with benches on either side took up another corner.

Not the Four Seasons, but heaven in Sophia's tired eyes. She trudged back to where she'd left the bike, pushed it under the lean-to and stacked several old tires against it to hide it from view. With nothing more than what she carried in her backpack, she reentered the cabin.

The door had neither lock nor latch to secure it. Too spent to care, Sophia shook out a thin mattress, tossed her blanket over it, placed the pistol Hector had given her on the floor beside the cot and lay down.

She stared up at the dark ceiling, thinking of Hector and Anna and all they'd sacrificed to get her away from Antonio. One tear fell, followed by another. Sobs rose up her throat and she let them come, allowing her fear and sorrow a release. Tonight she could grieve. Tomorrow, before sunrise, her journey continued.

THORN DRENNAN HADN'T planned on being out this late, but he'd promised his boss, Hank Derringer, that while he awaited his first assignment as a special agent with Covert Cowboys, Inc., he'd check the Raging Bull Ranch fences for any breaks.

With the number of illegal aliens and drug runners still crossing the border from Mexico into the United States, any ranch owner this close to the border could count on mending his fences at least two or three times a week, sometimes more.

On horseback, it had taken Thorn far longer than he'd anticipated. The sun had set an hour ago, and he still hadn't completed a full inspection of the southern border of the massive ranch. He'd continued on, despite how tired he was, taking it slow so that he didn't overtax his mount.

Since the stars shone down, providing enough light to see the fence, Thorn didn't have a reason to return to the ranch sooner. He'd just climb into his truck and head to his little empty house in Wild Oak Canyon and lie awake all night anyway.

Sleep meant nightmares. The kind that wouldn't let him get on with his life—the kind that reminded him of all he'd lost.

Tonight was the second anniversary of the murder of his wife and their unborn daughter. He couldn't have gone home, even if he'd completed the inspection of the fence. And the bars didn't stay open all night.

His house was a cold, grim testament of what his career had cost him. He'd slept on the couch for the past two years, unable to sleep in the bed he'd shared with Kayla. He'd loved her since high school. They'd grown up together there in Wild Oak Canyon. She'd followed him across the country when he'd joined the FBI and back home when he'd given up the bureau to take on the role of county sheriff. He'd made the switch so that he would be home more often, and so he and Kayla could start the family they both wanted.

Their plan had gone according to schedule—until a bullet aimed at Thorn had taken Kayla's life and, with hers, that of their unborn child.

Thorn stared off into the distance. His horse, Little Joe, clumped along, probably tired and ready to head for the barn. So much had changed, and yet South Texas remained the same—big, dry and beautiful in its own way. Never had he known a place where you could see as many stars overhead. Kayla had loved lying out at night, staring up at the sky, picking out the constellations, insisting they teach their daughter all about the world and universe they lived in.

Thorn didn't know much about the cosmos other than what he'd read in magazines, but he knew how to find the Big Dipper and Orion's Belt because of Kayla. And because of Kayla, Thorn never failed to marvel at the immensity of the universe, much less the galaxies beyond their own solar system.

Tonight the vastness only made him realize just how alone he was.

Little Joe ground to a halt, jarring Thorn out of his morose thoughts, and just as well. Coiled in big, loose curls was a tangle of barbed wire where the fence had been cut.

Thorn cast a quick glance around to make sure whoever had cut the fence wasn't still lurking before he went to work mending the break. An hour later, fence mended, he stretched aching muscles. The moon had risen high above, near full, shedding enough light that it could have been daytime. The light wouldn't last long. Thunderclouds looming to the west would change that soon. He'd have to hurry if he wanted to get back to Hank's before the storm reached him.

In the dust at Thorn's feet, a single tire track, probably a motorcycle, led from the break in the fence into the ranch. At that moment, the wind wasn't blowing and the track remained intact. Thorn stowed his tools in his saddlebag and swung up into the saddle. Hank's sprawling ranch house lay in the general direction of the tracks. With the moonlight illuminating the trail, Thorn chose to follow the tracks and see where they led. Perhaps he'd catch up with the trespasser.

After thirty minutes of slow riding, dropping to the ground to double-check the direction and climbing back into the saddle, Thorn spotted what looked like an old hunting cabin ahead in the distance. The motorcycle tracks were on a collision course.

Thorn pulled his rifle out of the scabbard and checked to make sure it was loaded and ready. When he got close enough, he dropped down out of the saddle and left the reins hanging.

Thunder rumbled, and Little Joe tossed his head and whinnied.

The flash of lightning reminded Thorn that the storm would soon be on him, obliterating the moonlight and any chance of finding his way back to Hank's ranch house in the dark.

Thorn crept around the cabin, checking for any sign of life. He spotted the motorcycle buried beneath a couple of old tires. His pulse quickened.

The person who'd cut Hank's fence was inside the cabin.

Standing to the side of the door, Thorn balanced his rifle against his hip, grabbed the doorknob, shoved open the door and darted out of range.

An explosion erupted from inside the cabin and wood splintered from the door frame, bouncing off Thorn's face. He ducked low, rolled through the doorway and came up in a crouch, aiming his rifle in the direction from which the last bullet had come.

"Vaya, o disparo!" Another shot blasted a hole in the wall near Thorn's shoulder.

He threw himself forward in a somersault, coming up on his haunches. The rifle lay across the cot, pointed at the side of the shooter's head.

"Por favor, no disparar!" a shaky female voice called out. "Don't shoot!" Slim hands rose above the other side of the cot.

"¿Hablas Inglés?" Thorn asked.

"Sí. Yes. I speak English. Please, don't shoot."

"Place your weapon on the floor and push it toward the door."

The thunk of metal hitting wood was followed by the rasp of it sliding across the floor.

Thorn hooked the gun with a foot and slid it toward himself. "Now you. Stand and walk toward the door."

She hesitated. "Do you promise not to shoot?"

"I'm not going to shoot, as long as you don't do something stupid."

A slim figure emerged from the shadows, rising above the cot. Long, straight hair hung down around her shoulders, swaying slightly as she moved toward the door, picking her way carefully. For a second, she stood silhouetted in the light filtering in from the moon, the curve of her hips and breasts in sharp contrast to her narrow waist.

She glanced toward him, moonlight glinting off her eyes.

Thorn stared, transfixed.

Then, before he could guess her intentions, she flung herself outside, slamming the door shut behind her.

Thorn shot to his feet, ripped the door open and ran outside. He turned left, thinking she'd go for the motorcycle under the lean-to.

Just as he rounded the corner of the house, he realized his mistake.

Little Joe whinnied, then galloped by with the woman on him.

Thorn tore out after them, catching up before Little Joe could get up to speed.

He grabbed the woman around the waist and yanked her out of the saddle, the force of her weight sending them both to the ground.

The wind knocked out of him, Thorn held on to his prize, refusing to let go, a dozen questions spinning through his mind. Who was she? What was she doing on the Raging Bull? And why did her soft curves feel so good against his body?

Chapter Two

When Sophia landed on the man, the fall forced the air from her lungs. She lay there for a moment, gathering her wits and her breath. Then she fought to free herself of the steel vise clinched around her waist. "Let go of me." She scratched and clawed at his arm.

"No way," the deep voice said into her ear, his breath stirring the hairs at the back of her neck. "You almost killed me twice and tried to steal my horse."

She jabbed her elbow into his gut and jerked to the side.

The man grunted and refused to loosen his grip.

Lightning flickered across the sky and a crash of thunder sounded so close, Sophia stopped fighting for a second.

The horse, standing a few feet away, reared and took off, probably racing for the barn as the sky lit again, this time with a thousand fingers of lightning.

Wind whipped Sophia's hair into her eyes, and the first drops of rain peppered her skin.

The cowboy gripped her wrist and rolled her off him onto her stomach.

He came down on top of her, straddling her hips, his pressing into the small of her back. "I'll let you up if you promise to behave."

She snorted and spit to the side. "And I should trust you?"

He chuckled. "You don't have much of a choice."

Sophia squirmed beneath him, trying to free her wrist from his ironlike grasp. "Let go. I'll leave and you will never see me again."

Thunder boomed so loud it shook the ground.

"Sorry, sweetheart, you're not going anywhere in this storm."

As if to emphasize her captor's point, the water droplets grew thicker, the wind blasting them against her skin.

The dry dust kicked up, stinging her eyes and choking her breath. "Okay." She coughed. "I'll behave."

The man's weight left her body and he jerked her to her feet.

As soon as she stood, the storm unleashed its full power in a deluge so thick she couldn't see her hand in front of her face.

"Get in the cabin!" her captor yelled over the roar.

Water streamed down her face, blinding her.

A shove from behind sent her stumbling toward the open door. Her heart hammered against her ribs; fear of the storm nothing compared to fear of being trapped with this strong, dangerous stranger inside the small confines of the cabin.

He stepped around her and dragged her along behind him.

Sophia planted her heels in the mud and jerked hard.

The rain allowed her to slip free of his grip, but she hadn't accounted for how easily. She teetered backward and landed hard on the ground, mud sluicing over her clothes, soaking her all the way to her skin.

The cowboy stood in the doorway, his arms crossed over his chest. "If you're not struck by lightning, the flash floods will get you!" he yelled.

"I'll take my chances." Sophia scrambled to her feet, slipped, almost fell and steadied herself.

The cowboy's lips quirked, and he shook his head. "Stubborn woman."

Sophia's chin tipped upward. Before she could think of a scathing reply, the cowboy moved, leaving the protection of the cabin to scoop her up. He tossed her over his shoulder like a sack of onions and spun back toward the cabin.

The wind again knocked out of her, Sophia bounced along with every one of his huge steps until they entered the cabin.

The brute of a man kicked the door shut behind him and set Sophia on her feet in the dark.

The temperature had plummeted with the rainfall, cooling her body. She shook, her teeth clattering against each other. "Don't try anything or I'll...I'll..." She strained her eyes to search the room for a weapon, the darkness hampering her efforts and only flashes of lightning giving limited relief.

Finally she straightened, holding her head high, not that he could see her. She'd come too far to fall victim to yet another man who wanted to use her. Sophia dropped her tone to one she hoped sounded tough and menacing. "I'll kill you." Too bad a shiver shook her as she said the words, making them sound weak and quivery.

"Sweetheart, I have no intention of 'trying' anything with you. You look like a drowned rat and you're covered in mud. You're about as appealing as a pig. Less so. I could at least eat a pig." He shuffled around the cabin, bumping into things.

Sophia stood close to the door, debating how to make her escape. The bellow of thunder and the rain pounding the roof intensified, making her think again.

Something rattled to her left, then a scraping sound

rasped in the darkness and a match flared. The cowboy held it up and stared at the potbellied stove. "Here, make yourself useful." He handed her a box of matches. "Light one."

She took the box from him as the match he held flickered out. Hands shaking, she removed a match from the box and scraped it on the side. The blaze from the match circled her and the cowboy in an intimate glow.

He grabbed a candle from the mantel and held it to the match, then stuck it in a tin holder. "That will do for a start, but it's cold, we're wet and we'll need a fire or we'll have a really bad night of it." He lifted the lid off a box beside the stove and grunted. "Nice." Several logs lay in the bottom, along with old newspapers. "Hank knows how to stock a cabin," he muttered as he lifted the logs out and stacked them in the stove.

Sophia's heart skipped several beats. "Hank?"

The man wadded up newspaper and jammed it beneath the logs before responding. "Yeah, you're trespassing on the Raging Bull Ranch. I take it you were the one to cut the fence?" He shot a narrowed glance behind him. "Illegal alien?"

She refused to be intimidated by his glare. "I am an American citizen."

"Even American citizens don't have the right to destroy other people's property or trespass. You can take it up with the law in the morning."

Could it be she'd found her way to Hank Derringer's land? Hope rose inside her. "I'd rather take it up with this man Hank."

The cowboy shrugged. "Suit yourself, lady. I don't care." He held out his hand. "I'll take those matches now."

She handed him the box and stood back.

He got the paper burning and the dry wood caught soon

after, crackling and popping. He left the door to the stove open, the blaze lighting the interior of the tiny cabin in a soft, cozy glow.

The heat didn't extend beyond a few feet from the stove.

Still leery about the cowboy's intentions, Sophia remained outside his reach, her arms clutched around her body, her teeth chattering.

The big man stood, holding his hands to the fire. "Sure is warm over here." He cast a glance at her and shook his head. "Good grief, woman, you're freezing. Get closer before you catch your death."

"I'm f-fine," she insisted, her gaze on the flames, mesmerized by the thought of warmth.

The cowboy unbuttoned his soaked shirt and peeled it off his shoulders.

Sophia gasped and backed even farther away until the backs of her knees ran into the side of the bed and she almost fell. "What are you doing?"

"Getting out of my wet clothes. I don't plan on freezing all night." He scooped her backpack off the floor and opened it. "Do you have any dry clothes in here?"

She darted forward and snatched at the backpack. "That's mine."

He held on to the strap, his eyes narrowing. "Seeing as we have to share this cabin for a night, I'd like to know you're not hiding a knife or another gun in here that you plan on using on me in my sleep." He peeled her fingers off the other strap and dumped the contents of the backpack on the closest of the twin beds.

Foil-wrapped tortillas, a can of *frijoles pinto* and two bottles of water fell out on the bed. Enough food for two people for a single day. Beside them, a flashlight, fifty dollars of American money and one extra T-shirt was all she had to her name.

"Not much to go cross-country on."

"I was backpacking in the canyon. I didn't plan on staying," she lied.

He dug in one of the side pockets of the backpack and brought out the wire cutters. "Something you carry on hikes?"

She shrugged. "A girl never knows what tools she'll need."

"Anyone ever tell you it's not safe to travel alone in this area? Especially if you're a woman."

Sophia swallowed hard on the lump forming in her throat. She hadn't planned on traveling alone. Hector was to guide and protect her until she found Hank Derringer. Now Hector lay dead back in the canyon. With no one to help her, she had to rely on herself. She lifted her chin. "I don't need a man to protect me." Especially one who wanted to control her and keep her locked away from the world.

"Glad to know that. I didn't plan on signing up for the job." He lifted the blanket she'd tossed on the bed earlier. "Since you have a dry T-shirt, I'll use the blanket until my jeans dry." He nodded toward the bed and the pile of supplies. "Get out of your wet clothes. Getting sick will do you no good." He reached for the button on his jeans.

Sophia's eyes widened and her breath caught in her throat. "What are you doing?"

He shook his head and spoke slowly, as if to a dense child. "I told you, I'm getting out of my wet clothes. You can watch…or not." He flicked the button open and ran the zipper down in one fluid movement.

Sophia gasped and spun away from him. "I don't even know you."

"It's not like I'm going to make love to you. I prefer my women willing, dry and preferably not covered in mud."

"All the more reason to remain in my wet clothing."

"Suit yourself." He tossed the jeans over a chair beside her. "If it'll help, I'll turn my back while you strip out of those muddy things. I might even be convinced to take them out in the rain and rinse them for you so that you'll have something semiclean to wear in the morning."

She did feel gritty and cold. The dirt she could handle, but the cold couldn't be good for her baby. "Fine." She turned toward him, happy to note he'd wrapped his naked body in the blanket. "Turn around."

She'd been raised in Monterrey by her Mexican father and her American mother, but the proprieties of life in Mexico demanded she didn't strip naked in front of a stranger.

Granted, proprieties had gone by the wayside when she'd chosen to move in with Antonio, despite her parents' objections. They'd begged her to wait until she had the ring on her finger before committing to such a drastic move. But Antonio had been eager to have her to himself, and Sophia had been young and stupid in love.

"Look, I'll turn my back," the man said. "But you have to promise not to stab me in it while I do."

Sophia snorted. "I don't have a knife, and you took my gun."

THORN KEPT HIS back to her, watching her movements through his peripheral vision and the movement of her shadow.

She eased along the wall toward the stove, wary of him and as skittish as a wild cat. If she didn't get out of the muddy clothes, they wouldn't dry by morning and she'd possibly get sick or suffer hypothermia from being cold all night.

Thorn didn't relish the idea of hauling a sick woman

back to the ranch. Especially if they were going to have to ride double on the motorcycle she'd hidden beneath the lean-to.

"Since we'll be sharing this cabin until the storm abates, it might help to know your name. I'm Thorn Drennan."

She didn't answer for a long time.

When he turned to see if she'd somehow slipped by him and left, his chest tightened.

The woman had shed her wet, dirty clothing and was slipping the dry T-shirt over her head and down her body.

Silhouetted against the fireplace, her curves were all woman and deliciously alluring.

A shock of desire ripped through him, and he closed his eyes to the image.

He hadn't felt anything for another woman since Kayla had died two years ago. Trapped in a cabin with a stranger, he wasn't prepared for the heat burning through his veins.

The woman turned toward him, her eyes narrowing. "You said you'd keep your back turned," she whispered accusingly.

"You didn't answer. I thought you might have bolted for the door."

"As you said, I'd be foolish to make a run for it in this storm."

He nodded. "You didn't answer my question."

She shrugged. "My name is not important. But you can call me…Sophia." The woman hesitated over the name, as if she wasn't used to giving it or using it.

Thorn didn't believe that it was her real name. But then, why would she keep her name from him unless she had something to hide?

Already uncomfortable with the situation, and not sure she wouldn't stab him in the back, Thorn carried her gun and his rifle to the door and laid them within reach.

"I'll take those clothes," he said.

Sophia gathered her dirty jeans and shirt and handed them to Thorn. Their fingers brushed, causing a jolt of electricity to shoot up his arm.

She must have felt it, too, because her eyes widened and her lips opened in a soft gasp.

Thorn brushed his reaction aside, blaming it on supercharged air from the lightning storm. He flung the door open, welcoming the cold rain that blew in with the fury of the storm.

With the blanket tied around his waist, he figured he'd get soaked no matter what. He held Sophia's clothes under the eaves, letting the rush of rainwater pour over the garments. When they were sufficiently free of mud, he wrung them out and closed the door.

Sophia moved another chair by the stove and hung her jeans across the back, then laid her shirt on the wooden seat. When done, she held her hands to the flames, her face pale, her jaw tight and determined.

Thorn scooped the gun she'd used to shoot at him off the floor and tucked it into the folds of the blanket around his waist. He leaned his rifle against the wall beside one of the two beds.

Sophia's gaze followed his movements, her brows knitted and her arms wrapped tightly around her middle.

Thorn liked that he made her nervous. She might be less tempted to take another stab at killing him if she was intimidated.

"Are you going to take me to the police in the morning?" she asked.

"I haven't decided." He crossed his arms over his chest, his brows raised. "Are you going to convince me not to?"

Sophia shrugged. "You have made up your mind already. Why bother trying?"

His eyes narrowed. "If you really are an American citizen, where are you from?"

She glanced to the far corner.

Thorn could almost see the cogs turning in her brain.

Finally she faced him, her brows raised. "San Antonio. *Sí,* I am from San Antonio."

"Vacationing in Big Bend, huh?" He raised a hand to his chin and stared down his nose at her. "I'm familiar with San Antonio. What section of town?"

Her eyes flared, then closed. She turned her back to him. "The north side."

"Ah, you must prefer shopping at Ingram Park Mall since it's closest to you, right?"

Her shoulders were stiff, and she remained with her back to him. "Right. Ingram."

Thorn's teeth ground together. If she really lived on the north side of San Antonio, the closest mall was not Ingram. She didn't know San Antonio any more than she knew where she was at the moment.

She dragged in a deep breath, her shoulders rising and falling with it. "What now?"

Thorn opened his mouth to call her out on her lie, but stopped when he noticed the dark shadows beneath her eyes and what appeared to be the yellowing remnants of a bruise across her cheek. He'd get the truth out of her, but it could wait until they both got a little rest. "Now we sleep."

He unfolded the second bed's mattress and stretched across it, laying the pistol beside him and lacing his hands behind his head. "You look done in. I suggest you get some shut-eye."

Her gaze swept over his naked chest, and lower. She hesitated, her tongue sweeping out across her lower lip.

The brief appearance of her pink tongue stirred a heated response low in Thorn's belly. Damn. What was wrong with him? He'd loved Kayla more than life itself. Why was his body reacting so strongly to this woman? Was it the vulnerability in her green eyes, or that she'd tried so determinedly to escape him that appealed to him on a deeper level? Whatever it was, he'd be glad when he handed her off to the authorities tomorrow. He closed his eyes to her image bathed in the glow of the fire in the stove. "I'm not going to sleep until you do, so move it."

"I'm not sleepy."

He opened his eyes. "Too bad."

Her glance darted from him to the bed beside his. "I have enough food for two people. Unfortunately, I don't have a way to open the cans. Hector—" Her lips clamped shut, and her face paled even more.

"Hector?" Thorn's eyes narrowed. He was up off the bed in a second. "You were traveling with someone else." He closed the distance between the two of them. "Weren't you?" Thorn gripped her shoulders, his fingers digging into her shirt.

Sophia, eyes wide as saucers, shook her head back and forth, tears spilling from the corners. "N-no. I was alone." She cowered, her eyes squinting, ducking her head as if expecting a blow.

"You're lying." He shook her. "Where is he?"

She gulped, the muscles in her throat working convulsively. "I don't know what you're talking about."

With her body close to his, her arms warm beneath his fingers, heat surged, followed by anger. "Damn it, woman, I'm tired of playing twenty questions. Spit it out. Where is this Hector? Do I have to stay awake all night in case he comes in and tries to kill me, too?"

"No!" Sobs shook her slight frame and her head tipped forward, her damp hair falling over her face. *"Madre de Dios."* She crossed herself. "He is dead."

The words came out in a whisper. Thorn thought he'd heard it wrong. He bent closer. "What did you say?"

A sob ripped from her throat and her head fell back, tears running like raindrops down her cheeks. "He's dead. They shot him. He tried to help me, and now he's dead! And it's my fault."

Chapter Three

Sophia swallowed hard, realizing her mistake as soon as the words left her mouth.

"Who shot him?" Thorn shook her. Not hard enough to hurt her, but enough to wrench another sob from her throat.

She looked away, the memory of Hector lying in a pool of his own blood far too fresh to erase. "I don't know." She choked back another sob, reminding herself that she couldn't cry forever. After all the time she'd spent as a captive in the compound, she'd learned one thing: crying didn't solve anything. What would it hurt to tell this man a few details? "Someone in a helicopter fired a machine gun at Hector."

His brows rose into the lock of hair drooping over his forehead. "A machine gun?"

Sophia nodded.

"Where is Hector now?" Thorn demanded.

"We were in the canyon. Hector had topped the ridge when the helicopter flew in. I h-hid beneath an overhang." She looked at him through her tears. "I should have helped."

"Against a helicopter?" Thorn's lips pressed together. "Not much you could do on your own unless you had a rocket launcher." He tipped his head to the side. "Question is, why did a helicopter fire on you and your friend

Hector if you were only out hiking in Big Bend country?" Thorn's eyes narrowed. "Now would be a good time to tell me the truth." He dropped his hold and crossed his arms. He waited a few seconds. "Neither one of us is going anywhere until you do."

She glanced toward the door. Thunder rumbled, rattling the doorknob. "I told you, we were hiking."

His lips thinned, and he shook his head. "I'm not buying it. There's a motorcycle in the lean-to that wasn't there a day ago. I'm betting you rode in on it."

She stared up at him, her mouth working, but nothing came out.

"Which brings me back to my original theory. You're an illegal alien."

"I'm not. My mother *is* American and, though I was born in Mexico, I have dual citizenship."

He held out his hand. "Then you won't mind showing me your passport."

She stared at his hand, her throat muscles working at swallowing the lump lodged in her windpipe. "I don't have it on me."

"Thought so. No documents, riding a bike across the desert near the border, helicopter in pursuit." He snorted. "You are definitely an illegal and possibly dangerous."

"Think what you will." She tossed back her long light brown hair. "Tomorrow I'll be away from here, and you won't have to worry about me."

"I wouldn't count on that."

She frowned. "Count on what?"

"That you'll be gone, or that I wouldn't worry about you. I've kinda taken a liking to you. Must have been the fall." He raised his hand to the back of his head.

"I'm sorry to say I have not taken a liking to you, *señor,*" she said, tipping her chin upward.

"Really?" Thorn leaned close, his eyes narrowing even more. He stared at her long enough to make her squirm.

Then he tilted his head back and laughed out loud. "You are entirely too naive and predictable, Sophia."

She harrumphed, clasping her arms around her body. "I'm happy you find me amusing."

Lightning flashed, sending shards of light through cracks in the boarded windows, followed by a deafening clap of thunder.

Sophia jumped, bumping into Thorn's naked chest. She raised a hand to steady herself and encountered smooth, hard muscles. Heat suffused her entire body. She might not like the man, but she couldn't help admiring his physique. She told herself it was nothing more than appreciation for a fine form.

Her belly rumbled loudly, reminding her that she needed to eat or risk dry heaves. And preparing food would allow her to put distance between herself and Thorn. She nodded toward the food on the bed. "I'm hungry."

"So you said." He reached out.

Sophia flinched, raising her hand to block his as she ducked.

Thorn's frown deepened. "Did you think I'd hit you?"

Sophia straightened, her body tense. "You wouldn't be the first man."

He continued to reach past her. Plucking a metal object from a shelf on the wall, he held it up. "I was reaching for the can opener." Thorn tossed the device on the bed and turned to grip her arms. "For the record, I don't hit women."

She planted her feet wide, her eyes narrowing to slits. "No? But you grab them and hold them hostage."

"Damn it, woman. For your own good."

"And how is being a captive good?" She snorted.

"You're like most men, thinking a woman must be controlled, that she doesn't have a brain to think for herself."

"You're putting words in my mouth." His hands fell to his sides. "Given that you could have died with your friend Hector and might have been caught in a flash flood or struck by lightning, I think I can prove my case for keeping you here."

She shrugged and ducked around him. "I don't care what you prove." Sophia grabbed the can opener and set it against the lid on the can of beans. After several attempts, she gave up, her stomach twisting, the hollow feeling making her nauseous.

"Good grief, woman." Thorn took the can and opener out of her hands. "It's not rocket science."

"No? Then you do it." She backed away from him, the nausea increasing until heat radiated through her body and she knew she couldn't hold back any longer. Sophia ran for the door, her footsteps drowned out by the pounding of rain on the tin roof. Her hand closed around the knob as the first wave hit.

Before she could yank the door open, a hand closed over hers. "Going somewhere, sweetheart?" Thorn asked, staring down at her, his brows drawn together in a fierce frown. "I thought we'd settled all this running away stuff, at least until after the storm."

She clawed at his hand. "Please." Sophia swallowed again and again, trying to force the bile back. "I have to get out."

He moved to stand in front of her, his arms locked over his chest like a barroom bouncer. "No."

"So be it." She heaved. What remained of the food she'd eaten the night before rose like a projectile up her throat. She bent in time to miss Thorn's face, but anointed his bare feet.

The heaving continued until Sophia's body shook so badly she fell to her knees on the hard wooden floor.

She cowered, waiting for Thorn to curse her and call her stupid for barfing on his feet. Sophia braced her body for the beating that was sure to follow.

The harsh words and beatings never came.

When the wave of sickness abated, she lay down on the floor, pressing her heated cheek to the cool wood.

Thorn crouched beside her, brushing her hair away from her face. "I'm sorry. Had I known you were sick—"

Thorn's voice washed over Sophia like a warm blanket. She lay with her eyes closed, one hand pressed to her mouth, the other to her belly, afraid to move and set off the nausea all over again. "I'll be okay. I just need to eat."

"You can't lie there on the floor." He touched her arm. "Let me help you to the bed."

"No." She brushed away his hand. "Leave me alone. It'll pass." After several minutes, her head quit spinning and she dared to open her eyes. "I'm sorry I threw up on you."

"I'll live." His frown had softened to an expression of concern. "Think you can move now?"

She nodded, lying there for a moment longer before attempting the simple task.

"I'm going to clean up this mess." Thorn moved about the cabin, the soft rustles giving away his location and negating the need for Sophia to look.

Before she could brace her hands on the floor and push herself to a sitting position, Thorn's strong fingers scooped beneath her legs and back, and he lifted her up in his arms in one smooth, easy motion.

Sophia closed her eyes, praying her stomach wouldn't churn and release again. "Please, put me down."

"I will." He crossed to the mattress he'd unfolded for

himself and laid her out on a blanket. "I found another blanket in a box."

With the back of her hand resting over her eyes, she breathed in and out several times, her mouth tasting so bad she feared she'd lose it again.

The snap of metal on metal made her glance across at Thorn.

With deft fingers, he had the can of beans open in a few quick twists of the can-opener key.

Sophia's lips tipped upward. "How is it you say…show-off."

"I never learned how to cook, so I had to get good at eating canned food or starve."

She smiled.

THORN'S HEART TUMBLED and came to a crashing stop.

Despite her pale face and slightly green complexion, her smile managed to light up the room, chasing away Thorn's natural distrust of the woman who'd done nothing but lie to him the entire time they'd been together. Something about her sad eyes and her inherent vulnerability called to his protective instincts. He still held the can, and his heart pounded against his ribs.

Sophia's smile faded. "You're staring at me."

He spun away, wondering what the hell had come over him. He rummaged in the wooden box where he'd found the blanket and emerged with a pot. He emptied the can of beans into the pot and set it on the potbellied stove. Then, using a stick from the box of wood, he stirred the embers inside the stove, making them glow brighter. Heat warmed his cheeks.

The bedsprings creaked behind him.

Sophia had pushed to a sitting position and was reaching for the foil-wrapped package on the other bed.

Thorn got to it before she did and unwrapped several soft tortillas. "Is this what you were going for?"

She nodded and peeled one off the top. Sitting with her legs pulled up beneath her, she nibbled on the corn tortilla, color slowly returning to her cheeks.

"How long has it been since you've eaten?" he asked.

She refused to meet his gaze. "I don't remember."

"And you were out for a hike on motorbikes." Thorn stared at her for a long time. "Still not talking?"

She finished the tortilla and nodded toward the stove. "You're burning the beans."

Thorn spun back to the stove and rescued the boiling beans. He scrounged up two tin plates and spoons from the storage box, held them under the eaves by the door to rinse them off and scooped beans onto each damp plate.

Sophia accepted the plate without complaint and dug her spoon into the fragrant beans, eating every bite.

Thorn sat back, his own plate forgotten. "How can you eat like that after being sick?"

She accepted another tortilla and sopped up the remaining juices from her plate. She finished the tortilla before answering. "I get sick if I don't eat."

"Are you anemic or something?"

"Something." Sophia set the plate on the floor, stretched out on the mattress and pulled the blanket over herself, closing her eyes.

"That's it?" Thorn asked.

"I'm working on, what did you call it? Shut-eye." Her eyes remained closed.

The fire burned down into glowing coals, heat from the stove filling the small space, making it cozy and comfortable despite the storm outside.

Thorn ate the beans on his plate, and then rinsed the pot and both plates and spoons in rainwater. Once he'd returned the eating utensils to the box, he cleared her back-pack off the remaining bed, gathered the handgun and rifle beside him and settled on his side, facing Sophia. In the fading light from the fire, he studied the stranger. Her Spanish accent led him to believe she'd spent the major-ity of her life south of the United States border, but her grasp of English made him want to believe her story that her mother was American.

Her dark blond hair and pale skin could mean either her mother was American, as she'd insisted, or she could be Mexican of Spanish decent.

Sophia's chest rose and fell in a deep, steady rhythm, her eyelids twitching as if her dreams were not all that pleasant.

What was she afraid of? Why wasn't she telling him the truth about her presence on the Raging Bull? Who had hit her to make her so skittish?

The more he reflected on Sophia and her possible rea-sons for being in the cabin, the more questions Thorn came up with. Finally, exhaustion pulled at his own eyelids, dragging them downward.

His final thought of the woman beside him was one that left him frowning into his dreams. She'd stirred in him a spark of awareness he hadn't felt since Kayla had died in his arms. And worse, he didn't understand the desire he felt inside to protect her from whatever she was running from.

Hiking in the mountains. *Not likely.*

With one hand on the rifle, the pistol tucked beneath him, he drifted into a fitful sleep, the storm outside rag-ing well into the early hours of the morning. His dreams were filled with the horror of the shooting that had taken his wife and unborn child, the nightmare of holding Kayla in his arms as she bled out. He'd held her so long that the

EMTs had to remind him where he was and that he couldn't stay in the middle of the street. He had to let go and get up.

"Get up!" a voice said into his ear. A hand grabbed his arm and shook him.

At first Thorn thought it was the EMT telling him they had to load his wife's body. As he swam to the surface of consciousness, he remembered his wife had been dead for two years. The hand moved from his shoulder, and something tugged in his fingers.

Thorn sat up and grabbed the hand trying to pry the rifle from his fingers. "Let go, or I'll shoot you," he said, pointing the pistol at his attacker.

Sophia raised her hands and backed up a step. She wore the jeans and shirt she'd spread out earlier to dry, and her gaze flicked to the door of the cabin, her eyes wide and filled with terror. "Please, don't let them take me back."

Thorn frowned. "What are you talking about?"

"Someone is outside. It might be the men who shot Hector." Sophia tugged at his arm. "Get up. Hurry."

As the fog of sleep cleared, Thorn realized the rain had stopped and, with it, the lightning. But what he'd thought was thunder was the rumble of an engine, like that of a heavy-duty diesel truck.

He jammed his legs into his jeans and boots, grabbed his rifle and reached for the doorknob. Before he could open the door, it was flung wide, slamming against the wall.

A towering figure filled the frame, backlit by the headlights of a truck standing a few feet behind him, engine running. From his silhouette, he appeared to hold an assault rifle.

His heart racing, Thorn raised his weapon and aimed for the middle of the man's chest. "Not a step farther."

The man froze in the doorway.

A voice behind the man in the door called out, "Thorn? Is that you?"

Thorn stared past the man with the assault rifle, his hand steady on his own gun. "Hank?"

The older man pushed past his bodyguard and held up his hands. "You gonna put that rifle down or shoot me?"

Thorn lowered the weapon, ran a hand through his hair and stared out into the darkness. "What are you doing here at this hour?"

"Thought you might need rescuing. When your horse came back without you on it, I sent out a search party, figuring you got thrown or bushwhacked." His gaze swung to the woman cowering in the corner by the potbellied stove. "Ah, you have company."

"Sorry to get you and your men out in that weather. The storm scared my mount, and he took off without me." Thorn turned toward Sophia. "I took shelter in this cabin, only to discover a squatter beat me to it." He waved toward Sophia. "Hank, this is Sophia. Sophia, this is Hank Derringer, the owner of the property you're trespassing on."

Before Thorn's last word left his lips, Sophia flung herself at Hank.

Hank staggered backward, his arms going around Sophia to steady them both.

The bodyguard reached for Sophia's arm.

"It's okay," Hank said. "She's not hurting me. Sophia, this is Max. Max, Sophia. There. You've been properly introduced."

Sophia buried her face in Hank's shirt, silent sobs shaking her body. "It is a miracle," she whispered, then her body went limp and she would have fallen to the floor if Hank hadn't had his arms around her.

Thorn stood by, his hands aching to go to Sophia's rescue, but he forced himself to stand back.

Hank stared over the top of the unconscious woman's head. "What the devil is going on here?"

Chapter Four

Thorn shook his head. "It's like I said, she was here when I got here." He explained about the damaged fence, the tracks leading toward the cabin, Sophia's wild story about hiking in the canyon and her guide being gunned down by a helicopter.

The whole time he'd been talking, Sophia lay limp in Hank's arms.

"Here, let me get her." Finally Thorn could stand it no longer and stepped forward, gathered Sophia into his arms and carried her to the bed. He stretched her across the blanket and tucked the ends around her. Her face was very pale in the light from the truck slanting through the door frame.

"If someone shot her guide, it might not be safe for her to stay out here," Hank said. "They might come back to take care of witnesses. We should get her back to the ranch house as soon as possible."

"Agreed."

"Max," Hank called out. "Check the perimeter."

Max nodded wordlessly and ducked out of the beams of the headlights.

Hank unclipped a radio hanging on his belt. "I'll let my foreman and security team know we've found you and to head back to base."

Thorn lifted his still-damp shirt from the back of the chair and shoved his arms into the sleeves.

Hank keyed the button on his handheld radio. "Scott."

Scott Walden, Hank's foreman, responded immediately. "Walden here."

"Found him. Notify the team, and let them know to head back to base."

"Will do," the voice crackled along with static over the radio.

"And be on the lookout for gunmen," Hank warned.

"Run into trouble?" Scott asked.

"Not yet." Hank stared at the woman lying unconscious in the bed. "But we could." When he'd finished, Hank nodded his head toward Sophia. "You got her?"

Thorn nodded. "If you can get the truck door."

"Got it." Hank exited, hurrying toward the passenger side of the waiting truck.

Outside the cabin, the air had a damp, rain-washed scent that stirred up all the differing aromas from the vegetation surrounding them. The dark sky of early morning sported an array of stars like a blanket of diamonds on black velvet from horizon to horizon.

Hank held the back door to the four-door pickup open while Thorn settled Sophia across the leather seat and climbed in beside her. He rested her head on his lap and buckled the seat belt around her middle.

Hank took the wheel while Max climbed into the front passenger seat, his M4A1 carbine assault rifle across his lap, his gaze scanning the horizon on all sides.

As Hank pulled away from the cabin, Sophia stirred, her head pressing against Thorn's jean-clad thigh. "Where… What happened?" She blinked up at him. "Hank." She tried to sit up but the vehicle bounced at that moment, keeping her from rising.

Thorn looped his arm around her to keep her from tipping forward. "You're in Hank's truck, headed for his ranch."

"Madre de Dios." She made the sign of the cross over her chest.

"Now that you're awake, you can tell me why you threw yourself at my boss." Thorn's lips pressed into a tight line. Sophia had given him so little information, he felt he was missing a big part of her story that could cause potential danger to all those around him.

"I was told he could help me." She laid her hand over her eyes, a sigh escaping her lips. "He is my only hope."

Hank glanced at Thorn in the rearview mirror. "Only hope for what?"

Sophia attempted to sit up again, this time succeeding. "To protect me from the man who would take me back to Mexico and imprison me."

"Why would someone imprison you? Have you committed a crime?" Hank asked.

"Only the crime of stupidity," Sophia responded. "Of trusting someone who promised to love me."

"And that would be?" Thorn asked.

"My fiancé."

Max snorted. "Nice guy."

Thorn's fingers tightened into fists. "What kind of man would imprison his fiancée?"

Sophia's face was pale and grave in the light from the dash. "Mine."

A loud metal pop sounded against the side of the truck.

"Gunshot!" Thorn shouted, and pushed Sophia's head back into his lap. "Stay down."

Hank punched the accelerator, shooting the truck forward. He swerved to miss a dwarf mesquite tree, ran over a clump of prickly pear cactus and raced on across the dark terrain at breakneck speed.

Max flicked the safety off his rifle, hit the down button on the window and swiveled in his seat. "They're coming at us from both sides." He fired off a burst of rounds.

Thorn ducked his head and turned right and left. "Two motorcycles on the near left. Three on the right from what I can see."

Max swung around, rising to his knees on the seat to get a better shot out the window, and sent another burst of rounds into the darkness.

Thorn struggled with Sophia to keep her low while trying to swivel against the restraint of his seat belt.

The windshield behind him exploded, showering him and Sophia with splinters of glass. "Don't move!" he shouted to Sophia.

Thorn punched the release on his seat belt and rotated in his seat, bringing his weapon to his shoulder. With the barrel of the rifle, he cleared the jagged edges of the fractured glass out of the way and aimed out the window. Without the headlights from the truck, he had to let his vision adjust to the near inky blackness before he could see the gang of dirt bikers closing in on the truck. He lined up his sights the best he could with the truck bouncing over every dip, rock and clump of vegetation. With a cyclist caught in the crosshairs, he squeezed the trigger.

The dirt bike swerved and flipped, sending its rider over the handlebars.

One down, nineteen to go.

A bullet winged past his ear. The bodyguard cursed behind him.

"Max," Hank called out. "You hit?"

"No, but it was close," the man said, his voice strained. "Punch it, they're gaining on us."

Another bullet nicked the broken glass of the wind-shield and scraped Thorn's shoulder before lodging in the back of Max's seat.

Thorn hissed, biting down hard on his tongue to keep from saying anything. For a moment, his rifle wobbled and almost fell from its position. Forcing the burning pain of the wound to the back of his mind, he focused on his targets.

Hank hit the gas and the truck leaped forward, pushing past their attackers.

Thorn prayed they'd get to the ranch compound before the bikers made Swiss cheese out of the truck and bullets started penetrating the thick metal sides.

"They're after me," Sophia said.

"Why?" Thorn aimed and fired off another round. The biker he'd been aiming for swerved to avoid a cactus at the last minute, and the bullet missed him completely.

"My fiancé doesn't let go of what he considers his. He won't stop until he has me or I'm dead."

"Well, he'll have to go through us first." Thorn's jaw tightened and he fired again, hitting the biker nearing the back of the truck. The biker's arm jerked backward, and he spun off the back of the dirt bike, hitting the ground hard.

Each time Thorn pulled the trigger, the pain in his right shoulder ripped through his arm. Warm liquid spread across his shirt and dripped down his arm to his elbow.

Two pairs of twin headlights shone across the land-scape, headed straight for them.

"Don't shoot at the trucks!" Hank yelled over his shoulder. "I think they're ours."

The cavalry arrived, bearing arms, plowing through the fleet of bikes, chasing them back.

Thorn held his rifle propped on the backseat, aimed out the shattered window in case the cyclists got close enough to be a danger. His blood hammered through his veins, pulsing through the open wound and sending shards of pain across his nerve endings, but he held steady and at the ready.

The assailants split up and scattered, dropping off to the east and west as the trucks closed ranks with the one Hank drove. Bullets continued to fly until the last motorcycle disappeared into the darkness.

Thorn settled back in the seat and brushed glass out of Sophia's silky hair.

She sat up and glanced behind them. "They're gone?"

"For now," Hank said.

Sophia glanced down at her arm, her eyes widening. "Blood," she whispered, checking her own skin for lesions. When she found none, she leaned away from Thorn, her gaze skimming over his body until it zeroed in on his shoulder. "You're bleeding." She ripped the hem of her T-shirt and wadded it up, pressing it to Thorn's shoulder.

"I'm fine. It just nicked me." Even as he played down the wound, he accepted the wad of fabric, covering it with his big hand. "Nothing major."

"I'll have Scott check it out." Hank shot a glance at Thorn in the rearview mirror. "We might want to take you into the clinic in Wild Oak Canyon and have them look it over, as well. Make sure the bullet didn't lodge inside the flesh."

"Walden can handle it," Thorn insisted.

"He's better with animals," Hank parried.

Thorn settled his weapon in his lap and winced. "What's a human but a glorified ape? Walden can do it. Besides, the bullet just nicked me." If he went to the hospital, Sophia would be exposed. He didn't want to leave her, not after killers had attacked them, possibly trying to get to her, like she'd said. He didn't know her and was under no obligation to protect her, but, somehow, he couldn't stop himself.

STILL SHAKING FROM the torturous ride and the anticipation of a bullet taking out one of the men trying to help her, Sophia reined in her fear and focused on the man bleeding on the seat beside her. She recognized the posturing of a male used to being shot at and shook her head. She'd witnessed too many of Antonio's men who remained doggedly at his side as they bled to death from rival gunshot wounds.

Hank's gunman had been harmed because of her, and Sophia felt responsible. He could have died. Despite the way he'd strong-armed her at the beginning, he'd done everything in his power to protect her since. She couldn't let Thorn die because of her.

Having lived in *la Fuerte del Diablo,* the desert hideout of *la Familia Diablos,* for over a year, she'd fished bullets out of open wounds, cleaned and dressed gashes caused by knife stabbings and even cauterized bleeders with a hot poker to save the lives of Antonio's servants and men. Some of the wounds Antonio had inflicted himself.

Sophia's back teeth ground together. Her fiancé had been anything but the charming, benevolent man he'd led her to believe he was during their brief courtship in Monterrey.

In front of her family, he'd been the perfect gentleman, catering to her every need, respectful of her, her family and her friends.

Once he had convinced her to leave her parents and join him at his home, he'd whisked her to the hidden desert compound and kept her prisoner. When she'd asked to leave, he'd flown into a rage and beaten her again and again until he finally wore himself out.

She'd barely survived that first incident and vowed to

never let it happen again. José, his second in command, had the audacity to tell her she was lucky he'd only broken her nose and ribs.

From that point on, she'd walked and spoken quietly, careful not to ignite the tempest of his full wrath. Her desire to remain quietly in the background had backfired. The more subdued she acted, the angrier Antonio became. Even the most insignificant of slights set him off.

Making love had settled into something more akin to rape.

Soon her own life seemed unimportant, but when Sophia discovered she was pregnant, she knew a baby wouldn't survive the hell she'd lived in for the past year.

That's when she'd vowed to escape or die, and take her baby with her rather than subject it to the terror that was its father.

An oasis of lights glowed in the distance.

"Is that your home?" Sophia leaned forward, her pulse quickening.

"That's it," Hank replied. "You'll be okay once we get you inside the perimeter of the security system."

A safe harbor sounded as near to heaven as she'd dreamed for months. Tears welled in her eyes. But she knew it wouldn't last long. Antonio would be after her, and he wouldn't stop until he had her back. She sat against the leather seats of the pickup, concerned for her rescuers and unwilling to see another wounded on her behalf. "Maybe you should leave me here."

Thorn's hand clasped her arm. "What are you talking about?"

"Those men shooting at us came for me." Sophia glanced behind them as if the bikers would appear again. "They'll be back to collect me."

Thorn's fingers tightened on her arm. "You're not going anywhere."

"You've already been shot because of me. No telling how many others have been injured. I couldn't live with myself if someone else died. My life is not worth that much. Stop the truck." She leaned forward, placing her hand on the back of Hank's seat. "Let me out."

Hank shook his head, his lips pressed into a tight line. "I'm not turning you over to those killers."

Sophia squared her shoulders. "Better one than many deaths."

"No one's dying on my watch," Thorn gritted out. "We'll get to the bottom of this. Until we do, you'll be safe in Hank's home."

Sophia sat back in her seat, biting her lip. As soon as she could, she'd leave the Raging Bull Ranch. Despite Anna's reassurances that Hank could help her, Sophia refused to let these good people die protecting her.

As they neared the large ranch house and its surrounding fences, Sophia's heart fluttered. The lights looked welcoming, comforting, not harsh and dangerous like those located around the outskirts of *la Fuerte del Diablo* in Mexico.

The closer they moved, the faster her pulse pounded in her veins, like racing for the finish line with an overpowering urge to shout, "I've won! I've won!"

For a long moment Sophia closed her eyes, her hand going to her still-flat belly. *It's going to be okay. I swear to you, baby, we're going to be okay.*

A hand on her arm made her open her eyes, and she stared up into the clear gaze of the man who'd saved her life.

"Are you feeling ill again?" Thorn asked.

She smiled and shook her head. "No. Just glad to be

safe for the moment." As soon as she got her bearings, she'd strike out on her own and find a safe place to hide. Maybe in Arkansas or Iowa. Someplace Antonio would never think to look for her. She'd change her name and start over.

A man carrying an assault weapon swung open a gate as they neared.

Hank barreled through and came to a halt in front of a huge barn. Two more men, dressed completely in black, surrounded the truck, also carrying assault weapons.

Sophia frowned, her confidence shaken at the militaristic stance of the gunmen. "Are you with the American military?" she asked.

Hank snorted. "No. I've made a few enemies through my business dealings that have cost me dearly." Hank's expression in the rearview mirror hardened. "These men help me keep that from happening again." The older man climbed down.

Thorn helped Sophia unbuckle her belt, brushing aside the fractured glass. He leaned close and spoke softly. "From what I've heard and read, Hank lost his family to intruders."

Sophia gasped and crossed herself. *"Madre de Dios."*

As Thorn helped her from the truck, Sophia's gaze followed the man Anna had asked her to contact, her hand going to her belly. How would she feel about losing her child to killers? The infant had yet to make its appearance, yet she already had an unbreakable bond with the tiny being growing inside her.

The other two trucks pulled up beside Hank's, and men piled out and gathered around their leader.

Sophia slipped toward the barn, hiding in the shadows. The fewer people who knew she was here, the better.

While Hank briefed them on what had happened, Thorn

stood back from the group, holding his arm. He glanced around as if searching for someone. When he spotted her, he closed the distance between them. "Why are you hiding?"

She shrugged, her heart squeezing in her chest at the amount of blood staining his shirt. "We should get you inside and treat your wound."

Thorn frowned. "I'm fine."

She shook her head. "Stubborn man." She reached out from the shadows and snagged Max's sleeve, dragging him back into the darkness with her. "Which man is Scott Walden?"

Max nodded toward a man standing close to Hank. "I'll get him." The bodyguard stepped toward the foreman and spoke to him quietly.

Scott Walden broke away from Hank and hurried toward Thorn. "Let's see to that wound." He hooked Thorn's arm and marched him toward the house.

Sophia hung back, lurking in the shadows of the barn, debating whether or not now was a good time to make her move to leave these people. Before she could make a move, Thorn dug his heels into the ground and came to a halt. "Not without her." He shot a glance back at her.

Why did the man have to be so stubborn? Sophia sighed. She'd have to follow, but she didn't want the other men to see her. The more people who knew she was there, the harder it would be to keep her presence low-key.

Thorn stepped back into the darkness beside her. "Why are you hiding?" he asked again.

"The fewer people who see me, the better."

Thorn waved Max and Scott toward him. They formed a force field of strength around her, shielding her from the lights shining overhead from the corners of the barn and house.

Once through a side door, Max disappeared back out-side, leaving her with the foreman and Thorn.

Sophia wanted to make sure the man got proper medi-cal care for the gunshot wound. It was the least she could do before she left. The man had saved her life.

Hank entered the house behind them. "I'll get on the horn with the local authorities. Let them get out there and clean up any bodies that might be lying around."

Thorn's lips pressed together. "You might want to put a bug in the Customs and Border Protection's ear. They might be more help than the local sheriff's department."

Sophia stopped in the middle of a hallway, her eyes widening, her pulse pounding. "Are you going to turn me over to them?"

Clutching his bleeding arm, Thorn stopped as well and gave her a half smile. "It's up to Hank. You're a trespasser on his property."

Hank patted her arm. "No, I won't turn you in to the authorities." His mouth turned down on the corners. "But I'll need to know everything. No lies, no holding any-thing back."

Sophia sucked in a deep breath and let it out slowly. "I'll tell you the truth if you promise not to tell the authorities I'm here." She'd tell him almost everything, but the most important piece of information she wouldn't tell anyone until she was safely hidden away in a new life as far away from *la Fuerte del Diablo* and Antonio as she could get.

"My men know you're here, and the men who chased us may have figured it out, as well."

Sophia twisted the torn hem of her shirt. "I won't go back."

"We won't let them take you back." Hank touched her arm. "You can trust me."

Scott cleared his throat. "We need to patch up Thorn

before we do anything. He's bleeding like a stuck pig, and I'm sure the housekeeper won't be happy about cleaning up the mess in the morning."

Hank nodded. "You're right. Let's get him into the kitchen. The first-aid kit is in the pantry."

Scott led the way, followed by Thorn and Sophia.

As they entered the kitchen, a younger man came hurrying down the hallway toward them. "Hank, got the sheriff's deputy on the phone wantin' to know what the hell's going on out here. Says he's on his way out."

Sophia's heart clenched, the blood leaving her head, her vision blurring.

"Brandon, get her to the basement," Hank said. "I'll handle the local law."

"You're not going to turn me over?" Sophia asked.

"Not yet," Hank promised. "I want to get to the bottom of this."

"Scott, get the first-aid kit." Thorn slipped his uninjured arm around Sophia. "I'm going with Sophia. We can do what needs to be done in the bunker."

Chapter Five

Hank guided them through the maze of secret doors and security locks to the hidden facility below his house with thick concrete walls and video cameras everywhere.

Thorn had been down there only twice since he'd started working for Hank. The place was built like a bomb shelter or fortress, capable of withstanding the impact of high explosives. It also had its own generators and satellite receivers should the electricity be cut off.

Hank had the money; he could afford every modern convenience and protective gadget a man could want, and his computer genius, Brandon, was tapped, or hacked, into just about every government database there was.

Having been the sheriff of Wild Oak Canyon, Thorn wasn't keen on the idea that Hank was breaking the law to get information. But from what he'd seen of Hank's operation, the man was really out for truth and justice, using whatever means he could to get there.

"Can you get out of that shirt while I wash up?" Scott asked.

"Sure." Thorn fumbled with the buttons down the front of his shirt.

Sophia stepped in front of him and brushed his fingers aside, making quick work of the buttons all the way down to where the shirt disappeared into his trousers.

Every time her knuckles brushed against his skin, an electric current zinged through him, setting his pulse pounding faster.

She tugged the shirt out of his waistband and shoved it over his good shoulder, then peeled it off his wounded shoulder. Some of the blood had dried, gluing the shirt to his skin.

Sophia's brows wrinkled, and she glanced up into his eyes with her own deep green ones. "This might hurt a little," she warned, capturing her teeth between her full, sensuous lower lip.

Thorn found himself wanting to bite her lip. Her fingers pressed against his skin, easing the fabric free of the caked-on blood. She stood so close that her breast brushed against his chest, the warmth of her body radiating through him.

His breath hitched in his throat and he fought to keep from grabbing her around the waist and crushing her against him, shocked as the urge washed over him.

He reached out, gripped her arms and set her away from him.

"But I'm not finished," she protested.

"Yes—you—are," he said through gritted teeth, and ripped the shirt from his shoulder, wincing at the pain, but glad for it because it helped take his mind off the way Sophia's hair slipped across her face, and the scent of her skin wafting over him.

Sophia glared at him. "You've started it bleeding again."

"I don't need you to fix it. Scott's the horse doctor."

"I've had experience treating wounds."

"Really?" Thorn shot back. "Where? What hospital?"

She glanced away, a shadow darkening her green eyes. "Not at a hospital. At *la Fuerte del Diablo,* where I was kept prisoner."

Thorn's chest tightened and he regretted his sharpness, wondering what Sophia had endured at the hands of her abusive fiancé.

Brandon entered the room, carrying a towel and a bottle of water. "Thought you could use this."

"Brandon, with all the gizmos you have down here, do you have a police scanner that picks up out here?" Thorn asked.

The younger man grinned. "As a matter of fact, I do."

"See if you can pick up anything about what's going on."

"All I've gotten is that the sheriff's department is sending a couple of units out this way to investigate gunshots fired." Brandon half turned toward the door. "I'll get back on it, if you think it's important."

"Do it. I'd like to know how the incident is being handled and what's being reported back."

"On it." Brandon left the room.

While Scott cleaned and examined his wound, Thorn studied the woman standing in the corner, gazing down at her fingers as she twisted the edge of her tattered T-shirt. She stood as far away from him as she could get without leaving altogether.

A twinge of guilt hit Thorn's gut at his shortness with her. He figured better short than act on impulses he'd thought long buried with his dead wife.

His instinctive reaction to her was a reminder of his need to keep his distance. Thorn pulled his thoughts together and winced as Scott applied a good dose of alcohol to the gash in his arm. "Sophia, do you have family here in the States?"

She glanced up, her eyes widening. "No."

"In Mexico?"

Her gaze lingered on him, and she chewed on that confounded lower lip again.

Damn.

Thorn dragged his attention back to her green eyes.

After a moment's hesitation, she answered, "In Monterrey."

"Why didn't you go back to them?"

She shook her head. "I had to get as far away from my fiancé as possible. I need to disappear completely to keep him from finding me." Her voice caught on the hint of a sob. "I'm not safe in Mexico."

She had family in Monterrey. Thorn understood how unstable the government was and how dangerous it could be if a cartel was after you.

"How will you get by here in the States without family? Do you have your own money?"

She shook her head. "No. I have a little, not much. Everything I own is in that backpack. I wasn't able to bring anything with me when I escaped."

Which meant she had a total of fifty dollars, and now, not even a change of clothes to start a new life in the States. Thorn tried to tell himself that it wasn't his problem. Sophia was not his responsibility.

Her gaze captured his, her eyes narrowing as if she could read his thoughts. "I don't need your help."

Her words stung as much as the antibiotic ointment Scott slathered onto Thorn's open wound. He winced and shot back, "I wasn't offering."

"Good." The sharp comeback was watered down by the shiver that shook her body. The hollows beneath her eyes made her appear tired, waiflike, in need of someone to protect her.

Brandon came back with a handheld scanner.

"What are they saying?"

"So far there've been a few communications warning the deputies to be ready for possible gunfire and to be on the lookout for a man and a woman, possible illegal aliens wanted for murder on the other side of the border."

Thorn's gaze shot to Sophia.

She shook her head. "That's not me. I've never killed a man in my life."

"And the man who helped you escape?" Thorn asked.

"I can't vouch for his record. All I know is that I owe him my life. He got me away from my fiancé and across the border into the States." Her head dipped as silent tears slid down her cheeks. "In my heart, he died a saint."

"Thanks, Brandon." After the foreman applied a wad of gauze and adhesive tape to his arm, Thorn stood. "I'm going up. I want to be topside when the sheriff gets here."

Sophia's eyes widened. "What about me?"

"Stay here until we give you the all clear." Thorn glanced from Brandon to Scott.

They nodded.

"We'll keep an eye on her." Scott started to pull his shirt off his back. "You might want a shirt."

"Thanks." He held up a hand, stopping the guy. "I'll get one from my room upstairs." The foreman was wiry thin. The shirt wouldn't go over his arms, much less his shoulders. Thorn cast a last glance at Sophia. "When the sheriff leaves, we're gonna have us a talk."

She nodded.

Thorn left, climbing the stairs out of the bunker and closing the hidden door behind him softly.

Voices sounded in the front foyer.

He hurried to the room Hank had assigned him and yanked a shirt on over the bandage, thankful the blood hadn't dripped onto his dirty jeans. Still buttoning the front, he strode down the hallway toward the voices.

Hank stood in the middle of the foyer with Max and three deputies dressed in the uniform of the local sheriff's department.

A twinge of regret rippled across Thorn. He'd worn just such a uniform not long ago and had been sworn in as the sheriff to protect the people of the county from crime.

Hell, he hadn't been able to protect his own family from a shooting that had taken the lives of his wife and unborn daughter. What made him think he could help protect a stranger?

"Drennan, good to see you." Deputy Sanders held out his hand and shook Thorn's as he came to a halt beside Hank.

"Sanders, how's the family?"

The deputy grinned. "Jordan turned two a week ago, and Brianna will be five next month. Can't believe they're that old already. Seems like yesterday Jessica and Kayla were pregnant—" The other man stopped in midsentence, his smile dying. "Sorry."

Thorn's chest tightened, and he glanced away for a moment before returning his attention to Sanders. "What brings you out here?"

"As we were tellin' Mr. Derringer, we had a report of gunfire out this way."

"Really?" Thorn asked. "Who called it in?"

"It came in on a blocked cell-phone ID. Anonymous." Sanders's lips twisted. "Since there was nothin' else goin' on, we decided to investigate. On the way out here, we got a report from the CBP that a man and woman wanted for murder had slipped across the border from Mexico."

"Who'd they kill?" Thorn asked.

"Two undercover DEA agents."

"Did they give you a name or description of them?" Thorn asked.

Sanders glanced at his notepad. "Antonio Martinez, five feet eleven inches tall, dark hair, dark eyes, slim and athletic. Elena Carranza, five feet four inches tall, dark blond hair, green eyes."

Thorn's gut twisted. "Murder?"

"That's what the CBP is reporting."

Hank tipped his head. "What about a photo?"

"They're working on it. We're supposed to get a photo or composite back at the station within the next couple of hours."

"I'd like to see that when you do." Hank glanced at Thorn. "My men and I will keep an eye out for them."

"In the meantime, we'll check into the incident you had earlier, although we won't be able to do much until daylight. At least we can check for bodies or any injured left behind. The CBP has representatives on their way, should be here momentarily."

"If you want to wait outside," Hank offered, "I'll send my foreman out to show you and the border patrol where we were ambushed."

"Any idea why they'd shoot at you?" Sanders asked.

Thorn held his breath, waiting for Hank's answer. "None."

"Why were you out that late?"

"One of my men was working the fences when that storm blew in. When his horse came back without him, I sent a search party out looking for him."

Sanders made notes on his pad. "Mind if we question him?"

Thorn raised a hand. "That would be me."

Sanders grinned. "Why were you out there working so late?"

"I was almost finished checking the entire southern fence line. Didn't see a need to head in until I got it done."

Thorn shrugged. "The storm moved in before I got back. To make matters worse, lightning struck, my horse threw me and took off."

"You're lucky you didn't break your neck."

Thorn touched his shoulder. "Just bummed my shoulder. Fortunately there was a hunting cabin close by. I holed up there until Mr. Derringer showed up to give me a lift."

"No sign of the woman or man?" Sanders asked.

"Never heard of this Antonio or Elena," Thorn replied, not exactly lying, but not telling the whole truth.

"Well, if you see them, call us, the CBP or the FBI." Sanders folded his pad and tucked it into his front pocket. "Don't try to capture them yourselves. They're supposed to be armed and dangerous."

"We appreciate the warning," Hank said. "Now, if you'll wait outside, I'll have my foreman meet you in front of the barn."

"Thank you, Mr. Derringer." Deputy Sanders shook Hank's hand, then held his out to Thorn. "When are you reclaiming your role as sheriff?"

Thorn shook his head. "Don't count on it. I've got a job with Mr. Derringer."

"Sorry, I didn't realize that. We don't have a sheriff right now. I'm sure if you wanted the job, you could get it back pretty easily."

"No, thanks." Thorn strode to the door and held it open. "Scott Walden will be out in a few minutes. He can show you where we were attacked."

Sanders gave Thorn another long look. "Kayla was my friend, too, you know."

Thorn's lips pressed into a thin line. The three of them had been inseparable in high school.

"She knew how much you loved being a cop. She

wouldn't have wanted you to give it up because of what happened."

Thorn held up his hand. "Don't."

Sanders nodded. "Just saying. We could use a good sheriff. And you were the best we've ever had."

"Why don't *you* run for the position?" Thorn asked.

Sanders shook his head. "I've only been at this job for a couple years. You're the one with all the experience."

"Not interested." Thorn held the door, his fingers so tight around the knob he thought he might crush it.

Sanders sighed. "Hasn't been the same since you left."

"Change is good," Thorn responded.

When the deputy finally walked through the door, Thorn let go of the breath he'd been holding and carefully closed the door behind his former employee. They'd been through a rough time with the previous sheriff being arrested for human trafficking. The lowlife had been responsible for allowing truckloads of women to cross into Texas and beyond, for sale into the sex-slave market.

After Kayla died, Thorn had quit the department, and a new, corrupt sheriff had been hired.

Too deep in his own misery and loss after quitting, Thorn hadn't brought his head up long enough to know what was going on. Another wave of guilt washed over him. He should have taken an interest in the town and county he'd loved. But he hadn't. How many people had suffered under the new sheriff's administration?

What Hank saw in this broken-down cowboy, Thorn didn't know. He was just thankful for a job at this point, wondering what assignment Hank would give him.

"Scott still in the bunker?" Hank walked toward a phone in the hallway.

Thorn nodded. "I asked him to keep an eye on Sophia while I came up."

As the two men headed for the secret doorway, Scott Walden blasted around a corner in the hallway. "Did she come this way?"

Thorn's brows knit. "Sophia?"

"Yeah. Said she had to use *el baño*." He shook his head. "Showed her where it was and spent a minute or two talking to Brandon. About the time I thought she'd been in there too long, I knocked. Got no response, opened the door to find she'd flown the coop."

Thorn raced around the corner, ripped the hidden door open and had to wait for Hank to press his thumb to the scanner.

When the heavy metal door opened, Thorn charged into the bunker, tearing through every room, startling Brandon at his desk.

"Did you see her?"

"No. I checked all the rooms, no sign. I was just backing through the security footage." Brandon sat back at his desk and clicked the mouse through several screens. "She might have overheard them talking on the scanner about the BOLO for the two murderers coming up from Mexico. She seemed to get really quiet after that. That's when she asked to use the facilities."

"How did she get out of the bunker?"

"I thought she'd take longer and wasn't keeping a close eye on the bathroom door. Then an alarm went off on my computer, so I was checking it. Guess that's when she made a run for it." Brandon shifted. "And, well, though you have to have clearance to get in, it's easy to get out."

Thorn leaned over his shoulder and stared at a dozen different views on the bank of computer screens. For the most part, nothing moved. Then a figure appeared in one of them, sneaking along a hallway toward a door.

"There!" Brandon pointed at the screen.

"Where is that?" Thorn asked.

"Near the back door by the kitchen," Brandon said.

Before Brandon had the last word out of his mouth, Thorn was halfway up the stairs leading out of the bunker.

Hank was waiting at the top. "Find her?"

"Back door." Thorn pushed past his boss and sprinted toward the back of the house.

As quiet as he could be in cowboy boots, he raced the length of the hall and skidded around the corner into the kitchen as Sophia reached for the doorknob to the back exit.

She gasped and turned to see who'd run in behind her. "You!"

"Going somewhere?" Thorn demanded.

She whipped the door open and would have run out, but Thorn got there first, his arm blocking her exit. And just in time.

Beyond the back door was the barnyard where the sheriff's deputies awaited the foreman's guide services to find the location of their earlier attack.

Thorn grabbed Sophia's wrist and tore it from the knob. Then he eased the door to the kitchen closed before anyone glanced their way. Once the door blocked their view to the barnyard and subsequently the view of them *from* the barnyard, Thorn crossed his arms and glared down at Sophia.

"Start talking now, or I'll let you walk right out there and turn yourself in to the deputies."

SOPHIA'S BREATH CAUGHT in her throat. The anger in Thorn's eyes seared a path to her heart. She'd been too damned close to being discovered by the authorities. Even if the big cowboy with the iron clamp around her wrist had been gruff about her escape, he had kept her from getting caught once again.

"Why did you try to run?" Thorn asked. "Who did you kill?"

Her chin dropped and she stared straight ahead, directly into Thorn's chest. "I'm not a murderer. I didn't kill anyone."

"Then why are you running? Why is it being reported that a woman named Elena Carranza and some guy named Antonio Martinez killed two DEA agents and fled Mexico?" Thorn stepped closer until he stood toe-to-toe with her. "What is your real name?"

She inhaled and let it out slowly. "My name is Sophia. I didn't lie. It's *Elena* Sophia Carranza. And I didn't kill anyone. I was running because I can't be caught. The authorities might send me back, and I refuse to go back. They'll kill me. Now it's even worse." Sophia closed her eyes and willed the headache building across her forehead to go away. "If they are looking for me as a murder suspect, who's going to believe my word against the border patrol who reported me as a criminal fugitive?"

"How can anyone trust you if you don't tell us the truth?" His hand tightened around her wrist, and a muscle twitched in his jaw as Thorn stared at her for a long, painful moment.

"What do you care if I stay or leave? You wanted to turn me over to the police. What's stopping you?"

"You know, you're right. I don't know why I should believe you. You've done nothing but lie and give me half-truths." He dropped her hand and stepped away from her. "Leave."

Sophia rubbed the red mark around her wrist, her pulse beating rapidly at the base of her throat. She'd pushed him too far because of her anger, and where would that get her? "I would leave," she said, then added on a whisper, "if I had somewhere to go."

"You seem to know what's best for you, and you claim you have it all figured out." He waved his hand toward the closed back door. "Go."

Sophia chewed on her lip. "But the police, the border patrol—"

"Will be gone in a few minutes. You'll be able to sneak out of here without disturbing a soul. Hank doesn't even have to know. I'll cover for you."

Her breath caught and she stared up at him, searching his face for some element of empathy but finding none. She straightened her shoulders and tipped her chin up. "Thank you. I will." She took a step toward the door and stopped, fear making her hands clammy and her feet drag.

As she reached for the doorknob, a sense of doom settled over her. Hector had given his life, for what? For her to get caught and sent back to face the cartel and Antonio's anger?

A hand caught her arm and spun her around. "Don't."

"But you want me to go."

"Yes, you make me crazy and I want you the hell out of my life." His lips thinned and the muscle in his jaw ticked. "But I can't let you go."

Sophia pressed her hands against the solid wall of his chest, her gaze finding and locking with his. "I didn't come here to mess up your life."

"Somehow, I think you did."

"Not intentionally. I can make it on my own. You aren't responsible for me." She couldn't let this man see how scared she was after coming this far. "I'm not afraid of anything," she said, biting down on her lip.

"Don't do that," he said, brushing his thumb across her bottom lip, forcing her to release her hold on it.

"Why?"

"Because it makes me want to do this." He bent and

claimed her mouth, crushing her against him, his arms tightening around her.

Her hands lay flat against his chest, pressing into him for the first few seconds. Then she curled her fingers into his shirt, her nails digging into the skin beneath. Despite the voices in her head telling her she was being stupid, she couldn't stop. He'd crashed into her world like a thunderous storm but kept her alive, protecting her when he didn't have to. He was a man of honor, unlike Antonio.

Sophia wanted to remain in the safety of his arms, to forget where she was and who was after her and just feel the warmth and security she knew in Thorn's embrace.

Thorn pulled her closer, smoothing her hair back from her face. He eased up on the kiss, ending it with a feathery brush of his lips.

For a moment, he rested his cheek against the softness of her hair while he gathered his senses and wits about him. At long last, he pushed her away, letting his hands drop to his sides.

She stood for a long moment, her lips swollen from his kiss, her eyes rounded, glazed with a wash of unshed tears. "Why did you do that?"

Guilt hit him with the force of an F5 tornado, and he stepped farther back. "I don't know."

She pressed her hand to her mouth and turned to yank the door open.

Thorn's heart tripped over itself and fell into his belly with the weight of a lead bowling ball. More than anything, he wanted this woman out of his life so that he could think about what he'd just done.

But when she stepped out the door, he couldn't let her go. She was in danger and needed him, whether or not he liked it.

"Wait."

She sucked in a breath and huffed it out. "What do you want?"

You.

The thought popped into Thorn's head before he could brace himself for the full impact. His breath caught and held in his chest, and he stared at her. "Stay."

Sophia paused. "Why? I thought you wanted me to go."

"I do. But you won't last two minutes against whoever is trying to kill you."

"You and I both know that by staying, I put you all at risk." She nodded toward his arm. "You got shot because of me."

"I'm willing to take the risk."

"And the rest of Hank's men? Are you speaking for them?"

"No. But they'd do anything for Hank." His lips quirked on the sides. "Even take a bullet for him."

"Well, I don't want anyone taking a bullet for me." She stepped through the door and out into the now-empty barnyard.

"Drennan, did you find her?" Hank stepped up behind Thorn.

"Yes," Thorn answered, without taking his gaze off the woman walking away from him.

"Where is she?" Hank asked.

He nodded to where Sophia was stepping off the porch onto the ground. "Leaving."

"Hell, no, she's not. I just lied to the deputies for that woman." Hank gave Thorn a push. "Get her back. I want answers."

His pulse quickening and a smile curling the corners

of his lips, Thorn stepped off the porch and caught Sophia's arm before she could take off. "Sorry, you'll have to leave later."

Chapter Six

Sophia sat in a wingback chair on the other side of Hank's desk in his study, her head drooping, the gray of predawn peeking through the blinds covering the windows in Hank's office.

"I didn't kill anyone," she said for the hundredth time. "I left my fiancé because he was cruel and part of the cartel. I knew if I wanted to live to be twenty-six, I had to get out."

"The CBP is searching for you and a man called Antonio Martinez."

Sophia gasped.

Hank pinned her with his stare. "Who is he?"

"My ex-fiancé." She frowned and sat up straighter, at a disadvantage with the cowboy towering over her. "He didn't come with me." Had he discovered her missing so soon and crossed the border looking for her?

"Thorn said you came across with a man named Hector. How does he fit in this picture?"

She swallowed hard on the lump rising up her throat. "Hector didn't kill anyone, either. He got me out. That man risked his life to get me across the border."

"Are you sure that's how it went? The CBP has an entirely different story. They say you and Antonio killed a couple undercover DEA agents."

"I swear, I am not with Antonio." Sophia shook her

head, fear making her breathing difficult. What if these men didn't believe her? Would they turn her over to the CBP? A sob rose up her throat, and she swallowed hard. "I left to escape him. Another captive told me to contact Hank Derringer, and Hector volunteered to get me out."

"How much did you pay him?" Hank fired off one question after another.

She snorted. "I didn't have any money. He told me he did it because I reminded him of his daughter." Her voice caught on a sob. "He gave his life for me, and for what?" She waved a hand. "I'm trapped here as if I traded one prison for another."

"You don't have to stay." Hank stood before her. "But if you want to live to be twenty-six, as you say, you might want to consider taking me up on my offer to provide your protection."

"How will you do that? Antonio has a network of people on both sides of the border willing to kill anyone who gets in the way of what he wants."

"You want to live?" Thorn asked.

Sophia touched her belly, reminding herself she wasn't alone. She had to consider the child growing inside her. "I can't pay you."

Hank chuckled. "I don't need your money. I have enough."

By the appearance of his house and the fully equipped bunker hidden beneath, he had more than enough. "What can you do to guarantee my safety?" Sophia asked.

"I'd start by assigning a bodyguard to watch over you."

Sophia's gaze darted to Thorn. "Him?"

Thorn snorted. "Please, don't look so enthusiastic."

Hank laughed. "Thorn was trained as a police officer and has served in the local sheriff's department before he came to work for me. He knows what it means to be under fire."

"What if he doesn't want the job?" Sophia's gaze swept over Thorn, challenging him.

"I'll do it," Thorn responded. "Whether or not I *want* to is beside the point. You need a keeper."

Sophia snorted. "I'm better off by myself."

Hank frowned. "Is there something going on between the two of you I should know about?"

Thorn shook his head. "Absolutely nothing." The look he pinned on Sophia dared her to refute that.

"Nothing."

"Then it's done." Hank crossed to his desk and sat behind it. "Thorn will be your bodyguard while we sort this mess out."

Sophia wasn't sure how she felt about Thorn being her bodyguard. Not after that kiss. What if he kissed her again? Her pulse fluttered and her cheeks warmed. She pushed aside the unwanted longing and focused on what Hank had said. "I don't know what you think you can sort out. I told you, my ex-fiancé will not stop until I'm either dead or back in his prison of a compound."

"This Antonio Martinez…he was your fiancé?" Thorn's eyes narrowed. "The name sounds familiar."

Sophia sat back in her chair, the fight gone out of her, exhaustion taking hold. "If you know anything about *la Familia Diablos,* you know that he's one of their leaders. Still want to protect me? Think you can?"

Thorn's brows dipped, and a snarl curled his lips. "I'm not afraid of the cartel."

She stared back at him. "You should be."

"I'll have Brandon do research on Martinez and *la Familia Diablos.*" Hank rose from behind his desk and stretched. "Once we've all had a little sleep, we can reconvene and figure out where we go from here."

Thorn nodded.

"Drennan, you can show Miss Carranza to the room next to yours. Security is pretty tight around here, but it doesn't hurt to have your bodyguard close."

Sophia opened her mouth to tell Hank she didn't want to be that close to Thorn but closed it again, knowing it would be a lie. The man might be stubborn and hardheaded, and kissed like the devil, but he'd come through more than once to save her life. Instead of arguing, she nodded. "Thank you, Señor Derringer."

Hank left the room without another word, leaving Thorn and Sophia alone.

Thorn glanced at her and sighed. "Lack of sleep leads to poor decisions. What say we get some rest?"

Sophia could have bet he was talking about the kiss, blaming his lapse in judgment on a sleepless night. A flutter of disappointment rippled through her. Having been awake for close to thirty-six hours, crossing rough terrain and dodging bullets had taken their toll. She trudged along behind Thorn. "Is there a possibility of getting a shower somewhere in this huge house?" The idea of scrubbing the dirt off her skin sounded like heaven.

"You're in luck. There's a bathroom in the suite." He led her along a hallway and stopped in front of a door. He twisted the knob and pushed the door inward.

Sophia stepped inside, her gaze going to the big bed with an off-white comforter spread across it. Exhaustion pulled her toward it. If she wasn't so dirty, she'd fall onto the covers and sleep like the dead.

"I'll be in the room beside this one." He nodded to a door on the wall inside her room. "There's a connecting door if you need anything."

Sophia's heartbeat fluttered. The thought of Thorn's bedroom being down the hall was quite different from a connecting door between the two rooms.

"Don't worry, I won't disturb you." His mouth slipped into a sexy smile. "Unless you want me to."

"I don't want you to," she was quick to say.

"Good." He stretched his arms over his head, winced and let them drop to his side. "I'm tired."

A twinge of guilt tugged at Sophia. "The wound?"

"Just a little sore. No more bleeding."

She nodded and stepped into the room.

Thorn turned to go.

Sophia paused in closing the door between the rooms. "Thorn?"

He glanced back.

"Thank you." Sophia shut the door and leaned her back against it.

The room was bigger than the living room of the apartment she'd shared with Antonio in the compound. The bathroom was on the opposite side of the room from the connecting door to Thorn's room. Sophia crossed to the connecting door and twisted the knob. It turned easily; it was not locked, and there wasn't a lock on her side.

A little uncomfortable with the idea of an unlocked door between them, she scooted off to the opposite end of the room and into the bathroom, where the lock worked perfectly fine. She twisted it and took a moment to appreciate her surroundings.

The bathroom had large pale cream ceramic tiles, granite countertops and a glass-brick wall surrounding the walk-in shower, large enough for six people, with two showerheads.

A two-person tub filled one corner of the room, with large fluffy towels draped over its side.

The grime of her trek across the Rio Grande and through the canyons of the Big Bend National Park prodded Sophia to strip her dirty clothes and step into the shower.

The water started out cold but quickly warmed, washing away the dirt, glass and blood that had been splattered across her over the past thirty-six hours. When her skin felt clean and her eyes drooped low, she shut off the water and dried off with one of the luxurious towels.

Then she remembered she didn't have clean clothes to wear. Too tired to care, she wrapped a dry towel around her and crawled into the big bed, pulling the comforter up over her body.

She lay still for several minutes, breathing in and out, trying to calm her racing heart. Light shone around the blinds covering the windows. The early-morning sun edged through every crack, but not quite enough to light the entire room. Shadows darkened each corner of the unfamiliar room. Every little sound—the crack of timbers as the house settled, a bird chirping outside the window, the lonely howl of the wind pushing against the glass—made Sophia's heart skip beats and her body tense. No matter how much she tried to relax, she couldn't.

The door on the other side of the room creaked open, and a head slipped around the panel.

Sophia squealed, pulling the comforter up to her chin. When the dim light touched his face, she realized it was Thorn.

"Sorry, didn't mean to startle you," he said.

"What are you doing in here?" she asked, her voice high and tight.

"Why aren't you asleep?" he countered.

She shook her head. "I don't know."

"New place make you nervous?"

She nodded. "That and the fact Antonio has his men looking for me."

He stepped into the room and glanced around. "Want me to check the closets and beneath the bed for monsters?"

She stared across at him, gauging whether or not he was being sarcastic. Thankfully, he wasn't sneering. *"Sí, por favor."*

Thorn moved about the room, padding softly in bare feet. He wiggled the doorknob to test the lock, tried the windows, which all remained securely closed, and opened the closet and inspected it thoroughly before crossing to where she lay in the bed.

Sophia's eyes rounded as he came closer, her hands clenching the comforter pulled up to her chin. "You don't have to look beneath the bed."

"How are you going to sleep if I don't make sure there's nothing or no one hiding beneath you?" His smile was no more than a gentle lift of the corners of his mouth, but the gesture was more calming than words. Thorn dropped to his haunches and ducked his head low, peering beneath the bed. "Dark but empty. Not even a single dust bunny to attack you."

Sophia laughed softly. "I know it's silly, but thanks for checking."

"You really should get some sleep. We could have a tough day ahead of us. You'll need your strength."

"I shouldn't have come here," she whispered.

"Based on all you said, you did the only thing you could."

"I didn't want to bring others down with me. My life is the way it is because of my own poor choices. No need for anyone else to suffer."

"You're here now, so stop worrying about it. Let Hank's team figure a way out of this mess for you."

"It's not easy turning over the reins to someone else. Not when your life depends on it." *Or the life of your unborn child.*

Thorn straightened beside her bed, so close he could touch her.

Sophia's blood heated, sliding through her veins like liquid lava, her skin twitching, aching for something.

When Thorn reached out and smoothed back a strand of hair from her forehead, Sophia's breath caught in her throat and she stared up into the most incredible blue eyes she could have imagined. As his fingers left her forehead, the warmth left with them. She'd never felt so safe as she did when she was with Thorn, and it scared her while simultaneously helping her relax. "Wh-why did you do that?"

His lips twisted upward on one side. "I don't know. It just seemed like the right thing to do."

She could get lost in his eyes. Her gaze remained on his for a long moment, all her muscles relaxing until a yawn rose up in her chest and nearly made her split her jaw. She covered her mouth and blinked, her eyelids drifting downward. She let them close for just a second. "Must have been sleepier than I'd thought."

Movement made her eyes flutter open.

Thorn no longer stood beside her bed. In the short time Sophia had closed her eyes, he'd slipped halfway across the room.

"Where are you going?" she whispered, hardly able to keep her eyes open.

"To my room. If you want, I'll leave the door open between us."

Her eyelids felt as if they had lead weights resting on them, driving them downward. *"Por favor."*

"Please, what?" he asked.

"Please stay until I go to sleep. It won't be long." She lay for a long time with her eyes shut.

The crackle of leather made her glance up.

Thorn had settled into the sturdy brown leather chair beside the bed. Sophia smiled.

"I'll stay until you fall asleep," he said, his voice low, caressing. Incredibly sexy.

A shiver rippled across Sophia's skin, and she closed her eyes to the alluring cowboy sitting so near.

"Sleep," he urged.

It felt more like a lifetime ago since she'd felt safe. Having grown up in a loving family, with an overprotective father and mother, she thought of violence and death as things that happened to other people. Not her. Until she'd made the mistake of trusting Antonio.

Sophia turned on her side, facing him, snuggled deeper into the comforter and drifted into the first deep sleep she'd had since she left her parents' home over a year ago.

THORN SAT FOR the longest time in the chair beside Sophia's bed, wondering what the hell he'd done. This woman had trouble written all over her. If he took the job of protecting her from whoever it was she was running from, there was a strong possibility he'd get shot at again, maybe killed.

As she lay with her palms pressed together and tucked beneath her cheek, she looked like a child, her thin cheeks and silky light brown hair fanned out on the pillow behind her. Gone was the little hellcat he'd fought in the cabin. In her place was an angel, with lips so soft, velvet didn't even describe them. Her hair feathered out to each side of her head in a spread of light brown strands. Though her eyes were closed, Thorn could envision the deep green of them boring into him as if he had the answers to all her problems. Trouble was, he had no answers. And if he didn't find some soon, she might not make it another day.

When her breathing became slow and regular, Thorn stood and stretched, ready to embark on a bit of intelligence gathering to discover just who Elena Sophia Carranza was. He'd asked Brandon to do some digging to see if she showed up on any wanted or missing persons lists in Mexico, the United States or Canada.

A soft moan rose from her throat.

Thorn leaned over her and stroked her hair. "Sleep. You'll be okay."

Her eyelids twitched but didn't open.

He bent and pressed a kiss to her temple, her soft skin making his lips tingle.

She smelled of honeysuckle, her hair still slightly damp from her shower. Sophia rolled to her back, the comforter sliding down to reveal the tops of her gently rounded breasts, the towel she'd wrapped around herself loosening.

Thorn made a mental note to ask Hank if he had some clothes she could borrow until they could get her to a store for something that fit. The woman had sacrificed her last T-shirt to use as a compress to stop Thorn from bleeding to death. It clearly was not the act of a murderer.

He brushed a strand of hair out of her face and straightened. If he stayed he'd be tempted to crawl into the bed beside her, something he hadn't been tempted to do since Kayla died.

Guilt swelled in his chest, driving Thorn out of the room and back into his own. He pushed aside the blinds and stared out at the South Texas morning sky, filled with purple, blue, mauve and orange. Steam rose from the ground from the rain they'd received during the night. Before long, the sun would soak up the moisture and the storm would be nothing more than a memory.

He lay on top of his bed, clothed in clean jeans and a T-shirt, and stared up at the ceiling. As soon as Hank was up and about, Thorn would ask him to find someone else to play bodyguard to the pretty fugitive. Already Thorn could feel himself getting too close to his client, a dangerous place to be should something happen to her. She stirred feelings in him he didn't want to face. He couldn't handle any more guilt and sorrow than he already lived with.

Fifteen minutes passed, and he still couldn't fall asleep.

Thorn rolled out of bed, checked on Sophia through the open doorway then slipped out into the hallway.

Noises drifted to him from the area of the kitchen. He headed that way, hoping for a piece of toast or cup of coffee.

Hank stood with his back to the doorway, pouring a cup of coffee from a glass carafe. "Want one?" he asked without turning.

"Please." Thorn hooked a chair with his bare foot, swung it away from the kitchen table and sat.

"How's our guest?" Hank set a cup of coffee on the table in front of Thorn.

"Sleeping." Thorn lifted the steaming cup and sipped. "I don't think she's slept in days."

Hank retrieved his cup and settled in the seat across from Thorn. Judging by Hank's well-worn jeans, button-up denim shirt and scuffed cowboy boots, no one would know the man was worth millions. "Scott should be back any minute from taking the border-patrol agents out to the shooting site. I hope to get an update then. In the meantime, we wait."

"Think they'll ask to search your house?"

Hank shook his head. "They'd have to show up with a warrant to do that." He glanced across his mug at Thorn.

"Don't worry—I won't let them know about Ms. Carranza."

"That puts you at risk for harboring a fugitive."

"I can handle it."

"Do you think the biker gang was after Sophia?"

"She seems to think they were."

"But do you?"

Hank sighed and set his mug on the table. "If they think I have her, they'll come after her here."

Thorn nodded. "Exactly my thoughts. Despite the amount of security you have, I don't think she's safe here."

"The sheriff said the CBP was setting up roadblocks on the highways leading out of this area. She'll never make it out by road."

"What about flying her out?"

"My helicopter is in the hanger in El Paso for annual maintenance and inspections." Hank shoved a hand through his graying hair and leaned back in his chair. "I could hire another one and move her, but that might draw attention she doesn't need."

"What can we do to keep her safe?"

Hank drummed his fingers on the table as the silence between the two men lengthened. "We need to hide her."

"Difficult when you have so many people around you. Any one of them could slip, whether on purpose or accidentally."

"Then we need to hide her in plain sight." Hank leaned forward, a light twinkling in his eyes. "Elena Sophia Carranza can disappear completely."

Thorn frowned, pushed his coffee aside and leaned toward his new boss. "What do you mean?"

"Right now, the only people who know she's here are you, me, Max and Brandon. She did a good job staying in the shadows when we brought her in."

"Right. So?"

"So we change her appearance and introduce her to the biggest gossips in town as your long-lost college sweetheart. Before you know it, the entire town will know her as…"

"Sally Freeman." Thorn smiled. "All we have to do is change her hair color and get her some clothes and a new driver's license, and we're good to go."

Hank stood. "I'll get my daughter PJ working on Sophia's transformation. She comes out often enough that they won't question why she's here. Once Sophia looks different enough to fool the sheriff's deputies and the CBP, she can move about Wild Oak Canyon without worrying."

"I don't know about that, but at least the authorities won't be looking at her as a murderer."

"I'll be back. I need to call PJ."

Thorn held up his hand. "Hank."

Hank paused.

"PJ needs to know not to leak any information about Sophia."

"She's good about keeping secrets. After all, she's her father's daughter." Hank's chuckle followed him down the hall until he disappeared around a corner.

Thorn collected his coffee mug and returned to his room.

He set his mug on the nightstand and strode for Sophia's room, a nagging feeling that something was wrong pulling him through the doorway. One glance across the room and his pulse ricocheted through his veins.

The bed was empty. Sophia was gone.

Chapter Seven

The compound lights blinked out yet again, as they did quite often, plunging her little room into complete darkness. Sophia swallowed a sob of terror, the sound of a little boy's cries cutting through her own fear, making her realize just how selfish she was to worry about how much she hated the darkness when a little boy cried in the night, unable to understand the instability inherent in a desert compound out in the middle of nowhere, dependent on generators and fuel. They were lucky to have any kind of electricity at all.

Though when the lights went out, Antonio usually returned to their room, intent on making love and further proving his power over her. She waited in the darkness, clutching the bedsheets around her, praying he wouldn't break one of her bones.

A woman's scream ripped through the night, penetrating the concrete-block walls and stucco.

Anna.

Sophia flung aside the covers and leaped out of the bed. The little boy's cries joined the woman's scream, galvanizing Sophia into action. She tore open her door and raced down the hallway to the rooms at the end where Anna and her son lived.

The door stood open, a flickering light illuminating the room within.

When Sophia barreled through the doorway, she smacked into Antonio, knocking him forward into a low table. He tripped and fell, landing with a grunt, the air around him reeking of cigarette smoke and stale alcohol.

"Pendejo!" he grumbled, pushing to his feet. More curses flowed from his lips as he closed the distance between them. "I'm going to kill you for that."

Sophia backed up and spun to race down the hallway and away from the fury etched in the man's eyes. Before she could take the first step, Antonio grabbed her hair and yanked her back.

She fell against him, pushing hard to throw him off balance. Her only hope was to get away and hide from him. Sophia fought, twisted and kicked, but his grip tightened, his fingers tangling in her hair like a knot.

"Leave her alone!" Anna screamed, pounding against the man's back with her fists. She tripped and fell to her knees.

Sophia planted her bare feet on the floor, tucked her shoulder and plowed into the man, sending him flying over Anna's body to land on his back on the hard Saltillo tile.

His hand, still tangled in her hair, dragged her backward and on top of him.

While Antonio caught his breath, Sophia scrambled free and shot to her feet. She gathered Anna and Jake and shoved them out the door in front of her, herding them down the hallway as fast as she could go. Their only hope was to find a place to hide until Antonio slept off the effects of the alcohol and drugs he'd been taking.

She stashed Anna and Jake in a storage room filled with sacks of pinto beans, flour and cornmeal. She piled the sacks in front of the two until no one would see them on a quick inspection of the tiny storeroom. There was only room for the two of them. Sophia backed toward the door.

Anna held out her hand. "Don't go. He'll kill you."

"Don't worry. I'll find a place to hide until he's sober." With a quick glance at the empty hallway, Sophia left the storeroom and ran down the corridor.

Antonio's roar echoed off the walls, and his footsteps thundered through the building.

She didn't have time to find another room. Once Antonio rounded the corner, he'd see her. And if he saw her, she was doomed to suffer another beating.

Sophia dove into their room, praying he wouldn't see her going there, hoping he'd think she'd left the main building to hide in one of the outlying structures.

With nothing more than a small cabinet that held her clothes, her only hiding place was beneath the bed she shared with her fiancé. With the footsteps closing in fast, Sophia dropped to the cold ceramic tile floors and rolled beneath the bed, pulling the blanket down to hide her in the shadows.

The door slammed open and Antonio bellowed, "Elena Sophia Carranza!"

She pushed herself as far back as she could go until her back hit the cool stucco wall. For several long minutes she lay as still as possible, afraid to move and even more afraid to breathe lest he hear her.

The man she'd been stupid enough to fall in love with tossed pillows, then flung the candlestick holder and her books across the room in his rage.

Sophia closed her eyes, as if that would help to hide her from Antonio's wrath.

Silence fell over the room. For a moment, Sophia thought Antonio had left, until she heard the sound of his breathing and the light scuffle of his shoes across the tiles.

With her breath lodged in her throat, Sophia waited.

A hand shot beneath the bed, grasped her ankle and yanked her hard, dragging her from her hiding place.

Sophia kicked and screamed, blinking back tears of fear and choking back sobs as she fought for her life, positive Antonio would make good his threat and kill her this time. His fingers closed around her throat and squeezed until she couldn't breathe. She tried to cry out, but nothing made it past her vocal cords. A gray shroud descended on her as her life slipped from her body.

"Sophia!" a deep voice called out.

Sophia strained to hear it again.

"Sophia, wake up!" A hand shook her shoulder. The one holding her arm was gentle, not the torture of Antonio's grip. She struggled to break free.

"Sophia," the voice said again, and strong arms wrapped around her, crushing her against a hard wall.

Sophia bucked and kicked, straining against the vise-like clamps around her body.

"Open your eyes, Sophia." The voice softened, and a hand smoothed the hair back from her forehead. "It's Thorn. Wake up."

She blinked, her eyes opening to the soft gray light of the shadowed room. A room far different from the one she'd shared with Antonio at *la Fuerte del Diablo* in Chihuahua.

A sob rose up her throat and shook her frame as tears slipped down her cheeks. *"¿Dónde estoy?"*

THOUGH SHE ASKED where she was in Spanish, Thorn replied in English. "At the Raging Bull Ranch. You're safe." He loosened his arms, allowing her to move and breathe more comfortably. Then he turned her to face him.

Her eyes were wide, her lips parted as she dragged air into her lungs as if she'd been running a marathon.

"You were havin' one heck of a dream." He kept his voice smooth, the same way he spoke when he worked with a frightened horse. "Must have been pretty bad for you to hide under the bed."

For a moment Sophia stared into his eyes, then she blinked and melted against his chest, burying her face in his T-shirt.

Her warm body shook against him. What kind of horrors had she endured to bring on such a terrible nightmare? The protector inside him wanted to find her nemesis and grind him into a pulp.

For several minutes, Thorn sat on the floor with Sophia nestled against him, trying not to think about the towel wrapped loosely around her, or the fact that it had inched up, exposing a significant amount of her thighs. He cleared his throat to break the silence. "Wanna talk about it?"

She shook her head and curled her fingers into the soft jersey, her fingernails scraping his skin through the fabric.

Okay, she didn't want to talk. Unfortunately, the longer she lay across his lap, the more his body responded to hers.

His pulse hummed along, driving blood to his lower extremities, making his jeans uncomfortably tight. He shifted her, easing her away from his growing erection.

Now was not the time to scare the poor woman. What if she'd been reliving the nightmare of rape?

Thorn tried to tell himself he'd been in love with his wife, and her memory could not be so easily set aside for a woman he barely knew.

The thought of Kayla usually had the effect of bringing Thorn back to the reality of his life and loss. Not so much at that moment. With Sophia so real and immediate stretched across his thighs, he could barely recall Kayla's pretty face. That bothered him enough to move.

He pushed Sophia off his lap onto the cool tile floor, stood and bent to gather her into his arms.

"I can get up on my own," she said, pressing her hands against his chest as he straightened.

"I know you can." He set her on the bed and pulled the sheet up over her gorgeous legs, as if hiding them would erase their image from his mind.

It didn't.

Sophia's cheeks reddened, and she tugged the towel over her breasts. "Do you suppose Señor Derringer would have some clothing I could borrow?"

"He sent for some. They should be here shortly."

"Has he heard anything else from the authorities?"

"Not yet. He expects them anytime, though." Thorn turned his back to her and walked toward the window. If he stared at her much longer, he'd be in a world of hurt. Why now, of all times, was he attracted to a female? Since his wife had died, he hadn't even looked at another woman.

Then Sophia had blown into his life and almost killed him. Why would he be attracted to her? She'd lied to him, shot at him and, if the CBP reports were accurate, could be a murderer running from Mexico to escape prison or a firing squad.

He glanced back at the woman lying in the bed, tugging at the towel across her chest, her cheeks a soft shade of pink.

No, he couldn't see her as a killer.

Movement out of the corner of his vision drew his attention back to the barnyard. "Looks like the CBP and the foreman are back."

Sophia's eyes widened, and she clutched the sheet in her hands.

He shot a frown her way. "Can I trust you to stay put while I go see what they found?"

Her lips twisted. "I have no clothes. I wouldn't get far in a towel."

Thorn's mouth twitched at the image of Sophia's escape in nothing but the fluffy white towel she could barely keep around her. He fought back a smile. "You didn't answer me. Do I have your word?"

Sophia's eyes narrowed and she studied him before she answered on a sigh. "Yes."

Thorn nodded. "I'll see about those clothes while I'm out." He left the house through the French doors in his room and hurried out to the barnyard.

Hank was there, standing beside Scott Walden. Max flanked his other side.

The sheriff's deputies and CBP men were gathered a few steps away around a topographical map laid out over their vehicle, pointing and discussing specific coordinates.

Thorn stepped up to Hank and Scott. "What did they find?"

Scott shook his head. "Not much. The bikers must have policed up their own. The only thing we found was a bike they couldn't haul out of there. The CBP took pictures and marked the spot on their maps. They'll send a truck out to collect evidence."

"Did they pull any slugs out of my truck?" Hank asked.

Scott shook his head. "They want to wait until the state crime-scene investigation team can get out here to process the evidence, since it's not certain the attackers were illegal aliens. Could be a local gang."

"Did you tell them about the man who helped Sophia escape?" Thorn asked, keeping his voice low enough that the CBP wouldn't hear.

Hank shook his head. "I thought we'd go find him first, so that they don't question how we knew he was out there."

"Good idea," Thorn agreed. The less the authorities knew about Sophia, the better. "If you think the woman is safe here with your bodyguards, I'd like to be in on that search party."

Hank glanced at him, his eyes narrowed. "We can hold her in the bunker." The ranch owner held up his hand. "And we'll keep a better eye on her this time. Plus, my daughter, PJ, is on her way out with some items I think will help us in our effort to camouflage our guest."

The leader of the CBP team broke away from those gathered around the map. "We had a call from the FBI. They want in on this investigation since it could be that the men who attacked you might have something to do with cartel members and the murder suspects." The man sighed. "I'd rather we handled it on our own, but I'm getting pressure from my supervisor. A regional director will be out here in the next couple of hours, along with the state crime-scene lab technicians. You'll need to be available to talk to them."

Hank's lips pressed into a line, then he shrugged. "We'll cooperate fully."

"In the meantime, keep your men clear of the attack site until the crime lab has a chance to gather more evidence."

"Can't keep the cattle from wandering," Hank warned.

The CBP officer shook his head. "Do the best you can."

"Will do." Hank stuck out his hand.

The CBP team lead grasped it and shook it briefly, then let go. "We'll be working out of Wild Oak Canyon for the short term until we get a handle on the murder suspects and where they might be headed." He directed his glance from Hank to Scott, then to Thorn. "If any of you see or hear anything, let us know immediately."

Thorn gave a single nod of acknowledgment, refusing to promise anything.

The CBP team folded the map, climbed into the government-issue SUV and drove down the gravel drive to the highway outside the gates of the Raging Bull Ranch.

Deputy Sanders stepped up to Hank. "Looks like the feds will be taking over. If they set up a task force, we'll assign a deputy liaison. In the meantime, call us if you have any more trouble. We're here for you." Sanders and his men climbed into their SUVs and followed the CBP off the ranch.

Hank sighed. "Let's get out to the canyon and find that body before the rest of the party shows. Maybe it will give us more of a clue as to the real identity of our guest."

"Will you report the body?" Having been an officer of the law, Thorn didn't like withholding information in an ongoing investigation. Then again, he'd have to explain how he knew about the body in the first place.

Though Sophia hadn't been completely up-front with him in the beginning and she could still be hiding something, Thorn wasn't ready to hand her over to the authorities. The nightmare that had caused her to crawl beneath the bed had to be rooted in some pretty bad stuff. There was more to her story, and he wanted to know what it was before he gave her to the sheriff, CBP or FBI.

The handheld radio clipped to Max's black utility belt chirped. He stepped away from the others and listened to the staticky call, answering with, "Let her in." When he rejoined the group, he leaned into Hank and said quietly, "Your daughter has arrived with Bolton."

"Good." Hank's mouth turned up in a smile at the mention of his daughter and her fiancé-bodyguard. "While PJ and Chuck keep Sophia company, we'll see about finding a body." He turned to Thorn. "It's rained pretty hard since she crossed the border, so we'll have our work cut out for us finding her trail."

Thorn stared out over the landscape, visualizing what he'd seen the previous evening before the sun had completely set. "We'll start from the point where she cut the fence and work our way into the canyon from there."

"Regroup in ten minutes?" Hank stared around at the men.

The foreman nodded. "I take it we'll be on four-wheelers?"

Hank nodded. "I think we'll get there and back faster."

"I'll get them ready." Though Scott hadn't slept in over twenty-four hours, the man sprinted toward the barn.

Thorn hurried back to the house and entered his room. The connecting door to Sophia's room was closed. He frowned and hurried toward it, his heart thudding against his chest. Had Sophia made another run for it?

He flung the door open and charged in.

Sophia stood naked in the middle of the room, her towel clutched to her chest, eyes wide and wary. "Don't you ever knock?"

Heat climbed up Thorn's neck to his cheeks and spread low into his groin at the sight of her slender legs, softly flared hips and narrow waistline. "Pardon me. I thought…"

"You thought I tried to run?" She turned her back, exposing the full length of her naked body to him while she dropped the edges of the towel in order to wrap it around her middle. "Kind of hard to do when you have no clothes." When she spun back to face him, tucking the corner of the towel in at her breasts, she glared at him. "A gentleman would look away."

More heat poured into his cheeks, and his lips tightened. He hadn't expected to see her naked and he certainly hadn't counted on his body's immediate reaction.

He summoned anger to push aside the lust threatening to steal his last brain cells. "You're covered now, and I'm in a hurry."

Her frown straightened, and she stepped forward. "What's happening?"

"Hank's daughter is here. You're to cooperate with her and stay in the bunker while we head out to find your dead accomplice."

Sophia tensed and bit down on her bottom lip. "You didn't inform the border patrol about Hector?"

"No. And we didn't tell them about the helicopter. All they know is that Hank was attacked by a group of dirt bikers on his property. That and what they'd been told about a couple of murderers possibly crossing the border near here."

The woman let out a long breath. "Thank you for believing me."

Thorn stared at her long and hard. "I wouldn't go that far. Until we find the body of your man Hector and determine his cause of death, I'm withholding my judgment."

Sophia frowned but nodded. "Understandable. You don't know me. I wouldn't trust me if I was in your boots."

"In the meantime, you'll stay in the bunker. The fewer people who know you're here, the better for all involved. I don't want Hank to be arrested for harboring a fugitive."

"I didn't kill anyone."

"So you say." Thorn hooked her arm and led her toward the door to the room. "Hank's daughter and bodyguard will be in charge of you today. If you want Hank's help, I suggest you cooperate fully."

Sophia shook off his hand and glared up at him. "Don't push me."

"Then move."

She tossed her long light brown hair back over her shoulder and reached for the doorknob, flicking the lock free.

After a quick glance down the hallway to ensure it was clear, she stepped out with as much pride and bearing as she could muster dressed in nothing but a towel, her hair uncombed and her face free of all cosmetics.

Sophia refused to let his autocratic ways cow her. She'd been beaten, cursed and held prisoner by a madman. Thorn Drennan didn't scare her one bit.

But when his hand cupped her elbow or pushed the hair out of her face, or when he pressed his body against hers…

Warmth sizzled across her skin and rippled through her nerve endings.

After all she'd been through with Antonio, Sophia couldn't understand the knot of desire building low in her belly for this taciturn cowboy marching her along the corridor.

He led her to the hidden doorway, pressed his thumb to the thumb pad and entered a combination. The door opened to the staircase leading downward into the basement beneath the ranch house.

He guided her down a long corridor and into a room with a large solid-oak table at the center. White dry-erase boards lined two walls, and a large white screen dominated the end of the room.

"Have a seat," Thorn ordered.

"Can't you say please? Or *por favor?*" When he didn't respond, Sophia tucked the towel closer and held her ground. "I prefer to stand."

He shrugged and left the room.

A moment later he returned with a lovely young woman with sandy-blond hair and soft gray eyes. A big man followed her through the doorway, his shoulders filling the frame.

Thorn turned to the two. "Sophia, meet PJ Franks and Chuck Bolton. They're going to stay with you until we get back."

Sophia gasped. "Get back?"

"I'm going with Hank and his men to find Hector's body."

"Oh." Her heart sank into her belly like a ton of bricks. Though Chuck and PJ looked fully capable, Thorn had been there for her from the moment she'd landed in his arms in the cabin. He'd kept her alive during the shoot-out with the biker gang and had held her through a nasty nightmare, soothing her brow and holding her until she'd stopped shaking.

His gaze captured hers, his eyes narrowing. "You'll be fine with PJ and Chuck until I get back."

Sophia swallowed the knot in her throat, turned away from Thorn and held out her hand to PJ. "Nice to meet you."

Thorn stood for a moment longer, and then left the room.

PJ took Sophia's hand in a firm but gentle grip. "Don't worry, he'll be back. Hank takes care of his own." PJ let go of her hand and turned to the man behind her. "We brought some things we thought you might need." To Chuck she said, "You can set the bag down and get out of here."

"Yes, ma'am." The big man grinned and set a couple of bulging plastic bags on the table. When he turned to leave, he captured PJ in a hold around her waist and kissed her soundly on the lips.

She slapped his shoulder, a smile spreading across her face. "Save it for later, cowboy."

Chuck stepped through the door and PJ closed it behind him, her smile still in place.

A pang of envy tightened Sophia's chest. "I take it you know each other."

PJ blinked as if she realized there was another person in the room. "Chuck's my fiancé and the father of our baby girl." She laughed. "Long story. If you plan on sticking around, I'll tell you all about it. In the meantime, I understand we have work to do."

Sophia frowned. "I don't understand."

"My father, Hank Derringer, told me you have a BOLO issued on you."

"BOLO?" Sophia shook her head, wondering if she had stepped into another world.

"Be on the lookout. It's a term law enforcement uses when they want all personnel to be on the alert for certain people they want to bring in for a crime or questioning." PJ's brows wrinkled. "He said the word is out that an Elena Carranza is wanted for murder in Mexico."

"I didn't kill anyone."

"So Hank said." PJ smiled. "You don't look like a killer to me, if that makes you feel better."

"Thank you." Sophia liked this woman with the open smile and the pretty eyes.

"The point is, Hank showed me the picture going around with your face on it. The features are a bit fuzzy, and your hair is really dark in the picture. If we make a few changes, you could pass for someone else."

"How will this help?"

"The roads in and out of this area have been set up with roadblocks. Until the dust settles, you'll be here awhile. We need to come up with a cover story for you."

Her pulse leaped and thundered through her veins. "I can't leave?" All the terror of leaving the compound in

Mexico returned, and her hands shook. "He'll find me," she whispered. "He'll find me and kill me."

PJ's brows knit. "Who will find you?"

"My ex-fiancé." Sophia shook her head. "I cannot stay here. I have to leave."

"Sorry, sweetie, it's not possible. There are cops, border patrol and FBI descending on this place. If you want to hide, you have to change your appearance and lie low."

"You don't understand." Sophia grabbed PJ's arm. "Everyone around me will suffer. No one is safe until he gets me back."

PJ held Sophia's hands steady. "My father won't let anything happen to you. That's why he's assigned Thorn to protect you outside these walls."

"Antonio has eyes and ears on both sides of the border." Sophia swallowed a sob. "It's only a matter of time before he gets word of where I'm hiding. I have to get away."

"And you will," PJ said. "When the hoopla dies down. And giving you a new identity will help keep the authorities out of your business should they see you."

Sophia breathed in and out several times to tamp down the rising panic. PJ was right. With so many people converging on the area, she wouldn't get out without running the gauntlet. If changing her appearance helped to hide her, so be it. It might also help her in her new life away from Mexico. "Okay, how do you propose to change me?"

PJ grinned. "Since Thorn has been assigned as your bodyguard, you'll be Thorn's old girlfriend from college come back to town to rekindle the romance." She held up a box with the face of a beautiful woman with flowing golden hair. "And you're going blond."

Chapter Eight

Thorn led the way out to the cabin where he'd first found Sophia. As he bumped along on the four-wheeler, his thoughts strayed to the woman, wondering if she'd try to escape again, and, if she succeeded, whether or not she'd make it on her own evading the men trying to kill her.

They skirted the area marked off by flags poking out of the ground, swinging wide to avoid disturbing potential evidence the state crime-scene investigators, CBP or FBI might use in their investigation of the biker gang and their possible connection with Mexican cartel members and the two reported murderers the Mexican government wanted extradited to face their crimes.

A small plume of smoke rose from the direction the cabin had stood the night before, providing shelter from the raging storm. Even before he reached the site, Thorn could smell smoldering wood.

His gut tightened. Had he not been the one to find Sophia first, she might have been burned to death in the rubble of the tiny hunter's shelter or dragged back to Mexico to a man who had abused her.

Thorn's fingers clenched around the four-wheeler's handles as he pulled to a halt in front of the charred remains of the shack.

Hank pulled in beside him. "Damn."

Without a word, Thorn dismounted and circled the blackened studs rising three or four feet from the ground. The roof had collapsed, and the corrugated tin twisted from the heat of the fire.

At the back of what was left of the building, Thorn kicked through part of the fallen roof to find the shabby dirt bike buried beneath, the tires and seat nothing more than melted black goo.

"Think Sophia was right and they were after her?" Hank stepped up beside Thorn.

"Looks like it. But we won't be certain unless they target her alone."

Hank's lips pressed into a thin line. "I hope the job PJ's doing on her will throw them off her trail a little longer until we can find the source of her troubles."

"Whoever's responsible has contacts on this side of the border."

"Stands to reason. Cartels wouldn't operate very well unless they had contacts on both sides of the border." Hank stared at the burned remains. "Most of the drugs they traffic end up in the States. The demand ensures the supply continues to flow."

Thorn nodded. He knew that. He'd busted his share of junkies and pushers in his job as the county sheriff before he'd quit. He'd even upset a few major drug runs on the highways headed north. Sadly, the drugs never stopped coming. In the losing battle to clean up the drug problem in his county, the price had been greater than the reward. His efforts had cost him the lives of his wife and unborn child, and his career.

For every bust, for every man taken out of the drug-running business, he could count on two more thugs filling that doper's shoes. When trafficking drugs exceeded anything an uneducated man could make in the States, and greatly exceeded the pathetic wages of an honest man in Mexico, the choice was easy.

"Come on. I'll show you where she cut the fence." Thorn straddled his ATV, swung wide of what was left of the cabin and sped toward the fence on the southern border of the Raging Bull Ranch.

The fence was still intact for as far as he could see in either direction.

While Thorn struggled with the barbed wire, Hank sent Max in one direction while he sped off in the other.

It took Thorn and Scott a few minutes to locate the spot he'd patched, and a few minutes more to unwrap the wire he'd used to pull the fence together. They were minutes he had the feeling he couldn't spare. Finding the body of Sophia's escort would prove time-consuming with her tracks effectively washed away by the previous night's storm.

By the time Thorn had the fence down, Hank and Max had returned.

"No breaks in the fence for at least a half mile to the west," Hank reported.

"None that far to the east," Max said.

"It appears the bikers didn't come from this end of the property."

"Which begs the question, were they really after the woman, or were they after Hank?" Thorn didn't expect an answer. He mounted his ride and gunned the throttle.

The group of men crossed the property line and entered Big Bend National Park, speeding toward the rugged hills and canyons heading directly south.

Thorn prayed they'd catch a break and stumble across the man's body soon, rather than spending hours combing over potentially thousands of acres.

He headed toward the pass leading down into a canyon, rationalizing Sophia's guide would stay low as long as possible before climbing out of the quasi protection of the canyon walls.

The path led downward, narrowing so much that their four-wheelers clung to the edges.

A sharp bend in the trail led to a straight stretch that climbed back up toward the top of a ridge. The roar of the four-wheeler engines echoed off the canyon walls, and buzzards lifted off the ground from the top of the ridge, spreading their wings to catch the thermals. They hovered above the approaching machines, watching, awaiting their turn to scavenge flesh from a dead animal.

Or in this case, the dead human.

Thorn reached the body first, skidding to a halt, thankful for the night's rain keeping the dust from rising and coating the man's body.

He lay sprawled across the trail. A motorcycle leaned against a boulder halfway down the steep hillside below, and the rocks between had a scraped or raked appearance as if the bike had slid on its side down the incline.

The ground around the man's body and what was left of his face was stained dark brown. Even the rain hadn't washed away the evidence of his demise.

"Jesus." Scott backed away from the gore and turned to purge his breakfast.

"Probably died instantly." Thorn's belly roiled, but he kept his composure, studying the ground around him a moment longer before he glanced around at the others. "See all we needed to see?"

Hank stood over the dead man. "How did she survive this attack?"

"Sophia said she was down the hill, in the shadow of an overhang when the helicopter flew over." Thorn stepped to the edge of the ridge and peered down another trail on the other side. As Sophia had indicated, a giant bluff leaned over the trail, providing a deep shadow beneath.

So far, Sophia's story checked out. Thorn turned around. "Let's get back. We can report this to the CBP, now that we know where he is. We can tell them a bull breached the fence and we went after him."

"Sounds good." Hank's face was pale and a little grayer than when they'd started out. "No man deserves to die like that."

And Hector had been helping Sophia escape.

Thorn leaped onto his four-wheeler, hit the starter and executed a tight turn on the narrow trail, heading back the way they'd come. Images of Kayla lying in a pool of her own blood stormed through Thorn's memory, spurring him on. He couldn't let the same thing happen to Sophia.

PJ SWITCHED OFF the hair dryer and laid her brush aside.

After an hour and a half of sitting in a chair, Sophia prayed the woman was done.

"What do you think?" PJ handed Sophia a mirror.

Sophia stared at the stranger in the reflection. Naturally a light brunette, the pale, golden blond strands fit her complexion and complemented her green eyes. She cupped the shorter ends falling only to her shoulders, liking the way it bounced. After one year in the compound, without a decent stylist, Sophia's hair had grown long and shaggy, down to the middle of her back. This shorter, lighter hair gave her an entirely different look.

"With the hair and those clothes, you won't look anything like the woman we started out with." PJ grinned. "You look fabulous."

Hope swelled in Sophia's chest and tears filled her eyes. "Thank you." She might have a chance of fooling people.

Maybe even starting over somewhere Antonio couldn't find her.

PJ turned to Max. "What do you think?"

Max had been leaning against the wall, his back to the women as PJ worked her magic on Sophia.

He turned to face them, his narrowed gaze widening when he saw Sophia. After a moment, he grunted.

PJ laughed. "I'll take that as approval." She turned back to Sophia and helped her out of the chair. "And I bet Hank knows someone who can fix you up with personal identification—a driver's license, social-security number, the works."

"He's already on it," Max confirmed.

Sophia straightened, her legs stiff from sitting so long, staring at a picture of the Grand Canyon on an otherwise-empty white wall in the cavernous conference room.

She smoothed the wrinkles out of the pressed khaki trousers and white short-sleeved ribbed-knit top PJ had provided for her. Sophia hoped the outfit gave her a casual, carefree, I'm-on-vacation look that would fool others enough they wouldn't think she was a cartel fugitive or illegal alien who'd slipped across the border in the middle of the night.

Her stomach rumbled, reminding her she'd better eat or risk being sick again.

PJ laughed. "I take it you're hungry."

Sophia's lips twisted. "I guess I am."

"Think it would be all right to go topside to the kitchen?" PJ asked Max.

The bodyguard's brows dipped. "Mr. Derringer gave specific instructions not to let Ms. Carranza out of the bunker until they returned."

"Then could you send Brandon up for something to eat?" PJ asked. "We could all stand a bite of lunch."

Max nodded, then frowned at them. "Don't go any-where."

Sophia gave the big guard a tentative smile. "I promise."

A moment later, Brandon entered the room. "Max asked me to keep an eye on you while he went to the kitchen. I thought you might be more entertained in the computer room, if you'd like to join me."

Sophia followed the young gadgets wizard, and PJ brought up the rear.

They entered the computer room, which was equipped with several workstations and a bank of a dozen monitors depicting alternating views of Hank's ranch from the corners of the house to what looked like the front gate.

Sophia was familiar with this kind of technology at *la Fuerte del Diablo*. Drug running was big business and the elusive *El Martillo,* the kingpin of the cartel, spared no expense to protect his investment. Though Antonio was one of *El Martillo*'s top men, he wasn't in charge. *El Martillo* slipped in and out of *la Fuerte del Diablo* under the cover of darkness to mete out his brand of justice to those who went against his wishes, serving as a reminder that he wasn't called The Hammer for nothing.

Sophia had never actually met *El Martillo.* She wasn't sure what his real name was or what he looked like. She'd only seen him in profile once. A tall man, he'd carried himself straight, almost like a businessman. But he was known for some unspeakable acts that kept his people in line when he wasn't around.

Her and Hector's escape from the compound would probably anger *El Martillo* and put Antonio under scrutiny, if not on notice, or even get him killed.

After all the abuse Antonio had heaped on her, she couldn't feel sorry for the man. He deserved whatever *El Martillo* did to him. If The Hammer allowed Antonio to live, he'd seek revenge on her for betraying him and putting him in danger of *El Martillo*'s wrath.

Sophia studied the monitors, searching for any signs of Antonio or the biker gang who'd attacked them the night before. "Do you also have some sort of radar to detect aircraft?" Images of the helicopter hovering over the top of the ridge strafing the ground with bullets sent a shiver over Sophia's skin.

Brandon shook his head. "No, not yet, but Hank has mentioned installing one. I'm in the process of evaluating what's available to come up with the best for the cost."

Movement on the screen overlooking the front gate drew Sophia's attention. "Are you expecting visitors?"

A large black SUV pulled up to the gate, and a man dressed in an olive drab shirt and dark sunglasses leaned out the window to press the button on the keypad. A beeping sound alerted them to the caller.

Brandon frowned at the monitor. "Hank mentioned the FBI would be checking in, but he said it would be later today." He leaned over a microphone and hit the talk button. "May I help you?"

"FBI," a disembodied voice crackled over the speaker.

Sophia's heart skipped a beat, and she clenched her fists to keep her hands from shaking. Though the man at the gate couldn't see her, she felt exposed. Did he know Hank was harboring their suspected murderer? Had the ranch owner lied and sent them to collect her and ship her back to Mexico?

"We're here to speak with Hank Derringer," the FBI agent continued.

PJ stepped up beside her and slipped an arm around her shoulders. "You'll be okay," she whispered.

The woman's reassuring words helped, but Sophia knew what would happen if she was sent back to Mexico. Antonio would kill her and her baby. "I can't go back," she murmured beneath her breath.

PJ's arm tightened around her. "And Hank won't let them take you back."

Brandon shrugged. "I'm sorry, Mr. Derringer is not available at this time."

"Do you know when he'll be back?"

"He should be back after lunch," Brandon said.

"We'll wait." In the view screen, the agent's head ducked back into the vehicle. From the angle of the camera, Sophia could see him lean back and say something to the man in the backseat.

The window went up, the dark tint on the glass blocking the view of the driver and the interior of the SUV.

Brandon lifted a radio and hit the transmitter key. "Max, we have company at the gate. FBI. They're waiting there until Hank gets back."

Max responded. "Roger."

For a long moment, Sophia stared at the screen. The SUV didn't move. Good at their word, the FBI wasn't leaving until they spoke with Hank. After five minutes, the doors to the SUV opened and the men got out, stretching. Four of the five men wore jumpsuits with *FBI* emblazoned on their arms. The fifth man emerged, an imposing figure in khaki slacks and a polo shirt with *FBI* embroidered on the front.

Sophia didn't recognize his face, but something about his size, the way he stood and his movements struck a chord of memory she couldn't place.

The leader of the agents spoke with one of his men, a tall, slender, light-haired man with narrow eyes and an angular face. He didn't speak with any of the others, only the leader, and he held a military-looking weapon as if it were an extension of his body.

A chill slithered down Sophia's spine, but she put it off as paranoia because these men were with the FBI, and they had the power to take her to jail for a crime she hadn't committed.

Sophia's pulse hammered through her veins. Like an animal trapped in a cage, she paced across the floor several times, always ending up back at the monitors to view the men determined to wait as long as it took until Derringer got back.

When would Hank and Thorn return? And how would they get her out of there without the FBI noticing her?

Movement on another monitor drew her attention away from the front gate and the FBI. A line of four-wheelers approached a camera. Leading the pack was a tall, sandy-haired man with broad shoulders and a determined set to his brow.

Thorn.

Sophia let out a breath she felt she'd been holding since he left. The man might not be able to protect her from the FBI or the CBP, but having him around made her feel better, like someone was looking out for her, whether she'd asked for his help or not.

"They're back," Brandon stated.

The four-wheelers slipped past the camera at the rear of the barn and appeared in the view screen in the barnyard.

Max strode into view.

Thorn, Hank, the foreman and the two bodyguards who'd gone with them dismounted and converged on Max, all eyes turning toward the driveway leading into the ranch compound.

Hank nodded at Max.

Max unclipped the radio from his belt and lifted it to his lips. His words crackled over the radio in front of Brandon. "Let the FBI through the gate."

The young computer guru responded, "Roger." He hit a button on a control panel.

Sophia's gaze returned to the monitor with the FBI SUV view. The gate swung open, the men piled into the vehicle and the SUV pulled through. Her pulse quickened, and she had the intense urge to run.

"Don't worry. My father wouldn't turn you over to them." PJ's arm squeezed her shoulders. "Just keep calm and stay here until Hank has a chance to talk to them and we know what they want."

Though she appreciated PJ's encouragement, Sophia wished Thorn was there with her. After his actions to ensure her safety from the biker gang attack, she trusted his strength and fighting ability to keep her alive. For a moment she wished he'd stay with her all the way to her new life. Too soon she'd be on her own again, as soon as she could get safe passage out of the area.

WHEN MAX MET them at the barn, Thorn's first thought was that Sophia had escaped. His breath caught and held until he heard the bodyguard out.

He'd barely released his breath when Max assured them Sophia was still safe in the bunker, but the FBI had arrived and wanted to be let in.

Hank gave the approval.

"Are you sure that's a good idea?" Thorn asked.

"Sophia is to remain in the bunker. If you'd like to join her, please do. Max can stay with me."

"If you're sure she's okay…" Thorn turned to Max.

The other man's lips twitched on the corner. "She's fine, but you won't recognize her."

Hank grinned. "I knew PJ would come through." He tipped his head toward Max. "Resume your watch on our guest. I'll send Thorn down to relieve you as soon as we figure out what the FBI is up to."

Anxious to see Sophia and prove to himself she was still there and okay, Thorn waited impatiently for the FBI SUV to stop in the barnyard.

Four men climbed out, all wearing the green jumpsuits of a tactical team, with *FBI* emblazoned across one arm and Glocks strapped to their black utility belts. One man held the door for a fifth man to emerge from the middle of the backseat.

It was Grant Lehmann, a regional director for the FBI and an old friend of Hank's.

Hank stepped forward. "Grant, good to see you."

The man wore khaki slacks and a black polo shirt with *FBI* embroidered on the upper-left front. He wore sunglasses, which he removed as he stuck out a hand to shake Hank's. "Hank, you seem to keep this part of the country busy."

Hank dipped his head, his lips firming. "Just trying to clean up a little riffraff. Make this part of Texas a safer place to live."

Lehmann chuckled. "So how's that working for you?"

Hank shrugged. "One bad guy at a time."

"Sure you're not setting yourself up as a target by taking on the drug cartels?"

"Someone's gotta do it if the U.S. government isn't willing to engage." Hank's jaw tightened.

If Thorn hadn't been watching the exchange closely, he wouldn't have caught the slight narrowing of Lehmann's eyes before he laughed.

"You know how to call a spade a spade, Hank."

"And the drug running doesn't seem to end."

"Well, we're here to help." Grant glanced around the

barnyard. "We need a place to set up operations to bring in some of those bad guys you were talking about."

"Care to share what you know?" Hank brushed his cowboy hat against his leg, stirring up a cloud of dust.

"There's a BOLO out on Elena Carranza and Antonio Martinez. They were thought to have crossed the border from Mexico headed this way."

"What makes you think they're in this area?"

"Undercover contacts on the other side got wind they'd left a cartel compound headed north."

"They could have crossed anywhere."

"Eyewitnesses saw them on motorcycles at a low-water crossing of the Rio Grande yesterday morning, directly south of the Raging Bull. They should have come across the river and entered the Big Bend National Park canyons in the afternoon."

"Just two?" Hank waved a hand at the four men in tactical jumpsuits. "They must be special."

"They are. We've already briefed the CBP that these two are armed and extremely dangerous. They've been instructed to shoot on sight."

Thorn was shocked by the man's words. Shoot on sight? Pretty harsh command for an FBI regional director. Something about the man didn't feel right.

Hank placed his hat on his head, shadowing his expression. "From what the CBP said, the Mexican government was interested in extraditing them."

"If it comes down to your life or theirs…" Lehmann's eyes narrowed "…don't hesitate. Shoot."

"That bad?" Hank asked.

"The worst," the regional director confirmed. "I wouldn't be here if it wasn't that important."

"Does seem strange for them to pull in a regional director for a couple of Mexican fugitives." Hank scratched his chin. "Guess they wanted the best on the case."

Grant snorted. "They'd have thrown the entire department at them if they'd had the funding."

Thorn stepped forward. "Do you have photos of the two?"

Grant's brows rose.

Hank turned to Thorn. "Grant, this is Thorn Drennan, one of the men I've hired on as ranch security. Thorn, Grant Lehmann, FBI regional director."

"And old friend." Grant shook hands with Thorn. "Hank and I have known each other for years. Been through rough times together. Isn't that right?"

Hank nodded. "Grant led the search effort when my wife and son were kidnapped."

"Unfortunately, we never found them or any clues as to who took them and where." Grant shook his head. "Lili-anna was a beautiful woman and Jake was a smart little boy, just like his father."

"Photos?" Thorn prompted.

Grant frowned and turned to the man nearest the vehicle. "Hand me the case file."

Without a word, the agent reached into the SUV and retrieved a folder filled with documents.

Grant flipped it open and pulled out two grainy photos. The woman in the first was smiling, and she wore her hair up with long dangling earrings swinging beside her cheeks. She held a margarita glass in one hand. The photo appeared to be a scanned and enlarged photograph of a young lady partying at a bar.

Despite the graininess, Thorn could tell this woman was the one they had hidden in Hank's bunker.

"She looks about as dangerous as a college coed." Thorn handed the photo back to Lehmann.

"Looks are deceiving. She and her boyfriend, Antonio Martinez, killed two undercover DEA agents."

"Why would they kill agents then run to the States?" Thorn asked. "It doesn't make sense."

"They skipped out of Mexico with a suitcase full of drug money. They'd be more afraid of cartel retaliation than being caught by the U.S. government." Grant's voice dropped to a low, dangerous tone. "They have a million reasons in that suitcase to run."

Chapter Nine

Grant Lehmann and his team stayed another ten minutes before they loaded up and left the Raging Bull Ranch with a promise to return to set up operations.

"Are you sure you want them here?" Thorn asked.

Hank nodded. "As long as they're here, I get information about their operation. Even if they don't feed it to me, I'll have Brandon bug them. We'll know what's going on."

"Why didn't you tell them about the body we found in the canyon?"

"I'm going to let the CBP find it." Hank smiled. "I'm also going to let the CBP set up operations co-located with the FBI—joint operations forcing the agencies to work together. The more people they have on this operation, the more confused it'll be." His smile faded, and his gaze captured Thorn's. "We need to get Sophia out of here before they return."

"What if what Lehmann said was true? What if she's in on the murders and the theft of the drug money?"

"What do you think? What do you believe?" Hank fired back.

Thorn usually trusted his gut. And his gut told him Sophia had told him the truth. He ran a hand through his hair. "I think she's telling the truth."

"I have a hunch she is, too." Hank turned toward the

house. "And if she's telling the truth, who's feeding the FBI a load of hooey?"

"Lies that could get Sophia killed on sight." Thorn didn't like it. That the FBI would fall into it so solidly had him scared for Sophia.

"First of all, I don't trust that the FBI is getting the right information. I still think there's some bad blood floating around in the bureau. Someone knows something about Elena and Antonio. And call me a fool, but I still like to think, though it's probably wishful thinking, that someone might even have information on the whereabouts of Lilianna and Jake."

"Then, yes, it's a good idea to keep the FBI close."

Hank waved a hand toward the hallway. "Let's see how it went with PJ. We'll need someplace to hide her away from here, and a believable story in case someone does spot her."

Thorn followed Hank to the bunker and waited while Hank pressed his thumb to the scanner. When the door opened, Thorn stepped past his boss and practically ran down the steps into the concrete-walled basement.

Hank chuckled behind him. "Afraid she's gone?"

Hell, yeah.

Thorn entered the conference room where they'd left Sophia with PJ. It was empty except for the cape, empty bottles of hair color and lingering acrid stench of chemicals.

Voices carried to them from the computer room.

"I bet they're with Brandon." Hank moved past the conference room and down the long hallway to the computer bay.

Brandon sat at his desk while the two women gazed at the bank of display screens.

As Hank and Thorn entered, a beautiful blonde with

deep green eyes turned toward them, her eyes widening. Her lips parted on a silent gasp, and she flew across the room into Thorn's arms. "Thank God you're back."

Thorn held her for a long moment, dumbstruck by the transformation. "Sophia?" He pushed her to arm's length and gazed down at her face.

Despite the change in hair color and style, the same green eyes stared back at him, misted in a film of tears. "You were away for a long time. Then the FBI came…"

"They're gone for now," Hank said. "You can't stay at the Raging Bull. They're coming back to set up operations here on the ranch."

Sophia's gaze bounced from Hank to Thorn. "Is it safe to leave the area?"

"No," Hank replied. "There are roadblocks everywhere. If you try to leave, even with the new hair, they might figure it out. Especially since I don't have your identification documents yet."

PJ touched her finger to her chin. "I'd offer to let her stay in my apartment, but there's barely enough room for me, Chuck and the baby. Plus, it's smack-dab in the middle of town. She needs to stay where no one really goes."

"Thorn, don't you live on the edge of Wild Oak Canyon?" Hank asked.

"Yes." Thorn tensed.

Brandon pulled up a map of the area on the computer and keyed in Thorn's address. He switched the view to satellite. "The house sits on the edge of town. I believe the house next to yours is empty?"

His gut knotting, Thorn didn't like where this was going. "The house next door is for sale." And had been for over a year with no prospects.

"The road leading out of town is a farm-to-market road, not a major highway. Traffic will be minimal." Brandon spun in his chair to face Thorn. "I can set you up with some cameras, but it'll take time. Maybe tomorrow?"

A heavy feeling pinching his lungs, Thorn wanted to tell them no. The last woman in his house had been Kayla, before she'd been shot to death. Going home was his own self-torture, which he preferred to do alone. He hadn't emptied her closet of clothes, and he hadn't painted over the half-finished wall in the nursery.

Kayla had asked him to paint it pale yellow, a neutral color that would suit a boy or a girl. She'd insisted on being surprised by the sex of their child. No matter whether a boy or a girl, she'd love that baby with all her heart.

She'd been killed the day of her monthly appointment. Thorn had picked her up from the house, the proud daddy going to every obstetrician appointment throughout her pregnancy.

Thorn hadn't known that the previous day, a drug addict he'd put away for peddling drugs to the teens in town had been released from Huntsville prison after serving only two years of a five-year sentence. Marcus Falkner was met by his girlfriend and driven all the way from the prison north of Houston to Fort Stockton. There he'd met up with one of his old gang members who supplied him with a 9 mm Beretta and a fully loaded ten-round clip.

He'd made the trip from Fort Stockton to Wild Oak Canyon, flying low in his girlfriend's black, souped-up Camaro, strung out on a fresh batch of crystal meth, arriving just in time for Thorn to help his wife from their truck in the parking lot of the clinic.

He'd fired off two rounds before Thorn had known what was coming.

Thorn had thrown himself at Kayla, knocking her to the pavement, covering her body with his.

Too hyped up on meth to shoot straight, Marcus emptied the rest of the clip and squealed out of the parking lot, fishtailing on loose gravel. He drove straight into a telephone pole, snapping his neck. Marcus had died instantly.

When Thorn had risen from the ground, he'd known something was terribly wrong with Kayla. She'd been lying facedown, moaning, her skin pale, a pool of blood spreading out from beneath her.

"You okay, Drennan?" Hank waved a hand in front of Thorn's face.

Thorn shook himself out of the memory and focused on his boss. "Yes."

"Then you'll take her to your house, and if anyone asks, she's an old girlfriend from your college days."

Thorn gritted his teeth, the thought of bringing any woman back to the house he'd shared with Kayla grating against his nerves. He glanced at Sophia's deep green eyes, noting the shadows beneath them and the yellowish-green bruise on her cheekbone that her long light brown hair had covered. He reached out and brushed his hand against the spot. "Did Antonio do this to you?"

She nodded, her face turning into his palm.

Thorn couldn't tell her no. He had a duty to protect her. If taking her to his house and pretending she was his old girlfriend was how he did it, then so be it. "Let's go before the FBI and border patrol make camp here." He turned to leave.

Sophia touched his arm. "You don't have to do this."

Thorn stared at where her hand touched his arm for a long moment, every emotion he'd ever felt for Kayla and her loss warring with the need to protect this woman the law was after for murder. For all he knew, she could be a killer.

Maybe he was an idiot, but he believed her story.

SOPHIA FIDGETED IN the passenger seat of Thorn's truck, carefully studying the road as they neared the town of Wild Oak Canyon, watching for any signs of police, FBI, CBP and cartel thugs carrying automatic weapons. Every time they passed a vehicle, she had to remind herself not to duck or act as if she was hiding. For this disguise to work, she had to look like a happy, carefree young woman on vacation visiting an old boyfriend. She forced a smile on her face that she didn't feel, and her cheeks hurt as they drove through town.

"Relax." Thorn glanced her way. "Your hair color and haircut will make it hard for the FBI to match you to the photo they have. Let it hang across your cheeks a little to break up the lines of your facial structure, and you'll be good to go."

"Won't you and Hank be in big trouble if the FBI finds out you are harboring a Mexican fugitive accused of murder?"

"Only if they catch us." His hands tightened on the steering wheel, his knuckles turning white. "First test coming up." He nodded toward the black SUV sitting in front of the sheriff's office. Beside it was a green-and-white Customs and Border Protection vehicle. Grant Lehmann was talking with a CBP officer, looking none too happy.

Another man wearing a green jumpsuit, with *FBI* written in bold letters on one sleeve, stood with a wicked-looking weapon slung over his shoulder, his gaze scanning the road. When it locked on Thorn's truck, Sophia shivered.

"Just look toward me." Thorn draped an arm over the back of the seat and smiled her way, his blue eyes twinkling at her from beneath the brim of his cowboy hat.

Sophia's heart fluttered. She blamed it on nerves at having to pass the very agents she was trying to avoid, but she knew it was Thorn's smile that gave her a thrill. She could almost forget she was a fugitive.

She didn't have to force her answering smile. "You look so much younger when you smile."

"And you look beautiful when you smile."

The tingling sensation spreading through Sophia's body had everything to do with Thorn's compliment, given in that deep, rich voice. Too bad it was all for show. Not that it mattered. Sophia had no intention of starting a relationship with the man anytime soon, if ever. Her stay in Wild Oak Canyon was temporary, to be ended when she could get out safely. Then she'd start a life somewhere no one could find her. The thrill of the moment before faded into intense sadness. Her baby would never know her grandparents. As long as Antonio was alive, Sophia could never go back to Monterrey.

The cowboy returned his attention to the road ahead and made a left turn at the next street. "Other than the one man, the rest of them didn't look our way. So far, so good."

They drove to the western edge of town, where the road disappeared out into the desertlike landscape. A soft, cream-colored clapboard house sat back from the road, its antique-blue shutters giving the building a splash of color. In the front yard, a scrub oak tree shaded the swing on the wraparound porch. The structure had charm and a feeling of home, making Sophia want to sit on that porch and sip lemonade.

Thorn slowed as they approached the driveway.

"This is your home?" Sophia asked.

The cowboy's hands gripped the steering wheel, his knuckles white. "Yes." He dragged in a deep breath and turned down the driveway, pulling up beside the house. He stared at the house for a long moment before he got out of the truck.

Sophia scrambled out and grabbed the suitcase Hank had given her, filled with toiletries and a change of clothing PJ had provided. For a moment she almost felt like a woman on vacation. If not for the overwhelming sense of dread hanging over her head and a sad feeling that she was trespassing on Thorn's privacy, she would have enjoyed exploring this quaint little house.

Thorn started up the steps without offering to let her go first. He stuck the key in the lock and twisted, then stepped back, his jaw tight, his face set, inscrutable.

Sophia entered the house, curious about the way Thorn lived. Mail was stacked on a table by the door. Some of it had slipped to the floor unopened, as if Thorn hadn't been home for a while.

All the windows in the living room to the right had the blinds drawn, blocking out the sun. In the corner, a small upright piano stood with music leaning on the stand as if waiting for the player to return.

"Do you play?" Sophia nodded toward the piano.

Thorn's lips tightened, and he said curtly, "No." He took the suitcase from her and climbed the stairs to the second floor.

When she didn't follow, he turned back, frowning. "Your room is up here."

Sophia followed slowly, wondering what had Thorn so tense. She stepped onto the upper landing, a few steps behind him. "If you're worried about getting caught hiding me, I can make it on my own. You don't have to do this."

"I'm not worried about being caught." Thorn entered the first bedroom on the right. Though small, the room had all the charm of the early twentieth century. A full-size white iron bed was centered on one wall, the mattress covered in an old-fashioned quilt in beautiful shades of pastel blue, violet and green. Light, white eyelet curtains framed the window, and sunshine shone through, welcoming her.

He set her case on the floor. "Bathroom is down the hall. You'll find towels and soap in the cupboard." He performed an about-face and inched past her as if trying not to brush against her.

Before he could leave her, Sophia touched a hand to his arm. "Did I do something to make you mad?"

Thorn stared down at the hand on his arm for so long that Sophia let go. Then his gaze shifted to hers.

"I haven't had another woman in the house since…" His lips thinned, and he turned to leave.

"Since when?" Sophia asked. "Since your wife died?"

Thorn spun to face her, his eyebrows drawn down. "How do you know about her?"

Sophia's lips quirked upward. "PJ mentioned you'd been married but that your wife died a couple years ago." Sophia sighed. "I am sorry for your loss." She stared up into his eyes, noting the deep creases at the sides and how gray his blue eyes had become.

"It was a long time ago."

"Not long enough for the pain to pass." Sophia nodded. "I'll try not to be too intrusive."

Thorn closed his eyes. "You're not. It's my problem. I'll deal with it. In the meantime, make yourself at home. Kayla would have wanted you to." He left her in the room and returned to the first floor.

Kayla—his dead wife's name.

Now that Sophia had a name to go with Thorn's grief, she understood the glimpses of the woman's presence in the house. Many of the decorations were far more feminine than what she'd associate with the stern, often sad Thorn. The piano in the corner of the living room, the colorful pillows on the sofa all spoke of someone who had loved this home and wanted it to be a haven of happiness for those who lived there.

Sophia swallowed hard on the lump building in her throat. Thorn must have loved her so much that it hurt to bring another woman into the same house he had shared with Kayla.

A sense of yearning seeped into her consciousness. What would it feel like to be loved like that? Other than their first encounter, when she'd tried to shoot Thorn and he'd threatened to shoot back, he'd been a gentleman and surprisingly concerned for her safety. The night before, when Sophia had stayed in Hank's house and had the horrible nightmare, Thorn had held her until she quit trembling. He'd even stayed near the bed until she'd fallen back to sleep. From what she'd seen, he'd been kind, caring and gentle. A far cry from the man she'd almost married.

A shiver reverberated down her spine. Even had she married Antonio, she'd have left him, given the same opportunity. He was a monster without a heart. Sophia wouldn't subject her child to his bouts of rage or the life they'd lived in the cartel compound.

Her best bet was to be prepared for her next move. It wouldn't hurt to study the layout of the house and surrounding properties in case she had to make a run for it.

Sophia left the clothes in the suitcase and wandered down the hallway, trying to remember which door led to the bathroom. She opened the first door past hers and gasped.

The room appeared to be a work in progress, one wall painted part of the way in a pale yellow while the rest remained a light beige. What caught her attention was the white crib standing in the corner beside a white dresser covered in a pad that would serve as a baby's changing table.

Sophia's heart squeezed so hard in her chest that she pressed a hand to the pain, her eyes filling with tears. Had they been expecting a baby when Thorn's wife died? Not only had he lost his wife, he'd lost his unborn child, too.

She stepped into the room, drawn by the baby bed. A thick layer of dust covered the railing, which indicated it had not been disturbed for a while. Two cans of paint stood on the corner of a painter's drop cloth, as if whoever had been doing the work had stopped in the middle with the intention of finishing the job later.

As she stared down at the empty crib, a sob rose up Sophia's throat. She backed out of the room and closed the door softly, her hand hesitating before she let go and moved on to the next door. Her heart ached for the man who had to come home every day to an empty house and reminders of what should have been.

The next door revealed the master bedroom. Sophia could see a king-size bed standing in the center of the room and a cherry dresser with a silver hairbrush and picture frame in the center. His closet stood open. From where she stood, she could see both men's and ladies' clothing hanging inside. No wonder Thorn hadn't wanted another woman in his house. He'd kept his pain trapped inside the walls. He had yet to let go of his memories.

A noise below made her jump and scurry toward the bathroom, where she washed her hands and splashed water on her face, rinsing the tears from her eyes. She stared at the woman in the mirror, barely recognizing herself. With blond hair falling just to her shoulders, she could be that girl on vacation. Only she knew she wasn't.

She ran her fingers through the strands, liking the look and feeling more hopeful that she stood a chance of making good her escape to a better life.

When she left the bathroom, she followed the sounds of pots and pans clattering in the kitchen on the first floor.

Thorn had a pan on the gas stove frying hamburger meat, and he was filling another with water. "I hope you like spaghetti. It's all I know how to cook."

"I love spaghetti. My mother used to cook it for us. May I?" She took the pot of water from him, set it on the stove and lit the element. "Do you have tomatoes, bell peppers and onion for the sauce?"

"Sorry." He gave her a crooked smile. "But I do have ready-made sauce." Thorn reached over her head, his body pressing against hers as he retrieved a jar from the cabinet.

When he set it on the counter beside her, he didn't move away at first. "You smell good."

She laughed, the sound shaky even to her own ears. "It's the cooking food. You must be hungry."

He turned her to face him. "It's not the food, unless you're cooking honeysuckle and roses."

She stared up into his eyes and her breath caught in her lungs, refusing to move into or out of her chest. Her gaze shifted to his lips.

For once, they weren't set in a thin, tight line. His lips were full, sensitive and very kissable.

Sophia swiped her tongue across her own suddenly dry lips. "Thank you."

He cupped her cheek with his palm and thumbed the fading bruise. "No man should ever hit a woman."

"I agree. That's why I left." She reached up and captured his hand against her face. "Don't."

"Don't what? Do this?" His mouth descended and claimed hers in a soul-shattering kiss.

Her breath escaped her on a sigh and she leaned into him, craving more, wanting to feel his strong arms around her. Not holding her captive but holding her safe and warm, making her forget everything else around her. The fear of escape and crossing the border, the horror of the helicopter gunning Hector down and her dread of being caught and deported back to Mexico where the cartel ruled all melted away.

For the moment, she was just a woman kissing a man who wasn't going to hurt her.

Thorn's hands slipped to her shoulders and he set her away from him, his face tight, a muscle ticking in his jaw. "That was a mistake. It shouldn't have happened." He wiped the back of his hand across his mouth, his gaze still on her face, his blue eyes gray and distant.

"Do not worry." Sophia fought to keep from wincing at the pain spreading through her chest as reality set in and reminded her where she was. In the house Thorn had shared with his wife. "It will not happen again." She turned toward the stove and the sizzling meat, letting the heat of the cooking food warm her cold cheeks. "You belong here, and I'm leaving as soon as I can get out of here safely."

The sound of an electronic chirp made Sophia spin around.

Thorn pulled a cell phone from his pocket and hit the talk button. "Drennan." He listened for a moment, his face inscrutable. Then he looked across at Sophia.

Her pulse leaped and her hands trembled, dread building with each passing moment. What now?

"We'll be on the alert." Thorn clicked the phone off, slipping it into his jeans pocket.

Sophia pressed her hands together to keep them from shaking. "What happened?"

"The CBP and FBI have started setting up camp on Hank's property. Brandon tapped into their radio communications and got word they'd found an ultralight aircraft on a neighboring ranch with tire tracks leading away. Do you know anyone who flies an ultralight?"

Sophia's gut clenched and burbled. "I only know one person who owns such a craft." He'd followed her. Her vision blurred, and she would have fallen if Thorn hadn't reached out to catch her before she hit the ground.

"Who is it?"

"The man I was running from, Antonio Martinez, my former fiancé." Thankful for the steely arms around her, Sophia fainted away into blessed darkness.

Chapter Ten

Thorn lifted Sophia into his arms and carried her into the living room, laying her across the sofa. He smoothed the blond hair out of her face, pulled his phone from his pocket and speed-dialed Hank.

"What's up, Drennan?"

"Sophia says the ultralight could belong to her ex-fiancé, Antonio Martinez."

"The man the FBI says murdered two DEA agents?"

"That's the one."

"Poor kid. Not only does she have the feds after her, now she has to worry about her ex finding her."

"I'm betting her welcoming committee last night was some of his doing."

"I had Brandon look up Antonio Martinez. If he's the guy we're thinking he is, he's second in command to the head of the *la Familia Diablos* cartel. He could have been the one to send out the helicopter that killed her escort."

Thorn had thought about that. "If he had the access and authority to send the helicopter, why did he land an ultra-light nearby? Seems like he would have had the helicopter set him down and then bug out."

Hank was silent for a moment. "Antonio is only second in command. Maybe his boss sent the helicopter."

"That's my bet. And I'd also bet that his boss isn't too

happy he couldn't keep his woman in line. She could lead people back to their hideout."

"Could be," Hank said. "Which would explain the leak to the FBI combining Martinez with Sophia and telling them that they were dangerous. What better way to get rid of two traitors?"

"Right. Shoot first, ask questions later." Thorn didn't like it.

"Do we need to change our plans? With the FBI and CBP here, I'm not certain she'd be any safer here."

"For now, she can stay with me." Much as he didn't like another woman in the house he'd shared with Kayla, he couldn't let Sophia roam the streets with so many factions after her. "If you could put feelers out to your local informants to be on the lookout for Martinez, that might help. The FBI and CBP might not see past Sophia's disguise, but Martinez would."

"Right. I'll circulate a copy of Martinez's photo to my contacts. In the meantime, keep a low profile."

"Will do." When Thorn ended the call, he found himself standing in front of the piano Kayla had loved playing. A photograph in a wooden frame stared back at him. He lifted it from the piano, memories flooding over him. They'd taken the picture on their honeymoon to South Padre Island. He and Kayla were smiling in the photo—two young people with their whole lives in front of them. They'd dreamed of owning a house, raising children and growing old together. His fingers gripped the frame, and his heart hurt. Kayla shouldn't have died.

"She was beautiful."

Thorn spun toward the voice.

Sophia sat up on the sofa, her gaze on the photograph in his hand. "That's Kayla, isn't it?"

Thorn nodded, afraid to speak around thickened vocal cords.

"You two look good together. You must have loved her very much."

"I did."

"How did she die?"

For a long moment he hesitated, not wanting to talk about Kayla and that horrible moment when he'd held her in his arms as she'd bled out.

Sophia rose and touched his arm. "I'm sorry. You don't have to tell me if it's too painful."

The warmth of her hand on his arm loosened his tongue. "Drug addict aiming for me, got her instead."

"I'm sorry."

"Why? You didn't do it."

"I'm sorry for your loss." She squeezed his arm. "I've been thinking about Antonio."

Thorn's brows descended. "What about him?"

"He's coming for me." Sophia stepped away from Thorn. "He'll kill anyone who gets in his way of taking me back. I should leave now, before anyone else gets hurt."

"You can't go. They'll be looking for you at the checkpoints."

"Then I'll get out on foot."

"It's a long way between towns. There's little vegetation to hide behind, and if the heat doesn't get you, the coyotes might."

Sophia shrugged. "I'd rather face the coyotes than Antonio."

"We've been through this. You're staying. No arguments." He turned at the sound of something hissing in the next room. "We'd better save the spaghetti before it burns the house down." Thorn placed the photo facedown on the piano, hurried into the kitchen and switched on his own police scanner, which he'd kept from his days as sheriff. As he salvaged the charred hamburger meat and poured sauce over it, he listened to the chatter between the deployed units and dispatch.

Sophia joined him and poured a handful of noodles into the pan of boiling water, stirring to keep them from sticking together. For the next ten minutes they worked side by side at the stove, preparing a meal like any married couple.

Kayla had always had supper ready when he got home from work. She'd never invited him to help, always letting him relax.

Despite himself, he couldn't help that he liked having Sophia there. He'd gone too long without company.

As Sophia drained the water from the cooked noodles, the scanner erupted with an excited deputy announcing, "Checked out that report of trespassers at the old Fenton place and found something interesting. You might want to send the FBI this way."

Thorn took the pan from Sophia and laid it on the stove quietly as he listened to the exchange.

Dispatch responded, "What did you find?"

"Empty cartridge boxes, wooden crates that could have held weapons and a few blasting caps scattered on the ground. The kind they use with C-4 explosives."

"I'll notify the FBI."

Thorn removed his phone from his pocket and hit redial. Before the call went through, a loud explosion rocked the house.

Sophia screamed, dropped to her knees and pressed her hands to her ears. "What was that?"

"I think someone found the explosives." Thorn ran out the front door onto the porch.

A truck skidded to a stop in front of the house, and PJ

flung the door open and stepped out on her running board, looking back over her shoulder. "Did you hear that?"

A thought struck Thorn. "Where's Charlie?"

"Thankfully, I left her with Hank's housekeeper at the Raging Bull. I was just coming by with a few more things your guest might find useful."

Thorn shaded his eyes and studied the plume of black smoke rising above the rooftops, his sense of duty toward the city and its inhabitants urging him to check it out. He couldn't stand back and let the town burn down and do nothing to stop it. "I need to see if anyone was hurt."

"Go." Sophia opened the screen door and peered out. "I can take care of myself."

Thorn frowned, knowing he should stay. Even with her changed appearance, she could still be in danger.

Sophia smiled. "You probably know everyone in town. You can't stay with me when someone you care about could have been injured." She touched his arm. "Go. I'll be okay."

"Are you sure?"

"I'm sure."

Thorn ran out to PJ. "Can you stay here with S—my guest while I check it out and see if anyone was hurt?"

"Sure, take Chuck's truck." PJ grabbed a canvas tote bag from the backseat and hopped out.

Thorn jumped in and turned the truck around, leaving a trail of black tire marks.

An explosion big enough to rock his house on the edge of town had to have done some major damage downtown. God, he hoped everyone was all right and that Sophia stayed safe while he checked it out.

SOPHIA BACKED BEHIND the screen door as Thorn drove away.

PJ stood in the middle of the street for a few moments

longer before she sauntered across the yard and climbed the stairs. "God, I hope no one got hurt."

"Me, too."

PJ closed the door behind her and handed Sophia the bag. "More clothes. Hope they fit."

"Thank you. I'm sure they'll be fine." Sophia set the bag on the sofa and stepped to the window, lifting one slat on the wooden blinds to peer out at the empty street. "I wish I knew what was going on."

"You and me both."

Sophia frowned. She left PJ standing in the living room and hurried to the kitchen, where the police scanner was blaring with reports from the deputies responding to the explosion.

A loud blast of static was followed by a man's voice. "A woman reported an explosion at Cara Jo's Diner on Main."

PJ gasped. "Cara Jo's. Oh, dear God."

"Sanders here. I'm almost there—holy hell."

"What's going on?" Sophia assumed the voice was the dispatcher.

"The diner's nothing but rubble," Sanders said. "We'll need the fire department and ambulance ASAP."

"On their way."

"Oh, my God." PJ's face paled, and she pressed her hand to her lips. "I work there. Today was my day off." She paced the kitchen floor, stopping to stare out the window toward the smoke now billowing toward the sky. "I hope Cara Jo and Mrs. K are okay."

"Don't stay on my account." Sophia waved PJ toward the front door. "Go. Check on your friend."

"I shouldn't. You need someone—"

"No. I don't. I can look out for myself." Sophia walked her to the door and opened it.

PJ reached for the screen door and stopped so fast

Sophia bumped into her. "Uh, Sophia, we might have a problem."

"What do you mean?" Sophia stood on her tiptoes and glanced over the taller woman's shoulder. A black truck with dark tinted windows and four motorcycles were headed their way.

PJ backed away from the door, then closed and locked it. "I'm not sure they're coming here, but we don't want to take the chance. Let's head out the back door. Go!"

Sophia ran through the house to the door leading away from the street into the backyard.

Since the house was on the end of the street, there was only one direction they could go to escape being seen. Back toward town.

Sophia ducked behind a scraggly holly hedge in back of the house next to Thorn's and crawled to the edge of the property. A ten-foot gap stretched between the bush and a storage shed at the back of the house next door. From where she stood, she could see the black truck getting closer.

"Holy cow," PJ whispered.

"If we're going, it better be now." Sophia grabbed PJ's arm and hustled her across the expanse to the back of the shed. The truck passed by and pulled into the yard in front of Thorn's cute little cottage.

The four motorcycles spun out in the front yard. Men piled out of the truck carrying wicked-looking guns aimed at the house. Another man stepped from the truck.

The air whooshed out of Sophia's lungs and blood rushed from her head, leaving her dizzy.

"What?" PJ whispered.

"He found me."

"Who? Your ex-fiancé?" PJ peered around Sophia.

"Antonio." Her world seemed to crash in around her and her feet felt leaden, glued to the ground. He'd found her and he'd take her back to Mexico, beat her until she bled and then kill her and the baby she carried. "I can't let him take me back."

PJ pulled her back from the edge of the shed. "I won't let him take you. We'll watch and wait for our chance to run."

Sophia stared out at the landscape, her heart slowing, her breathing becoming more labored. "He'll kill you, me and—" She clamped her lips shut before she blurted the word *baby*.

PJ grabbed Sophia and shook her. "Look, I'm not letting him kill anyone. I have a little girl waiting for me at Hank's. I'll be damned if anyone takes away my chance to see her grow up." PJ shook her again. "Snap out of it." Then PJ peeked around the corner of the shed. "We have to wait for our chance."

"Elena!" Antonio yelled.

Sophia flinched and eased forward, hate welling up inside. This man had claimed to love her and instead had beaten her until she lost her will to live. The only thing keeping her going was the baby growing inside her. Her child would live without fear, damn it.

"Elena, mi amor, salir." Antonio waited a moment, then waved forward his men with the ugly guns. They broke through the front door and disappeared inside. Footsteps could be heard pounding on the wooden floors, going up the stairs and back down. Then the men reappeared, shaking their heads. One shouted, *"Nadie aquí!"*

Antonio jerked his head and the four men crossed the yard to where he stood. He said something that sounded low and angry, but Sophia couldn't make out the words.

The four men faced the house, stood with their feet braced and fired their weapons, unloading their clips into the building. Glass shattered and wood splinters flew.

Sophia half rose, horrified at the damage they were

leveling onto Thorn's home. The home he'd shared with the only woman he'd ever loved. A woman who'd been pregnant just like Sophia when her life had been cut short.

When the gunmen stopped shooting, Antonio spoke lowly again, following his words with a sharp, *"Rápidamente!"*

The men raced to the truck and lifted out plastic jugs. They ran back to the house and doused the walls with liquid.

"Gasoline," PJ whispered. "They're going to burn it."

"No." Sophia lunged for the house.

PJ grabbed her and forced her back behind the shed. "Thorn can build another. Your life is more important."

Antonio pulled a matchbox from his pocket, kissed it then struck one against the side. *"Para ti, mi amor."* He threw the match, igniting the gasoline. Flames leaped into the air, and black smoke rose.

Sophia's heart broke as the house went up in flames, everything Thorn held dear burning within.

If she wanted to stay alive for her baby, they had to move before the fire spread or Antonio and his men saw them. Sophia waited for the moment when all the men turned toward Antonio, awaiting his next instruction. Meanwhile the fire flared, blocking her view of them and theirs of her and PJ. "Now!" Sophia hooked PJ's arm and ran as fast as her feet could carry her.

She didn't look back to see if they were being followed, instead running as if her life depended on it. She refused to be a victim ever again.

THORN SKIDDED CHUCK'S truck to a stop a couple of blocks from what used to be Cara Jo's Diner on the corner of the Wild Oak Canyon Resort on Main Street. A fire truck from the all-volunteer firefighting department was there, along with half a dozen firefighters still pulling their suits up over their street clothing. Pickup trucks with rotating red lights on top of them lined the street, and more were coming. Deputy Sanders was talking with Raymond Rausch, the Wild Oak Canyon fire chief, who was pointing at the gutted structure.

Cara Jo was one of Thorn's friends. He'd had coffee at the diner every morning for the years he'd been sheriff of Wild Oak Canyon and at least once a week since he'd quit his job on the force.

Thorn dropped down out of the truck and ran toward Sanders and Rausch, his heart thumping against his ribs as he scanned the faces, searching for Cara Jo and Mrs. Kinsley, the cook. It was late afternoon, before the typical evening dinner crowd converged on the diner. Hopefully there weren't many injured, or injured seriously.

Thorn stopped next to the fire chief. "Sanders, Raymond, what happened?"

Sanders frowned. "An explosion in the rear of the diner. We're not certain yet as to the cause."

"Cara Jo and Mrs. Kinsley?"

"Mrs. Kinsley was off this afternoon. We found Cara Jo in the dining room. The paramedics are loading her up now into the ambulance." Chief Rausch pointed toward the waiting ambulance. "She's pretty banged up, but the EMTs think she'll be okay. They're taking her to the hospital for further evaluation by a doctor."

Thorn ran to the paramedics wheeling the gurney toward the back of the waiting ambulance. He caught up with them and touched the shoulder of one of the paramedics. "What's the verdict?" he asked.

"Hey, Sheriff." Fred White, a man Thorn had known since high school, knew Thorn was no longer sheriff, but old habits died hard and Thorn didn't want to waste time arguing.

Fred nodded toward Cara. "Several lacerations on her arms, legs and face. Nothing life threatening, possible cracked ribs and a concussion. We're taking her in for X-rays and to give docs a crack at her." Fred leaned over Cara Jo. "Pun intended."

"Ha. Ha." Cara Jo wore a neck brace and was strapped down, completely immobile. "Thorn? That you?" Her voice was gravelly and weak.

Thorn leaned over her face so that she could see him without straining. "Hey, Cara Jo, going all dramatic on us?"

"Darned tootin'." She attempted a smile through her split lip. "Always aimed to go out with a big bang."

"Fortunately, you're not going out yet. Do you know what happened?" Thorn looked before he touched her hand to make sure he wasn't going to hurt her.

"I heard someone in the back. Thought for moment Mrs. K had returned, then all hell broke loose and everything went black for me." She snorted and grimaced. "Woke up lying in the street, with Fred shining a light in my eyes."

"A little unnerving?" Thorn shook his head. "They say you'll be okay."

"Then why do they have me strapped down? It's not like I'm gonna run anywhere anytime soon."

"Just a precaution," he reassured her.

"Yeah, yeah." Cara Jo's eyes closed for a moment. "Thorn?"

"Yeah, Cara Jo?"

"Heard you had a girlfriend in town. Sally Freeman, huh?"

News traveled fast in Wild Oak Canyon. Thorn hated

lying, but in this case, Cara Jo would understand. "Sally's a friend from college."

Cara Jo opened her eyes and raised her hand to clasp his. "Don't sell yourself short, hon. You deserve to be happy."

Thorn's heart contracted at Cara Jo's words. She was thinking of him when she was the one lying on a gurney with injuries from an explosion.

"Sorry, Sheriff." Fred nudged his arm. "I need to get Cara Jo to the hospital."

Thorn squeezed his injured friend's hand carefully and let go. "I'll be by to see you later."

"Countin' on it," Cara Jo whispered.

Fred and his partner loaded the gurney into the back of the ambulance and drove away.

Seeing Cara Jo covered in blood, cuts and bruises, lying strapped to the gurney, brought back memories of Kayla and the ambulance that had taken her to the hospital, where the doctor had pronounced her dead on arrival.

Anger slammed through his veins. This was his town, the town he'd grown up in, the place he'd played football, fell in love and got married in. He'd be damned if he lost another one of his people to senseless violence.

Thorn stalked back to the fire chief, ready for answers, and he wasn't going anywhere until he had some.

Chief Rausch leaned toward Deputy Sanders, his brows furrowed.

Sanders was on his radio, a frown creasing his forehead. He spun toward the west, his gaze scanning the rooftops.

Thorn turned, too, and his heart sank to his feet. More smoke rose over the roofline, from the direction he'd just come.

Holy hell.

He ran for his truck as other vehicles turned in the middle of the street. Sirens blared from the direction of the firehouse as another truck left the station.

As Thorn climbed into his pickup, he sent a fervent prayer to the heavens. *Please don't be my house. Please spare PJ and Sophia.*

Chapter Eleven

Sophia kept running until she was within a couple blocks of the center of town. Her sides ached and her lungs burned, but she refused to stop until she was certain they hadn't been followed.

When she looked back, no one was behind her and PJ. No black truck, motorcycles or Antonio. When she finally slowed, Sophia staggered to the corner of a house and leaned against it, heaving air into and out of her lungs. Then she bent double and lost what remained of the contents of her belly.

"Are you all right?" PJ pulled Sophia's hair away from her face and ran her hand over her back like a mother soothing her child.

Sobs rose up Sophia's burning throat. She moved away from PJ, stumbling toward the next house, determined to get as far away from Antonio as possible.

PJ caught up with her and grabbed her arm. "You can't keep going."

The wail of sirens cleaved the air, and Sophia watched through the gaps between the houses as vehicles raced by on the main roads, two blocks away.

Not knowing whether Antonio and his gang were still looking for her, she wasn't willing to step out of hiding onto Main Street to flag someone down.

"We need to make a call, but I left my purse and cell phone in Thorn's house. We have to get to a phone." PJ stared at the house across the street. "I think I know how."

"How?" Sophia asked.

PJ pointed at a small white clapboard cottage with a splash of bright gold lantana and marigolds growing in the front garden. "Mrs. Henderson and her husband live in that house. She works for Kate Langsdon. Mr. Henderson is retired. Hopefully he'll let us hide there until we can get in touch with Thorn or Hank." PJ patted Sophia's arm. "Stay here until I wave you over."

Sophia sagged against the wall. "I don't think I could run another step even with a gun pointed at me."

"Fatigue is hard to battle in your first trimester. Let me handle this." With a reassuring smile, PJ scanned the street before leaving the shadows and stepping out into full sunlight.

Sophia's belly tightened. *She knows I'm pregnant.* But how? She'd told no one. And throwing up once in front of the other woman wasn't necessarily a clue. She couldn't tell anyone. If Antonio learned the truth, there'd be no stopping him.

Too drained to consider running again, Sophia propped herself against the wall of the house she stood beside, half-hidden by a bushy crepe myrtle, whose bright fuchsia blooms spoke of carefree summer days.

Sophia would have laughed at the irony of her thoughts of the pretty pink flowers if two fires weren't still burning and she had enough lung power to summon humor.

PJ stepped out into the street, hands in her pockets, looking like anyone out for a stroll. She looked both ways before she crossed the road to the Hendersons' house and knocked on the door.

Her head jerked back and forth, and she turned completely around once before the door cracked open and an older man peered out.

PJ spoke to the man, turned and scanned both ends of the street, then waved Sophia forward.

Sophia's pulse raced as she left the security of the shadows and ventured out into the wide-open street. She tried to look natural, but by the time she was halfway across the pavement she was running again, fear driving her feet faster.

PJ and Mr. Henderson stepped to the side as Sophia fell through the open doorway, landing on her knees.

PJ slammed the door behind her. "I'm calling Thorn and Hank." She pointed at Sophia and gave her a stern look. "You stay there until you catch your breath."

Too exhausted to argue, Sophia rolled onto her back and sucked in air, filling her starving lungs.

Mr. Henderson leaned over her. "Are you okay? Want me to call nine-one-one?"

Sophia and PJ answered as one. "No!"

The old man's eyes widened, and he held up his hands in surrender. "Just tryin' to help."

"I'm sorry, Mr. Henderson." PJ touched the man's arm. "It's a long story, and someday I'll tell you all about it, but right now we need a telephone."

"It's on the counter in the kitchen." Mr. Henderson pointed to a doorway down the hall. "Help yourself."

PJ disappeared through it and Sophia sat up, her breathing slowly returning to normal.

Mr. Henderson held out his hand and helped her to her feet. "You could sit in the living room and rest while you're waiting. Mrs. Henderson should be home soon."

"No, thank you. I'd like to join PJ." She headed for the sound of PJ's voice. When she reached the kitchen, PJ was replacing the phone in the charger. "Hank's already halfway to town. He's going to take us out to the ranch. Apparently the explosion in town was at Cara Jo's Diner. Cara Jo was sent to the hospital. It destroyed the diner and part of the Wild Oak Canyon Resort." PJ sighed. "I wonder how my apartment fared. It's at the back of the resort, close to the diner."

A lead weight settled in Sophia's empty stomach. She couldn't help feeling as if it was all her fault. She'd brought disaster to this nice little town. "What about Thorn?"

"I couldn't reach him on the phone. I left a message on his voice mail that he could find us at Hank's."

"Is it safe for me to go out there? The FBI and border patrol have set up operations there."

"I asked him the same question." PJ smiled. "Hank seems to think he can sneak you past them." She hooked Sophia's arm and steered her back down the hall to the living room. "Sit. You look all in. If you're not careful, you'll lose that baby."

Sophia halted, bringing PJ to a standstill, as well. "How did you know?"

PJ smiled. "Honey, you've got pregnant written all over you."

Tears welled in Sophia's eyes. "You can't tell anyone. If word gets back to Antonio, I'll never be free of him."

The other woman's eyebrows dipped. "That bastard is not going to get his hands on you. Not if Hank, Thorn or I have anything to say about it."

Sophia's heart warmed at PJ's passion, even as she shook her head. "My being here has already caused too much damage. I need to leave."

"Sophia, you're carrying a child. You can't do this on your own. I won't let you." PJ hugged her. "I know what it's like to lie in a hospital without anyone by your side. It's hard enough to give birth. It's even harder to do it alone."

For a long time Sophia hugged PJ back. After suffering so long at Antonio's hands, the warmth of a hug was more than she could have hoped for. "Thank you."

"Can I get you ladies a drink?" Mr. Henderson hovered in the hallway. "The missus would be mad if I didn't offer."

"That would be nice." PJ stared at Sophia. "And if you have a few saltine crackers, we'd be appreciative."

Sophia smiled, touched by PJ's concern.

"Got those. I'll be right back." The man shuffled off with a purpose, and soon the sound of cabinet doors opening and closing and the beep of a microwave oven drifted into the hallway.

"You need to sit for a few minutes." PJ led Sophia into the living room and eased her into a chair. "Hank should be here any moment."

"Why do you call him Hank?" Sophia asked. "Isn't he your father?"

"That's a long story. I'll tell you about it someday over a cup of coffee." PJ laughed. "I guess we all have long stories to tell. Right now, what's important is that you rest. You're so tense—it can't be good for you."

Sophia breathed in and out, willing her muscles to relax after the terrifying race across the town. "I'm fine. Really."

Mr. Henderson entered the living room carrying a tray with two teacups and a plate of plain saltines. "I'm sorry, but we're fresh out of cheese to go with the crackers."

Sophia smiled at the old man. "They're perfect just as they are." She accepted a cup of tea and bit into a cracker, thankful that it absorbed the churning acid in her stomach.

"Mrs. Henderson just drove up with groceries. I have to help her unload."

"Don't worry about us." PJ waved him out the door. "We'll be fine."

After Mr. Henderson left the room, PJ leaned forward

in her chair, her eyes sparkling. "Do you know how far along you are?"

The excitement in PJ's eyes made Sophia's heart flutter. She'd dreamed about having a baby ever since she was a little girl. It was supposed to be a happy time, filled with anticipation, not fear. "If I'm right, I'm about two and a half months along."

"Does Thorn know?" PJ asked.

Sophia shook her head, sadness creeping in on her. "No. And the fewer people who know, the better."

"You really should tell him. He's responsible for your protection. How can he take care of you if he doesn't have the full picture?"

"I can't." An image of a half-painted baby room in Thorn's house rose up in Sophia's mind. "What happened to Thorn's wife?"

PJ's eyes misted. "It was so sad. He was working as the sheriff of Wild Oak Canyon. One of the drug dealers he put away was released from prison. He came back after Thorn."

Sophia's hands clenched around the teacup as she listened to PJ's words, pain radiating through her for the big cowboy who'd lost everything.

"Somehow the guy got a gun and went after Thorn, but got Kayla instead. She died instantly."

"And she was expecting a baby." Sophia didn't ask. She knew.

PJ nodded. "She was four months along. I'd never seen such a happy couple. Thorn was over the moon about it all. Until…"

"Kayla and the baby died."

"Yeah, he hasn't been the same since. He quit his job as sheriff shortly after and has been doing odd jobs, kinda aimlessly, until Hank hired him."

Sophia stared across at PJ. "You see why I can't tell him?"

"I guess I get your point." PJ sighed. "I still think he needs to know."

"I'm not going to be here forever." Sophia set her cup on the tray. "Why cause him more pain?"

Mr. Henderson's voice carried through to them from the kitchen, along with a woman's voice and the sounds of plastic bags being settled on the counter.

A moment later Mrs. Henderson entered the room, her face creased in a frown. "Are you two ladies okay? What a nightmare. Cara Jo is in the hospital, and it looks like half the town is on fire." She flapped a hand in front of her face. "I was leaving the grocery store when the explosion went off."

"We're okay, Mrs. Henderson." PJ rose from her seat. "We're just waiting for my father to come pick us up." She hugged the older woman. "I'm glad you're okay, as well."

"I don't know what this world is comin' to." Mrs. Henderson held out her hand to her husband, who took it. "My husband tells me you two were running from someone when you showed up on our doorstep." She glanced toward the front window. "Do you need to borrow a gun?"

PJ smiled. "Thanks, but I think Hank and his bodyguards will be able to handle things for us."

Mrs. Henderson looked around the room. "Where's that sweet baby of yours?"

PJ chuckled. "Charlie's safe at Hank's house. I wouldn't be nearly as calm if she wasn't." She glanced toward the window. "There's Hank now."

Sophia rose from the couch, her gaze following PJ's.

A big, black, four-wheel-drive truck rolled to a stop on the street. Three bodyguards dressed in black jeans, black T-shirts, sunglasses and shoulder holsters piled out, pistols drawn, setting up a perimeter around the truck. Hank climbed out and spoke to the bodyguard closest to him. That man disappeared around the side of the house while the others closed in around their boss.

Hank Derringer wore cowboy boots, pressed blue jeans and an equally pressed blue chambray shirt. On his head he wore a straw cowboy hat. If not for the bodyguards in defensive position around him, he could have been any Texas cowboy instead of the millionaire he was.

"I thought his truck was ruined in the shoot-out last night," Sophia noted.

"Honey, Hank has more than one truck. It takes a lot of people and equipment to run a ranch the size of the Raging Bull." PJ met Hank at the door. "Glad you came. We need to get Sophia somewhere safe."

"Where's Thorn?" Hank removed his hat and entered the house, leaving his two bodyguards out front.

"He headed for the explosion," PJ said. "We haven't seen him since."

"I tried to reach him on his cell with no luck." Hank glanced at Sophia. "I headed into town as soon as I heard dispatch on the scanner announce an explosion on Main. Thought you might be the target."

Guilt twisted like a knife in Sophia's gut. She almost wished she *had* been the target instead of the woman who'd been taken to the hospital. But she had her defenseless baby to consider. "No, Señor Derringer, we weren't anywhere close. I think it might have been a diversion to give my ex-fiancé a chance to find me."

The lines in Hank's forehead deepened with his frown. "In which case, it was effective."

"Unfortunately, our attempt to hide Sophia in plain sight didn't work." PJ's shoulders sank. "I'm sorry."

Mrs. Henderson waved them farther into the house. "Come in and have a seat. I'll make some coffee."

With a hand held up, Hank smiled politely at the older woman. "No need, Marge. We're headed back to the ranch. With all that's goin' on in town, we need to get Sophia somewhere safe. And I'm sure PJ will want to see Charlie."

Mrs. Henderson nodded. "You're right. I'd want to get to my baby, as well."

Sophia thanked the Hendersons and allowed Hank to hustle her out the door and into the backseat of the waiting truck. Two of the three bodyguards who'd arrived with Hank got in on either side of Sophia. PJ settled into the front passenger seat.

Hank took off, bypassing the circus responding to the aftermath of the explosion on Main Street, and headed out of town toward the Raging Bull Ranch.

Sophia craned her neck to look back at the trucks and vehicles crowded around the small town, hoping to catch a glimpse of Thorn. The farther away they got from town, the more alone she felt, even surrounded by PJ, Hank and his bodyguards. She hoped Thorn was okay.

As if reading her thoughts, Hank announced, "I left a message on Thorn's cell phone that I would be taking you two out to the ranch. Hopefully he'll get it."

Sophia wanted to see him and tell him she was sorry about his house. Her stomach roiled at the thought of all his photos and memories turned to ashes. It was hard enough to lose the one you loved, but to lose everything from your life with that person would be devastating. Knowing she was responsible for bringing this wave of destruction to the good people of Wild Oak Canyon, Sophia knew it was time to leave. To take the dark cloud of death that followed her and get out of the area.

As soon as she could figure out an exit strategy, she'd do it.

THORN JAMMED HIS foot on the brake and skidded to a stop a block away from the flaming inferno of his house.

Firemen had just arrived, jumping down from their seats and going straight to work, unrolling hoses and shrugging into their fireproof jackets.

Flames consumed the old porch and rose up the curtains inside the shattered glass of the front window. All along the front of the house, it appeared as if someone had fired a machine gun into the exterior.

Thorn's pulse pounded against his eardrums as he dropped down from his truck and ran toward the building. He scanned the yard and the vehicles parked nearby but didn't see Sophia or PJ. Had they gotten out? Or were they lying on the floor having been shot, maybe alive but too injured to move? He should never have left them alone.

"Anyone inside?" he asked as he ran past Cody West, a volunteer fireman he'd had drinks with on occasion.

"Don't know. We just got here."

Another fireman called out after him, "Hey, don't go in there. It's too dangerous!"

Thorn ignored the fireman, ran up the porch and grabbed the front doorknob, the heated metal burning his palm as he shoved open the door.

A black cloud billowed out, forcing him to crouch as he entered. Before he'd taken two steps, his lungs took a hit of smoke and his eyes stung and watered. Thorn pulled his shirt up over his mouth and ducked as low as he could get, blinking as he moved through the house. The living room and kitchen were empty, leaving the upstairs, where all the smoke rose. He ran back to the staircase and would have raced up to the burning second floor if hands hadn't grabbed him from behind and dragged him back out the front door.

Thorn fought to get loose, coughing the smoke out of his lungs. "Have to find them."

"They're not there." Chuck Bolton spun him around, maintaining a viselike grip on his arm.

"Then where are they?" Thorn reached for Chuck's shirt collar, ready to shake the man, his mind in a panicked haze of possibilities, all equally bad. "Did the cartel get them?"

Chuck shook his head. "No. They're okay. Get hold of yourself, man." He pulled his cell phone out of his pocket and held it up. "I got a text from Hank. He has Sophia and PJ and is taking them out to the Raging Bull Ranch."

All the tension left Thorn. He released Chuck's shirt and nearly dropped to his knees. "You're sure?"

"Read it yourself."

His eyes still burning, Thorn blinked several times before he could focus on the words in the text message.

"Man, Hank's been trying to get hold of you on your cell phone for the past twenty minutes."

Thorn reached into his back pocket for his cell phone. It wasn't there. He stared at the burning house. He must have left it in there.

"Come on, I'm in one of Hank's trucks and I've got a bodyguard with me. I need to get back to the Raging Bull. You can ride with us or follow me out there." Chuck frowned at the truck parked on the curb behind the fire truck. "Is that mine?"

"Yup." Thorn glanced at the side of the house where he'd parked his vehicle. His own truck had been hit with the same gunfire the house had suffered. Even if it wasn't covered in smoke, ash and debris from the fire, he doubted it would run. "Guess I'll follow you out to the ranch in your truck."

As Thorn pulled away from the burning house, he was hit afresh with a wave of grief so strong he had a tough time breathing. Everything from his life with Kayla had gone up in flames. The pictures, her jewelry and clothing, their wedding album and the quilt her grandmother had given her.

Tears trickled down his cheeks. Thorn rubbed his sleeve over them, smearing soot on his arm.

He was no better off than Sophia. No clothes but the ones on his back, no home to go to, no one waiting for him there.

But Sophia wasn't wallowing in her loss. She was fiercely determined to move on with her life, start over somewhere away from the tragedy of her past.

The woman was not only beautiful, she had spunk and grit. She'd been through hell and come out a survivor.

It hit Thorn, then—he hadn't been living his life. He'd been going through the motions, more of a spectator than a participant, letting everything pass by and refusing to engage.

How had he let himself sink so low?

He hadn't been raised a self-indulgent man, prone to pity. His father had raised a cowboy, rough, ready and willing to tackle any challenge.

It had taken a woman to remind him of that. A woman who was being chased by an abusive cartel thug. Whether or not Thorn had a life to go back to, he had one to protect. And he'd be damned if he let any more harm befall her.

With renewed purpose, he pressed his boot to the accelerator and spun Chuck's truck around, headed toward the Raging Bull and Sophia.

Chapter Twelve

Hank's housekeeper and PJ ganged on up on Sophia, insisting she eat a sandwich and drink a glass of milk. The food helped to settle her stomach and replenish the energy she'd been lacking earlier.

PJ had urged her to take a nap while she waited for Thorn to return from town. Sophia had refused, preferring to sit on the floor of the living room with PJ and Charlie as the baby played with her toys and made many attempts to roll over.

Sophia's chest swelled and her hand drifted to her belly, wondering what her baby would be like. Would it be a boy or a girl? Would she have green eyes like her mother or the dark, angry eyes of his father?

Too twitchy to lie down, Sophia rose from the floor and wandered through the house, careful not to stand too close to the windows should the FBI or border patrol wander by and see her. They'd been lucky the fire in town had drawn most of the agents that direction on the off chance their assailants were involved. Hank had no problem sneaking Sophia through the side door of his spacious home.

The one-story ranch-style house, with its cathedral ceilings and hardwood floors, had an open, airy floor plan with lots of thick, double-paned windows letting in the Texas sunshine but not the oppressive heat. The living room was bigger than the entire apartment Sophia had rented in Monterrey. A huge stone fireplace took up the majority of one wall, gray stone rising to the peaked ceiling.

The couch was bomber-jacket brown leather and as soft as a woman's skin. Tables scattered around the room were solid wood, possibly mesquite and beautifully handcrafted.

Sophia wandered from the living room into a foyer and across to an open door that led into a study. A massive desk made of the same mesquite sat squarely in the center of the room. On three of the four walls, bookcases rose to the ceiling, filled with books. Some were bound in leather; others were paperbacks with well-worn bindings.

The room smelled of leather, wood and the aftershave Hank used.

With nothing to do, Sophia continued her self-guided tour of Hank's abode, glancing toward the foyer every few minutes to see if Thorn had arrived.

Another door farther down the hall was mostly closed, the shadowy interior teasing, beckoning Sophia to glance inside.

As if drawn by an invisible string, Sophia entered, pushing the door wide. The curtains in this room had been drawn over the windows. Sophia found the light switch, flipped it and let out a soft gasp.

Light from a delicate crystal chandelier that hung from the center of the ceiling filled a room that looked to be straight out of a Victorian storybook. The soft, ivory walls were the background for deep red curtains and a red patterned settee with a carved wooden back and arms. Against one wall, an antique cherry secretary desk stood with the desk folded down and stationery spread across the wooden surface, as if whoever had started writing a letter had been interrupted but was expected to return.

Sophia entered the room, enchanted by the difference between the warm masculinity of the other rooms and the delicate beauty of this one. It felt like she'd walked into the room of a princess in a fairytale.

Though her family in Monterrey had been considered well-to-do, Sophia had never seen such beauty and luxury in one place.

She'd lived in the best part of Monterrey, attended private schools and partied with the same families growing up. But this little piece of antiquated heaven was like something straight out of a Victorian countess's home.

"Lilianna loved this room." Hank's deep voice filled the space.

Sophia jumped and turned toward the door, her face heating. "I'm sorry. I should have asked if it was all right to look around."

The older man smiled softly. "You're welcome to look wherever you like on this level."

She returned her attention to the beauty of the antiques and decor. "This room *es muy bonito*."

Hank stared across the room at a portrait over the fireplace. "My wife inherited much of the furniture. It was passed down through her family for centuries. She treasured it all, and could tell you a story about every piece."

For a moment Sophia studied the wealthy man, the sadness in Hank's voice and expression ultimately making her turn away. It hurt to witness his pain. The loss of his family reminded her too much of her own. "You loved her very much, didn't you?"

"Family is everything," he said quietly.

Sophia's chest ached. "I miss my family, too."

"Why don't you go back to them?"

"I will never be safe in Mexico." She pressed a hand

to her belly and the baby growing inside. "As long as Antonio is looking for me, I cannot go back to my family."

"Do they know you're alive?" Hank asked.

Sophia shook her head. "I haven't been allowed to contact them since Antonio imprisoned me. They must think I'm dead." Her voice caught on a sob.

"You should let them know that you're alive and well."

"I don't wish to give them hope." Sophia's gaze shifted away from Hank. "I don't know how this will end."

"Think about it, Sophia." Hank touched her arm. "I'd give anything to know whether my wife and son were still alive." His gaze drifted again to a large portrait over the mantel.

Sophia glanced at the image, her throat tightening. Her family had a portrait similar to this hanging over the mantel in her home back in Monterrey. She had been eight; her brother had been a baby. A young family, full of hope and promise.

Unlike the other things in the room, the picture, though encased in an antique oval frame, wasn't old and it wasn't painted. It was a professional photograph printed on canvas of a family—Hank, a woman and a small boy.

"That's your wife?" Sophia moved closer, struck by something in the way the woman in the portrait smiled. Her heart skipped a beat and then pumped faster the closer she got to the picture. "What did you say her name was?"

"Lilianna." Hank ran a hand through his hair, looking older than he had a moment before. "God, I miss her."

"Does she have a sister?"

"No, she was an only child. I met her in Mexico City while she was vacationing with friends."

"Did she die?"

"No." His voice grew terse. "She and my son were kidnapped a little over two years ago." He pointed to the toddler in her lap. "He was five on his last birthday."

Sophia couldn't mistake the deep sadness in Hank's voice, nor the overwhelming sense of something familiar in the woman's eyes and the way she held the child. As if a memory teetered on the edge of her consciousness, Sophia's eyes rounded. "What was your son's name?" She held her breath, knowing before he answered what it was, and she whispered it at the same time as Hank.

"Jake."

Hank stepped back as if she'd struck him, his eyes narrowing. "Why did you ask his name if you already knew?"

"It could be a coincidence." Her heart hammered against her ribs, her instincts telling her this wasn't a fluke. *Madre de Dios,* if it wasn't…

Her gaze met Hank's as she said, "I know them." Sophia clapped a hand to her stomach, the food she'd just eaten threatening to rise up to the sob stuck in her throat. "That's Anna and her son, Jake. I know them." Sophia ran from the room, racing for the bathroom in the hallway.

"Wait!" Hank yelled. "What do you mean?" He ran after her.

Behind her, Sophia could hear voices. One sounded like Thorn's, but she couldn't hold in the contents of her stomach, the truth of what she'd just learned making her insides riot. She flung open the bathroom door and made it to the toilet just in time to lose the sandwich and milk PJ and the housekeeper had insisted she eat.

Movement behind her made her moan. "Go away."

"You're going to have to try harder than that to get me to leave." Thorn's voice sent a wave of warmth over Sophia's suddenly chilled, trembling body.

"I'm sick. I'd rather you didn't see me this way." She heaved again, hating that she couldn't stop herself.

"Too bad." Work-callused fingers pulled her hair back from her face. "I'm not going anywhere."

"Stubborn man," she whispered.

He chuckled. "Hardheaded woman."

When she thought she could, she sat back on the cold tile floor and leaned her head against the sink cabinet.

Thorn released her hair and reached for a washcloth, running it under the tap. "Now, tell me what happened."

She closed her eyes, all the fight gone from her. "Where do you want me to start?"

Thorn pressed the cloth to her face, the warm, damp fabric a balm to her cool, clammy skin.

"Start with what you said to Hank," he prompted. "He looks like he saw a ghost."

Sophia looked up at the man who'd brought her and Thorn together.

Hank stood in the doorway, his face pale, his blue eyes intense. "What did you mean, you know Lilianna?" he demanded.

"Give her a moment." Thorn brushed the cloth across Sophia's lips.

Sophia clasped his wrist. "Let me." She took the rag from his fingers and pressed it to the side of her face as she stared up at Hank, her heart racing as she spoke. "I know them as Anna and Jake, but they are the same. Hank, I know where your wife and son are."

THORN TURNED IN time to see Hank Derringer take a step backward, his face blanching even more. "Please tell me you're not lying."

Sophia shook her head. "I'm not lying. Anna was the one who set me up with Hector. She helped me escape *la Fuerte del Diablo.*"

Hank ran a hand over his face. "Dear God, they're alive?"

"They were when I left Mexico." She couldn't vouch for anyone at the moment.

Thorn looked from Sophia to Hank, and back to Sophia. "Are you well enough to take this conversation to another room?"

She nodded and tried to rise. Before she could, Thorn scooped her up and carried her into the large living room where PJ stood beside Chuck, who held Charlie in his arms.

"Are you okay, Sophia?" PJ asked.

Sophia nodded. "I'm okay." She stared up at Thorn. "You can put me down. I can stand on my own."

Thorn slowly lowered her feet to the ground but refused to remove his arm from around her waist.

"You know Lilianna? She was where they held you hostage?" Hank grasped her hands in his.

Sophia squeezed his fingers. "*El Martillo* keeps her in his quarters. She's rarely allowed to go outside the walls."

"But she got you out." Hank's head moved side to side as he stared at their joined hands. "Why didn't she come with you?"

"I begged her to come, but she refused."

Hank frowned. "What?"

Sophia knew it would hurt Hank, but she had to tell him. "Anna told me she could never leave."

Hank straightened. "Why would she say that? I know my Lilianna. She loved me—she loved our home, our family and life together."

"I don't know why. When it came time for me to escape, she hugged me and told me to find you, that you would help me."

Hank's jaw tightened and he let go of Sophia's hands, his own clenching into fists. "Who is this *El Martillo?*"

"I never saw him. I only knew when he was there because everyone in the camp got nervous, even Antonio. The man came in the night by helicopter. He stayed in his quarters. Those closest to him went in and out, but he never did, leaving again under cover of night."

"He probably threatened to harm Jake." Hank slammed his fist into his palm. "The bastard!"

Thorn's arm tightened around Sophia, his attention captivated by the man who'd hired him. Knowing it was a huge risk and that the likelihood of being killed was high, he knew what had to happen. "We have to go after her."

Sophia stiffened against him. "Do you know what you're saying?" She stepped out of his arms and stood in front of him. "*La Fuerte del Diablo* is surrounded by members of the cartel. Those men were trained in the Mexican army. They're equipped with deadly weapons, and they don't hesitate to kill."

Thorn looked over her head to the man who'd taken him on when he hadn't been employed in two years, shown faith in him and given him a chance to start over. "If Hank's wife and son are in that compound, we have to get them out."

"Drennan's right." Chuck Bolton kissed his daughter and handed her to PJ. "She's been missing for more than two years. This is the first real lead Hank's had on her whereabouts."

"We have to move fast." Hank paced the living room floor to the fireplace and back, his head down and his body tense.

"Agreed," Thorn said, then added, "Before *El Martillo* realizes we know."

"If he hasn't already moved her." Hank strode from the room. "I'll call the other members of this team. We'll meet in the war room in the morning."

"What about the FBI and the border patrol?" Chuck asked.

The boss stopped and turned toward them. "None of this information leaves this room. Understood?"

Everyone answered as one. "Yes."

Hank spun, heading for the front door.

Thorn called out, "Where are you going?"

"I want to know if they caught up with the man responsible for the explosion and fires in town."

Thorn glanced down at Sophia. He wanted to know, as well.

"Go with them. I'll be okay."

"I'm not leaving you."

"And I can't step outside without being detected. I want to know if they caught Antonio. I won't be safe until they do."

"If you're sure." Thorn waited.

Sophia turned him around and gave him a gentle push. "I need a shower and some rest. If you're hanging around, I won't get either."

Thorn took off after Hank.

Chuck kissed PJ and Charlie. "I'll be back in a few minutes to take you two home."

"Take your time. I'm not even sure we have a home." PJ smiled. "And Charlie's about ready for a feeding."

Chuck caught up with Thorn and the two men stepped out into the fading light, crossing the yard to the long van the FBI had brought in as the base of operations. Two generators hummed loudly, providing power to the computers, lights and air-conditioning. Apparently only a skeletal staff had remained behind. One agent sat at a folding table outside the van, cleaning his M4A1 rifle. He glanced up as the three men approached. "Lehmann isn't here."

"Mind if I check with the computer operators?" Hank asked.

The man shrugged and refocused his attention on the rifle in his hands, sliding the bolt back into place. "Knock yourself out."

Hank stepped into the van first, followed by Chuck and Thorn.

"Any news on Martinez?" Hank asked.

The man at the computer nodded. "Had a sighting in Wild Oak Canyon right before the explosion, and then again near the house on the edge of town that got torched."

Thorn's fingers clenched. He wanted to ask if they'd seen Elena Carranza, but didn't want to draw any more attention to her plight than necessary.

The agent continued. "They think Martinez recruited a gang to help stage the explosion and fires."

That corresponded to what Sophia had related about the fire at Thorn's house.

"I take it they didn't catch him." Hank's words were a statement.

"No, but Lehmann was following a lead on one of the gang members. He should report in soon."

"What about the woman?" Hank asked.

The man shook his head. "Nothing yet. Seems to have disappeared. They probably split up to throw us off their trail."

Hank backed toward the door. "Thanks."

Thorn dropped down out of the van first. The man who'd been sitting at the folding table had disappeared.

Two long black SUVs rolled to a stop next to the van, and Grant Lehmann stepped out of the lead vehicle. "Hank." He nodded to the other two men, his attention returning to the ranch owner. "We've had a confirmed sighting of Martinez in the area. Again, I stress, he's dangerous. If you see him, don't hesitate to shoot. He's already put one citizen in the hospital."

"You think he set the explosion in town?" Hank asked.

"I don't only think it, I know it." Lehmann slipped his sunglasses off his face. "We canvassed the area and learned that a man fitting his description, along with two others, was seen around the back of the diner right before the explosion. They took off on motorcycles."

"Were they the same gang that burned the house on the edge of town?" Thorn asked, his teeth clenching.

The director nodded. "Thorn Drennan, right?"

Thorn nodded.

"That was your house, wasn't it? Sorry we didn't catch him before he torched it." Lehmann's eyes narrowed. "What had us puzzled was why he targeted your house. Do you have a connection to Martinez or his gang?"

Thorn kept a poker face, refusing to show any signs of emotion or indications that he was about to lie. He'd learned how to do this by some of the best and worst criminals. "Not that I know of. But I was sheriff for several years. Someone could have carried a grudge against me." That wasn't a lie. His wife's death had been because of a drug dealer's grudge. His training as an officer of the law made his gut clench at the thought of withholding evidence and the location of Elena Carranza, but something told him now wasn't the time to reveal her. His instincts had never been wrong.

"Seems strange Antonio would fill your house with bullets. He must have thought someone he wanted dead was inside." Lehmann pinned Thorn with his gaze. "Some neighbors down the street said they saw you enter with a woman."

"An old friend from college." Thorn gave him the story.

"Sally Freeman. She and I left the house to check out the explosion."

"The fire chief said you went back into the house after someone. Was there more than one woman inside?"

Thorn smiled. "As a matter of fact, there was. PJ Franks had loaned me her truck to check out the explosion. It wasn't until they dragged me out of my house that I learned she'd left before the shooting began and walked over to a friend's house."

Lehmann stared at him for a long time as if processing Thorn's story to see if it added up.

"Your man inside the van said you had a lead on one of the gang members with Antonio?" Hank asked, drawing the director's attention back to him.

Thorn released the breath he'd been holding.

"Yeah. Someone recognized one of the men on the motorcycle based on a snake tattoo on his arm. We did some digging and found a cousin of his on the south side of town in a trailer park. We were late by five minutes. The bikers had just left, Antonio with them."

"Any idea which direction they went?" Chuck asked.

"They could have gone anywhere." Lehmann rolled his neck, pressing a hand to the base of his skull. "They were all on dirt bikes. For all we know, they could have headed back across the border. CBP is sending a chopper out from El Paso. Hopefully we'll have a better chance of finding them from the air."

Hank snorted. "There's still a lot of ground to cover, and a dirt bike can go almost anywhere."

"It's all we have to go on for now...unless your team's come up with something to add to it." Lehmann's gaze traveled from Hank to Chuck, and then came to rest on Thorn.

"Nothing you haven't already discovered." Hank stuck

out his hand to the regional director. "Thanks for keeping us up-to-date."

Lehmann shook Hank's hand. "If you'll excuse me, I need to brief my agents and get out of here for a while."

"Not much to offer in town with the diner out of service." Hank nodded toward the house. "I could have my housekeeper make up some sandwiches for your guys."

Thorn waited for Lehmann's response. They'd have to hide Sophia if the FBI was traipsing through the house.

The director put one foot on the step to the van. "Thanks, but I'm pretty sure the men would prefer pizza. I thought I saw a place off Main."

"Joe's Pizza Shack stays open until nine," Chuck offered. "They make a mean pie."

Lehmann disappeared inside the van.

Thorn headed back to the house, anxious to get Sophia back in his sights. After what had happened with his house and the diner, he didn't want to risk leaving her for too long, even in as safe a place as Hank's security-wired home.

Once inside, he found PJ standing in the living room staring at Sophia playing with Charlie on the floor. "She's good with babies."

Thorn braced himself as he watched Sophia lying on her side on an area rug, propped up on her elbow. She was leaning over Charlie, tickling her.

Charlie giggled, her eyes sparkling, her dark brown hair sticking out in all directions in soft wisps. She batted at Sophia and giggled again.

Sophia smiled down at the baby and stroked her chubby cheek, her own cheeks flushed with pleasure.

Thorn's heart squeezed so hard he pressed a hand to his chest to ease the pain. PJ was right—Sophia looked natural playing with the baby girl. She would make a good mother.

Then it hit him. She'd thrown up the night he'd found her in the cabin and again today. She'd passed out when she'd been hungry, and she was desperate to get away from her abusive ex-fiancé. So desperate she'd risk escaping out from under the cartel.

Thorn's lips pressed together to keep him from blurting out the question foremost in his mind.

Charlie giggled once more and Sophia smiled up at PJ, her smile freezing when she spotted Thorn.

For a moment her eyes widened, then her smile faded and she looked away, her expression guarded. Sophia rose from the floor, lifting Charlie in her arms. "Did they find Antonio?" She kissed the baby's cheek and handed her to her mother.

"No," Thorn replied, his voice clipped, barely controlled.

Sophia looked at him again, her eyes narrowing. "Is something wrong?"

"You're pregnant," he blurted accusingly.

Sophia's gaze shot to PJ.

PJ hugged Charlie. "I didn't say a word."

Thorn glared at PJ. "You knew?"

"I figured it out when she was at the Hendersons'."

Chuck entered the house, calling out to PJ. "Ready to hit the road and see if we have a home to go to?"

"Good timing." PJ touched Sophia's arm. "You'll be okay."

Sophia's gaze followed PJ through the front door as she left, finally returning to Thorn when they were left alone.

Not wanting their resulting argument to go public, Sophia headed for the bedroom, assuming Thorn would follow.

He did, catching up to her as she entered. "We're not done here."

"I know." She waved him through the door.

Once he was inside, she closed the door and faced him, her gaze steady, her face inscrutable. "Yes. I'm pregnant."

Thorn closed his eyes as the flood of emotions washed over him. Pain, guilt, anger and, strangely, hope. "Why didn't you tell me?"

"I didn't want anyone to know." Sophia's finger twisted the hem of the clean shirt she was wearing. "The fewer people who know about it, the better. Should Antonio learn I'm pregnant with his child, he'll stop at nothing to get me back."

Sophia stepped up to Thorn. "I don't want to go back to *la Fuerte del Diablo*." Her hand lifted protectively to her abdomen. "I left to give my baby a better life. One where she's not afraid all the time." Her jaw tightened even as her eyes filled with tears. "Please...don't tell anyone."

Thorn's anger dissolved, and his hardened heart melted into her watery green eyes. *Damn her!* Damn her for opening him up to pain again. Having lost Kayla, their child and the house filled with memories, he couldn't do it again. He gripped her arms, anger bubbling over. "I won't tell anyone, but understand this—I'm not getting involved with you or anyone else." He shook her slightly.

Tears tipped over the edges of her eyelids. "I know, and I completely understand."

Thorn recognized the strength it had taken for her to come this far and her fierce desire to provide a better life for her baby, but he also knew how vulnerable she was and that she wouldn't last much longer on her own against a cartel out to kill her, with the FBI and CBP ordered to shoot on sight.

As much as he wanted to have Hank reassign him so that he didn't have to dig his own emotional grave deeper, he was stuck. He'd gone way past being able to hand her off to someone else. So far past that all he wanted was to hold her in his arms and keep her safe from anyone who wanted to hurt her.

"I can leave. You don't have to help me." Her fingers dug into his shirt, belying her suggested solution.

"You know damn well I can't let you leave." Thorn pulled her into his arms, crushing her mouth with his. He dragged her body close to his, melding them together in an embrace far more flammable than a lit match to a stack of dry tinder.

When at last he let her up for air, she sighed and leaned her cheek against his chest. "This should never have happened."

"No," he agreed, inhaling the scent of her floral shampoo. "It shouldn't have happened."

"And I don't expect it to continue." She pressed her palms to his chest and leaned back to gaze up into his eyes. "Once I leave here, I have to disappear."

A hollow feeling settled in Thorn's gut and spread to his heart. She'd been telling him the same information from the beginning. Sophia had no intention of sticking around once she was free to hit the road. Why, then, did it hurt more now?

He brushed the hair from her face, tucking it behind her ear. "We'll talk about that later. Right now, we have to keep you safe from Antonio and away from the FBI and border agents."

"Is that even possible?" She snuggled closer to him, a shiver shaking her body. "Antonio tracked me to your house in town. He has to know I'm here. It's only a matter of time. Why doesn't Hank turn me over to the FBI or the CBP? He wouldn't have to worry about Antonio, and maybe they would see the truth and not shoot me."

Thorn shook his head. "Rumor has it there's a mole in

the FBI, someone who's been allowing coyotes to move people and drugs across the border into the States. Hank doesn't trust anyone past his own inner circle of men."

"From what Brandon said, the regional director is Hank's friend."

"Maybe, but he's not part of Hank's inner circle—people Hank trusts with his life."

"I'm not part of his inner circle. How does he know I'm not lying?"

Thorn traced her lips with his finger, mesmerized at how they moved with each word she spoke. "He trusts his instincts."

"I don't know why," Sophia said. "I've done nothing to build his trust."

"You've given him hope." Thorn gave in to the temptation and brushed his lips across hers.

She closed her eyes and whispered, "As long as I am here, you are all in danger." Sophia pushed her hands against his chest until she could stare into his eyes. "Antonio will find me."

"Hank won't let him get to you." Like a moth to flame, Thorn was drawn to her as he grazed her lips with his, loving how soft, full and warm they were. "And I'll do everything in my power to keep him away from you."

"Even help me leave when the roadblocks clear?"

Chapter Thirteen

Sophia's arms twined around his neck, pulling him closer, her breasts pressing against his chest. Fire burned inside her as the ridge beneath his jeans nudged her belly. She wanted to be closer to this cowboy who'd saved her life and treated her with gentle respect. "You'll help me when I have to leave?" she repeated.

"If it comes to that." He buried his face against her neck and moaned. "Right now, all I can think about is how your skin feels against mine." His mouth touched the pulse pounding at the base of her throat and he moved lower, sweeping across the swell of her breast beneath the soft cotton of her T-shirt. He lifted the hem, dragged it up over her head and tossed it onto a chair.

Her heart thumped against her ribs as if it would break free of its restraints. Sophia stood in a black lace bra, the cool waft of an air-conditioned breeze feathering across her nakedness. Thorn's coarse hand skimmed down her waist and over the swell of her hip, disappearing into the waistband of her borrowed jeans to caress her bottom.

"If you just weren't so darned stubborn…and beautiful…and brave." He trailed the fingers of his other hand along the curve of her throat and across her shoulder, sliding the strap off.

Beyond frustrated and way past impatient, she reached

behind her and flicked the clasp free, releasing the garment to fall to the floor, her breasts bobbing free.

Thorn groaned. "I'm in so much trouble with you, Sophia."

"You are?" She felt empowered as she tugged his shirt free of his jeans and flicked the buttons open one at a time. "I'm on the run from a man. I sure as hell never planned on getting involved with another." She freed the last button and gripped the openings of the shirt, pulling him closer. "I'm not staying," she said, her words fierce, determined, more to remind herself than him.

"Okay, okay." He held up his hands in surrender. "You're not staying. I'm not in the market for a relationship. What's keeping us from doing this?" He bent to take one of her nipples between his lips and tongued the pebbled tip.

Sophia arched her back, pressing closer to his warm, wet tongue. She cupped the back of his head, holding him as close to her as she could get him. "Exactly," she breathed. "No strings, no expectations."

"Just mutual lust," he muttered around the nipple.

"The other L word." She guided his other hand to the second breast, then reached for the rivet on his jeans. "Think they'll miss us for a little while?"

"Hank's in the bunker." He nuzzled her cleavage while backing her toward the bed.

"It's too early for supper." She pushed the top button loose on his jeans and gripped the zipper tag. "Who else would care?" She didn't have family standing outside ready to criticize her actions, or a husband she was cheating on. All loyalty to her ex-fiancé had ended the first time he'd hit her.

Clothes flew off and Thorn swept her off her feet, laying her across the neatly made bed. "I thought you'd died in that fire." He came down over her, balancing, a hand on either side of her.

She gave him a crooked smile and cupped his cheek. "You'd have been free of your duties if I had."

"Don't." He touched a finger to her lips, his brows drawn together. "You have a baby to think about."

How well she knew. "Does that bother you?" Her gaze slipped to his neck, refusing to look him in the eye. Afraid he'd be hesitant to make love to a woman carrying another man's child.

"Hell, yeah."

Her heart cramped and she lay very still against the softness of the blanket. What did she expect? She'd been with another man and was pregnant with his child. What man wouldn't be bothered?

He lay down beside her, his hand smoothing over her cheek where the bruise had all but vanished. He trailed his fingers over the fullness of one breast and down to her still-smooth belly. "Scares the hell out of me."

"Because it's someone else's baby?" she asked, her breath catching in her throat as she waited for his answer.

"No." Thorn's lips clamped together in a thin line.

Even more softly, she whispered, "Because of how you lost your wife and child?"

For a long moment, he didn't answer. When he did, he spoke so softly that she had to strain to hear. "There was no reason for them to die." He stared at her belly, but he must have been reliving the past. Shadows descended over his eyes. "I didn't react fast enough."

She grabbed his hand, threading her fingers through his. "It wasn't your fault." She brought his hand to her cheek. "You didn't pull the trigger."

"I might as well have." His fingers tightened around hers.

"But you didn't."

"Now I'm expected to keep you safe." His gaze shifted to hers. "You're pregnant, just like her. Only this time, you're the target of an entire cartel and the U.S. government, not just collateral damage of a bullet meant for me."

"Again, whatever happens to me will not be your fault."

"Maybe."

"Do you still miss her?"

"Kayla?" His finger traced her collarbone. "I always will."

The tightness in her chest was expected, and she understood and accepted it. He'd loved his wife. That was one of the reasons she found herself falling in love with him. A man who loved his wife that much was a man worth giving your heart to. He'd never willingly break her heart if he loved her.

Oh, if only he loved her as much as he'd loved his wife. As quickly as the thought emerged, she pushed it to the back of her mind. Theirs was not a forever commitment. It couldn't be. "Kayla was a very lucky woman."

"Kayla died," he said flatly.

"I'm truly sorry for your loss. But she always knew you loved her. For that, she was very fortunate. Not all married couples can claim they still love one another."

"I'll never forget her."

"Nor should you." Sophia smoothed the frown from his brow and pressed a kiss to his lips.

"I'll never understand a man who hits a woman. Especially one he's promised to love." He pulled her into his arms and rested his chin on the top of her head. "Your ex hit you often, didn't he?"

"Yes."

Thorn's arms tensed around her. "I can't let anything else happen to you."

She pressed her palms against his chest, shoving him

away with a smile. Then she drew a line with her finger from the middle of his chest down his taut abs, to the line of hair angling downward to the thick, straight shaft jutting upward. "I was hoping something *would* happen."

Thorn grasped her hand and pinned it above her head, not so tight that it would scare her. "I think I've got this." With careful, deliberate moves, he kissed and nipped his way the length of her torso, stopping to feast on her breasts before moving downward. He pressed his lips to her belly, gently skimming over it to the triangle of curls at the apex of her thighs.

Sophia squirmed against the mattress, wanting more, faster. Never had she felt the amount of raging desire she experienced at Thorn's touch. The past few months with Antonio had been a nightmare of sexual demands she'd been forced to perform or suffer the consequences—a bruised cheek, broken rib, busted lip or swollen eye.

Thorn treated her body like a delicate flower to be held with the lightest touch, to be revered and cherished as if it would break with too much pressure.

When he parted her folds and stroked her core with the tip of his finger, she dug her heels into the mattress, arching her back off the bed.

The time of gentle persuasion was over. "Please, I want more."

He chuckled, his warm breath stirring her nether curls. "Patience." He dipped into her channel, stirring her juices, dragging them up to the sensitive strip of flesh between her folds, throbbing from his initial attack. "I don't want to hurt you."

"You won't." With his next stroke, her head rolled back and her thoughts winged away, lost in the haze of desire building inside.

When he replaced his fingers with his tongue, she

moaned, coming apart with each thrust, swirl and stroke until she exploded in a burst of sensations so intense all she could do was gasp. She grasped his hair, her fingers convulsing around the strands, holding him steady one moment, urging him on the next.

When she thought she could stand no more, he reached over the side of the bed, grabbed his jeans and ripped his wallet from the back pocket. He rifled through the contents until he came out with a small foil packet.

"I can't get pregnant because I already am."

"For your protection and peace of mind."

Her heart warmed. He cared enough to protect her and her baby.

He slipped the condom over his erection and settled between her legs.

As he hovered at her entrance, he bent to claim her mouth.

She swept her lips over his, her tongue pushing through his teeth to tangle with his.

As their tongues collided, he plunged inside her, gliding in, stretching and filling all the emptiness she'd endured over the year of her abduction.

Pressing her feet into the mattress, she rose up to meet him thrust for thrust, her hips rocking to his rhythm, her fingers digging into his buttocks, guiding him deeper.

As the heat increased and she neared the precipice, tingling started at her center and spread like wildfire throughout her body to the very tips of her toes and fingers. She grew rigid, holding on to the fevered euphoria of their most intimate connection.

Thorn impaled her one last time, remaining deeply rooted inside her. He dropped down on top of her, holding her close, crushing the air from her lungs.

Sophia didn't care. If she died right then, she'd die

happy, fulfilled and intoxicated with what making love should always be like.

After a moment Thorn rolled to his side, bringing her with him, allowing her to take a deep breath.

She lay for a long time in the haven of his arms, her eyelids fluttering closed, the deep exhaustion of pregnancy claiming her. Never had she felt so incredibly... loved. Her elation faded to despair as she reminded herself that this feeling was destined to be a one-time event. As she drifted into sleep, from the corner of her eye, a single tear dropped.

THORN LAY FOR a long time, drinking in the beauty of Sophia as she slept, her green eyes shuttered, the salty track of a tear like a scar on her perfect skin.

He wanted to take away her pain, to hold her until all the terror subsided, to keep her safe always. Inside, Thorn realized that until the cartel thug Antonio Martinez gave up his quest to reclaim his hostage, Sophia would be on the run, constantly in fear of discovery.

Thorn would have stayed cocooned in the sheets with Sophia had a knock not disturbed his perusal. He rose from the bed, slipped into his jeans and padded to the door barefoot.

When he opened it, Zach Adams, one of the men Hank had hired as a Covert Cowboy, stood with a grimace on his face. "Hate to interrupt, but Hank wants us in the bunker. Now."

Thorn nodded. "I'll be right there." He closed the door, found his boots and finished dressing in less than a minute. Then he bent over Sophia's bed and pressed a kiss to her forehead, careful not to wake her.

Pregnant, running from an assault and making love all in one day had drained her. She needed sleep.

He drew the curtains over the blinds, blocking out the last of the sun's rays. "Sleep, sweetheart. We'll figure this out together."

He left the room, closing the door softly behind him, and hurried to the bunker, his pulse speeding as his resolve solidified. Antonio Martinez couldn't continue to make Sophia's life hell. If the FBI and the CBP couldn't nail the bastard, it was up to him and the Covert Cowboys to do the job.

In the bunker, he found Hank, Chuck, Zach and Blaise Harding gathered around a large-screen monitor on the wall of the computer lab. Hank had called in all the new members of CCI.

Brandon manned the keyboard at his desk. "Based on Ms. Carranza's accounts and the amount of time she and her escort were on the run and the direction they came, I pulled satellite images from across the border in the Mexican state of Chihuahua, locating a small village called Paraíso." Brandon chuckled. "It translates to paradise, which is ironic, considering it's in the middle of a desert with nothing much around it."

Hank waved a hand impatiently. "Get to the point, please."

Brandon cleared his throat and clicked the mouse. The view on the big screen zoomed in on a location to the west of the town. The clarity of the satellite image sharpened until a fortified compound came into view.

"You think that's it?" Hank leaned closer. "Is that *la Fuerte del Diablo?*"

"Can't be absolutely certain, but given the parameters, I can't find anything else that remotely resembles a drug cartel fortress within a three-hundred-mile radius. And if you look closely inside the walls, there's a space large enough to land a helicopter. And to the south is a dirt landing strip for fixed-wing aircraft. The place is big enough to house a small army of cartel members and stage a boatload of drugs for delivery. From what I can tell, there isn't a cow, horse or goat in the area. They aren't trying to disguise it as a ranch, meaning the Mexican government either doesn't have them on their radar or they're paid off to turn a blind eye. What better location to ship drugs into and out of the U.S.?"

"And what better place to hide hostages?" Hank's voice was low, angry. "How soon can we get our team in there?"

"They'll be heavily armed and possibly booby-trapped," Zach stated.

Hank turned to the man. "Is this the same place you were held captive and tortured?"

"No, I was captured by *Los Lobos,* archrivals of *la Familia Diablos.* But this compound is very similar, and the two cartels play for keeps. They shoot first and ask questions later."

"Trigger-happy," Chuck added.

"They have to be, or they die." Zach's jaw and fists tightened. "And they show no mercy to prisoners."

"Do you think we'll find Lilianna and Jake there?" Thorn asked.

"It's the only lead I've had on them in the past two years. I have to check it out."

"It could be a suicide mission," Zach warned.

Hank faced Zach. "If Jacie was kidnapped by *La Familia Diablos* or *Los Lobos,* would you leave her there?"

"I'd die trying to get her out," Zach responded, his face grim.

From what Thorn knew, Zach had been an undercover agent with the FBI seized by *Los Lobos,* along with his female partner over a year ago. Held captive for weeks, he'd been tortured for information regarding a government insider allowing *la Familia Diablos* cartel free rein across the border into the U.S. His partner had been tortured to death while Zach had been forced to watch.

When *la Familia Diablos* had attacked the *Los Lobos* hideout, Zach had escaped back to the States. If anyone knew the extent of suffering the cartels could impart, it was Zach.

Hank faced the gathering of Covert Cowboys, his six bodyguards and ranch security men. "Together, we have eleven of us."

Chuck blew out a stream of air. "Any idea how many are inside the fortress? What we'd be up against?"

"I asked Sophia. She said it varied anywhere from fifteen to thirty, depending on what was going on," Hank said. "Brandon's working on verifying numbers, but we have to go on limited intel for now." He looked into the faces of each man in the room. "I can't ask any of you to do this. Like Zach said, it's a suicide mission at best."

Zach stepped forward. "I'm in."

"Me, too," Chuck agreed. "I can't imagine if PJ was the one stuck in that hell for two years."

One by one, the bodyguards and ranch security team added their names to the list.

Blaise raised his hand. "Count me in."

"Me, too." Thorn moved forward.

"I can't let you go." Hank stared at Thorn. "We need you with Sophia. She doesn't stand a chance on her own, and with all of my ranch security on the team, this place won't be safe."

Thorn itched to be with the team storming *la Fuerte del Diablo,* but he'd promised to keep Sophia safe no matter what.

"What about me?" Brandon stood with the rest of them, his face set, his young body not nearly as intimidating as the hardened warriors of the Covert Cowboys and ranch security.

"I need you to man the computers and feed us information as you get it," Hank said. "We can lock down the bunker. It's fireproof and hardened, so a direct attack won't penetrate it."

"When do we start?" Zach asked.

And the planning began.

SOPHIA WOKE TO a dark room and reached out a hand for the warm, solid comfort of Thorn. As she touched the empty pillow, the loneliness of the empty room threatened to overwhelm her.

Who was she kidding? He was only obligated by his job to protect her, not provide comfort and emotional support. That's what family was for. In her case, it wasn't an option—she was on her own. And at that moment, it was a very lonely feeling.

She flicked on the reading lamp on the nightstand and stared around the room. Tall ceilings, walls painted a pale terra-cotta and rich mahogany furnishings made it as warm as an air-conditioned room could be. Without personal touches, it might as well have been a very nice hotel room.

Sophia would give anything for a photograph of her mother, father and baby brother. She missed them so much it hurt. What she wouldn't give to hear her mother's voice telling her everything would be all right, just like when she'd been a little girl and had fallen and scraped her knee.

The light from the lamp glanced off something black and shiny on the nightstand. Thorn's new cell phone that Hank had given him to replace the one that burned in his house. He wouldn't have gone far without it.

Hungry and in need of the facilities, Sophia rose from

the bed and slipped into the jeans and T-shirt Hank's housekeeper had unearthed from Lilianna's wardrobe. She opened the connecting door to Thorn's room, hoping he was there. He wasn't.

As she passed back through her room, the light once again glanced off Thorn's cell phone.

If Antonio already knew she was there, what would it hurt to call her parents? It wouldn't trigger him to find her because he already had.

And what was it Hank had said? He'd give anything to know his wife and son were still alive, to hear their voices.

All the time she'd been incarcerated in *la Fuerte del Diablo,* Sophia had dreamed of hearing the voices of her mother, father and brother, Ernesto. Had her family had the same dreams?

Did cell phones have reception this far out in the country? As wealthy as Hank was, had he had a cell phone tower installed nearby to enable his communication with the outside world?

Could she place a call to Mexico?

Her heart pounded as she took first one step, then another toward Thorn's phone. The closer she moved, the faster she went until she pounced on the device and held it in her hand.

Her parents' number was as clear in her mind as it had been a year ago. She dialed it and got a message that the number she had dialed was not a working number. Had they disconnected or changed numbers? Then it dawned on her that a call from the United States to Mexico would require the country prefix.

Her hands shook as she dialed the full number and waited.

"Hola." When her mother's voice sounded in her ear, Sophia almost dropped the phone.

Her throat closed, and she fought to push words past the sobs. "Mama."

A long pause followed, then a tentative, "Sophia?"

"*Sí*, Mama, it's me."

"Oh, dear God, Sophia!" Her mother's sobs crackled into Sophia's ear.

"I'm okay, Mama." Sophia almost regretted the call. To give her mother hope when she had very little herself of coming out of her situation free or alive.

"We thought you were dead." More sobs.

Sophia cut through them, unsure of how long she could talk or if it put her or her parents in further danger. "Mama, how's Papa?"

"Sick with worry about you and Ernesto."

Sophia's hand tightened on the cell phone at the mention of her younger brother. "What's happened to Ernesto?"

"He's gone, too!" Her mother hiccupped, her breath catching. "Where have you been? Why haven't you called?"

"I can't go into that now. Just know that I'm alive. Tell me what happened to Ernesto."

"He had gone to work for the bank where your father works, but he fell in with a bad crowd at a local night club. He went there last night. We haven't seen him since."

A deep voice sounded in the background of the call and Sophia's heart skipped several beats. Her father. He spoke in rapid-fire Spanish. Her mother answered, her mouth away from the phone. Sophia couldn't follow the conversation.

"Mama?" she said into the phone. "Mama!"

"Sophia?" Her father's deep voice filled her ear. "Where are you? Why haven't you called?" He spoke in Spanish.

After several days around people who only spoke English, it took Sophia a moment for her mind to process and reply back in Spanish. "I'm in Texas. I'm okay for now. What about Ernesto?"

"I just got off the telephone with someone who said that if you do not return to the fortress, they will kill your brother."

Like a punch to the gut, Sophia doubled over. The cartel had her brother. She should have known Antonio would be monitoring her home in Monterrey and that he'd use her family against her. He knew how much she cared about them.

"Did they say anything else?" she asked, barely able to force the words past her heartbreak.

"If you don't go immediately and alone, he will be dead by sunset tomorrow." Her father paused. "Who are these people? Why are they doing this to you and Ernesto?"

"Papa, I can't go into it. Just know this. I love you." She fought to make her voice strong when her entire body shook. "Tell Mama I'm going to make this right."

She didn't wait for his response, pressing the button that would end the call. Sophia tossed the phone to the nightstand, knowing what she had to do.

She had to return to *la Fuerte del Diablo*.

Chapter Fourteen

When Thorn went back to Sophia's room to check on her, he was surprised to see her out of bed, dressed and looking as if she was going somewhere.

"I thought you'd be sleeping," he said.

"I couldn't." She paced across the room, parted the curtains and stared out at the night. "Why are there men still moving around the barnyard?"

"Brandon located *la Fuerte del Diablo.* Hank's getting a team together to cross over and free Lilianna and Jake."

"I want to be with them," she said.

Thorn shook his head. "Won't happen. Hank's leaving me behind to keep you safe."

"I'm the only one here who knows what room they keep Anna and Jake in. They need me."

"The odds are against them as it is. You don't have the combat training most of those guys do." He gripped her arm and forced her to look at him. "Think of your baby."

Her gaze met his, tears swimming in her green eyes. "I need to be there."

"You have to trust them. If you go, they'll be worried about what might happen to you. They won't be able to focus on their mission. That could get more people killed, and they'll already be outmanned and outgunned." He gathered her in his arms and smoothed his hand through her hair. "Don't worry, I'll be here with you. Antonio won't have a chance to get anywhere near you."

"When are they going?"

"Hank's arranging for a team to be transported via airplane late tomorrow evening."

"Isn't he afraid tomorrow will be too late?"

"Given the numbers they'll be up against, it might be too soon. He needs time to charter the transport plane he'll need to drop the men in on the other side of the border."

Sophia lowered her head. "I need to eat."

"I'm glad to see you're feeling well enough. Your baby needs the nutrition as much as you do."

He escorted her to the kitchen, where Hank's housekeeper had left a tray of sandwiches in the refrigerator. After Sophia had eaten an entire sandwich by herself in silence, Thorn began to wonder what had her so preoccupied. Perhaps the thought of Hank's men storming the compound had her worried for Lilianna and Jake.

Sophia's face was pale throughout the meal, the shadows beneath her eyes deeper and her eyelids slightly red rimmed, as if she'd cried recently.

When they'd finished and cleaned up their plates, Thorn hooked her arm and headed toward their rooms. "I think you could use more rest."

She halted before they'd gone too far, bringing Thorn to a stop. "I'm not tired."

"Then what's wrong?" He faced her, tipping her face up to the light and brushing his thumb across her cheek. "Have you been crying?"

A film of tears washed over her eyes. "No."

"Liar." He touched his lips to hers in a brief kiss. "Were you upset when you woke up and didn't find me there?"

She pulled her chin away from his fingers and looked away. "A little."

"I wouldn't have gone, but Hank called a meeting to discuss the plan." He cupped her cheek. "If it helps to know, I'll be with you from here on out."

She stared up into his eyes, the tears spilling down her cheeks.

Not exactly the response he'd anticipated from his statement.

"Thorn," Hank called out from near the hidden door to the bunker. "Ah, Sophia. Good. You're awake." He waved them over. "Feeling better?"

Sophia wiped the tears from her cheeks and crossed to the ranch owner. "Have you learned anything else about where they're keeping Anna and Jake?"

He smiled. "I take it Thorn filled you in on what Brandon found?"

"He did."

He turned to the hidden door and pressed his thumb to the pad on the wall. "I'd like you to look at what we've been working on." The door swung open, revealing the staircase.

"Of course." Sophia followed him into the bunker, Thorn close behind.

Again, Thorn was struck with a sense of something not being quite right with her. Until she told him what it was, though, he'd only be guessing.

Hank led them into the conference room with the big screen at the end. Brandon was still there, his fingers alternating between the keyboard and the mouse. "I accessed records of the satellite images for the past few days and put together a day-by-day progression of activity I thought you might find interesting."

Hank held out a chair for Sophia and sat in the one beside her. Thorn sat across the table, the better to study Sophia.

Brandon clicked the keyboard several times and an image came up, very much like the one he'd seen earlier at the meeting of the team.

The compound sat at the center of the image, concrete walls surrounding it.

"It's a fairly large complex with several buildings." Brandon moved his cursor, pointing at the largest building in the center. "This appears to be the main residence." He moved the cursor to a large empty spot to the right of the big building. "Now watch this."

He clicked the keyboard, and another image that looked exactly like the first appeared on the screen. Only the empty space had something in it that resembled the shape of a helicopter.

Sophia leaned forward. "A helicopter landed at *la Fuerte* each time *El Martillo* paid a visit."

"This image was from two weeks ago." Brandon turned to Sophia.

Sophia's face blanched and her body trembled. "*El Martillo* was there two weeks ago. From what Antonio told me, he had four of his men executed for passing information to *Los Lobos*."

Thorn couldn't imagine what this *El Martillo* would do to her if she were captured and returned to the fort.

Brandon clicked the screen. The helicopter disappeared, and in its place a tractor-trailer rig materialized with what appeared to be boxes lined up to be loaded into the back.

"Drugs?" Hank asked.

"Probably." Zack entered the room and took the seat beside Thorn.

"And notice the men gathered around." Brandon zoomed in.

The image blurred, but Thorn could still make out men carrying what looked like AK-47s. "Well armed."

"And probably trained by the Mexican army. The cartels pay better," Zach added.

"There are roads into and out of the compound," Brandon continued.

"But we won't be taking those." Hank tapped his fingers against the hardwood tabletop. "In order for us to maintain the element of surprise, we have to come in cross-country."

"Are those the exact coordinates?" Sophia pointed to the numbers on the top right corner of the screen.

"Yes," Brandon responded. "Smack-dab in the middle of the desert, south of Big Bend."

Sophia focused on the screen, then she closed her eyes. When she opened them again, she glanced around the table to Hank. "I never saw the place from this angle, so I can't be certain, but from the layout of the buildings it looks like *la Fuerte del Diablo*. And If I'm not mistaken, you'll find Anna somewhere in the main building."

Hank captured her hand and squeezed it.

Thorn tensed. He knew how much Hank loved his wife, but seeing him cling to Sophia's hand like that sent a jab of jealousy through Thorn he didn't know he had in him.

"Thank you," Hank said.

Sophia's lips thinned. "Don't thank me until you get them out alive." She glanced across the table at Thorn. "If you'll excuse me, I'm very tired."

"Come on, I'll take you topside." Thorn rose and led Sophia out of the room. Once they'd climbed out of the bunker, he slipped an arm around her. "Are you sure you're okay?"

"Why do you ask?"

"You seem preoccupied." He continued walking with her toward the bedroom they'd shared a couple hours ago. "Having regrets?"

"About?"

"What happened?"

She stepped through the door and pulled him inside, closing the door behind him. "If there's anything I'm not regretful about, it's you." She rose up on her toes and planted a kiss on his lips, lacing her hands behind his head to deepen the contact.

When she broke it off, she dropped her forehead to his chest. "I don't know what I would have done without your help that first night. I'd most likely be dead or on my way back to *la Familia Diablos*." A shiver shuddered through her at the thought, knowing it was exactly where she had to go. She wouldn't let her brother die for the mistakes she'd made. Her parents had gone through too much already.

"Then why were you preoccupied at the meeting with Hank?"

Sophia glanced away. Lying had never been easy for her. With Antonio, her life had been a lie in order for her to survive his abuse. With Thorn, she couldn't look him in the eye and tell him an untruth. "I was remembering all the horrible things that happened while I was there. The brutal beatings of men who didn't follow orders exactly right. The executions of rival cartel members caught on the wrong side of an imaginary border. The cries of the women whose men were found with their heads cut off."

Thorn pulled her against him, his arms wrapping around her waist, his touch more comforting than sexual. Just what she needed at that moment.

She closed her eyes, trying to block out all that was the worst of what she'd endured. "I never wanted to go back." And she would never consider it, if not to save her brother from a similar fate. If going back to Antonio kept him from killing Ernesto, so be it. The only bargaining chip she held to keep him from beating her to death was the fact that she was pregnant with his child. Surely he wouldn't kill her until after the birth.

"You're safe with me," Thorn said.

"Yes, I am." She tipped her head up, inviting his kiss. As she'd told him, she wouldn't be around forever. This would be their last time together, and she planned to make it a memory that would last.

Sophia stepped away from him.

"Do you have to be anywhere anytime soon?" she asked.

Thorn's lips curled upward on the edge, and he reached for her. "No."

She dodged his hands and slipped out of the T-shirt and jeans, slowly sliding her panties over her hips.

Thorn stood still, his gaze following every move, the ridge beneath his fly growing with each passing second. When she stood naked in front of him, he growled and swept her up in his arms. "I thought you were tired."

She laughed and nipped his earlobe. "I was."

He carried her to the bed and laid her across the mattress, then straightened. "Then maybe I should leave you to your sleep." His eager expression belied his words.

Sophia climbed to her knees, ran her hands down her naked flesh then flicked a button loose on his shirt. "If that's what you really want…"

"No. It's not." He finished the buttons, tossed the shirt and shed his boots and jeans in record time. Then he slid into the bed beside her. "You know what I want?"

"I could guess." She climbed up over him, straddling his hips, his member nudging her behind. "But I'd rather you showed me."

"Seems you're the one on top of things." He tweaked her nipple. "Perhaps you'd rather show me."

Their casual banter made it easy to make love to Thorn, a far cry from their first few encounters rife with tension and distrust. Now all she wanted to do was lie with him, making love into the dark hours of the morning.

One kiss at a time, she showed him how much he'd come to mean to her in the very short time they'd been forced together. If only they had more days together. If she wasn't headed back to the very place she'd sworn never to return to. A place she may never leave again. A lump blocked her throat, and she fought the rising sob.

This was to be their last night together. Sophia wanted to remember the joy, not the impending doom and sorrow. She started with a kiss, her lips tasting his, her tongue seeking the warmth and strength of his. Her body moved over his as she rose up on her knees and came down on him, guiding his shaft to her entrance.

Their coupling was intense, fiery and beyond anything she'd experienced in her life. When she lay spent beside him, in the comfort of his arms, she wondered how she could walk away from him without dying inside.

Thorn held her curled into his side, his chest rising and falling in a smooth, even pattern of deep sleep.

For a long time, Sophia drank in the sight of him in the dim light managing to find its way through the drawn curtains. The cowboy was handsome, dedicated and had a heart of gold.

She'd miss him, but she had to go.

Carefully, she extricated herself from his embrace and eased out of the bed.

Thorn rolled over, his eyes opening slightly. "Where are you going?" he asked sleepily.

"To the bathroom," she whispered. "Sleep."

His eyes closed. "Don't be gone long."

"I'll be right back." She dressed in the jeans, shirt and the tennis shoes Hank had loaned her from his wife's closet. Carefully, she lifted the pistol Thorn had laid on the nightstand before he'd gone to bed. Then she slipped from the room into Thorn's and out the double French doors onto the wide deck, tucking the gun into the back waistband of her jeans.

Trying to remember where all the security cameras were, she stuck to the deepest shadows and headed away from the house, moving from the bushes to a tree and across to the fence.

A shadow moved near the edge of the house.

Sophia tensed and stopped, hunkering low to the ground, her gaze on the house, watching, waiting for whatever was there to move again. After a moment, a cat emerged from behind a bush and sauntered toward the barn.

With a sigh Sophia continued, hugging the fence and working her way back to the barn, slipping in the back entrance where the four-wheelers were stored.

Hoping the foreman kept them topped off with gasoline, she shifted one into Neutral and pushed it through the door and out the back entrance into the night.

Each of the ATVs was equipped with GPS. All she had to do was enter the coordinates she'd memorized from the screen Brandon had shown her and follow the trails through the canyons and across the Rio Grande back into Mexico. Nothing to it—as long as she could dodge the border patrol, evade the FBI and, most of all, escape the notice of the cartel members set on killing her.

For the first quarter mile she pushed the vehicle, the strain on her muscles nothing compared to the pain in her heart. Thank goodness the land around the ranch house was flat, no hills, or she'd never have gotten as far as she did.

For the first time in her life, she'd met a man she could trust. A man who had a huge capacity to love and knew how to treat a woman right. How she wished she'd had more time to get to know him better, to show him that she was worth the trouble of loving again.

She envied Kayla and she envied her friend Anna the love of their husbands.

Sophia had to placate herself with the knowledge that she had a baby to love. Someone she'd give her life to save. She had to focus on getting her brother out of trouble, then she'd find a way to remove herself from the cartel's clutches.

If she did manage to get back to Wild Oak Canyon, she'd look up Thorn. Yeah, and miracles happened to people like her.

At what she guessed to be a quarter of a mile away from the ranch, she climbed onto the four-wheeler, her hand hovering over the starter.

A shiver of awareness slipped across her skin, and she turned back to see if anyone had followed.

In her peripheral vision, a shadow moved. Her focus jerked to track it, scanning the horizon between her and the ranch. All she could see was one lonely, dwarf mesquite tree huddled close to the dry earth, its tiny leaves brushed carelessly by the breeze. Nothing else moved.

A nervous chuckle left Sophia's lips as she hit the start button. The engine cranked immediately. She pressed the gas lever, and the vehicle leaped toward her fate.

THORN WOKE IN the darkness and blinked several times before he realized where he was. The clock on the nightstand read five minutes after three.

Sophia had gotten up to relieve herself, saying she'd be right back. He hadn't checked the clock then. How long had she been gone?

His pulse quickening, Thorn rose from the bed and

slipped into his jeans. A quick peek into the bathroom and he was no closer to finding Sophia. The light was off—it was empty.

His heartbeat thumping hard now, he returned to her room and checked inside the connecting room. She wasn't there. Out of the corner of his eye, he noticed the curtain on the double French doors was stuck between the two doors, as if someone had gone out in a hurry.

A lead weight sank into his gut as he reached for the doorknob he'd locked earlier. The knob turned easily, opening to the outside. Thorn returned to Sophia's room, shoved his feet into his boots, grabbed his shirt and headed outside in search of his missing charge.

He'd have woken if she'd been abducted. Which meant she'd slipped out on her own. Perhaps to get some fresh air? He prayed that was the case. Deep down, though, he knew it wasn't. She'd always said she didn't want to put anyone else at risk.

One of Hank's night guards stepped from the shadows. "Halt. Who goes there?"

Thorn recognized him as one of the men Hank had hired straight from a gig in Afghanistan. The man had been a marine, fearless and determined. But he walked with a limp. Another stray Hank had collected to fight his good fight.

"Did you see a pretty blonde come this way?" he asked, hopeful the guy's keen sight had picked up her whereabouts.

"Just came on duty about an hour ago." He shifted the M4A1 to a resting position. "Only movement I've seen was the FBI director's SUV pulling away from the ops tent."

"Working late hours, isn't he?"

"There were some raised voices in there for a few minutes before the director left."

"I need help locating the woman. I think she might be in danger."

Hank stepped out on the porch wearing jeans, a T-shirt and slippers. "What's going on?"

Thorn gritted his teeth. "Sophia's gone." On his watch, and she'd gotten away.

Within minutes, everyone on the ranch staff, including the housekeeper, had been alerted and was now checking every nook and cranny for her. Every last bodyguard and security guard reported finding nothing.

The group gathered in the barnyard. Hank walked over from the Joint Operations tent, his face grim. "I spoke with the crew on duty, thinking maybe Ms. Carranza turned herself over to them." Hank shook his head. "They never saw her, and the director left alone."

"She ran," Thorn said. "She couldn't have gone far. All the vehicles are accounted for."

"Except one." Scott Walden, the foreman, stepped into the middle of the crowd. "One four-wheeler is missing from the barn. I followed the tracks out the back door into the pasture. Whoever took it headed south."

Thorn's heart sank. "She is going back to Antonio. Back to *la Fuerte del Diablo*."

"Why?"

"She was worried that by her being away from there, others would be hurt and that Antonio wouldn't stop hurting people until he had her back." Thorn's fists clenched. Antonio would beat her, regardless of her pregnancy. Sophia and the baby might not survive. "I'm going after her."

Hank put a hand on his arm. "You can't."

He jerked his arm free. "Like hell I can't."

"More than Sophia's life will be at stake in the compound."

"You don't understand—she might not make it back to

the compound. Traveling at night in the Big Bend canyons, she could run off a cliff, be bitten by a snake, get attacked by wolves or, worse, cartel members."

"Each of my ATVs is equipped with GPS tracking devices. Let's get Brandon to pull up her location on the computer and see how far she's gotten."

Thorn fought the urge to jump on the next available vehicle and storm after her. "Okay, but I'm going after her."

"And you will, but with a better understanding of where she is and what's at stake." Hank led the way into the bunker.

Brandon was already at his computer, clicking away on the keyboard. One final click and a screen displayed a topographical map and a red dot in the middle. "There. I guesstimate she's close to two hours away from us, deep in Big Bend country."

"If you follow her now, you may or may not catch up to her," Hank said.

"But she could be hurt."

"Brandon will keep an eye on her progress."

"I can do better than that." Brandon jumped up from his desk and headed into another room, emerging with a handheld device. He clicked the on button and waited, then handed it to Thorn. "You can follow her progress on this."

"But it's only the progress of the vehicle. We don't know if she's the one driving it."

"It's the best we have," Brandon said. "Short of going after her yourself, you'll have to trust that she can make it back on her own."

Two hours might as well be two weeks. She'd cross the Rio Grande while still under cover of darkness. If he started now, he'd cross in daylight. Stronger chance of being discovered by the trigger-happy cartel or diligent border-patrol agents.

"Hank," Brandon continued, "I just checked with your guy at Charter Avionics. They've been so busy that he's been up all night. But he was pleased to let you know that you can have the cargo plane today."

"What time?"

"They're pulling the preflight now. It can be ready in one hour, and they've located a cargo to pick up in Monterrey. Say the word and they'll file the flight plan."

"Tell them we'll be there in an hour." Hank turned to his foreman. "Scott? Is your flying license still current?"

"You know it," Scott replied.

"He's a pilot?" Thorn asked. What else didn't he know about Hank and his team of mercenaries?

"One of the best." Hank clapped his foreman on the back. "Flew missions in Iraq."

"And now I'm a foreman. A long way from my duties in the air force." Scott grinned. "I grew up on a ranch. I prefer working with horses and cattle, but I keep current on my flight skills, thanks to Hank."

"Drennan, you ever jump from a plane?" Hank asked. Thorn nodded. "I did back in college a couple times."

"Chuck will give you a quick refresher with the equipment we have. If all goes well, we could get to the fort before Sophia." Hank faced the team. "Our timeline has just moved up. We leave as soon as we gather our gear and weapons."

Chapter Fifteen

Sophia had the feeling again that someone was following her. Doing her best to stick to the shadows of bluffs, she still had several long stretches of open ground to navigate. Thankful for the full moon lighting her path, she pressed on, hoping and praying the four-wheeler wouldn't run out of gas or someone wouldn't stop her from reaching her destination.

Her brother's life depended on her return to *la Fuerte del Diablo*.

She'd found her way along the trail she'd taken a few days earlier with Hector and now faced the long, somewhat flat stretch leading to the low-water crossing they'd forged on their dirt bikes. With the recent rain, Sophia couldn't be sure the river would be low enough to cross on the four-wheeler. The best she could do was cross on the ATV. If it was too deep, she'd lose the bike and have to continue on foot, without the aid of the GPS.

She slowed as she neared the river, her gaze darting left and right, searching for movement. At this point she'd be exposed, out in the open for anyone to see, including the United States border patrol. Although she couldn't imagine why they'd stop her crossing into Mexico. Didn't they concentrate on people *entering* the United States?

She gunned the throttle, sending the ATV out across the

open expanse and into the water. Halfway across the river, the vehicle's forward momentum slowed and it started floating sideways.

No. Just a little farther. *Come on,* por favor.

The wheels hit a sandbar beneath the water's surface and sent the vehicle forward again and into shallower water.

When she emerged safely on the Mexican side, Sophia paused as the engine chugged and choked. Setting the shift in Neutral, she revved the throttle until the engine ran smoothly again.

As she reached for the shift to set it in Drive, something stung her shoulder. She clapped her hand to the sharp pain and felt warm, sticky liquid. When she held her fingers up in the moonlight, she knew. She'd been hit. Another shot kicked up the rocks in front of the ATV. The next shot hit the handlebar, missing her fingers by half an inch. The bullets were coming from the other side of the river.

With too much open space to navigate before she reached cover, Sophia knew she'd never make it. She threw herself off the vehicle on the shadowy side. As soon as she landed on the rocky ground, she lay flat and pulled Thorn's handgun from the back waistband of her jeans. If she remained still enough, maybe whoever was shooting at her would assume he'd hit his mark and killed her, then maybe he'd move on.

With nothing but the four-wheeler as cover, Sophia lay still, the minutes stretching by like hours. Then she heard it. The sound of an engine splashing in the river. Only one engine.

Carefully, so that her movements wouldn't be detected, she eased around the knobby tire.

A man with a rifle slung over his shoulder hydroplaned across the river on a four-wheeler much like hers. Only his ATV wasn't lucky enough to catch a sandbar. Instead, it was caught in the current and drifted down the river.

The rider jumped off, holding what looked like an automatic rifle that soldiers carried over his head.

Sophia waited until he was close enough, then she aimed the pistol at the man—knowing she had only one chance to get it right—and pulled the trigger.

The bullet hit him in the leg and flung him backward into the water. His rifle flew into the air, landing with a splash in the current.

Sophia leaped to her feet and ran to the man, who was flailing and grasping for a handhold as the current carried him farther downstream.

At last he scratched his way to the shore, dragging himself up on the Mexican side.

Sophia was there, waiting for him, and she pointed the gun at his head.

When he turned to look up, the moonlight glanced off his features.

Sophia gasped. "I saw you at the ranch. You're with the FBI."

He grunted, his face creased in pain. "Help me."

"Why should I? You tried to kill me." She refused to get close enough to let him grab her and take her weapon away.

"Please." He reached out a hand. "My radio went down with the four-wheeler. If you leave me here, I'll die."

"Don't the feds know you're out here?" Her heart fluttered and she studied the horizon, searching for more agents like him.

"No." He dragged himself farther away from the river, leaving a thick trail of blood on the rocks. When he'd gone a couple feet, he collapsed facedown, his voice muffled but clear. "I'm not one of them. I'm a mercenary, a sharpshooter for hire."

"Then why the FBI outfit?" She nodded at his official-looking coveralls with the FBI lettering on the shoulder.

"Lehmann wanted everyone to think I was one of them."

"Why? Don't they have sharpshooters in the FBI?" she demanded, none of this making any sense.

"Yeah, but they usually shoot criminals."

Her stomach clenched. "And you'll shoot anyone who'll pay the price." She stood back, her weapon trained on him. "Are you telling me Lehmann wants me dead?"

"You and Antonio Martinez."

"Why?"

"Something about loose cannons and knowing too much." He groaned. "I don't know. Ask Lehmann." He looked at her with pleading eyes. "Just don't leave me here to die."

"*Lo siento, señor,* you are on your own." Much as she hated leaving an injured man, she had her brother to think of. "I have to go." Weighted by guilt, she turned toward her ATV.

"It's not safe to go back to the cartel," the man called out.

"I know." She didn't have a choice. It had been made for her when they'd taken her brother.

She returned to her vehicle and looked it over carefully, locating a storage compartment behind the seat. Inside it was a flare and a long, thick strap.

With the gray light of dawn creeping in from the east, she didn't want to stay long lest someone stop her to ask what she was doing there. She couldn't afford to be arrested. Not now.

Hurrying back to the downed man, she dropped the flare and the strap close to him and stepped out of his reach. "Use the strap as a tourniquet and the flare once

I'm gone. If I have a chance to send help, I will. Not that you deserve it."

She'd done all she could afford to do. With a last look at the man now sitting up, applying the tourniquet to his wounded leg, Sophia started the four-wheeler, shifted into gear and shot off toward the coordinates on the GPS.

Hungry, thirsty and exhausted beyond caring, she passed through the small town she and Hector had avoided on their escape route out of Mexico. The road leading to *la Fuerte del Diablo* lay before her. It was the path to hell, but hopefully one that would free her brother and spare her parents more grief.

She'd only gone a couple miles, kicking up a cloud of choking dust, when two men stepped out into the middle of the road, AK-47s pointed at her.

Sophia pulled to a stop and reached into her back waistband. She tossed the gun to the ground, and with her hand raised high in the air she spoke clearly. *"Me rindo. Quiero ver a Antonio."*

The men grabbed her, shoved her into their waiting truck and sped toward the compound, stopping at the gates, where more guards with high-powered weapons awaited, one with a radio who called ahead, warning of her arrival. Once inside, they drove straight to the main building.

Led like a prisoner being marched toward the firing squad, Sophia was shoved forward to face the man standing at the entrance.

Wordlessly, Antonio grabbed her arm and flung her through the door.

Sophia hit the cold, hard tile, resigned to the fact that he would take out his anger on her. She climbed to her feet and cringed when Antonio backhanded her, sending her staggering into a wall.

"You have embarrassed me." He spoke in English, knowing she would understand but his men would not.

"Let my brother go, and I will stay," she said, wiping the blood from her busted lip.

Antonio laughed, grabbed her arm and shoved her down the long hallway. "You are not one to give orders."

"I only came back to save my brother."

"He is not my prisoner to free."

Sophia stood tall, her head thrown back, all the rage she'd been hiding over the year surfacing. "Let him go, or I will leave again."

"You are *mi novia,* and you will do what I say!" he yelled, flinging her into the room she'd shared with him for the past year.

One of his men called out behind him.

Antonio turned all his fury on the poor man. *"¿Qué quieres?"*

The man spoke fast in a hushed, nervous whisper.

Sophia couldn't hear everything, only the name *El Martillo* voiced in a fearful tremor.

A thundering rumble shook the roof, the sound Sophia related to the arrival of the cartel kingpin.

Antonio's face blanched and he kicked at the messenger, sending him running away. He grabbed Sophia's wrist and tried to haul her out into the hall. "We must leave."

She braced herself against the door frame and yanked her arm free of his grip. "Not without my brother." Backing into the room, she put as much distance as she could between her and the man she'd grown to despise.

"You do not understand." Antonio lunged for her, his lips curling into a snarl. "I did not take your brother. He is not my prisoner to bargain with."

Sophia dodged him and rolled across the bed to land on her feet on the other side. The wound on her shoulder was nothing compared to what Antonio would do if he caught her.

The popping sound of gunfire outside made Antonio glance away.

Sophia grabbed a wooden chair and held it like a weapon in front of her.

Antonio's eyes took on a wild, frantic look. "We are all as good as dead if we do not leave now."

"Afraid of the people you associate with?" she asked.

"Only one." Antonio yanked the chair from her grasp and sent it crashing against the wall. Then he grabbed her by the arm and dragged her from the room, stopping so suddenly, Sophia slammed into him.

"Going somewhere, Martinez?" A deep voice speaking in English and devoid of all emotion echoed off the walls.

Sophia looked around Antonio to see a man wearing a black suit and sunglasses.

"I'm glad you two are here at the same time. You've led us on quite the chase." The man held a dark gray pistol in one hand. With the other hand, he removed his sunglasses.

"Oh, thank God, the FBI." She tried to rush forward. "It's over, Antonio. You will not hit me ever again."

Antonio's hand shot out, stopping her from passing him. "It's over all right. We should have left immediately." His gaze never strayed from the bigger man's face. "He's going to kill us."

"No." Sophia shook her head. "I'm not a criminal. I didn't kill those DEA agents. I'm a prisoner."

"*El Martillo* knows," Antonio said, his voice flat.

A loud bang shocked Sophia's eardrums.

Antonio jerked backward. The hand that had been holding hers dragged her with him as he fell to the floor, a bright red stain spreading across his chest.

"Get up," the man with the gun demanded.

Sophia looked back at him. "You're with the FBI. I saw you at Hank's ranch. You have to help me get Hank's wife and son out of here."

The man's lips curved. "That's why I'm here." He nodded toward the end of the hall. "But we must hurry."

Sophia didn't hesitate. She freed her arm from Antonio's death grip, stepped over his body and ran.

The reassuring sound of footsteps rang out behind her as she reached the rooms where Anna and Jake were held. "They're in here. But the door is locked."

"Not for long." The man in the suit shoved a key into the lock and turned it.

Too late, Sophia realized her mistake as he pushed the door open and shoved her inside.

The key, Antonio's mention of *El Martillo*...

"You're *El Martillo*," she whispered, her chest tight, refusing to allow air into or out of her lungs.

"Sophia!" Anna called out from behind her. "Oh, Sophia, you're back." The woman Sophia had seen in the portrait in Hank's house pulled her into her arms and hugged her close, along with her young son. "Leave her alone," she said over the top of Sophia's head, her tone fierce. "She's done nothing to you."

"On the contrary, she's compromised my operation. We're leaving now. Before they find us."

An explosion rocked the floor beneath them. Anna, Sophia and Jake dropped to their knees.

Anna linked her arm with Sophia's and then stood, pulling her to her feet, her face grim, a hint of a smile on her lips. "I think you're too late."

"Not as long as I have a hostage." He grabbed for Sophia, looping his arm across her neck and pulling her back against him, pointing his gun to her head. "Come on, Anna, you and Jake are leaving with me if you don't want to see your friend killed."

SCOTT DROPPED THEM from the sky far enough away from the compound that they wouldn't be seen drifting to the ground in their parachutes in the predawn gray sky. But that meant hoofing it to the cartel hideout on foot across the desert. When they got close enough, Hank sent two men forward to plant diversionary explosives to draw attention away from the rest of them advancing on the walled fortress.

Using an MK12 special-purpose sniper rifle, Zach took out the sentry on the northwest corner while Chuck nailed the man on the southwest corner and the rest of the team used grappling hooks and rope to scale the back wall while members of the cartel were responding to the explosion on the opposite side of the compound.

First inside, Thorn dropped to the ground, an HK MP5 submachine gun clutched in his right hand, six forty-round replacement magazines strapped to his body and an armor-plate carrier with an armor plate tucked inside, protecting his chest. On his head, he wore a ballistic helmet. Each man carried either an M4A1 or an HK416 carbine assault rifle, with a knife at his side and a Sig Sauer SP226R 9 mm pistol strapped to one leg. They were loaded with enough ammo to take down an army of cartel thugs.

With the submachine gun taking point and his knife in his other hand, Thorn kicked in a door at the back of the main building.

A man inside standing guard opened fire.

Thorn ducked back behind the door, giving the man time to spend a few rounds, then he dove in, rolled and came up shooting. He took the man out in a short five-round burst.

Yelling inside the building meant they only had a few minutes to locate the prisoners and get them to safety.

Thorn covered while Blaise kicked in the door the guard had manned. Inside they found a young Hispanic man in jeans and a Universidad Nacional Autónoma de México T-shirt. He held up his hands. *"No disparen!"*

"¿Dónde usted?" Zach demanded.

"Ernesto Carranza," the young man answered. "I speak English."

"Any relation to Sophia?"

"Elena?" He nodded. *"Sí."*

"Where are they keeping her?" Thorn demanded.

"I didn't think she was here. They grabbed me to get her to return."

A rush of relief washed over Thorn. So that's why she'd gone back to *la Familia Diablos*. Dread quickly followed. Antonio had used her brother to get her back. He'd never let either one of them leave alive.

"Stay here or follow and keep out of the way, but be warned, there will be bullets."

"I'm coming." He followed, leaving a good distance between them.

Thorn came to the end of the hallway and turned left. A body lay in the middle of the corridor. One he knew they hadn't shot.

A man in a suit emerged from a room with a woman in front of him, a gun pressed to her temple. He closed the door behind him.

Thorn recognized them immediately.

Grant Lehmann held Sophia at gunpoint.

"That's Antonio Martinez. He's dead, and I caught his accomplice." He nodded toward Thorn. "It's okay, you can put your guns down," he said with a smile. "Show's over."

"Don't trust—" Sophia gasped.

Lehmann's arm tightened, cutting off her words. "That's right, don't trust a cartel member. We need to get her back to the States and on trial for the deaths of the DEA team."

"Let her breathe, Lehmann," Thorn warned, his hand tightening on the submachine gun.

Hank came up behind Thorn. "Grant? What are you doing here?"

"I heard you were making a move into cartel territory. Couldn't let you go it alone," Lehmann said smoothly. Too smoothly.

"So where's your team?" Thorn asked.

"Handling things outside. I took lead on the inside to make sure the two most wanted didn't escape."

Sophia's eyes were wide and round. She clutched at Lehmann's arm around her throat, trying to shake her head.

"Let her go, Lehmann," Thorn said, taking a step closer.

"She's escaped you before. If I let her loose, she'll do it again."

Her face going from red to blue, Sophia sagged against Lehmann.

His heart in his throat, Thorn growled. "Let her go. Now." He raised his submachine gun and pointed it directly at the FBI regional director's head. "Or I'll shoot you."

Apparently Lehmann had loosened his hold when Sophia's body went limp. Color began returning to her face.

"Hank, call off your dog. He's not going to shoot while I'm holding his girlfriend." Lehmann's gaze narrowed. "I know you were harboring her, and you could be in a whole lot of trouble stateside should the word get out that you're a traitor."

Hank raised his pistol, leveling it at Lehmann's face. "I think I know a traitor when I see one."

"I don't know what you're talking about."

"You're the one who has been leaking information to *la Familia Diablos*."

"No," a muffled voice called out through the closed door. "He is *El Martillo*, leader of the *la Familia Diablos*. Don't trust him."

"Lilianna?" Hank stepped closer.

"Hank? Oh, God, Hank! It's me, Lilianna. I'm in here with Jake!"

"You!" Hank's face turned a mottled red. "You stole her away from me. All the time we were searching, you knew!" The pistol in Hank's hand shook, then steadied. "Bastard!"

Lehmann laughed. "And you thought I was your friend."

"You won't get away with this, Grant. You betrayed your country."

The FBI traitor snorted. "I've gotten away with it for years. How do you think drugs and human trafficking flowed so easily past the farce they call Customs and Border Protection? Not to mention beneath the noses of the FBI?"

"You arrogant bastard." Thorn's gut knotted. If he didn't get Sophia away from Lehmann, there wouldn't be anything left for him to save.

"Having a heart or a conscience doesn't make you rich, does it, Hank?" Lehmann's lip curled. "You stole the only thing I cared about when you took Lilianna away from me. Well, I got her back, didn't I?" His nostrils flared, his face reddening. "How did it feel?"

Thorn wanted to kill the man even if Hank didn't.

Hank stood with his fist wrapped so tightly around his pistol his knuckles turned white. "You know damn well how it felt. My life ended."

"You're through, Lehmann," Thorn said. "Your drug-dealing, human-trafficking days are over."

"You're a fool, Drennan. You and these broken-down

cowboys Hank's hired. Who do you think they will believe? It will be my word against yours. Besides, when all is said and done, there will be no witnesses." Lehmann stood his ground, the gun against Sophia's head. "Come any closer, and I'll shoot her." He struggled to hold her limp body in front of him.

Thorn refused to lower his weapon. He couldn't shoot for fear of hitting Sophia. And Lehmann would follow through on his promise to kill her.

Sophia's eyes opened and she blinked at Thorn, mouthing the word *now.*

At the angle she'd slid, she had a clear shot for an elbow to Lehmann's groin. She slammed her elbow back and ducked out of Lehmann's hold.

His gun went off, the shot going wide, hitting the other side of the hallway.

Thorn hit the trigger of the submachine gun at the same time Hank fired his pistol, both rounds clipping Lehmann in a shoulder, sending him slamming back against the wall. Lehmann slid, leaving two streaks of blood as he descended to the floor.

Thorn, his heart thundering, crouched beside Sophia, who lay facedown on the floor. "Are you okay?"

For a long moment she didn't respond.

He gently turned her over, and her eyes blinked against the light. "Thorn?"

"Yeah, darlin', it's me." He smiled at her. "You brave, stupid, hardheaded woman."

"Stubborn man." She gave a half laugh, half cough. "Did you get him?"

"Hank did." He brushed the hair off her forehead.

"Is he dead?" she asked.

"No. We need him alive to reveal the extent of his network."

"Ernesto?" She pushed against Thorn. That's when he noticed the wound on her shoulder.

"You're hurt." He pressed her back to the floor and ripped the sleeve away from the injury.

"Just a flesh wound." She smiled, but it faded quickly. "My brother…"

"I'm here, *mi hermana*." The young Hispanic knelt beside her and took her hand. "Mama and Papa…we thought you were dead." He carried her hand to his lips and kissed her fingertips. "I've missed you."

"Come on, we have to get you to a doctor." Thorn slipped his machine gun over his shoulder and rose, lifting Sophia into his arms and away from the front of the doorway.

Hank slid Grant Lehmann's gun into his back waistband and reached for the door. It was locked.

He aimed his pistol at Lehmann's head. "Where's the key?"

Lehmann clutched his arm and laughed. "Inside with her."

"Lilianna, get away from the door."

"I'm clear!" she called from inside.

Hank redirected his aim to the door handle and pulled the trigger. The door frame splintered. Hank kicked the door, and it flew inward.

In the next moment, he was engulfed in an embrace from the wife he'd almost given up on ever finding.

Thorn's heart swelled for the man who'd gone through hell. His own arms tightened around Sophia. For only knowing her the short time he had, he knew he didn't want to live another day without her. She was brave, caring and willing to sacrifice herself for the ones she loved.

"You'll never get back across the border with me," Lehmann said, his voice shaking, his face losing some of its color. "Who do you think they'll believe? An FBI regional director or a team of washed-up mercenaries?"

"He hired a mercenary sharpshooter to pose as FBI to kill me," Sophia said. "And he almost succeeded. He's back at the river crossing. And I'm sure he'd be happy to tell all for the price of saving him."

"I paid that man too much," Lehmann snorted. "I could have done a better job killing you. But still, it would be my word against yours. I have friends in high places."

"And so do I." Hank stood with his arm around his wife and son. He raised one hand to touch the high-tech helmet he wore. "I think they'll believe the video I've been recording since we stormed into *la Fuerte del Diablo*. It's being transferred back to my computer guy at the Raging Bull and by now is in the hands of my trusted friends in the FBI and the CBP. I'm sure they'll be waiting at the border with a welcoming committee. Especially since we'll be bringing *El Martillo* with us."

Lehmann's eyes closed, and his forehead creased as if in pain. "You'll never get out of here alive."

Hank held a hand up and squinted as if his attention had been redirected. After a minute, he spoke. "Thanks, Harding. I knew I'd picked the right men when I hired y'all."

Hank's gaze settled on his former friend. "While you've been bleeding and blabbing, my men reported in that they've subdued what *la Familia Diablos* members remain on the grounds. The rest ran. So much for loyalty, huh?"

Hank left the building, carrying his son and holding Lilianna close like he never wanted to let her go.

Thorn followed, hugging Sophia to his chest, Ernesto beside him.

"I can walk, you know." Sophia leaned into him and kissed his cheek.

"I like holding you." He scowled down at her. "At least I know where you are when you're in my arms."

"I had to come, or they would have killed my brother."

"I would have done the same. But promise me one thing."

Her arms slipped around his neck, and she feathered her fingers through his hair. "Anything."

"No more running."

"I promise."

"And when we get back to the States, I want to take you out."

"Out where?"

"On an honest-to-God date. I want to start over, get to know you, learn what your favorite color is, your favorite ice cream."

"Deal." She kissed his lips then pulled away. "On one condition."

"What condition?"

"You take me to see my parents first."

"That can be arranged."

She stared up into his eyes. "One more condition."

"No more conditions."

"Just one." She cupped his cheeks in both her palms. "Is there room in your heart to love another as much as you loved your wife?"

Thorn smiled down at her. "I'll never stop loving Kayla, but being with you has shown me that I could be open to loving another."

She looked away, her hand slipping to her belly. "How about two others?"

He laughed and spun her around. "I wouldn't have it any other way."

When he finally came to a halt and set her on her feet,

Sophia stroked the side of his face, her touch warming him through to the heart he'd thought dead forever. "Thorn?"

He turned his face into her palm and kissed the lifeline that had brought him back from the dead. "Yes, Sophia?"

"My favorite color is blue, I love chocolate ice cream and I believe I'm falling in love with you."

Chapter Sixteen

Hank Derringer leaned against the breakfast bar at the pre-grand opening of the newly reconstructed and improved Cara Jo's Diner in Wild Oak Canyon, three months after it had burned to the ground. He'd helped Cara Jo with the costs of reconstruction, allowing her to expand the floor space, update the kitchen equipment and give the diner a shiny new appearance with a fifties, retro feel.

Clearing his throat, Hank began speaking. "I called this meeting of the Covert Cowboys not only to celebrate the reopening of Cara Jo's Diner but to thank you for all the good work you've done over the past months we've been in business.

"Grant Lehmann is awaiting his trial, but with the evidence we've accrued from his hired sharpshooter and other FBI agents seeking a plea bargain, he's sure to get a fat sentence and be off the streets for a very long time."

Everyone in the room clapped and cheered.

"Most of all, I want to thank everyone for helping bring Lilianna and Jake home safely." His voice cracked as he continued, "I owe you so much."

"Thanks, Hank." Chuck Bolton was the first to speak. "But none of us could have been as successful without the confidence and support you've given us." He stared down at the baby on his arm. Charlie, now six months old and tugging at Chuck's collar, giggled and cooed, obviously loving her father. "Some of us wouldn't be here today if CCI hadn't come along to save our sorry butts."

Blaise Harding snorted. "Speak for yourself, Bolton."

"Admit it, Harding—you wouldn't be engaged to Kate if you hadn't gone to work for Hank," Zach Adams said.

Blaise kissed Kate with a loud smack. "You got that right." He bent to lift Kate's daughter, Lily, into his arms. "And I wouldn't have my sweet Lily to give me hugs."

Lily wrapped her little arms around his neck and pressed a kiss to his cheek. "I love you, Daddy."

Blaise's eyes rounded and he leaned back, staring at Lily, then Kate. "Did you hear that?"

Kate smiled up at him. "She wanted to call you Daddy." The beautiful strawberry blonde nodded. "I thought it was time."

Blaise squeezed Lily to his chest until she squealed, "Let me down. Pickles is getting away."

He set her on the ground, his eyes shining with moisture as he watched his little girl chase after the black-and-white border collie.

Hank laughed as his son, Jake, raced after the two.

"I owe Hank my life for assigning me to find Jacie's sister." Zach pulled Jacie's hand through his arm and smiled at the pretty brunette cowgirl. "I'd probably still be wallowing at the bottom of a whiskey bottle if not for Hank and the Covert Cowboys. And Jacie."

Jacie laughed. "Instead he's making me crazy, following me around when I'm leading big-game hunts. When's his next assignment, Hank?" She winked and pinched Zach's arm.

Hank tipped his head toward Thorn. "How's the house comin' along?"

Thorn rested his hand on Sophia's thick waistline. "Should be finished in a month."

"Cuttin' it kinda close?" PJ smiled at Sophia. "You'll be havin' that baby before you move in."

Sophia laughed. "Thorn's got ten weeks to make that deadline."

"Do you know what you're having?" Kate asked.

Sophia glanced up at Thorn, smiling. "A girl."

Thorn's lips twisted. "Don't know what to do with a little girl."

Chuck laughed. "Trust me, they'll know what to do with you. Isn't that right, Charlie?" He lifted his baby girl high in the air.

"Hey, I'd like a little of that affection, too." PJ groused good-naturedly.

"Darlin', you know I love you," Chuck said.

"Oh, yeah?" PJ crossed her arms. "When are you going to make an honest woman of me?"

"Soon as you set the date."

Hank's bark of laughter got everyone's attention. He cleared his throat and nodded at Thorn.

"There's my cue." Thorn dug in his pocket, winked at Hank and dropped to one knee. "Sophia, love of my life, the only woman I can see myself shackled to for the rest of my days, will you marry me?" He held out an open ring box with a beautiful diamond engagement ring inside. "I already have your father's blessing, if that helps."

Sophia pressed her hands to her chest, tears welling in her eyes. "Really? You want to marry me?"

Thorn nodded. "We might have had a rocky start with you almost killing me, but I'm willing to take the chance if you are." He removed the ring from the box and held it out. "So what's it going to be? Yes or no? And please say yes, 'cause I can't wait much longer to make you my wife."

"Yes!" Sophia gave him her hand, and he slipped the ring on her finger. Then she flung her arms around his neck and kissed him.

Chuck tipped his head toward PJ. "So, is it going to be a double wedding?"

PJ smiled. "I'm in, but Sophia and Thorn might want the day all to themselves."

Sophia shook her head. "A double wedding will be twice as much fun as a single. Do you agree, *mi amor?*"

"I do." Thorn held her as close as he could without squishing her belly.

Tears welled in PJ's eyes. "I'm gonna have more family than I know what to do with."

Lilianna slipped an arm around Hank and leaned into him. "She's got a good heart, just like her father."

"Yes, she does. I'm about the luckiest man alive." He kissed his wife and hugged her close.

Slowly Lilianna had settled back into her old life. She'd be seeing a therapist for years to come, but she was happy to be home, and Jake was recovering from his two-year ordeal with the cartel. Hank had taught him to ride horses, and it was helping him to open up and be a regular little boy.

While the ladies gathered around Sophia, congratulating her on her engagement, the men circled Hank.

"So, Hank," Blaise said over the chatter of the women, "what's next?"

"I have assignments waiting for each of you, and I'm thinkin' of hirin' a couple more cowboys and maybe even a cowgirl." He stood straight, his arms crossing over his chest. "Y'all still in?"

As one, the cowboys yelled, "Hell, yeah!"

* * * * *

"Whatever threat is jeopardizing the peace of this town and the law, you can be sure I'll be out there fighting it." Bree pressed her full lips together.

Jamie wondered what she'd do if he tried to kiss her. His pulse quickened. As unpredictable and unreasonable as she was, she might just shoot him.

Not that kissing those lips wouldn't be worth the risk. Not that he was going to do it. He was in town on serious business. And women were no longer part of his life, anyway. He had too much baggage, too many nightmares. He had no right to bring that into a relationship and mess up somebody else's life along with his.

He was a trained killing machine. That was about it. He planned on living the rest of his life using what skills he had in the service of his country. He stood.

"Forget about me and my team."

Although, he was pretty sure he wasn't going to be able to forget about her.

MY SPY

BY
DANA MARTON

MILLS & BOON

First published in Great Britain 2013
by Mills & Boon, an imprint of Harlequin (UK) Limited,
Eton House, 18-24 Paradise Road, Richmond, Surrey TW9 1SR

© Dana Marton 2013

ISBN: 978 0 263 90378 2
ebook ISBN: 978 1 472 00753 7

46-1013

Harlequin (UK) policy is to use papers that are natural, renewable and recyclable products and made from wood grown in sustainable forests. The logging and manufacturing processes conform to the legal environmental regulations of the country of origin.

Printed and bound in Spain
by Blackprint CPI, Barcelona

Dana Marton is the author of more than a dozen fast-paced, action-adventure, romance-suspense novels and a winner of a Daphne du Maurier Award of Excellence. She loves writing books of international intrigue, filled with dangerous plots that try her tough-as-nails heroes and the special women they fall in love with. Her books have been published in seven languages in eleven countries around the world. When not writing or reading, she loves to browse antiques shops and enjoys working in her sizable flower garden, where she searches for "bad" bugs with the skills of a superspy and vanquishes them with the agility of a commando soldier. Every day in her garden is a thriller. To find more information on her books, please visit www.danamarton.com. She loves to hear from her readers and can be reached via email at danamarton@danamarton.com.

With many thanks to my wonderful editor,
Allison Lyons.

This book is dedicated to my readers who
are my support, my inspiration, my true friends,
online and off. Your kindness means more to
me than words can say.

Chapter One

He had two weeks to gain the information he needed to stop terrorists with weapons of mass destruction from entering the country. But everything his six-man team had done so far had been a bust.

Undercover operative Jamie Cassidy sat with his back to the wall in the far corner at the Yellow Armadillo, a seedy, small-town bar on the backstreets of Pebble Creek, Texas. Country music streamed from overhead speakers; the place was dark and dingy, the food was fried within an inch of its life. But the beer was cold, the only nice thing that could be said about the joint.

"So you have no idea who the new boss is?" he asked the scrawny farmhand across the table.

Billy Brunswik fingered the rim of the tattered Stetson on his lap, his eyes on his empty glass. A cowboy tan left the top of his forehead white, the rest of his face several shades darker. His checkered blue shirt was wrinkled and smudged with dirt, as if he'd been wearing it for more than a day or two. He silently shook his head.

Jamie had his own cowboy hat and jeans and shirt to fit in, a far cry from his usual commando gear. In a place like this—a known hangout for smugglers—being spotted as a government man could quickly earn you a bullet in the back.

He waved the perky blonde waitress over for another round for Billy but didn't return her flirty smile. His attention was on the man across the table. "It's tough. Believe me, I know." He waited until the waitress left. "In this economy, and they cut off work. Hell, what are you supposed to do? Who do you go to now?"

"Nobody knows nuthin'." Billy set his empty glass down and wiped his upper lip with the back of his calloused hand, then pulled out a tin of chewing tobacco and tucked a pinch between gum and cheek. "I can barely buy groceries for the girlfriend and me, I'll tell you that."

Jamie watched him for a few seconds, then slid three twenties across the table. "I know how it is."

Billy was on the cash like a duck on a june bug, the bills disappearing in a flat second. He looked around nervously, licking his crooked yellow front teeth. "I ain't no snitch."

Jamie gave a sympathetic nod. "A man has to live. And I ain't asking for nothing that would get you in trouble. Just need enough to show the boss I've been working." He shrugged, playing the halfhearted customs agent role.

Billy hung his head. "I do work a little," he admitted. "When nobody's lookin'. Just some weed."

"Who do you kick up to?"

"Ain't nobody there since Kenny."

And no matter how hard Jamie pushed the down-on-his-luck farmhand after that, Billy didn't give up anything. Although he did promise to get in touch if things changed.

Developing an asset was a slow and careful business.

Jamie left the man and strode across the bar, looking for familiar faces as he passed the rows of tables. The two border towns his team watched, Hullett and Pebble Creek, had their share of smugglers, most of them lying low these days. He didn't recognize anyone here today.

He paid the waitress at the bar, stepped outside into the scorching heat then shoved his hat on his head and rubbed his eyes. He'd spent the night on border patrol, then most of the morning running down leads. His legs hurt. The doc at Walter Reed called it phantom-limb pain.

He resisted the urge to reach down and rub his prosthetic limbs. It did nothing for the pain, and he hated the feel of the cold steel where his legs should have been.

He strode up to Main Street, came out by the bank and drew a hundred out of the ATM while he was here, since Billy had cleaned him out. Then his gaze caught on the bookstore across the street. Maybe a good read would help him fall asleep. When on duty, his mind focused on work. But when he rested, memories of his dark past pushed their way back into his head. Sleep had a way of eluding him.

He cut across traffic and pushed inside the small indie bookstore, into the welcoming cool of air-conditioning, and strode straight to the mystery section. He picked out a hard-boiled detective story, then turned on his heels and came face-to-face with the woman of his dreams.

Okay, the woman of every red-blooded man's dreams.

She was tall and curvy, with long blond hair swinging in a ponytail, startling blue eyes that held laughter and a mouth to kill or die for, depending on what she wished.

His mind went completely blank for a second, while his body sat up and took serious notice.

When his dreams weren't filled with blood and torture and killing, they were filled with sex. He could still do the act—one thing his injury hadn't taken away from him. But he didn't allow himself. He didn't want pity. Foreplay shouldn't start with him taking off his prosthetics—the ultimate mood killer. And he definitely didn't want the questions.

Hell, even he hated touching the damn things. Who wouldn't? He wasn't going to put himself through that humiliation. Wasn't going to put a woman in a position where she'd have to start pretending.

But he dreamed, and his imagination made it good. The woman of his dreams was always the same, an amalgamation of pinup girls that had been burned into his brain during his adolescent years from various magazines he and his brothers had snuck into the house.

And now she was standing in front of him.

The pure, molten-lava lust that shot through his gut nearly knocked him off his feet. And aggravated the hell out of him. He'd spent considerable time suppressing his physical needs so they wouldn't blindside him like this.

"Howdy," she said with a happy, peppy grin that smoothed out the little crease in her full bottom lip. She had a great mouth, crease or no crease. Made a man think about his lips on hers and going lower.

He narrowed his eyes. Then he pushed by her with

a dark look, keeping his face and body language discouraging. Who the hell was she to upset his hard-achieved balance?

He strode up to the counter and paid with cash because he didn't want to waste time punching buttons on the card reader. He didn't want to spend another second in a place where he could be ambushed like this. The awareness of her back somewhere among the rows of books still tingled all across his skin.

"I'm sorry." The elderly man behind the counter handed back the twenty-dollar bill. "I can't take this." He flashed an apologetic smile as he pushed up his horn-rimmed glasses, then tugged down his denim shirt in a nervous gesture. "The scanner kicked it back."

"I just got it from the bank across the street," Jamie argued, not in the mood for delay.

"I'm sorry, sir."

"Everything okay, Fred?" The woman he'd tried to pretend didn't exist came up behind Jamie.

Her voice was as smooth as the kind of top-shelf whiskey the Yellow Armadillo couldn't afford to carry. Its sexy timbre tickled something behind his breastbone. He kept his back to her, against enormous temptation to turn, hoping she'd get the hint to mind her own business.

Then he had to turn, anyway, because next thing he knew she was talking to him.

"I'd be happy to help. How about we go next door and I'll help you figure this out?"

The police station stood next door. All he wanted was to go home and see if he could catch a few winks before his next shift. "I don't think so." He peeled off another twenty, which went through the scanner without trouble. Next thing he knew, Fred was handing back his change.

"I really think we should," the woman insisted.

Apparently, she had trouble with the concept of minding her own business. He shot her a look of disapproval, hoping she'd take the hint.

He tried to look at nothing but her eyes, but all that sparkling blue was doing things to him. Hell, another minute, and if she asked him to eat the damned twenty, he would have probably done it. He caught that thought, pushed back hard.

"Who the hell are you?" He kept his tone at a level of surly that had taken years to perfect.

The cheerleader smile never even wavered as she pulled her badge from her pocket and flashed it at him. "Brianna Tridle. Deputy sheriff."

Oh, hell.

He looked her over more thoroughly: the sexy snake-skin boots, the hip-hugging jeans, the checkered shirt open at the neck, giving a hint of the top curve of her breasts. His palms itched for a feel. If there was such a thing as physical perfection, she was it.

Any guy who had two brain cells to rub together would have gone absolutely anywhere with her.

Except Jamie Cassidy.

"I'm in a hurry."

"Won't take but a minute." She tilted her head, exposing the creamy skin of her neck just enough to bamboozle him. "I've been having a hard time with counterfeit bills turning up in town lately. I'd really appreciate the help. I'll keep it as quick as possible, I promise." The smile widened enough to reveal some pearly white teeth.

Teeth a man wouldn't have minded running his tongue along before kissing her silly.

Another man.

Certainly not Jamie.

Okay, so she was the deputy sheriff. The sheriff, Kenny Davis, had been killed recently. He'd been part of the smuggling operation Jamie's team was investigating. A major player, actually.

After that, Ryder McKay, Jamie's team leader, had looked pretty closely at the Pebble Creek police department. The rest of them came up squeaky clean. A shame, really. Jamie definitely felt like his world would be safer with Brianna Tridle locked away somewhere far from him.

She was too chirpy by half.

He didn't like chirpy.

But if she wasn't a suspect, she could be an ally—if he played his cards right. Although poker wasn't the first thing to spring to mind when he thought about playing with her. He could no longer feel the air-conditioning. In fact, it seemed the AC might have broken since he'd come in. The place felt warm suddenly. Hot, even.

He loosened the neck of his shirt. "Fine. Five minutes."

He held the door for her, regretting it as she flashed another gut punch of a smile. She better not read anything into that basic courtesy. He'd been raised right, that was all. He couldn't help it. He wasn't falling for her charms, no way, he thought as she walked in front of him, hips swinging.

The gentle sway held him mesmerized for a minute. Then he blinked hard as he finally focused on one specific spot. Was that a small firearm tucked under her waistband, covered by her shirt? Hard to tell with his eyes trying to slide lower.

He looked more carefully. Damn if the slight bulge wasn't a weapon. She'd been armed the entire time and he'd never noticed. He was seriously losing it.

He drew in a slow breath as they walked into the station. On second thought, forget developing her as an asset. Working with her would probably be more trouble than it was worth.

He was going to tell Brianna Tridle where, when and exactly how he'd come into possession of the stupid twenty-dollar bill in question. Then he was walking out and not looking back. If he had even a smidgen of luck coming to him, he'd never see her again.

"I REALLY APPRECIATE this." Bree measured up the cowboy with the bad attitude.

Not a real Texas cowboy, actually. He was missing the Texas twang, his general accent making it difficult to pin down from where he hailed. And he wore combat boots with his jeans. It threw off his cowboy swagger. He had shadows all around him, his aura a mixture of dangerous and sexy. He was hot enough to give women heart palpitations on his worst day.

Not that that sort of thing affected her. She was a seasoned law enforcement officer. "And your name is?"

"Jamie Cassidy." He didn't offer his hand, or even a hint of a smile as he scanned the station.

She'd bet good money he didn't miss many details.

Fine. She was proud of the place, clean and organized. The dozen people working there were the finest in South Texas. She would trust each and every one of them to have her back.

While he examined her station, she examined him.

He stood tall, well built, his dirty-blond hair slightly mussed as he took his hat off. When he ran his fingers through it in an impatient gesture, Bree's own fingertips tingled.

He had the face of a tortured angel, all angles and masculine beauty. His chocolate-brown eyes seemed permanently narrowed and displeased. Especially as he took in the metal detectors she'd had installed just last week.

Lena, the rookie officer manning the scanner, held out a gray plastic tray for him.

Bree offered a smile. "We just upped our security. If you could hand over anything metal in your pockets and walk through, I'd appreciate it."

She was in charge of the station until the new sheriff was elected. They'd had an incident recently with a drunk housewife who'd come in to file a complaint against her husband, then ended up shooting a full clip into the ceiling to make sure they believed her when she said she *would* shoot the bastard if he came into her new double-wide one more time with muddy boots.

She'd been a bundle of booze and wild emotions— the very opposite of Jamie Cassidy, who seemed the epitome of cold and measured.

He scowled as he dropped his cell phone, handful of change and car keys into the small plastic tray. "I'm going to set the alarm off." He tapped his leg. "Prosthesis."

That was it, then, Bree thought as she watched him. The reason why his walk had been off a smidgen. "Not a problem, Lena," she told the rookie, who was staring at him with dreamy eyes. "I'll pat him down."

"No." His face darkened as his gaze cut to hers.

They did a long moment of the staring-each-other-down thing. Then his lips narrowed as he fished around in his shirt pocket and pulled out a CBP badge.

Customs and Border Protection. *And the plot thickens.* She tilted her head as she considered him. Why not show the badge sooner?

Maybe it was a fake. She'd worked pretty closely with CBP for the past couple of years. She'd never seen him before. If she had, she would have definitely remembered him.

She widened her smile. Defusing tension in a bad situation always worked better than escalating it. "I need to check you just the same. New procedure. Sorry."

For a second he looked like he might refuse and simply walk away from her. She kept her hand near her firearm at her back, ready to stop him. She preferred to do things the easy way, but she could do it the hard way if needed. Up to him.

But then he seemed to change his mind and held out his arms to the side. She wondered if he knew that his smoldering look of resentment only made him look sexier.

"It'll only take a second." She ran her fingers along his arms first, lightly. Plenty of muscle. If he did change his mind and began causing trouble, she would definitely need her service weapon.

She moved her hands to his torso and found more impressive muscles there. She could feel the heat of his body through his shirt and went faster when her fingertips began to tingle again, a first for her during pat down. What on earth was wrong with her today? She tried to focus on what she was doing. Okay, no shoulder holster, no sidearm here.

"Almost done." She squatted as she moved down his legs, pausing at the sharp transition where the living flesh gave way to rigid metal. *Both* of his legs were missing. Her gaze flew up to his.

He looked back down at her with something close to hate—a proud man who didn't like his weaknesses seen.

"Enough." He stepped back.

But she stepped after him. "One more second."

Awareness tingled down her spine as she pulled up and reached around his waist, almost as if she were hugging him. And there, tucked behind his belt, she found a small, concealed weapon.

She removed the firearm carefully, pointing it down, making sure her fingers didn't come near the trigger. "When were you going to tell me about this?" She checked the safety. *On.* Okay.

"I'm so used to carrying, I forgot," he lied to her face.

Which ticked her off a little.

She dropped the weapon into the gray plastic tray Lena was holding. "You can claim these on your way out." If she let him leave. "This way."

They went through the detector, which did go off, as he'd promised. Curiosity, wariness and even some unwanted attraction warred inside her as she led him into interview room A at the end of the hallway. He was not your average Joe. This man had a story. She wanted to know what it was.

"How about I get us something cold to drink?"

He didn't look impressed with her hospitality as he scanned the small white room. "I'm in a hurry."

She left him anyway, and swung by Lena on her way to the vending machine. "Let me see that." She took his weapon, grabbed two sodas then stopped by her office and ran the gun.

Unregistered firearm. On a hunch, she called her friend Gina at the local CBP office. "Hey, you got someone over there by the name of Jamie Cassidy?"

"Not that I know off the top of my head. Why? Anything to do with the counterfeiting thing you're working?"

"Don't know yet. Might be nothing. I'll talk to you later." She hung up and walked by Lena again, looking at Jamie Cassidy's car keys in the plastic tray.

"You'll need a warrant to look in his car," Lena remarked, now sitting by her computer, answering citizen queries.

"Or his permission. Least I can do is try," Bree said as she walked away.

Mike was coming from the evidence room. "What you up to?"

"Picked up someone with a fake twenty."

"Need help?" He was a few weeks from retirement, but not the type to sit back and count off the days. He was always first to offer help and never said a word if he had to work late.

"Thanks. But I think I can handle him." She hoped. She was ready to roll up the counterfeiting thing.

She was sick of the recent crime wave in her town lately: a rash of burglaries, several acts of unusual vandalism and sabotage, arson even, and then the counterfeit bills showing up suddenly. Whatever she had to do, she was going to put an end to it.

She grabbed her shoulder holster from the back of her chair, shrugged into the leather harness and stuck her weapon into the holster to keep it within easier reach. Time to figure out who Jamie Cassidy was and if he'd come to town to cause trouble.

She had a sudden premonition that prying that out of him wasn't going to be easy. She'd been a cop long enough to know when somebody was lying, and the man waiting for her in interview room A definitely had his share of secrets.

HE WAS SITTING in an interrogation room, fully aroused. That was a first, Jamie thought wryly. Because, of course, she'd *had* to put her hands on him. At least she hadn't noticed his condition; she'd been too focused on his weapon.

He leaned back in the uncomfortable metal chair. The place was small, the cement brick walls freshly painted white, the old tile floor scuffed.

The metal door stood open, but the station was full of uniforms. He wouldn't get far if he tried to walk out, not without violence, and he wanted to avoid that if possible. He watched as the deputy sheriff reappeared at the end of the hallway, her gaze immediately seeking out his.

And there it came again, that punch of heat in the gut.

"Stupid," he said under his breath, to snap himself out of it.

He'd never been like this. Back when he'd been whole, he'd enjoyed the fairer sex as much as the next guy. Since he'd been crippled, he kept to himself. He was half machine, half human. Who the hell would want to touch that?

Yet she'd touched him and hadn't flinched away. She'd felt his prosthetics and her face had registered surprise, but not pity. He pushed that thought aside. What would Miss Perfection know about physical deformity?

He watched as a uniformed cop, dragging a loud-mouthed drunk, headed her off halfway down the hall.

"No needles," the drunk protested, then swore a blue streak, struggling against the man who held him, trying for a good swing, the movement nearly knocking him off his unsteady feet.

Brianna Tridle smiled sweetly.

Yeah, that was going to work. The man needed someone to put the fear of God into him. Jamie could have gotten the job done in three seconds flat. Possibly two. He relaxed and got ready to enjoy watching the deputy sheriff fail.

"Come on now, Pete." She kept up the all-is-well-with-the-world, we're-all-friends routine. "Big, tough guy like you. Remember when you had that wire snap at work and cut your leg open? You didn't make a sound all the way to the hospital when I took you in. Pretty impressive."

The drunk pulled himself together a little and gave her a sheepish look. "It's just the needles. You know I can't stand them, darlin'."

"Tell you what. You do the blood test, I'll drive you home. You won't have to wait here until Linda gets off shift."

"Can't give no blood." He shook his head stubbornly. "I'm dizzy. Haven't even eaten all day."

"I bet Officer Roberts hasn't had lunch yet, either. How about you swing by the drive-through and grab a couple of hamburgers? On me."

The drunk went all googly-eyed. "You'll always be a queen to me, darlin'," he promised, and this time followed Officer Roberts obediently as he was led away.

Jamie stared. *Enforcing the law with sweet talk.*

What kind of monkey-circus police station was this? And then he stilled as he realized he was even now sitting in an interrogation room, where he'd had no intention of being. Hell, the woman had done it to him!

He glared at her with all the resentment he felt as she came in with a couple of drinks. He was out of here.

"Got the money out of the ATM at the bank across the street five minutes ago. You can check their security video." He rose. "That's all I know."

She put a can of soda in front of him with that smile that seemed to have the ability to addle everyone's brain around her. She sat, folding her long legs under her seat. "Just a few minutes. Please?" she asked very nicely. "As a favor from one law enforcement drone to another."

Establishing common ground in thirty seconds flat. Nice work, he had to admit. He sat, but only because he was beginning to be intrigued.

"What do you do, exactly, at CBP?" She fitted her supremely kissable lips to the can as she drank, keeping an eye on him.

"I'm on a special team," he said, more than a little distracted.

"Dealing with?"

"Special stuff."

She laughed, the sound rippling right through him. He resented that thoroughly.

"Why do you carry an unregistered firearm instead of your service weapon?" she asked as pleasantly as if she was inquiring about his health.

She got that already, did she? A part of him was impressed, a little. Maybe she wasn't just surface beauty.

"Took it off someone this morning. Haven't had a chance yet to turn it in," he lied through his teeth. He was in town as part of an undercover commando team. What they did and how they did it was none of her business.

She smiled as if she believed his every word. "All right, that's it, then," she said brightly. "I better clear you out of here so you can get back to work. I know you guys are busy beyond belief."

She stood, taking her drink with her. "Just to make sure I have all my *T*s crossed and *I*s dotted, would you mind if I took a quick glance at your car?" she added, as if it was an afterthought. "With all this counterfeit stuff I'm struggling with…" She gave a little shrug that another man would have found endearing. "It's really helpful to be able to cross people completely off the list."

"Go ahead," he said, regretting it the next second. But part of him wanted to test her. No way in hell she was going to find the secret compartment that he himself built. "It's a black SUV in front of the bank." He gave her his plate number. "You already have the keys."

She walked out, ensuring him of her gratitude and sincere appreciation. And this time, she closed the door behind her. Which locked automatically.

And just like that, he was in custody.

His mouth nearly gaped at her effortless efficiency.

He had to admit, if he was normal, if he was the type who believed in love, she would be the exact woman he might be tempted to fall in love with.

Of course, with everything she had going for her, chances were she was already married. No wedding ring—he couldn't believe he'd looked—but people in law enforcement often skipped that. No reason to advertise to the bad guys that you had a weakness, a point where you could be hurt.

Married. *There.* He found the thought comforting. He liked the idea of her completely out of his reach. Otherwise, the thought of her would drive him crazy during those long nights when he couldn't sleep.

He waited.

Looked around the small room.

Looked at the locked door.

It'd been a while since he'd been locked up and tortured, but the more he sat in the interrogation room, the more uneasy he felt. *It's not like that.* He swallowed back the memories. Rubbed his knees.

But a cold darkness seemed to fill the room around him little by little, pushing him to his feet. *Think about something else. Think about work.*

Plenty there to figure out. His six-man team was putting the brakes on a serious smuggling operation that planned on bringing terrorists, along with their weapons of mass destruction, into the country, information that had been gained on an unrelated South American op.

To stop the terrorists, his team had to work their way up the chain of command in a multinational criminal organization. They'd gotten the three low-level bosses who ran the smugglers on the United States side of the border. What they needed now was the identity of the Coyote, the big boss who ran things on the other side.

He paced the room, forcing himself to focus on what they knew so far. But too soon his thoughts returned to Brianna Tridle. He moved to the door to look out the small window through the wire-reinforced glass. What he saw didn't make him happy.

She was coming back in with a uniformed cop, carrying his arsenal, down to his night-vision goggles that had been hidden in a separate secret compartment from the rest. She called out to the handful of people in the office as she deposited the weaponry on a desk.

He couldn't hear her, but he could read her sexy lips. He was pretty sure she'd just said *terror suspect*.

Oh, hell. That definitely didn't bode well for him.

Chapter Two

"Officer Delancy here is going to take your fingerprints," Bree informed Jamie Cassidy, if that was his real name, once she was back in the interview room with him, feeling a lot more cautious suddenly than the first time around.

"I noticed earlier that you had a wallet in your pocket. I'd appreciate it if you handed that over, please." She kept as pleasant an expression on her face as possible, even if she felt far from smiling.

The kind of weapons he had in his SUV were definitely not standard government issue that CBP would use. And they were far too heavy duty for the kind of criminals she usually saw around these parts. He didn't just have weapons—he had an arsenal with him. For what purpose?

"I need to make a phone call," he demanded, instead of complying.

"Maybe later." If he *was* a domestic terrorist, he could set off a bomb with a phone call. She wasn't going to take chances until she knew more about him. "Let's do those prints first and have a little talk. Then we'll see about the phone."

He scowled at her, looking unhappier by the second. An accomplishment, since he'd been in a pretty sour mood even when she'd first laid eyes on him.

"How about we talk about your weapons first?"

He held her gaze. "How did you find them?"

He clearly hadn't thought she would. At the beginning of her career, it had annoyed her that men tended to underestimate her. Then she'd realized that it was an advantage.

"Just came back from special training with the CBP. They spent three entire days on tips and tricks for spotting secret compartments. Same training you received, I assume? Since you claim you work for them?"

Smuggling had been getting out of hand in the area until a sudden recent drop she didn't think would last. And now with the counterfeit money nonsense… She needed skills that would help her put an end to that. As she watched him, she wondered if he was a CBP agent gone bad. It happened.

"You're making a mistake here."

"Oh, Lord," she said easily. "I make at least ten a day, for sure." She smiled. "Why are you in Pebble Creek, Jamie?"

"I told you. I consult for CBP," he said morosely, but sat back down and let Delancy take his fingerprints.

Consulting now, was it? His story was subtly changing. There was more here, something he wasn't telling her.

"And you needed those guns for…"

"I spend a lot of time on the border."

"Doing what?"

"Monitoring smuggling."

Or helping it along, most likely.

Sheriff Davis was dead, the new sheriff elections mere weeks away. She'd been away for training and out of the loop, way too much dropping on her lap the day she'd come back. Like counterfeit twenties showing up.

She'd notified the CIA as soon as she'd caught the first. They were sending an agent before the end of the week to investigate. Acid bubbled in her stomach every time she thought of that. She wasn't a big fan of outsiders messing around in her town.

And if that wasn't enough, now she had Jamie Cassidy to deal with. She was starting to feel the beginnings of a headache.

He was watching her, his eyes hard, his face closed, his masculine mouth pressed into a line—not exactly a picture of cooperation. If this went the way she thought it would, she'd be here all day and then some. Which meant she'd have to call her sister and let her know she'd be late. Not a good thing with Katie being so bad with even the slightest change in her routine.

"How long have you been in town?" she asked as Delancy left with the fingerprint kit, closing the door behind her.

"A couple of weeks."

Which coincided with the counterfeit money showing up.

He rubbed the heels of his hands over his knees, drawing her attention there. How much did she know about what was really under his jeans, anyway? She'd felt metal. But was all of that his prosthetics?

She stood to walk around the desk. "Would you mind rolling up your pants?" she asked in her friendliest tone.

"In light of the weapons we found in your car, I'd feel more comfortable if I made a full search. Just to set my mind at ease."

If he'd been cold before, he went subzero now, his gaze turning to black ice. Every muscle in his body tensed. She'd definitely hit a nerve.

Would he hit back? She was ready to defend herself, not that she was looking forward to tackling him. He looked strong, quick and capable.

She should have asked Delancy to stay as backup, she thought too late. Jamie was already on his feet.

ANGER AND HUMILIATION washed over Jamie as he stood. He'd played along long enough. He didn't have time for this. "You need to let me make that call."

The next thing he knew, he was shoved face-first into the wall, his right hand twisted up behind his back, his cheek rubbing into the brick. Air whooshed out of his lungs, more from surprise than anything else.

Her transformation from sweet to tough cop was pretty spectacular and stunned him more than a little. For a second her body pressed against his full-length from the back, her soft breasts flattened against his ribs. Another place, another time… Heat and awareness shot through him, pure lust drowning out the aggravation that she would try to manhandle him.

He could have put her down. He could have put her down hard.

But she was an officer of the law, and they were on the same side. And frankly, he was beginning to respect her skills.

"Take it easy," he said. "I'm cooperating."

He let her pull down his other hand and put plastic restraints on him, even if the thought of being tied up made him uneasy. Any undercover commando who couldn't get out of plastic restraints in under a minute needed to quit. He said nothing when she edged his boots apart with her foot.

Then she bent and grabbed on to the hem of his jeans, and that set his teeth on edge. "That's not necessary. I'm not the enemy."

She rolled the denim up briskly. "Just a quick check. Then you give me that number you want to call and I'll call for you. How about that?"

Over his dead body. She called Ryder and Jamie would never live it down that he'd gotten nabbed and interrogated by Deputy Sheriff Hot Chick.

He held still as she moved his pant leg up. He knew what she would see: cold steel alloy, nothing human, a well-engineered machine. He'd received his prosthetics as a major favor from a friend of the colonel his team reported to. It was the best technology Olympic athletes used, taken up another notch. A prototype, the first and only set to receive the designation combat ready.

"Fancy hardware," she commented as she covered up his left leg and moved on to the right. "How did this happen?"

None of her business. "Car accident." He said the first thing that came to mind.

"I would have thought war injury." She finished and straightened, expertly sliding her hand into his pocket and retrieving his wallet. "You move like a soldier."

And suddenly he had enough of her prying into his business. He twisted his wrist to expose the link on his metal watchband that he kept sharp. Another twist, applying pressure to the right places, and he was free.

He reached for her as he turned, caught her by surprise and had her trapped against the wall in a split second, holding her hands at either side of her head, preventing her from going for her weapon.

Their faces were inches from each other, their bodies nearly touching. She stared at him with wide-eyed surprise that quickly turned to anger, then back to calm strength again, the transition fascinating to observe.

God, she was even more beautiful up close—those sparkling blue eyes and all that flawless skin.

"Not a smart move," she said calmly, the words drawing his gaze to the crease in her bottom lip that begged to be kissed. "I call out and there'll be half a dozen officers in here in a second."

"Why don't you?" He knew the answer, the exact same reason why he hadn't given her the number to call Ryder at the office. She didn't want to embarrass herself.

Her cell phone rang in her pocket.

He thought about kissing her, which was really stupid. He held her for another long second before he stepped back and let her go as a gesture of good faith, but took his wallet back.

She pulled her phone out with one hand, her gun with the other, pointing it at the middle of his chest.

She glared at him as she took the call. "Yes. Yes, sir," she said, the look on her face stunned at first, then quickly turning speculative. She lowered her gun. Her sparkling blue eyes narrowed when the call ended, and she turned her full attention back to him.

She stepped around to put the desk between them once again. "Want to guess who that was?"

He raised an eyebrow.

"Homeland Security. I've been ordered to release you immediately, without any further questions. Want to tell me what that's about?"

He winced. He would rather have that nobody know about his brief time in Brianna Tridle's custody, but, hell, he'd take whatever break he could get at this stage.

He sauntered by her on his way to the door. "Looks like you won't get to keep me. Life is full of disappointments, Deputy Sheriff."

HE ALMOST DIDN'T even mind having to see her again, Jamie thought as he ran a quick background search on her once he was back at his office that night, after having caught a brief nap at his apartment.

She hadn't returned his weapons, probably just to spite him. The orders on the phone had been only about releasing him, she'd said. He could claim his property after a twenty-four-hour waiting period, some rule she'd made up on the fly, he was sure.

"So she hauled you in?" Shep, one of his teammates, was asking with a little too much glee.

They worked out of a bulletproof office trailer in the middle of nowhere, close enough to the border to be able to reach it within minutes, far enough from prying eyes in town.

They had a pretty simple setup: one office for Ryder McKay, the team leader, an interrogation room, a bathroom and a small break room in the back, the rest of the space taken up by desks for the six-man team.

Ryder was locked up in his office, on the phone. The rest of the team was out.

Jamie shrugged as he scrolled down the screen.

"She questioned you?"

"Interrogation room." He spit out the two words as if they were broken glass in his mouth. He read the search results on his screen, scanning the scores of photos of her. *Miss Brianna Tridle accepts her crown.* She'd been Miss Texas. No joke.

She'd been younger—different hair, more makeup, but the smile was the same. He felt a tug in places that hadn't tugged in a long time, just looking at her on the screen.

"Handcuffs?" Shep asked.

He refused to answer, opening the next document that detailed everything from her family circumstances to her education. She was single, the sole guardian of one Katie Tridle, twenty-three years old.

Sister?

There was something there, he thought. Normally a person didn't need a guardian at twenty-three.

"Seriously, she had you in handcuffs?" Shep gave a belly laugh. "Oh, man, I would have given money to see that. Why didn't you just call in?"

Because she wouldn't let me, was the answer, words he wasn't about to say. He shut down his computer instead and pushed to his feet. "Patrol time, funny boy. Move it."

Shep picked up his handgun and shoved it into his holster, grinning all the way. It burned Jamie's temper that he had to get his backup weapon out of his drawer because most of his stuff was in the deputy sheriff's custody.

"Good thing she ran your prints and the flags went off in the system." Shep was having way too much fun with the incident to let it go, giving another gloating smirk as he got into his own SUV while Jamie hopped into his.

Yeah, flags had gone off. Homeland Security had called. They'd called both Brianna Tridle and Ryder at the office, unfortunately.

Jamie turned on radio contact as they pulled out of the parking lot. "How are you doing following up on the Kenny Davis angle?" he asked, ready to change the topic of conversation.

"Running into a lot of dead ends."

The Pebble Creek sheriff had been killed in a confrontation with Mo, another teammate, when the sheriff had gotten involved in the smuggling and kidnapped a little boy to use as leverage to regain a drug shipment he'd lost.

Mo did gain some clues out of his investigation: a code name, Coyote, the head of the smuggling operations on the other side of the border, and a date, October 13.

Something, but not enough. They needed to unravel the Coyote's identity and take him into custody, and they needed to figure out what the date meant.

"You think October 13 is the transfer?" He asked the same question they'd asked each other a dozen times since Mo had come up with the date.

"What else?"

"Why would the sheriff reveal it?"

"A sudden pang of patriotism? He knew at the end that he was dying. Money had been his main motivator for going bad. At that last moment, he knew money was no longer any good to him. He did this one thing to appease his conscience."

That made sense. But October 13 was only three weeks away. They had credible intelligence that several terrorists, along with some weapons of mass destruction, were going to cross this section of the border, the few hundred miles they were patrolling and investigating.

Now they had the date. Hopefully.

They needed an exact location.

To get that, they needed to find the Coyote.

"We'll catch as many smugglers as we can. One of them will lead us to the boss on the other side. He'll have the details of the transfer. Once we have him, I'm not worried. We'll get what we need out of him." Shep was more optimistic than Jamie.

"The smugglers we catch are small potatoes. None of them had a straight line to the Coyote so far."

"Patience is the name of the game."

Not one of his strengths, Jamie silently admitted.

They could have called in the National Guard and closed down the border in this area. But the bad guys would see that and simply bring over the terrorists and their weapons someplace else.

Which was why Jamie's six-man team was handling things quietly. According to their cover, they were here to observe illegal border activity and make budget recommendations to policy makers, while closely working with the CBP. In reality, they were a small, fast-hitting unit of a larger undercover commando team that protected national security all over the globe.

They wanted the terrorists to have no idea that they were expected. They wanted the bastards to come as planned so they could be apprehended and neutralized, taken out of the action for good—the only real solution.

Jamie and Shep talked about that and strategy as they reached the border, then radioed Keith and Mo to return to the office. The night shift was in place.

The full moon had come up, illuminating the landscape: some limited grazing land with large patches of arid ground thrown in that grew nothing but prickly pear and mesquite.

The Rio Grande flowed to the south of them, its dark waters glinting in the moonlight. Cicadas sang in the bushes. Up way ahead, deer were coming in to drink, but hearing the two cars, they darted away.

The place could look so peaceful and serene, belying how much trouble this little strip of land was causing on a regular basis lately.

Jamie pulled into a mesquite grove to observe for a while. Shep drove ahead and disappeared from sight after a few minutes. They were at one of the known crossing spots where the river was wide and the water low, the crossing relatively easy.

He got out his binoculars and used those for the first scan, then switched to his old, cracked night-vision goggles he'd grabbed from the office. He was mostly panning the river's southern bank, so he almost missed the three men who stole forward from the bushes on his other side, carrying oversize backpacks and an inflatable raft.

"Got three here," he said into the radio to warn Shep. "Be right back."

Jamie didn't wait for him. He started his car and gunned the engine, caught the trio halfway between the bushes and the water, squealed to a stop then jumped out, aiming his weapon as he rushed forward while they scattered.

"Guns on the ground! Hands in the air! Now!"

But the idiots seemed to find courage in the fact that they outnumbered him three to one. The nearest one took a shot at him.

Jamie ducked, ran forward and fired back, aiming for the extremities. They needed information, which dead men couldn't give.

He hit the guy in the leg and the smuggler went down, then Jamie was on top of him, maybe a little rougher than he had to be. His already damaged night-vision goggles broke and fell into the dirt.

Disarming the idiot took a minute, cuffing him another as the man struggled pretty hard while swearing and complaining about his injury.

"I'll feel sorry for you later." Jamie finished securing him. "Now shut up."

By the time he was done, the one who had the raft was at the edge of the water, the other one running in the opposite direction, back into the bushes where they probably had a vehicle hidden.

"Halt!" he called after him, not that the guy obeyed.

Jamie swore as he pushed to his feet. He'd already taken one down. He could have waited for Shep to go after the others together. But he wasn't in the habit of holding anything back.

He took after the guy who was going for the getaway car. With his prosthetics, he was no good in water, a weakness he hated.

He caught sight of Shep's car flying back, kicking up dust, just as the man he was chasing turned for a second and squeezed off another shot at Jamie.

He slowed, steadied his arm and shot back, aiming at the guy's gun and hitting it, a miracle considering the distance and lack of light. Then he darted forward once again, after the man who had already disappeared in the bushes.

The brush he entered was as tall as he was in places so he slowed, watching for movement up ahead. Nothing. The moon sliding behind a stray cloud didn't help. He had his high-powered flashlight clipped to his belt. Too bad turning that on would just make him a target.

Waiting for Shep and hunting as a team would have been smarter, but once again something—a need to prove himself, pride—pushed him forward.

He moved slowly, step by step, careful not to trip.

Somewhere behind him, Shep beeped his horn to let him know he got his man. That blare turned out to be Jamie's undoing.

He didn't hear the smuggler jump out of the bushes on his right, so he caught the collapsible paddle full in the face.

Pain shot up his nose and into his brain. He sprinted after the bastard anyway, shaking his head to clear it. The uneven ground tried to trip him; he focused on his balance, on closing the distance.

The man dropped his backpack and picked up speed.

Jamie didn't slow to see what he'd been carrying. That could wait.

Dark shadows surrounded them; there was no other sound but their boots slapping on the ground and their harsh breathing. Thorny bushes tore at him, ripping flesh and fabric. He paid no mind to anything but the man in front of him.

When he came close enough, he dove forward. They went down hard onto gravelly ground, rolled. Jamie was stronger, but the guy could maneuver his legs easier. A few minutes passed before he could subdue the smuggler.

"What's your name?" He flipped the guy onto his stomach and yanked the plastic cuff around his wrists. "What are you doing here? Who do you work for?"

But the man didn't respond, just snarled with impotent fury.

Jamie pushed himself up with his hands, then stood, the movement ungainly. Walking and running were his strengths; other things still didn't go as smoothly as he would have liked. He pulled the guy to standing and drew his gun at last to speed things up. "Talk and walk."

The guy did neither, so Jamie shoved him forward.

He picked up the backpack on their way back to the SUV. Judging from the metallic clanking, it held weapons, probably a few dozen small handguns.

Drugs and illegal immigrants were smuggled north; guns and money were smuggled south, in ever increasing quantities, fueling massive empires of crime on both sides and causing untold human misery.

The three they'd caught tonight were a drop in the bucket.

"Got him. Coming out." He called a warning before stepping out of the cover of the bushes.

Shep had been waiting. He lowered his weapon. Looked like he'd already stashed the other two guys in the back of his SUV. He holstered his gun as Jamie came closer.

"You okay? Your nose doesn't look too good."

"Feels like it's been driven into my brain." It really did. He was seeing a couple of extra stars than what were in the sky tonight.

"Broken?"

"Nah." But his cheekbone might have gotten cracked. He flexed his jaw. His face burned like hell.

"Could have waited for me."

Yeah, they were a team. *Whatever.* Just because he was no longer whole didn't mean he couldn't handle a chase by himself. Although that probably wasn't what Shep had meant.

He drew a deep breath. After his injury, he'd spent some time in the darkest pit of depression. Then he'd gotten his new legs and…fine, he'd been overcompensating. "We got them. That's what counts, right?"

Shep was panning the brush with his spotlight. "Did you find their car?"

"Didn't get that far. Has to be back there somewhere. I don't think they walked far." The man he'd chased down had had plenty of energy left in him for a good sprint.

"I'll go and take a look." Shep took off running, keeping both his flashlight and his weapon out.

Jamie shoved the smuggler he'd caught up against his SUV, searched the man's pockets for ID but found nothing but a small bag of weed. He locked the guy in the back of the car then went through the backpack and came up with three dozen brand-new small arms: Ruger .380, the perfect size to be carried concealed.

A small-time operation, but something. These three had to have a link on the other side. And that link would have an uplink. Follow the trail, and it might lead to the elusive Coyote.

He stayed on patrol while Shep ran the smugglers in, bringing Mo back with him so Mo could take the smugglers' car for a thorough search and fingerprinting. They would follow even the smallest lead. The stakes were too high. There were no unimportant details.

They kept an eye out for others. Sometimes smugglers worked in separate teams. They figured if one team got caught, the others would slip through while the border patrol was busy with the unlucky ones.

But the rest of the night went pretty quietly, the borderlands deserted. When Keith and Ray came to take over at dawn, Jamie drove back to his apartment to catch some sleep. His ringing phone woke him around midmorning.

"A friend of yours stopped by to see me earlier," Ryder, the team leader, said on the other end, sounding less than happy.

Jamie tried to unscramble his brain as he sat up and reached for his prosthetics. "Who?"

"Brianna Tridle."

An image of her long legs and full lips slammed into his mind. Okay, now he was wide awake.

"She kept calling up the chain at CBP until they gave her our contact number. Tracked us down from there.

She's demanding to be involved in our investigation. If her town and her people are part of whatever our mission is here, as she put it, she wants in."

"How did she take being disappointed?" With her looks, she probably didn't often experience a man saying no to her. Jamie almost wished he could have been there to see when Ryder had done it.

But Ryder said, "Actually, I agreed."

"Say that again?" His hand halted over the straps.

"She grew up around here, knows everyone. People respect her. Record clean as a whistle. We're pressed for time. She could be an asset."

"More like a pain in the asset."

"Possibly. She's pretty protective of her town. In any case, I don't plan on that being my problem," he added cheerfully.

A dark premonition settled over Jamie, immediately justified as Ryder said, "Since you're the one who got her all riled up, you'll be her liaison on the team."

"I don't think it's a good idea to involve her."

"You have my permission to try to talk her out of it. Tomorrow. Right now I need you to drive up to San Antonio. I got a new name from one of the men you and Shep caught last night on the border. Rico Marquez. He's a known gangbanger."

Which translated to: be ready for anything.

He was just as likely to come back with Rico as he was with a bullet in his back.

"Want someone to go with you? I could pull Keith from border detail," Ryder offered. "This is a pretty promising lead."

"Nah," he said, unable, once again, to shake the need to prove himself, even if nobody but him thought that was necessary. "I can handle it."

Chapter Three

Jamie tracked Rico to an abandoned warehouse where the man was apparently hiding out at the moment due to the fact that a rival gang member was hunting him. Information unwittingly supplied by his mother, who'd thought Jamie had come to help her son.

Jamie picked the lock on the rusted emergency door on the side of the building and eased inside little by little, as silently as he could manage. The temperature had to be close to a hundred; there was definitely no air-conditioning here. The cavernous place smelled like dust and machine grease.

The carcass of a giant and complicated-looking piece of machinery took up most of the floor; the ceiling was thirty feet high, at least. A metal walkway ringed the building high up on the wall, and some sort of an office was tucked under the corrugated metal roof in the back.

Jamie caught sight of a faint, flickering light up there—a TV?—so he moved that way. Where the hell were the stairs?

He walked forward slowly, carefully, listening for any noise that might warn him that he wasn't alone down here. Nothing.

Once he was closer to the back wall, he could hear
the muted sounds of the TV upstairs. Good. Maybe they
wouldn't hear him coming.

Now all he needed was to find a way up. He wished
he had more light down at ground level, but all the windows were up high, just under the roof, and all were
covered with enough grime to let through precious little light.

There were a million hiding places for someone to
wait to ambush him. Then again, he'd also have plenty
of cover if it came to a close-quarters shootout in here.

He scanned all the dark corners and found the stairs
at last, hiding behind a bundle of foot-wide pipes that
ran up along the wall. He approached it with as much
care as possible.

The corner was a perfect place to ambush someone
if anyone was down here, watching him. But he reached
the bottom of the stairs without trouble.

Next came the tricky part—he had to go up the stairs.
No more cover. He'd be in plain sight the whole time.
The metal steps would rattle, drawing attention to him.
He could be picked off with a single shot.

He took his gun out and moved up facing the main
floor, ready to fire back if anyone took aim at him.
Maybe he could keep them pinned down until he
reached the top. But he made it all the way, walking
backward, without anyone taking a shot at him.

Okay. That had to mean there were no lookouts on
the lower level. If there were, they wouldn't have let
him get this far, not when taking him out would have
been a piece of cake.

So far, so good. But the next step was even more

difficult—sneaking by a wall of office windows that stretched from floor to ceiling and left no place to hide as he made his way to the door.

Anybody in the office would see him as soon as they looked this way.

He stole toward the windows and stopped as soon as he reached glass. He poked his head out a little to see what waited for him inside the room.

Overturned office furniture and stacked-up file cabinets cut the office space in two. He could see behind them through the gaps, could see part of a television set in the far corner, a mattress on the floor and naked bodies entwined in the act of lovemaking.

He blinked. Okay, that was unexpected. *Awkward.*

But also lucky.

He could make it across the walkway, passing in front of all those windows, without being seen. Nobody was paying the slightest attention to him.

He twisted the doorknob. Locked, which he'd kind of expected. But it was a simple office door lock and he had it picked in a flat minute.

Heck, a secretary with a hairpin could have done it.

He moved inside silently and kept down as he inched forward, using file cabinet for cover. Any noise his boots made was covered by some moaning and a lot of heavy breathing, not to mention the TV running a Mexican soap opera and a fan that was going somewhere behind the pile of furniture.

The scent of sex hung in the air, which made him think of Deputy Sheriff Bree Tridle, for some reason.

He pushed her out of his mind as he pulled his

backup weapon and stepped forward with a gun in each hand. "Freeze!"

The woman screamed and scampered off her man in a panicked rush, nearly kicking him in the head as she grabbed for the sheet to cover herself.

Jamie's eyes were on the guy. "Freeze! Hands in the air!"

Rico was in his early twenties, covered in gang tattoos, his gaze rapidly clearing as he grabbed for the handgun next to the mattress. He wasn't concerned with modesty.

Jamie shot at the gun and the force of the bullet kicked the weapon out of reach. Rico went for a switchblade that had been hidden under his pillow, apparently. He was nothing if not prepared.

He lunged toward Jamie.

"No! *Mi amor?*" the woman screamed, scampering farther away from them, looking shocked and horrified at the scene unfolding in front of her.

Jamie deflected the knife and knocked Rico back. "I don't want to have to shoot you, dammit!"

That slowed the guy down a little. "You no come to kill us?" He held the blade in front of him, ready for another go.

Jamie kept his gaze above neck level. "Customs and Border Protection. I'm here to talk about the smuggling your gang is involved in. You look like a nice couple. Nobody has to die today."

Wow, he was getting downright soft here. He sounded almost as optimistic as the deputy sheriff.

Rico didn't look convinced. "Her brother didn't send you?"

Jamie stashed his backup gun into the front of his waistband, then reached for his CBP badge and held it up. "I'm only here for information, man."

Rico raised his knife and his chin, sneering with contempt. "I don't talk to pigs."

"That's generally a good policy. Snitches don't live long in this business." Jamie glanced for a split second at the young woman who was white with fear, pulling her clothes on with jerky movements, and he did some quick thinking. "But it looks to me like you have something to live for. What if you two could get away both from your gang and your father?"

"Mi amor?" The woman's gaze flew to Rico, hope mixing with alarm in her voice.

"Can't be done." Rico reached for his jeans, didn't bother with underwear. He was tough enough to rough it, seemed to be the message.

Since he wasn't sneering anymore, Jamie took that as a good sign. "A chance at true love, the two of you together. What's that worth?"

Rico considered him through narrowed eyes. "You let Maria go. Right now."

"Okay," Jamie agreed, as a gesture of good faith. Maria probably had zero useful information for him, anyway. He looked at the woman. "Go."

She cast a questioning glance at Rico, who repeated the order in Spanish and explained that he would find her later, but she stubbornly shook her head.

A rapid argument followed before she finally ran for the door. They could hear her footsteps on the metal walkway, then down the stairs.

"I could kill you now," Rico said, still holding the

knife, a nasty-looking piece that had probably seen plenty of business on San Antonio's backstreets.

"You could try," Jamie answered calmly, feet apart, stance ready. He actually preferred Maria out of the way. No sense of her getting in the middle of this and maybe being killed.

Rico measured him up again. Swore in Spanish. "What the hell do you want from me?" he asked at last.

"I'm looking for a man called Coyote."

"Don't know him." But the corner of his left eye jumped.

"Any information would help. All I need is a link I could follow to him."

"And if I give you this, me and Maria go to witness protection?"

He nodded.

"Where?"

"Someplace where nobody can find you. You can get rid of the tattoos. They'll hook you up with a job and a place to live. You can get married."

Rico still hesitated.

"Ask yourself this," Jamie gestured at the ratty, messed-up room with his free hand. "Is this the life you want for your children? Or do you want something better? Doesn't she deserve more than this?"

God help him, he was appealing to true love. Something he wasn't even sure he believed in. But maybe Rico did, and that would be enough to settle matters here.

The man lowered his knife and filled his lungs, his ink-covered shoulders dropping as he exhaled. He looked pretty damn young with all the bluster gone out of him. He barely looked twenty. "There's no way out for guys like me."

"There is now. This must be your lucky day."

Tension-filled silence stretched between them.

"Okay," Rico said. "Let me think. I might be able to get something for you. If you can keep us safe. Maria the most."

An opening. "I'll talk to my people. But I need a solid lead."

More silence, then, "How do I find you?"

Jamie reached into his back pocket, pulled out a business card with his number on it and tossed it on the mattress between them.

Rico didn't move to pick it up. He'd do that when he was alone.

"Don't wait too long to call," Jamie warned. "I found you once, I will find you again. If I have to track you down, I'll be coming to bring you in." Then he backed away, gun still in hand.

He didn't relax until he was down the stairs and out of the building.

Damn, he hoped this would get them results. Because otherwise he would have to explain to Ryder why he wasn't taking Rico back to the interrogation room with him.

He'd just taken a hell of a gamble.

BREE WAS HEADING back to her office with her first cup of coffee of the morning, thinking about the talk she was giving at the middle school later about crime prevention, when Jamie Cassidy strolled into the Pebble Creek police station.

"I'm armed and I'm not handing my weapon over," he advised Lena by the metal detector, looking as surly and aggravated and sexy as ever. He took off his cowboy hat and ran his fingers through his hair to straighten it.

"Let him through," Bree called out before Lena could tackle him.

Or something. The officer had that dreamy-eyed look again that said she wouldn't mind seeing Jamie Cassidy on his back. There were probably a million women out there who shared the sentiment, although today he looked somewhat worse for wear.

Bruises and cuts marred the right side of his face—looked like he'd taken a beating since Bree had last seen him. Given his attitude and general disposition, she could see how a person would be tempted.

She flashed him her "this is my station and I'm the boss here" look, but when she spoke, she kept things cordial. "Mr. Cassidy. Nice to see you again. Why don't we talk in my office?"

"Jamie." He strode in past her, his mouth set in a line that was suspiciously close to a snarl.

A part of her that was apparently easily distracted wondered what it would take to make him happy. Not that she was volunteering for the job. Not even if those sharp eyes and those sculpted lips of his could have tempted a saint.

She closed the door behind them. "Please, take a seat. How can I help you today?"

He lowered his impressive frame into the nearest chair as he gave a soft growl of warning that he probably meant to sound threatening.

She found it kind of sexy, heaven help her. "Are you all right? What happened to your face?"

"Somebody whacked me."

"While the rest of us can only dream," she said sweetly. "Life is nothing but unfair." She set her mug down. "Came to share information?"

"Came for my equipment."

"Heavy-duty stuff." She didn't want him to leave until she got at least *something* out of him, so she grabbed the first-aid kit from the bookshelf on the back wall and went to stand in front of him, half sitting on her desk. "Let me see this. Look up, please."

He did, but only to send her a death glare. "I'm fine."

"Of course you are, mucho macho and all that. Which is how I know you won't be scared of a little sting."

He'd cleaned and disinfected his injuries from the looks of it; the smaller scrapes were already scabbed over, but she didn't like the larger gash over his cheekbone where his skin had split.

"I assume you didn't go get stiches because you don't have the time, not because you're scared of the needle?"

He shot her a dark look. He did that so well. Must have been part of his training.

"Why don't I slap on some butterfly bandages, as long as we're both here. Then you won't have to go see a doc. You'll save a ton of time that you can use to glare at people. I'd hate to see you slip off schedule."

His eyes remained stoic, but the corner of his sculpted mouth twitched. "Make it quick."

"How about you tell me who you guys are for real? Who do you really work for?"

"That's on a need-to-know basis."

"You're in my town, on my turf. I need to know."

"I don't think you have the right clearance, Deputy Sheriff."

He said *deputy sheriff* as a slur, as if he was calling her *babe* or maybe some other word that started with a *b*.

She focused on the disinfecting and the butterfly bandages to keep herself from engaging in contact unbecoming a police officer. When he was good to go, she closed her kit and walked back behind her desk.

"How about you tell me the basics," she suggested. "Something to get started with."

"I'm here for my equipment," he repeated.

Okay, then. He wasn't going to be an easy nut to crack.

She shoved aside a manila envelope somebody had left on her desk and folded her hands in front of her. "Just so we're clear on this one thing, this is my town. You make trouble here and I'll know why."

Being a Southern belle and a lady came naturally to her. She'd been raised on the beauty-queen circuit, but some days she did have her lapses. Looked like it was going to be one of those days.

His eyebrow slid higher. "Do I look like trouble?"

"Double serving. With whipped cream and cherry on top."

A bark of laughter escaped him, softening his face, and she caught a glimpse of what he might have been at one time, without all the darkness he was now carrying. It took her breath away.

Phew, all righty, then. She shook her head to clear the image.

So unfair that she would find him attractive. He was in her town doing secret things. He was about as pleasant as a wild boar with a toothache. He was high-handed. She didn't want to like him, not even a little.

"What's your team really doing on the border?" she asked again, and waited.

And waited.

"Ryder McKay said that you'll be my liaison. Liaise." She raised her eyebrows into her best schoolmarm look.

He still waited another couple of stubborn seconds before he finally said, "We're here about the smuggling."

"But not to make policy recommendations," she guessed.

He shook his head, watched her, measured her up again. "We're here to intercept a special transfer."

"And you work for Homeland Security?"

He just stared at her.

So, okay, she could pretty much guess the rest. Whatever his team had come for probably had something to do with terrorism. "Is my town safe?"

"Yes."

"And you know this how?"

"We have *some* information. You're not a target."

Made *some* sense. Terrorists would be going for one of the major cities.

Anger coursed through her. She was a patriot and a Texan, sick of people who tried to mess with her country. "Is there anything I can help with?"

He hesitated for a moment. "Maybe. I'll let you know if we come across something where we could use your assistance."

"And you'll let me know of any developments?"

He hesitated longer this time, but said, "Yes."

"Thank you." She pulled out the bottom drawer that was about filled to the rim with his weaponry and one by one set them on the desk between them, grabbing an old canvas bag from under the desk and dropping it on top. "I'd appreciate it if you carried that loot out of here concealed."

He gave a brief nod and stepped forward to pack up his things. The string on his night-vision goggles caught on her manila envelope. They reached for it at the same time, their fingers touching.

She barely had time to register the zing as she jerked back, the contents of the envelope spilling all over her desk.

She stared at the photos for a disjointed moment as her brain registered the images: snapshots of her in her kitchen, taken from outside her house. She grabbed for them, but not fast enough.

He snatched up the last one and took a good look at it before holding it up for her. "What the hell is this?"

The photo showed her standing in her bedroom next to the bed, changing, wearing nothing but a skimpy bra and blue jeans, holding her favorite checkered shirt.

She grabbed the picture from him as her heart sped suddenly. *Oh, God. Not again.* She so didn't have time for her past to rise up to claim her. "That's on a need-to-know basis."

HE DIDN'T LIKE the way she suddenly paled, or the idea that she had a stalker.

"When do you think these were taken?" Jamie asked.

She didn't think about it long. "Last night. That's the shirt I was wearing yesterday."

"And you went to see Ryder McKay earlier in the day?" He gave her a pointed look.

"The two have nothing to do with each other."

The hell they didn't. "Smuggling is a multibillion-dollar business. It's a dangerous business."

"Really? I must have been sitting behind my desk, filing my nails, and I missed that briefing," she said with that overly sweet smile he'd come to learn meant she was mocking him.

He shot her a look that told her he wasn't amused. "Look, people around here know we're investigating smuggling. Someone saw you visiting the office. They didn't like it. You need to stay out of what we're doing."

"I'll take the risk."

"I'm not asking. I'm telling you. Don't involve yourself. Forget everything we've talked about earlier."

"Or what?" A laugh escaped her and trilled along his nerve endings. "You'll spank me? For heaven's sake. I'm an officer of the law. I'm trained to handle myself."

The visual of the spanking bit left him both speechless and breathless for a second.

"I'm a big girl, Jamie." She switched to dead serious and ticked off in a split second, which did nothing to lessen the wave of lust that threatened to drown him. "Whatever threat is jeopardizing the peace of this town and the law, you can be sure I'll be out there fighting it." She pressed her full lips together.

He wondered what she'd do if he tried to kiss her. Throw him against the wall again? His pulse quickened.

On the other hand, as unpredictable and unreasonable as she was, she might just shoot him.

Not that kissing those lips wouldn't be worth the risk, he decided. Not that he was going to do it. No way. He was in town on serious business. And women were no longer part of his life, anyway. He had too much baggage, too many nightmares. He had no right to bring that into a relationship and mess up somebody else's life along with his.

He didn't have much left. He was a trained killing machine, that was about it. He planned on living the rest of his life using what skills he had in the service of his country.

"Stick to speeding tickets," he said as he stood. "Forget about me and my team." Although he was pretty sure he wasn't going to be able to forget about her. He was going to try, anyway, he promised himself as he walked away from her.

His shift was starting in half an hour.

He walked out of the station to his SUV parked up front. At least he'd gotten a possible lead in San Antonio.

He would have to figure out the witness-protection thing with the U.S. Marshals Service. And Rico had to think about what he had and come up with enough that would buy him two witness-protection tickets.

Jamie needed to talk to Ryder about that. And forget about Bree. He would. After he made sure she was safe.

Chapter Four

Stick to speeding tickets, Jamie Cassidy had said. He had a singular ability to get under her skin, Bree thought as she went about her business.

She didn't have to worry about speeding tickets, as it turned out. Just as she finished her crime-prevention presentation at the middle school, the town's streetlight system went down, snarling traffic, cars barely inching along. She spent most of the rest of her shift cleaning up the mess.

A dozen fender benders got tempers flaring; a couple of arguments ended in fistfights before it was all over. Bree didn't have too much time to think about Jamie Cassidy, and thank God for that, because the man was enough to raise any sane woman's blood pressure.

She was exhausted by the time she made it back to the station, and then a whole other hour went to waste with writing up reports. She'd just finished when Hank, the contractor whose company managed the town's traffic-control system, walked into her office.

"Hey, Bree." He was short and round, the mocha-skinned version of Danny DeVito, a family guy who was always hustling, always working on something, if not for his kids and small company then for the town. He was a tireless volunteer.

"Everything up and running?"

"Almost. I wanted to talk to you about something." He stopped in front of her desk. "Looks like several of our control boxes were shorted out on purpose."

She stilled. "Are you sure?" Why on earth would somebody want to do that? "Can you give me the locations?"

He rattled off the crossroads and she wrote them down. "I'll look into it. Thanks for letting me know. Can I get you a coffee from the break room?" The least she could do. She appreciated the work Hank did and the fact that he took the time to come in to talk to her.

"Lena already fixed me up with coffee and a Danish." He patted his round belly with a quick grin. "I better get going. I still have a couple of things to fix."

She gave him a parting wave. "Thanks. I really appreciate it. Give me a call if you run into any trouble."

"Will do. Say hi to Katie for me," he said as he left her to her work.

She shrugged into her harness and slipped her weapon into her holster as she stood and scanned the major intersections on her list. Several stores in those spots would have external security cameras. She needed to check the footage.

Most of the officers were out on calls and the station was close to deserted.

"I'm off to look into the traffic-light business," she called to Lena on her way out. "Back in an hour, I hope. Want anything?"

"A hot guy with an oil claim on his ranch?"

"If I see one, I'll send him your way."

The traffic was clearing up at last so she didn't have any trouble reaching the first address, just three blocks from the station. The owner of the small pawnshop handed over his security video without insisting on a warrant. Bree had cut him a break a month or so ago when he'd taken in stolen merchandise without knowing.

She moved on to the next address, a place that sold used video games and gaming equipment, and got the recording there, too. She'd been buying Katie games there for years. She knew her community and was nice to people. And they were nice to her when she needed something.

The next place after that was a specialty shop, selling high-end, artisan cowboy boots, run by one of her old schoolmates.

Rounding up the half-dozen recordings took a little over an hour, including taking some time to talk with people. She liked knowing what was going on in her town.

Then it was back to the office to view the footage. Another half an hour passed before she had her men, two twenty-somethings from Hullett—Jeremy and Josh Harding, brothers. She knew them from a round-up brawl that had sent six men to the E.R. last year.

She headed out to Hullett to pick up the boys. She let them sweat it out in the back of her police cruiser—didn't start questioning them until they were in the interview room.

They both wore scuffed boots and jeans and identical ragged T-shirts, no brand, cheapest stuff money could buy. They looked down on their luck. If they were going to commit a crime, why not one that would benefit them financially? Try as she might, she couldn't figure out the traffic-light angle.

"Little old for pranks, aren't you?"

Jeremy shot a meaningful look at his younger brother before looking back at her. "Dunno what you talkin' about."

"What do you Hullett boys have against Pebble Creek these days?" They had an arson investigation going, the fire started by someone just like these two, last week. Then there were the half-dozen cases of random vandalism she couldn't tie to anyone. Investigations that kept her busy, like she needed extra work with smuggling and the counterfeit money coming in.

"You're messing up my crime-rate statistics," she told them, putting away her softer side. "I don't like it."

The younger one, Josh, brightened. "We are?" He sounded a little too eager. Even pleased.

She looked from him to Jeremy. "Okay. What's going on here?"

"We have an alibi. We were at a friend's house, hangin' out and shootin' beer cans," the older brother said, smug as anything.

"Is that so?" she asked calmly. "Because I have half a dozen security tape recordings showing you two messing with the traffic-light control boxes."

The younger brother paled. "I can't go to no jail. Jenny's gonna have a kid. Ma's gonna skin me alive if I get into trouble again. She said it."

"Shut up, idiot," Jeremy barked at him.

Bree raised a placating hand. "How about we start

with cooperation, then discuss restitution? Things don't have to come to jail."

"Sounds good, ma'am," Josh hurried to say, all manners, suddenly.

His older brother whacked him on the shoulder. "You don't even know what it means."

"Can't be worse than jail."

Bree shook her head. "It means you two have to pay back the repair costs, and then never cause trouble in my town again." She thought that was a fair deal, but Josh's shoulders sagged.

"We ain't got no money. That's why we did it in the first place," he whined, earning another smack from Jeremy.

They were only about ten years younger than she was, but she felt like she should ground them or something. "No more hitting." She held up a warning finger. "Now, explain to me how you make money from stopping traffic?"

They looked down. Looked at each other.

She pulled out her cell phone. "How about I just call your mother?"

"The mill," Josh blurted out, then slumped as Jeremy shot him a dark look that said, "I'll make you regret this later."

"The wire mill?" Hullett had a wire mill. She failed to understand what Pebble Creek traffic had to do with it.

"It's going under," Josh explained.

Not a surprise. The owner was in prison for human trafficking. A shame for the workers and their families. The Hullett wire mill was the town's largest employer.

"You two work there?"

Jeremy pressed his lips together and sulked, but Josh responded. "We already got our pink slips."

Bad timing with the baby coming, she thought. "I'm still waiting on how this connects to traffic."

"Word is, there's gonna be a paper mill comin' in. Choice is between Hullett and Pebble Creek."

She knew about that. Some rich Chinese guy, Yo Tee, who owned a big paper mill on the other side of the border, was thinking about building a smaller one over here. Probably to get a tax break or whatever. He had some team that was scouting for a location. She'd run into them the week before when an overeager citizen spotted them at an abandoned factory and reported it as a possible burglary.

"We want the paper jobs in Hullett," Josh told her. "They could put new machines into the wire mill and keep the workers on. We could do trainin'. We ain't stupid."

Clearly. She narrowed her eyes at him. "So you're making a mess of my town to make Hullett look better. Is that it?"

He looked down at his hands sheepishly. "We need the work."

They went about it in a completely wrong and idiotic way, but she could certainly understand their motivation. "What else?"

Josh looked up, confusion on his face.

"What else have you done?" she clarified.

"The lights were it. I swear."

He looked earnest enough that she believed him. But she would bet good money that Pebble Creek's recent troubles with vandalism had been caused by some of his buddies—bunch of geniuses.

She told them she'd take them to holding, one at a time, while she figured something out. She took Jeremy first, then Josh. With Josh, she swung by the break room on their way to holding.

He walked with his head hanging. "Just don't call my ma, all right? She can't pay no bail."

"Want some coffee?"

He looked up with surprise. He'd probably expected chastisement. "Thank you, ma'am. I would."

"How about something to go with it?" She gestured toward the box of doughnuts on the counter.

"For real?"

"I'm not here to abuse people whose biggest crime is wanting to work."

Relief filled his face as he cautiously reached into the white paper box for an apple fritter.

She drew a slow breath. "But you and your brother did go about it the wrong way. Replacing those fuse boxes will cost a mint."

Josh looked like the first bite got stuck in his throat. "I told you, we ain't got no money."

"And the baby's coming," she said with sympathy. "I'll talk to the judge. You could be booked and released today, no bail. I could put in a strong recommendation for community service only. You and your brother could work off the damage." She paused. "Thing is, if I'm that nice, I need to know everything you know."

But instead of giving her information on other recent vandalism in Pebble Creek like she'd expected, he said,

"I know about the bad money they were talkin' about on TV." He looked around nervously.

Pay dirt.

She hurried to the door and closed it, all ears. "Sit." She put the whole doughnut box in front of him.

But he looked really scared now, just holding on to his fritter. "If anyone finds out…"

"Not from me. I promise."

He swallowed hard and looked to the door as if to make sure nobody was coming in. "I was at Ronny's house last week for some grillin' and beer." He paused.

"Ronny who?"

"Brown. Down by the reservoir."

She knew Ronald Brown. They were old friends. She'd arrested him on drug distribution last year. He'd gotten off on a technicality. "How is he linked to the fake money?"

"I don't know. I swear." Josh put his free hand to his chest. "I went into the house to take a leak. He was in the kitchen with this other dude. The other guy was givin' him a roll of twenties and tellin' him they needed to be spent slowly and carefully."

"That's it?"

He nodded. "I didn't think nothin' of it until they said about bad money on the news."

"What did the other man look like?"

"Mexican. Short and scruffy. He had some tattoos. Ain't never seen him around before."

"How about you look at some pictures for me?"

She led him back to her office then had him look through the mug shots on her computer.

Scrolling through the pictures, and doing a lot of

handholding so Josh wouldn't renege on his promise to help, took some time. By the time they ran out of mug shots to look at and she'd processed then released the brothers, her shift was over. Too late to go and see Ronny Brown. She put away her files. Tomorrow was another day. Right now, she had to go pick up Katie.

The drive over took less than ten minutes.

"Did you have a good day?" Bree asked when they were in the car, heading home.

Katie worked at a facility that employed handicapped people. They shipped small machine parts all over the country and were responsible for wrapping and packaging. The people running the place were fantastic with the employees. Katie loved going to work since all her friends were there. They had fun together.

"Mrs. Mimms said I did good work," Katie said. "I think she was happy. She made the happy face."

They'd been working on emotions with cue cards and internet pictures in the evenings. Katie was high functioning, but she did have autism. She had trouble with emotions, both displaying them appropriately and telling the mood of others.

"I'm sure she was very happy. Did you have a good lunch?"

Food was a touchy subject. Katie only liked a handful of things, and she wouldn't eat at all if the food on her plate was touching.

"Chicken fingers. Good."

Bree relaxed a little. It worried her when Katie skipped meals. She was such a skinny little thing already.

"We got someone new," her sister informed her.

"He's just like me. Except he doesn't talk to anyone. His name is Scott."

"Do you like him?"

"He's quiet."

Which meant she liked him. She gave a full report on the way home, then went through her coming-home routine, putting her things away, washing her hands, setting the table, while Bree made some hamburgers for dinner.

"Can we do a puzzle later?"

"Sure." Bree pulled the French fries from the oven— baked to save some calories—and thought how much she liked their evenings together. Katie was sweet and gentle, and part of her life irrevocably.

She didn't care if the few boyfriends she'd had over the years couldn't deal with that. They'd wanted her, but they hadn't wanted her "baggage," as the last one had put it. Thing was, she would rather have her sister than a jerk in her life, anyway. She *had* said that. With a Southern-belle smile on her face.

Still, the good things in her life far outweighed the bad.

She thought of the pictures in the manila envelope, the first time she'd allowed herself to think of them since she'd gotten them away from Jamie Cassidy.

Trouble was coming again.

Just thinking about that made her tired.

Why now?

She would end it for good this time, she promised herself. She wasn't going to let this touch Katie, put her in danger.

As she turned to put the food on the table, movement outside caught her eye.

Did someone just step behind her garage?

She set the fries on the table. "I'm going to put the garbage out, then we can eat."

"Okay," Katie called back, cheerful and oblivious to danger, which was the way Bree meant to keep things.

She bagged up the garbage. Then she slipped her service revolver into her waistband before she walked outside through the back to confront her past that was rising up once again to claim her.

Chapter Five

Her mother's oversize garden sculptures populated the backyard, same as the front, their shapes too familiar to look eerie, even in the twilight. Bree opened the door without a sound and ducked to the right, into the warm evening air and the cover of the bushes. And then recognized the man standing by the shed—Jamie Cassidy.

You have got to be kidding me. She ground her teeth together.

She nearly sprung up to yell at him. But maybe teaching him a lesson would be a more productive way to prevent him from spying on her again. So she kept down, skulked around the rock garden and snuck up behind him, using the statues as cover.

She didn't have much in the backyard as far as tall plants went, just a few butterfly bushes, with more color added by generous clumps of black-eyed Susans and asters that were putting on quite a show of yellow and purple this fall.

She moved as silently as a copperhead, raising her gun when she was but a step behind him, anticipating the jolt he'd give when she pressed the cold metal against the back of his skull. That ought to take the cocky bastard down a peg.

Except when she was an inch away, he said, "Hey, Deputy," and reached back at the same time, clamped his fingers over her wrist and shoved her against the side of the shed, holding her hand above her head, their faces inches from each other.

His cheekbone had turned purple since she'd last seen him. He still wore her butterfly bandages. And he still looked too handsome by half. *Deal with it.* She normally wasn't a shallow person.

"What are you doing at my house?" She shoved against him with her free hand but he wouldn't budge. "I could have shot you."

"I didn't think you were the type to shoot a fellow law enforcement drone."

"How did you know I recognized you?"

"You never took the safety off your weapon."

Dismay and aggravation tightened her jaw. He'd probably seen her and tracked her movements from the moment she'd come outside.

She didn't often get caught off guard. That Jamie Cassidy had had her back against the wall twice now in the space of a week aggravated the living daylights out of her. "What are you doing here?" She repeated the question he still hadn't answered.

"Trying to catch whoever took those pictures. I think this might be connected to your visit to Ryder. Someone doesn't want you to share your local expertise with my team. Whoever is trying to mess with you might be just the guy we're looking for."

"You're just trying to scare me off so I don't stick my nose into your team's business."

"One can dream," he said lightly.

"Maybe *you* sent the pictures to intimidate me," she said, although she knew that wasn't the case.

He leaned another inch closer. His sharp gaze raked her face. "When I want to scare someone, I'm a lot more direct about it. I don't leave them guessing."

His powerful body completely blocked any escape, his fingers holding her right hand above her head as effectively as handcuffs. He wasn't trying to look threatening, she didn't think. The words had been said straight-faced, yet alarm tingled down her spine nonetheless.

Okay, and a little bit of lust, too. She didn't think he was going to harm her. He could have done so already, countless times if that was his intention. The twinge of attraction she felt was a pure evolutionary response of a female to a display of power from the alpha male.

So unfair.

She tried to resist the magnetic field that drew her to him.

The faint scent of his soap tickled her nose, mixed with some barely there, understated aftershave. She could almost swear she could smell the testosterone coming off him, he was so ridiculously male.

He had a warrior's body, a warrior's stance, a warrior's eyes. And definitely a warrior's strength. She tried to pull away and failed once again.

"You're trespassing," she pointed out, a little testiness mixing with the twinges of lust she didn't appreciate.

He opened his mouth to respond, but Katie appearing at the back door stopped him short. He let Bree's hand go immediately and she moved out of the shadows while he disappeared into them. She appreciated that tremendously. She didn't want him upsetting Katie.

"We're having dinner," Katie said. "It's dinnertime."

"Yes, it is, sweetie. I'm coming." She hurried toward her sister. Having her schedule interrupted could send Katie off-kilter for the rest of the evening. Better to keep everything running smoothly.

She glanced back from the doorway one last time, but Jamie Cassidy had disappeared completely.

She wasn't enough of an optimist to think permanently.

JAMIE WENT AROUND the back of Bree Tridle's modest two-story home. He'd gone off and grabbed something to eat, then came back. This time her upstairs lights were all out; there was just one light on downstairs, in her kitchen. He knocked quietly on the back door before trying the doorknob. Unlocked.

"Bree?" He didn't want to get shot.

"In here."

He moved down the dark hallway and came out into the kitchen, bathed in light. The space was plain and spotless, Mexican tile floor, simple pine cabinets. A handful of small, crystal unicorns hung in the window.

She sat at the kitchen table, a bottle of beer and a bottle of strawberry wine cooler in front of her. Looked like she'd been expecting him.

"How did you know I'd come back?" he asked as he sat, taking the beer.

"You don't look like the type who walks away without getting what he came for."

He leaned back in his chair. "I like smart women. I'm glad we understand each other."

"Let's not get carried away." She drank straight from the bottle.

Good. He didn't have the patience for prissy women. She was trying his patience in so many ways already, the last thing he needed was for her to start putting on airs.

"So why are you here, exactly?" she asked.

"I need that envelope." He should have taken it when he'd been in her office. He'd been distracted. By her. That wasn't going to happen again. He was here on a mission.

"Why would you think I brought it home? Things like that are entered into evidence."

He watched her for a long second. "You strike me as the kind of woman who would handle her personal business herself."

"I'm glad you understand that it *is* personal. I'll take care of it."

She said that with a little too much confidence. He watched her for a moment. "So you know who your stalker is?"

She shifted in her seat, reaching for her bottle again, saying nothing.

Okay, she did know. "Has this happened before?"

She gave a reluctant nod. "Back when I was competing."

Beauty pageants, she meant. She looked different now from the super made-up, big-hair pictures he'd found on the internet. She was still beautiful without a doubt, but in a hometown-girl kind of way.

She wore her hair in a simple ponytail, the blond her natural color, he was pretty sure, little makeup, dressed plain and comfortable. The kind of woman who could dazzle the hell out of a guy yet somehow make him comfortable when sitting with her. And could probably beat the stuffing out of him if he got fresh with her.

"Want to tell me about it?" he asked.

"If it gets you out of my hair."

He promised nothing. Not about keeping out of her hair, or her pants, for that matter. There was a part of him, getting louder and louder, that wanted to keep his options open.

"When I was doing the pageants," she said after a minute, her expression turning sober, "I had a young fan, Lilly Tanner, who wanted to be just like me. She wrote me several times, and I wrote back. We even met. Her room was apparently covered with my posters. She wore T-shirts with my picture on them."

She paused to draw a slow breath. "She was bullied in school and ridiculed. They called her ugly, and worse. A lot worse. Just really mean and nasty stuff." She folded her hands on her lap. "She ended up committing suicide."

"And one of her friends blamed you for it."

"Her twin brother, Jason. He's not—" she paused "—he doesn't always understand what he's doing. He was born with some mental disability and the added depression pushed him off balance after Lilly's death."

Not a comforting thought. "You need to make him stop before this escalates."

"I know." She took a drink. "I called his parents while I was waiting for you to show. They don't know where he is. He moved away from home six months ago and only keeps in touch sporadically. I'll find him."

She didn't seem scared or upset as much as sad.

"You feel some responsibility for the sister," he guessed. "The parents lost their daughter and you don't want to be the one to put their son in prison."

"Maybe." She glanced toward the stairs. "I met him before. He wasn't some evil kid. He just didn't know how to relate to the world around him."

"I don't think you're taking this seriously enough."

"We'll just have to agree to disagree."

That little crease in her bottom lip kept drawing his gaze. He looked up into her eyes. "I don't do that when I'm right."

She raised an eyebrow. "Are you ever wrong?"

"Not that I can remember."

He got the quick laugh from her that he'd been aiming for. He hadn't liked the darkness on her face, the idea that she would carry the guilt over the girl's death. She had nothing to do with that. Her happy, peppy personality might have annoyed him before, but it looked good on her. She needed to go back to that.

If anyone had a past to feel guilty about, it was him. An entire family had been killed because of him: husband, wife, four kids. He pushed away the memories, rubbed the ache in his knees, even if there was nothing there but metal.

"I like modesty in a man," she observed, irony in her tone.

He almost asked what else she liked in a man, but

decided he'd better not. He needed to focus on the business at hand. "I'm going to need that envelope."

Her forehead pulled into an annoyed frown. "I know who sent it. I said I'll take care of it."

"I still need our lab to confirm whether any prints on the envelope really belong to your old stalker. Once I know this has nothing to do with my job, I'll cross it off my to-do list and you can handle it any way you want to."

"I don't need your permission to do that." But she got up and walked to the kitchen counter and pulled out an evidence bag with the manila envelope inside it. She grabbed a plastic bag from the counter, carefully transferred the photos into that and kept them. She gave him the envelope only.

He didn't feel like arguing with her for the rest. He took the bag and walked to the door. "I'll be in touch."

"Phone is good," she said.

He lifted an eyebrow as he looked back at her. "Why, it's almost as if you didn't like me, Deputy Sheriff," he said as he left her standing in her kitchen.

He walked across her small front yard, where she had almost as many garden statues as she did in the back, mostly unicorns and angels. He wondered what the story behind those was, but he couldn't wonder for long. His phone interrupted.

Rico Marquez.

"Made up your mind?" Jamie asked as he got into his car.

"Yeah, man. I got something."

"I'm on my way. Same place as before?"

"At the chop shop across the road. Come in through the back."

He hung up, then sent a text to Ryder to let him know where he'd gone. At this time of the evening there wouldn't be much traffic on the roads, but it'd still be well past midnight before he made it to San Antonio and back.

He had plenty of time to think on his way into the city. Mostly he thought about whether the meeting was a trap. But no matter which way he turned it in his head, he didn't see what reason Rico would have for taking him out. Unless his whole plea was bogus and he wanted a high-score kill to get a promotion within his gang. A possibility.

Yet the chance that he did have something on the Coyote and he was willing to share it was worth the risk. So Jamie made sure his weapons were checked and ready and that he was wearing his bulletproof vest before he pulled into the dark alley behind the chop shop and got out, sending his exact location to his team first, as insurance.

He got out of the car slowly. When he didn't immediately get hit from one of the windows, he counted that as a good sign.

The rusty steel door opened before he could knock, and Rico gestured for him to hurry inside. The lights were off in the main bay, and the smell of motor oil hung in the air. Rico led him to the office in the back but only turned on the small desk lamp there. It barely illuminated the room. The cavernous shop stretched in darkness on the other side of the glass partition.

Rico scratched his tattoo-covered neck. Pretty much

every part of him that was visible was inked, including the backs of his hands. "Anyone follow you here?"

Jamie shook his head.

"You wired?"

Jamie pulled up his shirt.

Rico's glance caught on the gun first, tucked into the waistband, before he raised his gaze to scan the rest. That they would both be armed had been understood from the beginning.

Jamie dropped his clothes back into place. "What do you have?"

Rico rubbed his fingers over his mouth. "If this checks out, I get protection? For both of us?"

"That's the deal."

The man shifted from one foot to the other. "You said you're looking for the Coyote. What for? He's bad news, man."

"Let that be my problem."

Rico measured him up. A couple of seconds passed in silence.

"Last year I was in the can," he said at last, then drew a long breath. "Enrique led the gang then. He wanted to move some of our guys down south, take over. Wanted to control both sides. He wanted to be king."

"So?" Gangs looking to expand weren't exactly big news. "Where does the Coyote come in?"

"In prison, the man in the cell next to me worked for the Coyote."

Jamie leaned forward and listened.

"He wanted revenge. The Coyote killed his brother. He said he'd pass information to Enrique, help Enrique take territory from the Coyote."

"Did he?"

"He got stabbed the next day." He banged his fist against his chest several times to demonstrate. "The guards never figured out who stabbed him, but I know. A guy called Jimenez. On the Coyote's orders."

"Where is Jimenez now?"

"Nobody knows. He went underground when he got out. Might be he was killed."

Another dead end. But there was something else here. Orders got delivered through visitors. All he had to do to find the Coyote's messenger was search the visitor records at the prison, see who'd come to visit Jimenez just before the murder. Then the messenger could lead him to the Coyote himself.

"So when do we get out?" Rico asked. "I don't want to wait. Maria's ready. Tonight?"

"Give me a couple of days to finalize everything. I'll call you to let you know how and when to come in."

The thought that they would soon have a direct link to the Coyote was enough to keep Jamie awake on the drive home, no coffee needed. Even if they couldn't dig up enough evidence to charge the man with smuggling, they would have murder one if they could prove that the Coyote had ordered the execution of that man in prison. It didn't much matter under what charge the bastard was put away, as long as he was taken out of circulation.

And, most important, once they had him, they would do whatever it took to get enough information out of him to catch the terrorists they were hunting.

He thought about that, and about Bree's stalker. He didn't like the idea of Bree in danger. She was way too nice. If some bad guy came into her house she'd be more likely to offer him coffee than shoot him between the eyes.

Yet if anyone could talk her way out of a situation with smiles and politeness, it was her. He didn't fully understand how she did what she did, but he had to admit it worked.

That was a whole different approach from how he operated. He'd been trained to identify the enemy, aim, shoot and kill. She needed someone like that to back her up, just in case.

Not that he was volunteering.

He just wanted to make sure her stalker wasn't connected to her recent cooperation agreement with his team. He hoped she was right. He hoped it was something else, a misguided regular Joe, like she'd said, and not some professional criminal sent to harass her.

He had work to do and she was a distraction. He wanted to figure out what was going on so he could close the door on the whole business and walk away from her. As soon as possible.

Chapter Six

She'd planned on going out and finding Ronny Brown
to ask him about the suspicious roll of twenties Josh had
seen him receiving, but by the time Bree dropped off
Katie at work and got to the office the morning after
Jamie's surprise visit to her house, she had a visitor
waiting. The CIA had sent an agent in response to her
call about the fake twenties.

He was a full head taller than she, clean shaven,
blond hair cropped, black suit crisp. He carried a black
leather briefcase and wore the exact kind of CIA sunglasses actors wore on TV. He had a strong jaw, straight
nose, good build.

Hot, Lena mouthed from behind him, grinning.
Looked like she wouldn't have been against a full-body
search if the opportunity presented itself. Not that she
was a lecher or anything, or someone who flitted from
guy to guy. She just had a cheerful personality and a
zest for life, and she noticed and appreciated pretty
things and hot guys and whatever else made life good
to live. She fostered rescue puppies and went skydiving
on the weekends. Working with her was fun, because

she was fun, and because she was also an extremely competent officer.

Sexy, she mouthed next with a wink.

Not as sexy as Jamie Cassidy, Bree thought. Not that she was here to check out men. Or that she was interested in either of them. But she wasn't blind. Especially to Jamie, whose dark gaze had managed to haunt her dreams all night, damn him.

The visitor nodded at her. "Deputy Sheriff."

"You must be Agent Herrera." She shoved Jamie out of her mind and returned the agent's smile as she showed him into her office. Since he was already holding a disposable cup he'd probably picked up at a drive-through, she didn't offer him coffee. "Why don't you take a seat?"

She turned on her computer, then unlocked her top drawer and extracted the three evidence bags that held the three twenty-dollar bills she'd seized so far. "I have time and date, and the circumstances of how and where the bills were obtained, including names and contact information."

"I appreciate it. It's always good to work with competent people." The agent held one of the bags up to the light and examined the banknote.

"Can you tell anything just by looking at it?"

"Just that it's pretty good quality. We'll have to run some tests. Could be leftover from an old batch we've already seized."

She thought about Ronny Brown, the clue Josh had given her. What had Josh seen in that kitchen? Somebody handing over a roll of bills. Ronny hadn't been caught with any fake money, and most vendors in town were checking. She'd put the word out right after the first case.

More likely than not, the money Ronny had received had to do with drugs. That was his usual speed. She would check him out before she said anything to Agent Herrera and look like a small-town rookie, too eager to jump the gun. The agent wouldn't appreciate having his time wasted.

And she didn't need to look like a fool just before sheriff elections. Not that she was running. Being sheriff took more time than she could give. First and foremost, she wanted to be there for Katie. But the new sheriff would be her boss, and she didn't want his first impression to be that she was an imbecile.

"You find a lot of counterfeit money?" she asked the man.

"Not that much. But when we do, we take it seriously. Out of every ten thousand dollars in circulation, about three are fake."

He glanced through the window of her office at Lena, who caught the look and smiled at him. The agent's gaze lingered.

Well, what do you know? "Will you be staying?"

"For the rest of the week." He laid his briefcase on his knees, opened it then carefully placed the three evidence bags on top of some papers before looking across the desk. "If I need a place to interview people?"

"Feel free to use our facilities." Lena could show him around.

"Thank you, Deputy." He stood. "I'll be in touch." He pulled a card from his suit pocket and set it on her desk.

"If you come across any information that might be relevant to this case, I'd appreciate it if you'd let me know."

"Of course."

He left with a parting nod.

Okay, definitely handsome, if a little dry for her taste. But Lena was a big girl and had the right to pick her own poison, Bree thought with a smile as she stood to go for coffee.

The corner of a manila envelope in her in-box caught her gaze.

Her stomach clenched.

So stupid. Now she was going to be scared of envelopes? It could be anything.

But she used her shirtsleeve to carefully tug the envelope from the pile. Unmarked, it was the same size and color as the one the photos had come in. Lumpy. *Not pictures this time.*

She stepped over to close her door, then pulled two rubber gloves from the box in her drawer and put them on before she opened the clasp.

Visual first. She peered inside and could see some kind of fabric. Dark. She carefully tilted the envelope, holding it by the corners until the contents dropped onto her desk.

Black lace panties, she registered a split second before recognizing them as hers.

Jason had been in her house. Anger and concern pulsed through her in alternating bursts, her teeth clenching.

He was getting braver. Of course, he was nine years older now—no longer the adolescent kid she remembered, but a man.

When her phone rang, she picked it up without looking at the display, her attention still on the slip of black cloth in front of her. She eased it back into the envelope in case someone came in, while balancing the phone between her shoulder and ear. "Bree."

"Just wanted to make sure you got to work fine and everything's okay," Jamie said on the other end.

Because an arrogant outsider keeping tabs on her was what she really needed. He was on some superteam. If he thought just because she was a small-town deputy and a woman she was clueless, he had another think coming. She didn't need his "protection."

"Thanks for the concern, Mr. Cassidy." She exaggerated her Texas drawl. "I might have strained my pinky, holding it out while I was sipping tea. Also, my corset pinches a little, but other than that I'm okay."

A moment of heavy silence passed. "Don't mock me." Then another pause. "And don't talk to me about corsets."

The deep timbre of his voice as he said that sent a not-altogether-unpleasant tingle down her spine. She was as bad as Lena out there with Agent Hottie. Uh-uh, not going to happen. She didn't even like Jamie Cassidy. And she had way too much going on to get tangled with a man right now.

She filled her lungs. "Is there a particular reason you're wasting my time this morning? Did your team find anything you'd like to share with me?"

"Any new contact from the stalker?"

She shoved the envelope into her top drawer. "No." She didn't want or need Jamie Cassidy's help. He was too much of a distraction.

"You hesitated."

She rolled her eyes, even though she knew he couldn't see it. "My stalker is my problem."

"Not until I'm sure he's not coming after you because you got involved with my team."

He was like a dog with a bone. She closed her eyes for a second. "He's not. I told you."

"We'll see when the envelope comes back from the lab. I'm on border patrol today. I'll stop by tonight to talk about whatever happened since I last saw you."

"Nothing happened."

"Put another beer in the fridge for me," he said before he hung up on her.

She was an upbeat person normally. She really was. But Jamie Cassidy was getting on her last nerve. If he showed up at her house tonight, they were going to have to have a serious talk about boundaries.

She was *not* going to let him keep on distracting her. She drew a deep breath and refocused on her work, then walked out of her office to check with Lena about a bail-bond issue they hadn't yet resolved from the previous week. Then she would track down Ronny Brown.

Lena was just hanging up the phone when Bree exited her office. "Discharge of a firearm at the Yellow Armadillo," she said in a "what else is new" tone.

"Bail-bond agent come in yet?"

"All taken care of."

"I'll see about the Armadillo." And off Bree went, without her morning coffee.

Traffic was light, the sky a clear blue, yet tension stiffened her shoulders. Jason was going to be trouble. And Jamie Cassidy... Not thinking of him on her drive over to the bar was more difficult than she'd anticipated. Those eyes and that fallen-angel face...

She was normally pretty good at self-control. The fact that he was rapidly getting under her skin aggravated her more than a little. She put all that away when she reached the Yellow Armadillo.

She found about two dozen guys wasting away their lives inside the dingy space when she walked in with her weapon drawn. She focused on Ronny Brown, who was standing in a group of three people in front of the bar. Okay, so maybe her day was turning for the better. Except for the small problem that two of the men had their guns drawn.

"Just the guy I want to see," she told Ronny in her calmest tone. He was the only one in the group who was unarmed, and he looked less than happy about that, his gaze darting around as he tried to find a way out of his predicament.

She flashed them all her best smile. "Gentlemen, what seems to be the problem here?"

A young Mexican guy with gang tattoos she hadn't seen before was pointing his gun at Ronny. Both their lips were bleeding. Shorty, the bartender, a grizzly ex-oil-rig worker who stood over six feet tall, was holding the mother of all rifles on them, keeping them in check.

"How about we all put our weapons down? Just as a matter of common courtesy." She was trying to set a good example by lowering her own.

Tattooed Guy swore and swung his gun to point at her then squeezed off a shot. As she ducked, not shooting back since there were people all over the bar, the bartender squeezed the trigger on his rifle. The boom made glasses rattle all over the tables and her ears ring.

But instead of hitting Tattooed Guy, Shorty somehow ended up shooting Ronny, who must have gotten in the way. Ronny went down screaming. A light hit in the leg, nonfatal, Bree registered, yelling, "Somebody call 911!" as Tattooed Guy ran for the back door.

"Keep Ronny here." She threw the words at the apologetic-looking bartender, as she took off after the gangbanger. "And, for heaven's sake, nobody shoot anyone else," she called back as she ran. "I mean it!"

She burst through the back door into a narrow alley between rows of buildings, into a wall of heat and the stench of garbage. The place hadn't grown any more pleasant since the last time she'd made a bust back here.

Tattooed Guy was dashing forward a hundred yards ahead of her, somewhat encumbered by pants that had been below his waist earlier but now were slipping lower. Not the first time she was grateful for the stupid pants-on-the-ground fashion. It was definitely a boon for law enforcement.

"Stop! Police! Drop your weapon!"

Instead, he shot back over his shoulder.

The bullet slammed into the wall next to Bree, sending wood slivers spraying. She felt a sharp sting at her neck but didn't bother to check. Injuries would have to wait until later.

Feet set apart, she braced both hands on her weapon. *Aim. Shoot. Bang.*

She took the shot without emotion, the only way to do it—no aggravation now, no anger, nothing but the job. The man sprawled onto the gravel face-first, sliding another foot or two, carried by his momentum. He was going to leave some skin behind, she thought as she ran forward.

She'd hit him on the back of his right arm. Blood leaked from the sleeve of his T-shirt. But he pushed himself up, ready to run again.

Too late. She was on top of him by then.

"You have the right to remain silent," she started, and kept on going with his rights as she tied his hands behind his back, ignoring his moaning and complaining, yanking him up just as he progressed to threats.

Fortunately for him, she was a good enough shot to have caused only a light injury. Unfortunately for her, that meant he was well enough to dish out a heap of verbal abuse.

"Hey! Is that any way to talk to a lady? You kiss your mother with that mouth?" She had a badge and she had a gun. She didn't need to take sass from anybody.

She got him back to the bar but pretty much had to shove him the whole way. The bartender still had Ronny at gunpoint. Ronny sat on the floor, pale and looking as if he was in shock, holding his bloody thigh with both hands.

She looked around at the patrons, most of whom had gone back to drinking and talking, although they were keeping an eye on her and the proceedings. "Anybody else hurt?" she called out.

"Nah."

"No, ma'am."

The replies were all negative.

She shoved Tattooed Guy onto a chair and made sure he wasn't bleeding heavily enough to bleed out before the ambulance got there. Then she hauled Ronny up and cuffed him before letting him drop back down to the floor.

She glanced over her shoulder. "Dammit, Shorty, put that rifle away. I got this. They're not going to cause any more trouble." She searched the men's pockets and dropped the contents into separate evidence bags: money, bullets, cigarettes. The stranger was Angel Rivera, according to his driver's license.

She turned back to the rest of the patrons when she was done. "All right, cowboys, start lining up for your witness statements."

She called Lena, then took statements painstakingly, had each person sign theirs, not that she got much out of them. Ronny and Angel had apparently been sharing a drink in one of the more secluded booths when they'd started arguing. Then Angel had fired a shot at Ronny before Shorty took matters into his own hands and restored the peace.

Lena arrived at about the same time as the ambulance. Bree let her take over Shorty and the witnesses while she went to the hospital with the two men.

She started grilling them while waiting for the E.R. doc. No sense in wasting time. There'd be a dozen new things waiting for her when she got back to the office. Crime didn't take a break just because she got busy.

She started with Ronny. "Want to tell me what that was about?"

The man shrugged.

"The Angel guy looks like bad news to me. He disliked you enough to take a shot at you. And that was before. Now he's going to the can for it. How much you think he's going to like you when he comes out?"

Ronny stayed silent.

"Looks like a gangbanger to me. You know his type. They come with a lot of close friends, and revenge is their middle name."

Ronny was beginning to look nervous, squirming on the bed—a good start. A little more motivation and he would probably break.

"I don't like outsiders coming into my town, causing trouble," she said, hinting that she was willing to take Ronny's side on this.

That seemed to help.

"He says I owe him money," Ronny said at last, then swore colorfully and at length. "Lyin' bastard. I ain't owe him nuthin'."

"Where is he from? I haven't seen him around here. His tattoos don't look familiar." She knew most of the gang tattoos for the groups that were active in her county.

"San Antonio."

"I don't like it," she said, half to herself, half to the man. San Antonio gangs moving down this way was the kind of trouble she didn't need. "Are you getting into something over your head, Ronny?"

His shoulders sagged, his expression turning miserable. "My leg hurts."

"I know. They'll look at you in a minute." She patted his arm. "Look, I got enough problems already. CIA's here, pain in the neck. They're investigating all that counterfeit money business. I got my hands full.

How about we clear this up right fast and we all go our own way?"

His gaze cut to hers, panic crossing his face. "CIA's investigatin' here? In Pebble Creek, you mean?"

"Yeah." She shrugged. "They take counterfeiting seriously. Thing is, you've kind of been implicated. I've been looking for you, actually."

He cast a desperate glance around, opened his mouth, closed it, opened it again. "I have nothin' to do with it, I swear."

She nodded. "Then none of the bills I took off you will have any trouble going through the scanner? You know I'm going to have to check them."

He froze, panic written all over him. Then Angel cleared his throat on the other side of the green divider and Ronny caught himself, sat up a little straighter in the propped-up bed. "I don't know anything about that."

"I have an eyewitness."

He closed his eyes and grimaced, then, after a moment of hesitation, lifted his hands, palms out. "It was all Angel, I swear," he said, obviously having come to a decision. He was more scared of the CIA than his gangbanger associates, apparently.

Something rustled on the other side of the green divider hanging from the ceiling. "Shut up," Angel called over, his tone plenty threatening.

"I'll get to you, Mr. Rivera. You just hang in there," she told the man and made sure she didn't turn her back to him.

He could try to grab her—even with one hand cuffed to the bed—if he was stupid enough to go for it.

She made sure she was ready for anything as she

tried a few more tricks with Ronny, but he really did seem to be clueless. He got the bills from Rivera, and that was all the information he had.

When she was done with him, Bree pulled the divider open and stepped over to the other bed. "How about you continue the story? Ronny got the money from you. How did you come by it? You just took a shot at me. That's assaulting a police officer. You want to be very helpful now." She waited.

"No hablo inglés."

"Yo hablo español. See? It's your lucky day." She flashed him her nicest smile, even though she didn't feel like it.

But Angel just stared daggers at her and wouldn't answer any questions no matter what language she asked them in or what she promised or threatened. If looks could kill, she would have been lying at the foot of the bed in a sticky, red puddle.

She kept on until the doctor finally showed up to check on the men. While he did that, she stepped outside and called the CIA agent to fill him in. Now that Ronny had confirmed a connection to the fake money, she had something solid to pass on to the agent.

She might not have gotten a ton of information, but they were one step closer to the source of the bad money. Progress.

Agent Herrera could come and see if he might get further with the two dimwits if he felt like it. She also called Delancy to stay with Rivera until the man could be taken into custody. She needed to get back to the office and take care of other business.

BORDER PATROL WAS a bust: no movement all day. Jamie used some of the time to call the lab to check on Bree's envelope. Several times. They had a partial print, too smudged to be of much use, but they were trying to digitally enhance it before running it through all the databases again.

At least he made some progress with setting up witness protection for Rico Marquez and his girlfriend, calling around to make sure all the pieces were in place for a problem-free extraction.

He could have left it to the U.S. Marshals Service; they ran the program just fine. But he'd given Rico a promise, so he made sure he kept an eye on the process and was part of the decisions. He sure hoped Rico would have something usable for him in exchange.

When his shift was over, Jamie swung by his apartment—a utilitarian, sparsely furnished space he basically only used for sleeping—took a shower and changed before heading over to Bree's place. He checked the perimeter first. She kept her property tidy, as did the rest of her neighbors. Seemed like a nice, family kind of neighborhood. She should have been safe enough here.

When he was sure all was clear and nobody suspicious was hanging around, he walked up to the front door and knocked.

"I should have locked you up for that fake twenty and all those weapons," she said as the door opened. "Just to keep you out of my hair."

She wore a pink T-shirt with jean shorts, her long shapely legs making his mouth go dry as they caught his attention, his brain barely registering the words she was saying. Then he blinked and caught up.

"You think of me and you think of handcuffs?" He wanted to see her off balance for once. "A man could take that as encouragement."

But she just burst out laughing.

She was way too cheerful by half. Thing was, he kind of liked it. He'd lived in darkness for so long, she felt like sunshine on his face.

As she lifted her chin, he caught sight of a bandage on her neck and his whole body went still, his protective instincts plowing forth like a steam engine. "Are you hurt?"

She raised a perfect eyebrow. "Chill. Just a scrape. The bullet didn't even hit me."

He didn't like the thought of a bullet anywhere near her. He wanted to ask how it'd happened, but he was interrupted.

"Who is that?" came a call from somewhere in the house.

He had thought they would be alone, that her sister would be asleep by now.

"That's Katie, my sister. She stays up late to watch her favorite shows on Fridays." Bree eyed him with hesitation.

He had no doubt she wanted to kick him out. But she was too much of a lady to do it—the beauty of Southern hospitality.

"It's been a long day." He piled it on. "Hot out there on that border. I sure could use a cold drink."

Her sister stepped into the foyer and stopped, her eyes fixed on Jamie. She looked a lot like Bree in her coloring but shorter and slighter. She wore jeans and a T-shirt with a pink unicorn in the middle.

"Katie, this is Jamie, a friend from work," Bree said.

"Are you a police officer?" She watched him without blinking, as if she had X-ray vision.

"Kind of," Jamie answered. "How are you, Katie? Nice to meet you."

"I'm watching my show," she said after some time, then padded away, barefooted on the Mexican terracotta tile.

"She likes you," Bree said, a frown smoothing out on her forehead. "If she didn't trust you, she would have stood there until you left to make sure you were out of our space."

He followed her into the kitchen, spacing out a time or two when his gaze slipped below her waist. Those shorts should be illegal. Then again, she was wearing them in the privacy of her home. He was the idiot for coming here and asking for trouble.

Katie paid little attention to them, sprawled on the rug on the living room floor in front of the TV, watching some crime show as intently as if she was memorizing every word.

Bree brought him a cold beer, along with a glass of orange juice for herself as they sat down, the same as before.

She caught his gaze on Katie. "Autism. She's very high functioning. She really doesn't need a lot of help," she said with a proud, loving glance toward her sister, not as someone who was bitter or embarrassed. "She's as good as you and I in a lot of things, and in some things she's better."

He wouldn't doubt it. "You're lucky to have each other."

She tilted her head, her shoulders relaxing. "Most people say she's lucky to have me." She watched him for a second or two. "They don't know anything."

"I have seven brothers and a sister."

She muttered something that sounded like, "God help the women of the world," under her breath.

He added a silent amen. His brothers were... His gaze slipped to her legs. With a view like that, who could think about his brothers?

"Seven brothers and a sister," she repeated, sounding more awed than snarky this time around. "That must be great."

It was, even if he'd spent the past couple of years pushing his family away. He'd been in a dark mood after he'd come back from Afghanistan without his legs.

"We have our moments."

He didn't ask if she was from a big family. He'd read her file. She only had Katie. Her parents had both passed away a decade ago in a house fire. He glanced at Katie, who was watching her show, completely mesmerized. "You're close."

Part of him envied that connection. He'd had that before. And he couldn't blame anyone for losing it. He'd been the one to push his family away.

"That's the best part of having a sister." She was smiling, but a shadow crossed her eyes.

"And you would want to keep her safe." He came around to the purpose of his visit. "So if there was anything strange going on, you'd tell me."

She straightened in her chair. "I don't need your protection. Seriously, Jamie, you're handsome and all, have that whole warrior thing going, but we have to stop meeting like this."

She thought he was handsome? That tangled up his thought process for a few seconds. "Where would you like to meet?" A certain part of him was voting for her bedroom.

"On the phone when you call to update me on what your team is doing in my town," she said deadpan.

She was a tough nut to crack. Good thing he didn't mind a challenge. "How about your case? Any progress with the counterfeit money?"

"The CIA is here." She gave a small shrug. "I caught two guys today who are connected. One doesn't know anything, the other one isn't talking."

His gaze slipped to her neck again, the muscles in his face tightening as he reached out and touched the edge of the bandage for a second before drawing back. "You had a tough day. Might as well tell me about it. Chances are, if I get what I came for, I'll leave faster. I want to know about what's going on with your stalker."

She rolled her eyes at him. But then her face grew somber as she thought a little before saying, "I got another envelope today."

His body tensed as he watched her closely. "More pictures?"

She shook her head. "Something more personal. He took something from the house this time."

His fingers tightened on the cold bottle. "He's escalating. He came in. He's getting closer."

"I don't think he'll make contact. He didn't before."

Which meant absolutely nothing. "What did he take?"

"None of your business."

He had to ask. "Anything that could be considered sexual?"

She nodded with reluctance.

Anger cut through him. "You know what that usually means in cases like this. He wants you and he hates you at the same time. It's not a good combination."

"I know. I thought about that. He was an adolescent boy the first time he became obsessed with me. Now he's all grown-up."

He turned that over in his head a couple of times, considering the implications. "Why come back now, after all these years?"

"He's been living with his parents until recently. He took off without notice. I'm guessing he stopped taking his meds."

More bad news. "What if he pushes even closer?"

"I'm a trained officer of the law. I'm always armed. Katie is never home alone. If I have to go back to the office for something, Eleanor, our neighbor, comes over. And Jason is not after Katie, anyway. He's after me. He just wants to scare me and have a good laugh about it. He gets off on showing how clever he is."

"You're sure it's Jason Tanner?"

"Pretty sure."

He hoped so. A messed-up average Joe would be easier to handle than if the smugglers, ruthless killers, were coming after her.

"You got the envelope for me?"

She got up and brought it to him with a resigned shake of her head.

"Whatever he took is still inside?"

"Not a chance, buster."

Of course, the more secretive she was, the more his imagination tortured him. He watched her from across the table, held her gaze. There were enough sparks between them to set her kitchen on fire.

He wasn't sure what to do with all that heat. He'd never wanted anyone with this intensity before. He would have liked to think he had enough self-control to not cross certain lines, but the hell of it was, he wasn't sure.

"I'm not relationship material," he said, just so they understood each other. If anything were to happen, he wanted her to be forewarned.

She flashed him an amused look. "Good thing I'm not looking for a boyfriend. I'm not looking for a man at all, in fact." She tilted her head. "Your being here is more like harassment than a date. We're clear on that, right?"

"I don't want you to be upset."

"Because you don't want to be my boyfriend? I think I'll live."

"I meant if we end up sleeping together."

She was just taking a sip of her juice, which she coughed up, some of it through her nose. She grabbed for a napkin and dabbed her face, then wiped the droplets of juice off the table. "You think we're going to sleep together?" She looked at him, bewildered.

She'd never looked sexier.

"I'm pretty sure," he said miserably, with all the resentment he felt. She was the one who'd barged into his life at that bookstore. He hadn't asked for any of this.

"No."

"Okay." He nodded. "That's good." He didn't need that kind of grief.

BRIANNA TRIDLE, THE most beautiful woman in the world, had a guy in her house.

The man watching her from the outside didn't like that. His hands tightened on his camera as he observed through the kitchen window, hidden in the darkness. Clouds covered the moon, and he'd picked a good spot, wedged between two tall bushes. He was good at hiding. He was good at a lot of things. He didn't care if people called him stupid.

Brianna was inside in the light. She was pretty. He wanted more pictures of her. He liked looking at her. He always had. But he didn't want pictures of her with the other man.

She belonged to him. She was supposed to be waiting for him. He'd come back to forgive her. But she was betraying him.

Rage washed over him so hard it had him grinding his teeth.

The doctor said he had to control his rage. The doctor said a lot of things. He didn't like the doctor. He wanted to do what he wanted to do, and not what other people told him.

Chapter Seven

Tracking down Jimenez—Jamie's one lead to the Coyote—proved to be a difficult task. He'd been released from prison two months before, unfortunately, current location unknown. Jamie was running down leads all day, calling Jimenez's family and dropping in on his known associates, trying to get a bead on him.

Nobody knew where he was or, if they did, they weren't telling. He drove back to the office in a bad mood, which didn't improve when the first thing he heard was, "Why the long face? Deputy Hot Chick slapped the cuffs on you again?"

Shep grinned at him from behind his computer. "She can do a full-body search on me anytime she wants," he finished.

"Beauty Queen Babe?" Keith joined in, coming from the back with his coffee. "Oh, man. She's a walking fantasy."

"Watch it before you get lovebug fever," Shep shot at Keith. "It's going around in the office."

He wasn't lying. Ryder and Mo, two guys as tough as they came, had recently been bitten.

"You look at a woman too long, next thing you know

you're shopping for a ring," Shep warned Keith, the youngest man on the team.

"Not me, old man," Keith vowed as he plopped into his chair. "Spending your life with one person is like… medieval. Who does that anymore?"

Keith had a playboy side. He was young and full of energy, and had the looks to pull it off. Jamie had seen women walk up to him and hand over their phone numbers on more than one occasion when they'd been in town together, running down leads.

Not that Jamie'd had any trouble in that department, either, before. He'd meant to get married. Coming from a big Irish family, marriage and kids had always been the assumption, the expectation, even. He'd been in love, or he'd thought he'd been. He'd been on the verge of getting engaged.

Then he'd come home without his legs and given Lauren her freedom back. She hadn't protested. And her leaving hadn't destroyed him.

He hadn't been seriously interested in anyone else until now. Good thing he and Bree had been able to clear the air between them. There was some attraction, fine, but neither of them wanted to see where it might lead.

They both had other things to do. They were both content with the way things were. Big relief.

He booted up his laptop and let Shep and Keith argue over the merits of serial dating. He tuned them out when he saw that he'd been emailed the prison visitors' log for the day he'd requested. Since he couldn't find Jimenez, he had to figure out who carried the hit order to him from the Coyote.

But as he opened and scrolled through the file,

he soon realized that the logs weren't overly helpful. Jimenez had had two visitors on the morning of the day when he'd killed the inmate who'd been about to betray the Coyote.

Neither of the visitors were fellow gang members, but a priest with a prison reach-out program, and Jimenez's girlfriend, Suzanna Sanchez. Jamie checked the address given in the log—San Antonio—looked up the phone number online and made the call.

"I'd like to talk to Suzanna," he said when the line was picked up on the other end.

"Wrong number." The male voice sounded elderly.

He confirmed the address and was assured he'd gotten that right. And after a few moments of conversation, it became apparent that he was calling an apartment building where tenants rotated in and out on a regular basis.

He thanked the man and hung up, entered Suzanna's full name and last known address as well as approximate age into the most comprehensive law enforcement database he had access to. He had a new address and new phone number within seconds. As luck would have it, she was living farther south now, less than twenty miles from Pebble Creek.

This time he hit the jackpot.

"I need to talk to you about your boyfriend, Jimenez, ma'am."

"You found the bastard, ay? You gonna make him pay child support now?" She misunderstood him.

He didn't correct her assumption. "Could I stop by so we could talk in person?"

"*Sí.* I'm at home. Where else would I be? He left me

with three *niños*. I can't afford no daycare to go work no more." She went on cursing Jimenez both in English and Spanish.

Keith was still trying to convince Shep of the beauty of open relationships. Jamie tracked down information about Jimenez's other visitor, the priest, via the internet, grabbed his address, too, then took off to see Suzanna.

She lived in an immigrant neighborhood where people ran into their houses when they saw Jamie's truck roll down the street. They were afraid of immigration. He slapped his fake CBP badge on. Better if they think he was here checking on her immigration status than if they thought she was snitching on her old boyfriend to law enforcement. Jimenez was a hard-core gang member. His buddies wouldn't take well to traitors.

He checked his gun before he got out, then walked to the patched-up trailer that looked like it was on its last legs; the roof was repaired with corrugated steel, the siding was missing in patches. One good storm and the thing would collapse. He didn't like the idea of little kids living in a place like that.

When he knocked, a young woman in her early twenties came to the door with a baby on her hip and two toddlers clinging to her legs. She wore thrift-store clothes, nothing but suspicion on her face.

Her gaze slid to his badge.

"I'm green-card citizen," she said. "My children all born here."

"May I come in, ma'am?"

She stepped aside to let him in and closed the door behind them. She didn't ask him to sit. "You said you wanted to talk about loco bastard Jimenez."

"When was the last time you saw him?"

"In the spring. I went to visit him in prison. Told him I needed money for the *niños*."

"Was that all you discussed?"

"He said he give me money when he free. But he never came here when he got out, not even a once." Frustration tightened her voice, tears flooding her eyes. "He's no good *hombre*. You see him, you tell him I want to put knife in his heart."

The anger seemed sincere. "Did anyone ask you to take him a message?"

"No, *nada*. He no family here. His mother lives in Mexico. His brothers all shot dead." She crossed herself.

"How about his friends?"

She rolled her eyes. "He no let me meet no friends. He's jealous man. He hit me if mailman brings package to door. He wants me to him only. Much love before." She shook her head. "Now he want me no more."

He stayed for another twenty minutes, asking what she knew about Jimenez's job, his friends, the people the man hung out with. He asked about messages in prison again, but she knew nothing and he believed her. She didn't seem like a seasoned criminal, just a woman on the edge after making too many bad choices.

Jamie ran the information he had so far through his head as he walked to his car. Jimenez executed one of the Coyote's men in prison, one who'd been on the brink of betraying the Coyote. Jimenez was one of the Coyote's men, but couldn't be found. If Jamie caught the messenger who took him the hit order, that guy could lead him to the Coyote instead.

Jimenez's girlfriend didn't pan out. Jamie drove up

to see the priest at the mission next, which was nothing but an abandoned pizza store in a strip mall.

The front windows were busted, possibly shot out, now patched up with cardboard. Father Gonzales, an older man sitting inside, sported a blue sling, but his face immediately stretched into a smile as Jamie walked in.

Jamie introduced himself then gestured at the windows with his head. "Rough neighborhood?"

"We do gang rescue," the sixty-something priest said. "The gangs don't like it. The Lord's work is not always all puppies and rainbows, I'm afraid."

The priest seemed to have a good sense of humor about it, even if sitting in a storefront unarmed while ticking off some of the most ruthless criminals in the state didn't seem like a smart plan to Jamie. He kept his opinion to himself. He asked about Jimenez instead.

The priest remembered him. "A troubled young man. Yet so much to live for. All things can be forgiven."

"Did you try to convince him to leave his gang? Is that what you were talking about when you went to visit him in prison?"

"That and Jesus. You'd be surprised how many of these young men wear the cross. I try to convince them to live by its principles. We talked about that and his children's future."

"Do you keep in touch? Have you talked to him since his release?"

"No." He sounded genuinely saddened. "I'm afraid I wasn't good enough. We might have lost him. But the Lord doesn't give up on anyone. And neither will I."

"You might be fighting a losing battle, padre."

But the old man smiled with full conviction. "That

cannot be. It's too important a battle to lose. There are thirty thousand gangs in this country, did you know that? Eight hundred thousand gang members. Do you know what the life expectancy is for these young men?" He paused for a second before he went on. "Twenty years. Just enough to leave some orphans behind."

The sad truth. "Jimenez has three small kids."

The priest shook his head. "I lost contact with the mother. I would have liked to help her. She moved at one point. I think paying the rent is difficult for her."

Jamie considered him. He seemed like a good guy. "I can give you their new address. They looked like they could use a little help."

He talked to the priest some more to get a better feeling for him. He definitely seemed to be the genuine article, believing in what he was doing, even willing to give up his life for the men he was trying to save. Jamie couldn't see him passing a kill order.

But then, who?

Could be the order hadn't gone straight to Jimenez. It could have gone to one of his buddies inside, then passed on to him. Who did Jimenez hang with in prison?

Rico Marquez might have the answer. And he wanted that new chance through witness protection enough to cooperate.

Jamie called him on the drive back to Pebble Creek but Rico didn't pick up his phone. He'd have to try again later.

He returned to the office just in time to go out on patrol with Shep.

"I'll meet you by the river," he told his teammate

as they got into their cars. "I need to check on something first."

He wanted to drive by Bree's place to make sure everything was okay there. He tried to make a habit of doing a drive-by check every time he was passing within a few miles of her house.

Not because he liked her. She was annoyingly cheerful. She fought crime by being nice. What was that? Utter nonsense. She was a disaster waiting to happen. That was the only reason he was checking on her. *Not* because he cared or had more than a passing interest in her.

Yet his blood ran cold as he turned the corner and saw the police cruisers lining her street.

Her front yard was destroyed. Tire marks crisscrossed her rock garden, her collection of garden statues scattered around in pieces. Violence and destruction hung in the air.

He noted her car in the driveway as he came to a screeching halt and jumped out, Officer Delancy running to block his path. He was about to shove the woman out of the way when Bree appeared in the doorway.

She had a tight look on her face, her beautiful smile missing. "It's okay. You can let him pass."

He hurried to her, assessing the damage, trying to figure out what he'd missed. "What the hell happened here? Why didn't you call me?"

"Just got home. I have to get back inside. Katie is upset." She turned back in.

When he followed her, she didn't protest.

"We need to talk." They needed to have a serious discussion. Her stalker was progressing from bad to worse pretty fast. He'd gone from watcher to invader to violent attacker in the space of a few days.

Whether she wanted to admit it or not, she was in serious trouble.

BREE WATCHED AS Katie rocked herself in the living room, tears rolling down her sweet face.

"The unicorns are broken," she repeated.

The mess outside was a major disruption in her life, and she didn't deal well with disruption.

Bree wanted to give her a hug, and she could have used a hug herself, but Katie didn't like when people touched her in general, and she didn't allow anyone to touch her at all when she was upset like this.

"What can I do to help?" Jamie asked quietly behind her.

"She's—" Bree folded her arms around herself, her throat burning. "Those statues are pretty much the only thing we have left of Mom. She made her own molds. It was her hobby. She made all those unicorns because they're Katie's favorite."

She drew a slow breath and let her arms down. She needed to be strong and to take charge. They couldn't get stuck in this terrible moment. They had to keep moving forward, get past it.

"How about we get ready for dinner?" she called to Katie, trying to sound as cheerful as she possibly could. "Let's start cooking." They needed to get back to their regular schedule. The familiar chores would offer comfort.

"You need to go someplace safe," Jamie said in a low voice that only she would hear.

She'd thought about that already. "I don't know if Katie could handle that right now. She's not good with change under the best of circumstances. I asked for police protection. We should be okay here as long as we have that."

"You need something 24/7."

She shook her head. "That might be overkill, I think. Jason has done what he set out to do—he scared us. I really don't think he'll come back."

He frowned at that assessment. "And if he does?"

"I can handle things when I'm home. If I have to go in and leave Katie with Eleanor, there'll be a cruiser sitting by the curb with an officer." Bree had responsibilities at the station. Her job didn't always conform to a nine-to-five schedule.

Jamie was watching her with worry in his eyes. "What can I do?"

She searched his face. He seemed to genuinely care. She didn't want to be touched by that, but she was, anyway. "I don't know."

"But you'll let me know?"

Why? They weren't friends. They were nothing to each other. And yet, she nodded.

"I have to go on patrol."

"Go. There's nothing you can do here right now. It's all over." She hoped.

He didn't look convinced. He left her with a dark look on his face. Through the window, she could see him check over her yard and talk to Delancy before he got into his car and drove away.

"Everything's okay," she told Katie. "We'll fix this. We always fix everything, right? We're the superteam."

They'd gotten through worse, like their parents' deaths in the fire.

Yet whatever they'd faced in the past, they'd never been in physical danger.

She went to the kitchen and started preparing dinner. Regaining normalcy was the key. "How about you set the table?" she asked Katie again. They needed to get back to the mundane. She needed to settle Katie down before she could start thinking about how to solve their problems.

She wanted to be out there, securing the crime scene, taking tire casts, looking for prints and clues. But her sister would always come first.

She could hear her front door open. Probably Delancy. She called out, "Back in the kitchen."

"Just me." Her neighbor, Eleanor, shuffled into view, wearing one of those ankle-length flowery dresses she preferred. She was in her sixties, kind faced with pixie-cut hair and lots of artsy jewelry.

She always cheered Katie up, as she did now. Katie stopped rocking as soon as she saw her.

"How are you, Katie, sweetie?" Eleanor asked her.

"Somebody killed my unicorns."

"Oh, I don't think so, honey. Unicorns are magic. I bet they're just sleeping."

The distress on Katie's face didn't ease. "Magic doesn't work. It's a trick."

"Sweet mackerels, did you hear that nonsense on TV? You just wait. Unicorn magic is special." She winked, pulling a bag from behind her back. "Guess what I brought you?"

"Chocolate-covered pretzels!" Katie sounded excited at last. Then turned to Bree. "I can't eat dessert before dinner."

"That's right." Not that she wouldn't have let Katie eat absolutely anything to cheer her up, but rules were an important thing for them, something that provided Katie with stability in a world she didn't always understand.

"Here." Eleanor gave Katie the bag. "You keep this safe until after dinner. You're in charge. Somebody has to be the boss, right?"

Katie looked pleased about that.

Eleanor walked out into the kitchen. "How can I help?" she asked Bree.

"I think we're good. She's calming down. But I'm not looking forward to her going outside tomorrow morning and seeing the destruction again. She's going to Sharon's house to hang out." Sharon was Katie's oldest friend. They'd grown up together, and now they worked together.

She looked from Katie back to Eleanor. "Thank you for calling the station."

Eleanor reached a hand to her chest. "He was crazy. Shook me up." She shook her head. "Plowed right through the lawn with his big pickup. And then back and forth, back and forth. Sweet mackerels." She sank into a chair as if just thinking about it drained the strength from her. "Had to be drunk as a warthog."

"Did you see his face?"

"Young guy. I already told Officer Delancy. Honestly, I was too far away to get a good look at him. And he was turning back and forth, backing over things. Was he on drugs, do you think?"

"I don't know. But we'll definitely find him." Bree pulled a pizza from the freezer and popped it in the oven. "Why don't you stick around for a slice?"

"Don't want to be in the way." But she looked pleased as peaches at the invitation.

She lived alone, not that she was lonely. She had a flock of girlfriends and they were always off to some garage sale here or a flea market there. They had big dreams of finding something rare and making a big splash on *Antiques Roadshow*. Half of them were in love with the furniture-expert twins.

"You know we love you. And we love your company," Bree told her.

So she made the pizza, tossed a salad to go with it and they all ate together, and shared the chocolate-covered pretzels before Eleanor went home. She liked to turn in early.

Bree watched Katie's favorite prime-time crime shows with her and opened a new puzzle to keep them busy during commercial breaks. When Katie remembered the statues and got upset again, Bree gently guided her back to the picture they were putting together piece by little piece, a modern-art painting titled *Sisters*.

Not until Katie was asleep did Bree go out to Delancy. The others were gone by then, Delancy taking night shift for the protection detail. She didn't have much information, just that the forensic teams had done a good job and they should have something by the next day.

So Bree went back inside. She wanted to stay close

to Katie. Sometimes, when she went to bed upset, Katie had nightmares.

Bree thought about the attack, about how serious the danger was that they were in, about what she could do if things escalated further. While she'd been telling the truth when she'd told Jamie she didn't expect this to get any worse, she was smart enough to know that it paid to have a plan B, just in case.

If they needed to go somewhere for a while... She needed to make plans ahead of time, start talking to Katie about it now, prepare her that they might be leaving. Jamie would approve. He seemed to have been genuinely worried about them.

He seemed to always be here, whether she wanted him to or not. Not that long ago, she'd found that aggravating. But today, his checking up on her had felt nice, actually.

And then, since she'd thought about him just before bed, of course, she dreamed about him. In her dream, she definitely wanted him. She wasn't even surprised that he was the first person she saw in the morning when she looked out her window as she brushed her teeth.

Chapter Eight

It looked as if he'd come here straight from his shift on the border. He'd definitely been there for a while, because half the statues had been repaired and were back in one piece. The front yard no longer looked as if someone had swung a wrecking ball around. Huge, huge improvement compared to the night before. Bree couldn't believe her eyes.

She ran a brush through her hair, then checked in on Katie, who was still fast asleep. They didn't have to get up early on Saturdays since neither of them worked. She threw on a pair of jeans and her favorite red tank top, jumped into flip-flops and hurried outside.

Boy, it was getting hot already. But with Jamie there, she didn't spend much time thinking about the weather. He had a way of commanding a person's full attention.

"Thank you," she said as she reached him. He didn't have any new bruises, didn't look like he'd been in any fights last night with smugglers.

"You're messing up your lines," he said as he straightened, his clothes covered in dust. "Usually you ask me what the hell I'm doing here."

She made a face. "It's so unmanly to cling to the past like that."

And he almost smiled, which was big progress for Jamie Cassidy. He wasn't exactly the type one would expect to break out in a song and dance. Although if he did, she'd definitely watch.

"Thank you," she said again as she examined his handiwork. She could barely see the cracks. He'd fitted everything back together nearly seamlessly. There was something sexy about a man who knew how to do stuff. As far as she was concerned, competence had always been an aphrodisiac. "How do you know how to do this?"

"My grandfather was a mason, came over here from Ireland. I helped him build all kinds of things when I was a kid. He used to hire me in the summers. We worked on a couple of old churches together." He brushed a mortar-looking plop of white off his knee. Not that it made a difference. He was pretty much covered in grime.

She was a Texas country gal. Dirt never bothered her.

He wore dusty blue jeans and a black T-shirt with a sweat stain on his chest. Who knew sweat could be so sexy? Her gaze caught on his bulging biceps as he lifted a chunk of unicorn back onto its pedestal.

A decade ago, the kitchen fire that had killed her parents had taken the house. A tragic, freak accident. Katie had been on her first sleepover at Sharon's place. Bree had been away at college.

The fire marshal had said afterward that it looked like their mother had been overcome by smoke at the top of the stairs. And their father wouldn't leave the house without her. He was found with his arms around her, protecting her to the end.

The house had been the least the Tridle sisters had lost that day.

Everything had to be rebuilt, an exact same replica of the old house for Katie's sake. Bree had even replaced the furniture with similar pieces. She'd done a fair job, but it was only the statues that were part of the original property. Katie treasured them. They provided good memories and continuity.

Bree watched Jamie as he worked without pause, his focus on the job. "This will make Katie happier than I can tell you."

"It's good to be moving a little after sitting in the car all night on patrol. I don't have to be at the office until noon. I should be able to finish here."

She was pretty sure between night patrol on the border and office duty he was supposed to squeeze some sleep in there somewhere. Yet she didn't have it in her to send him away. Having the statues fixed would mean the world to Katie.

"I'm making breakfast," she told him. "Why don't you come inside in a little while and have something with us?"

He watched her for a second. "Will Katie be okay with that?"

She smiled. "She will when she sees this."

And then she walked back toward the house, her heart a little lighter. She walked by Delancy's cruiser and thanked the bleary-eyed officer for her help, then sent her home to rest.

"Are you sure?"

"Jamie will be here for a while."

Delancy shot her a curious look.

"It's not like that," she said.

"Sure it isn't. He's obviously just a concerned by-stander," Delancy said with a suddenly saucy grin, then drove away with a wave.

Bree went inside and cooked breakfast: scrambled eggs with salsa mixed in, home-style bacon and skillet cakes. She put on some coffee, too. Lord knew she needed some, and she had a feeling Jamie probably did, too.

Katie came downstairs just as Jamie was entering the house.

"You're Bree's friend," she said thoughtfully. "Your name is Jamie Cassidy."

"Yes it is. Is it okay if I visit?"

"Jamie is fixing Mom's statues," Bree told her sister, and watched as Katie ran to the window, her eyes going wide. She clapped her hands at the sight that greeted her.

Bree could barely talk her into coming to the table to have some pancakes. "Come on now, or they'll get cold and you don't like that."

That did the trick. Katie ran to the table and plopped onto her chair. "Unicorns sneeze Skittles," she said, her gaze snapping back to the window every five seconds.

"Mom used to say," Bree explained. Katie had loved unicorns for as long as she could remember. Because unicorns were different, but great. Just like Katie. Not worse than other people at all, just different and special. Her mother used to say that to her when she'd been younger and asked why some kids at school made fun of her.

There wasn't much bullying. For one, Katie's teachers simply didn't stand for it. And also because they'd had a neighbor kid at the time who was in the same grade and always stood up for her. Bree had been too many years ahead of Katie to be of much help. They had never been in the same school building together.

"Skittles come from unicorns? That's awesome." Jamie was playing along.

"Only not these ones," Katie explained with all seriousness. "Because they're made of stone. And also because unicorns are imaginary. They sneeze Skittles in our imagination. Having imagination is a good thing. And Skittles are real."

"Well, thank God for that," Jamie countered, not a trace of his dark looks and surliness in evidence.

Katie nodded as she ate. During breakfast her gaze kept straying back outside, then returning to Jamie again. They stuck to small talk, mostly Katie asking questions. She was good with questions. She wanted to know everything.

She would have made a good detective. Maybe that was why she liked crime shows. She followed a different one every night, had a TV schedule she stuck to religiously. She could usually guess the killer halfway through the story.

"What kind of car do you have?" she drilled Jamie.

He told her. "It's the blue one, out by the curb." He nodded toward the window.

Katie looked, nodded, then turned back to him. "Where do you live?"

"Are you married?"

"Do you have kids?"

"Do you have a sister?"

The questions kept coming. She was impressed with the seven-brothers-and-a-sister thing.

Then it was time for Bree to take her to Sharon's house, just a few blocks away.

Jamie was still working in her yard when she came home. He was pretty close to finishing. The improvement he'd made was amazing. With some minor cleanup on her part, the front yard would be back to normal in no time.

"I'm so grateful that you're doing this," she told him. "Katie is very impressed with you, by the way. She couldn't stop talking about you to Sharon."

He shot her a questioning look.

"Sharon is a friend from work. They hang out Saturday mornings together. We don't have a big family. I want her to have friends." Especially since she worked for the police. She wanted Katie to have a support system if anything happened to her.

He put the last chunk of concrete in place and smoothed down whatever white cement mixture he was using to glue the pieces together. The unicorn looked fully recovered. Even jaunty. Her mother would approve, she thought out of the blue, and the thought made her smile.

"Why don't you come inside to clean up?" she offered.

He looked down on his clothes. "Okay. That might be good. Thanks. I'll just go out back and clean off these tools with the garden hose first."

She went with him, helped then they walked inside together. She led him to the sink in the laundry room and brought him a towel. "Anything interesting happen out on the border? I see nobody whacked you," she teased. "Must have been a slow night."

"It was pretty quiet," he said as he cleaned himself up, taking the jab in stride. "Every night is not a full-blown monkey circus, thank God."

She had stepped to the window when she'd shown him in, which she now regretted. The space was too small for the two of them and he blocked her way out as he peeled off his T-shirt, washed it under the water then hung it on a peg while he cleaned off his amazing upper body.

Oh, wow. He was incredibly built. And scarred. She tried not to stare, but was pretty much failing miserably. Water droplets gathered on his dark eyelashes, making them look even darker.

When he was done, he shrugged into the wet T-shirt.

"I could toss that into the dryer for you," she offered, finding her voice.

"In this heat, it'll dry as soon as I go back outside. Actually, a little cold feels nice. I don't mind. It's been a hot morning."

It was still pretty hot, as far as she was concerned.

He finger combed his wet hair back into place. "How is the counterfeit investigation going?"

"The CIA agent is doing his stuff. How about your op?" She was so proud of herself for still being able to think. She definitely deserved a pat on the back for that one.

"More dead ends than you can shake a stick at. I got a lead, kind of." He shrugged, the movement of his muscles accentuated by the wet T-shirt. "It's a long shot, but it's better than nothing."

Quit staring. Say something intelligent. Semi-intelligent. Okay, anything that doesn't have to do with rippling muscles.

"Did I see your car up by the mission yesterday? I was up there at the tackle shop to pick out a pole for one of the officers who's retiring. Mike. We're doing a group gift. He likes fishing," she added inanely.

He watched her for a moment as he hung up the towel to dry.

Oh, right. "You probably can't say what you were doing up there."

But he came to some sort of decision, and said, "I was running down a lead on a prison hit. Someone from the outside brought the hit order during a visit. I need to find out who. Father Gonzales was on the visitor log so I checked him out. Do you know him?"

The thought of Father Gonzales being involved in any kind of criminal activity made her laugh out loud and distracted her from his body, at last. Okay, partially distracted.

"He's as antiviolence as they get. He would give his life for you, but participate in murder?" She shook her head. "No way. I've known him all my life. I'd stake my career on it that he didn't have anything to do with an ordered hit."

"Pretty much the impression I got." He nodded, frowning. "Except, here's the thing—there were only two visitors, the priest and the girlfriend. Every instinct I have says she's clean, too. So where does that leave me?"

"The message could have been transmitted through a third party. It might have gone to another inmate first, then he passed it on to the actual hit man."

"That's what I've been thinking. I need to follow up on that today. Man, that's gonna be a time killer. It's a big prison with a ton of inmates." He didn't look happy. "We don't have extra time on this."

"What does your ordered hit have to do with the border?"

"Nothing you need to worry about."

She stepped forward, her dander rising. "I thought we've been over that. Everything that happens in my county I worry about. Does this have to do with smuggling? I could help you with that. I have a pretty good grip on the usual suspects. I know the players. Look, I've been doing this for a long time before you got here."

His gaze dipped to her lips, and she realized she might be standing too close, but she didn't want to step back and have him interpret the move as her backing down.

"It's smuggling related," he said after a moment, with a good dose of reluctance.

Oh, she thought as she recalled his team's purpose here. She narrowed her eyes. "Does this have anything to do with terrorists?"

And then he kissed her.

For a brief second, she wanted to shove him away and demand answers. And then suddenly she didn't have it in her to pull away. A small part of her knew he was probably kissing her only to distract her, but most of her didn't care.

It was sooo good. *Oh, sweet heaven.*

His lips were firm and warm on hers. She hadn't been kissed in a long time, and it'd been even longer since she'd been kissed by a guy who could make her skin tingle just by being in the same room with her.

One second it was just kind of a brushing of lips, then his mouth slanted over hers and he went for it.

Sweet mackerels, as Eleanor would say.

The heat was crazy sizzling. She wouldn't have been surprised if her hair started smoking.

Why now? Why him? He was anything but uncomplicated.

She wasn't the instant-attraction type. She didn't fall for every handsome face. She was friendly when it came to…friendship. But when things went past that… It took her forever to warm up to a guy that way.

All the instant heat now caught her by surprise.

He tasted her lips, slowly, carefully, doing a thorough job of it. By the time his tongue slipped in to dance with hers, her nipples were tingling. She was helpless to do anything but open up for him. He sank into her with a soft growl that was out-of-this-world sexy.

As he tasted her fully, all her blood gathered at the V of her thighs. And he hadn't even put his hands on her yet. She was in so much trouble here.

Her head swam. Ridiculous. Deputy sheriffs didn't swoon. It had to be against regulation. Maybe the eggs she'd made for breakfast were bad. She'd rather consider food poisoning than admit that Jamie Cassidy could undo her like this.

Desire washed over her, again and again, in everstrengthening waves. He made her want things that…

Her brain stopped. Her body took over.

Wow, okay, she missed being with a man.

HE WAS SO turned on he couldn't see straight. Lust took over his body. Testosterone flooded his brain. What few brain cells were still working were overtaken by confusion. And surprise that he could still respond to a woman like this.

He wasn't sure if he felt hopeful or resentful about his body's overwhelming response to her.

Plain and simple, she knocked him on his ass.

He wanted her now, here, hard and fast. He couldn't see beyond that.

He eyed the washer hopefully. He could lift her on top of that, wrap her endless legs around his waist. His body hardened for her. "I want you," he said in a rusty whisper as he pulled his head back a little.

"Yeah, I think I got that," she responded in a weak tone.

Her beautiful eyes were hazy with passion, turning him on even more.

He swallowed a groan. "I don't want to want you." He didn't want the complications that would come with it. He kissed her again, anyway.

It felt a lot like falling. He didn't like falling. He'd spent months falling all over his face in physical therapy after he'd gotten his new legs. Thinking of that made him think of what would come next, in a normal encounter between a man and a woman who wanted each other.

Taking off their clothes somewhere upstairs.

She melted against him. Some feeling that was a lot

softer and lighter than he was used to lately pulled him forward. He pulled back. She made him want things he didn't want to need.

SHE WAS BREATHING hard and hoping he wouldn't notice. *He didn't want to want her.* Well, other than the part of him that obviously did. Was it pitiful that she desperately wanted him, aching with need between her legs?

She was so damn stupid. She'd tried this before. It never worked. And it was her fault. She would always put Katie first and whatever guy was in her life would want to come first. Completely reasonable.

The kiss had been great, but she couldn't, shouldn't, go too far down this road with Jamie. The longer she let this go on, the more hurt she'd be at the end. One guy she'd fancied herself in love with had asked her to put Katie into a home so he could move in and they would have some privacy.

That had caught her off guard, broke her heart, made her feel stupid that she'd thought he was different than the others. And here she was, thinking the same again, about Jamie.

"I'm sorry. I shouldn't have done that." She shouldn't have kissed him back. "This is not going to work between us. It's not working for me."

He stared at her. Shook his head. "I apologize if I read you wrong."

He hadn't. He'd read everything right, had done everything right. She'd wanted him, wanted him still, even right now, wanted nothing more than to go back into his arms and be kissed silly all over again.

She was tempted beyond words to throw all caution

to the wind and just do that, let the chips fall where they may. Except she'd done that before, and the chips always fell on heartache. She was an intelligent woman. She wasn't going to make the same mistake over and over again when it came to men.

He didn't need to know that her knees were still weak from his kiss.

Quick. Say something unaffected and clever.

Not a damn thing came to mind.

Then she blurted, "Did you check both lists?"

He blinked, looking at her as if she was from another planet. "What both lists?"

"The prison keeps two separate visitors' logs. One for general visitors, the other for the attorneys and whatever. That's maintained separately. And they won't show what attorney visited what prisoner."

The heat in his eyes simmered down little by little. "That sounds stupid."

"It's to maintain attorney-client privilege," she told him, proud of herself for sounding like a professional instead of a moonstruck teenager, even if on the inside she felt more like one than she cared to admit. "Could be Jimenez's lawyer was the one who took him the hit order."

Chapter Nine

On his way home, Jamie called into the office and asked Ryder to put in a request for the new set of visitors' logs. There also had to be court records that would show who had defended Jimenez during his incarceration. They would have to jump through a couple of hoops and wait for warrants, but they could definitely get the information. *Progress in the case.*

Which was a good thing, especially since his liaison with the deputy sheriff was getting worse and worse. He was definitely going in the wrong direction with Bree. She was completely right. He'd been way off base, way out of line.

He wasn't looking for a relationship. There was absolutely no reason to stir things up with her. Good thing she had a sober head on her shoulders and saw their mistake for what it was.

He'd gotten carried away with her. It wouldn't happen again.

The kiss… He drew in a slow breath then released it as he pulled into the parking spot in front of his apartment. It wasn't going to happen again. Definitely.

Maybe she'd forget.

Maybe she barely noticed, he tried to tell himself as he drummed up the stairs. Then he swore at his own stupidity. While the kiss had been completely unprofessional, it was also utterly unforgettable.

He'd been a hairsbreadth from pushing further. Common sense, mission objective and regulation be damned, he'd wanted her, then and there, all the way. Which meant one thing: time to take a giant step back from Bree Tridle.

He showered using a plastic chair since he couldn't stand under the water, drew the blinds, went to bed. He refused to think about her or how she'd felt in his arms, but then, of course, he dreamed about her. In his dream, their interlude didn't stop with kissing. He woke a little while later in a haze of heat and lust, pulled the pillow over his face and forced himself back to sleep.

This time, his dreams turned darker. He was in the torture chamber in the hills of Afghanistan, in the cave that had been converted into a prison just for him. Outside the iron bars, enemy fighters held the family who had sheltered him after his chopper had gone down. He was the sole survivor of his team. With two broken legs.

The first week, they tortured him to gain intelligence. He resisted. The second week, they tortured the family: husband, wife and children. He almost talked then. The third week, when the family had been reduced to bloody corpses, his tormentors had turned their attention back to Jamie once again.

They moved from hooking him up to batteries to chopping off body parts. They'd leave his tongue for last, so he could tell them what they wanted to know, they'd said. Everything else was fair game. They'd started from the bottom up.

By the time he was rescued, he was mad with pain and more than half-dead from blood loss. And a different man from the one who'd taken that chopper in.

Ex-beauty queen Brianna Tridle needed a man like him about as much as she needed a shot in the head, Jamie thought as he woke, then dressed grimly and got ready to go into the office, then out on patrol again.

He needed to pull back from Bree and keep his distance.

BREE HAD JUST gotten home with Katie when she got called into work.

"Jesse called in from the liquor store. He caught a fella with a fake bill. He's holding him at gunpoint. I can handle it if you want," Lena offered.

Bree always had the weekends off so she could be with Katie. She drew a deep breath as she thought for a second, then came to a decision. "I better go. I'm supposed to liaise with Agent Herrera on the counterfeiting." She watched Katie go into the kitchen for a snack. "I'll call Eleanor over to stay with Katie. I need someone to watch the house."

"I'm on my way."

"Thanks. I appreciate it." She hung up and called Eleanor. "Any chance you could come over for an hour or so? I have to go out on a call."

"Anytime, hon," her neighbor said on the other end. "You know how much I love that sweet girl. Spending time with her is a pleasure. I'd just be sitting home all lonesome, anyway."

"You're going to run into a good man one of these days."

"I'd take the one you had out in your front yard yesterday." She chuckled. "If you tire of him, you just send him my way."

"He's not my boyfriend or anything," she started to say, but Eleanor was already ringing the doorbell. "Okay, I'm out here."

Bree opened the door and they put away their cell phones simultaneously.

"Thank you. I really appreciate this."

"Just as long as you have cookies in the cupboard." Eleanor's sweet tooth was as bad as Katie's.

"Always."

"Hi, Katie, sweetie." The older woman walked in. "I was a little lonely tonight. Mind if I come over? I like your TV better, anyway. It's bigger."

That's how they played it lately, since Katie, twenty-three now, had been asking why she still needed a baby-sitter. Bree wouldn't have hurt her feelings for the world, but she wouldn't compromise her safety, either.

"I'm going to run out for a minute. You two have fun," she told her sister. "Leave me some cookies."

Eleanor walked her to the door to lock it behind her.

"Lena will be by in a few minutes," Bree said. "I just… With the vandalism thing…"

"We'll be fine," Eleanor said. "Don't you worry about us, hon." Then she added, "So about your young man?" And watched Bree speculatively.

"It's not like that. He's just a friend."

"Honey, a man puts in that kind of labor on your

front yard and he doesn't send you a bill in the mail, it's more than friendship."

"It's not the right time for me for anything more."

"You can't still be thinking that. It doesn't have to be either Katie or a man, Bree. You're so reasonable and flexible about everything else. You know what a guy like this is called?"

"Jamie?"

Eleanor gave a quick laugh. "A keeper. Think about it."

She promised nothing, but walked to her car and got in. She glanced back at the house as she waited for Lena.

She wasn't terribly worried about safety. Jason wanted *her.* If he ever escalated to the personal-attack stage, he'd be coming after her, and she could handle him.

She waited a few more minutes. Called Lena.

"I'm five minutes away."

"All right. I'm going to get going here. I don't like the idea of Jesse holding anyone at gunpoint."

He was an ornery old geezer who'd had a father and grandfather in the bootlegging business. Jesse had cleaned up his act and took his status as the first upstanding citizen in his family seriously. He was way past retirement age. He claimed he'd owned his small store since before the flood. He protected his turf. He'd been known to put the fear of God into any kid who showed up for liquor with a fake ID.

She called Agent Herrera on her way over. "Got a new counterfeit bill. I'm on my way to pick it up and take a statement from the person who tried to use it."

"I'll drive over."

She gave him the address, then turned down Houston Ave.

A small crowd had gathered in front of the liquor store by the time she pulled up front, gawkers watching through the glass as Jesse kept a young, gangly guy pinned in place by the checkout counter.

"Deputy Sheriff." She flashed her badge, although most of the people there knew her. "Nothing to see here. Please, disperse." She got out of the car and strode straight to the door.

She wasn't scared. It was South Texas. Most everyone out in the country had a gun or two. Most knew how to use it. Jesse was cantankerous, but he wasn't a hothead.

"It's Bree. I'm coming in, Jesse."

She put her hand on the door handle, pushed it in an inch, then said again, "Jesse? It's Bree. I'm coming in."

"Come on in, darlin'. I got you one here."

"I appreciate it. How about you put the gun down?"

Jesse lowered his rifle. "You takin' him in?"

"You bet." To get the man away from Jesse, mostly. She turned to the younger guy. This one she didn't know. "I'm Bree Tridle, deputy sheriff. How about we go down to the station and talk about that twenty?"

"Yes, ma'am." The kid seemed mighty motivated, looking between the door and her.

"Do you have ID?"

The kid dug into his pocket and handed over his driver's license. Garret Jones, age twenty-two, lived a few towns over.

"All right, Garret, I'm going to take you in for a short

interview." She looked at Jesse behind the counter and gestured toward the twenty in front of him. "Is that it?"

Jesse nodded. "Yep."

She pulled a rubber glove from her back pocket, an evidence bag from the right and bagged the money. "I appreciate the call. Go easy with the gun next time. Just a call would be fine," she added, just as Agent Herrera walked in.

He looked Garret over.

"You want him?" she offered.

"You take him in," he said. "I'll ask a few questions here, then I'll be coming in, too."

"See you later, then."

"Thank you, Deputy."

She got the kid in the back of her cruiser without trouble. He didn't say a word all the way to the station. She didn't push him, either. Agent Herrera would be questioning him, although she would ask to sit in on it. Whether counterfeiting fell under the CIA's jurisdiction or not, whatever happened in her town was her business.

Another hour, she figured. Then she'd be heading back home to Eleanor and Katie. Maybe she would take them to the mall for window shopping. They were all in need of a break.

JAMIE DROVE DOWN the deserted dirt road along the border. Everything was quiet. He'd been watching the flat expanse of arid land, keeping an eye out for the slightest movement as he talked to Shep over the radio.

"Ever been in love?" The words popped out of his mouth without warning, surprising even himself.

"Repeat that?"

"You ever been in love?"

A stretch of silence followed. "I had girlfriends."

"I mean real love."

"Hell, no. Who needs that aggravation?"

Exactly. "Come close?"

Another stretch of silence. "Kind of liked someone. Didn't work out. Bad deal all around."

"How bad?"

"She cost me my job, stole my car and set my house on fire. That's all I'm going to say about that," he added gruffly. "And I'm going to have to kill you if you ever repeat it."

"Understood," Jamie said with full sympathy, sobered more than a little. This was exactly the kind of confirmation he needed. Walking away from Bree was the right thing to do. He'd known that all along. And now Shep agreed.

His phone was buzzing. He glanced at the display. "Gotta go."

The labs at Homeland Security worked around the clock, and he'd marked his evidence "contact with results immediately." They were calling back.

"All right, give me the good news," he said.

"Both envelopes were sent by the same person. Jason Tanner."

Bree's old stalker. She was right. Better this Jason guy than the alternative. At least the mess at her house wasn't connected to the smugglers.

"Thanks." He hung up, a little relieved. Her stalker had nothing to do with the smuggling. He was free to walk away.

Except, no way was he going to be able to do that,

not after kissing her, not after meeting Katie, not after seeing the destruction in her front yard.

Despite his best intentions, he'd somehow gotten tangled.

Oddly, the thought of that didn't bother him nearly as much as he'd thought it would. Bree was one of a kind. She was... All right, so he had a soft spot for her. There, he'd admitted it. Didn't mean he had to act on it. Ever again.

While that thought felt very self-righteous, it also felt incredibly depressing.

He was about to call her to let her know about the fingerprints when his police scanner came on. He caught the code first.

Fatal shooting.

Then came the address in a staticky voice, and his blood turned cold. He whipped the car around and shot down the road like a rocket, calling Shep.

"There was a shooting at Bree's place."

"Go. I can call Mo to cover for you."

"Thanks."

His car couldn't move fast enough as he flew over the uneven road, his heart thundering in his chest.

When he hit the actual paved roads and had to worry about other cars, he kept hitting the horn in warning, flying around them, putting every bit of his training to use. Then he reached her street and saw the police cars in her driveway for the second time in two days.

Caring about someone was a heart attack and a half, he decided.

He squealed to a halt and jumped out, his blood running cold as he registered the shattered living room window. He pushed his way inside, but an officer stepped in his path.

Then Officer Delancy, coming in behind him, spoke up for him. "He's with Bree."

"Where is she? Is she hurt?"

Delancy shook her head.

He could breathe again. "Katie?"

"It's the neighbor woman."

He hurried down the hallway and into the living room. An old woman lay on the floor, her chest bloodied, cops securing the crime scene.

He went in as large a circle around them as he could, ran up the stairs. "Bree?"

"In here." The words came from the back.

He caught sight of a neat master bedroom and sparkling-clean bathroom as he made his way to her, to Katie's room where Bree was sitting next to her sister on a pretty pink bed.

Katie was rocking, wide-eyed, talking too loudly. "Eleanor. Eleanor. She. She. She…"

"Shh. I know. It's okay."

Katie's gaze flew to Jamie, and the look in her pretty dark eyes broke his heart. "Eleanor is not sleeping."

"No."

"You can fix her. With unicorn magic."

"I can't, Katie. I'm sorry."

She rocked harder and moaned, ground her teeth.

He flashed a helpless look to Bree. "What happened? What can I do to help?"

She had shiny tracks on her face. She shook her head as she stood.

He walked over to her, then stopped short. He'd almost pulled her into his arms. But she didn't want that. She'd been pretty clear about it. He shoved his hands into his pockets instead. That bullet had been meant for her, he knew without a doubt, and the thought about killed him.

"I have to stay with her," she said in a low tone. "Could you go downstairs and check out what's going on? There's an address book in the top drawer of the TV stand. Could you bring that up? I want to be the one to call Eleanor's brother."

He nodded. "We're going to talk about this. It's gone too far. I'm going to upgrade your security." She might not want his kisses, but she would have his protection. He had a team. They each could spare a few hours here and there. Starting with him.

She didn't protest. A good thing, because no way was she going to talk him out of this.

"DOES IT HURT?" Katie asked.

Bree knew what she meant. "She's not hurting. It's not like when you cut your finger. There's no pain at all in death."

"She has blood. When I cut my finger, it bleeds and it hurts."

"Only when you're still alive."

"She's dead."

"Yes, she is, honey."

"Why?"

The question was killing her. *Jason Tanner.* It had to be him. And if he'd been the one to shoot that gun, then she'd been the target. She'd underestimated him, underestimated the danger he posed. But she wouldn't do that again. She was going to bring the little bastard in.

Sitting inside while other officers processed the destruction outside her house had been difficult the other day. Sitting up here while they processed the crime scene downstairs was nearly impossible. She was a cop, had been a cop for a long time. Everything she was pushed her to go, to hunt, to bring in the man who'd done this.

"Where did Eleanor go?" Katie asked. "The window broke and then she fell down. And then she wasn't there."

No, not in the lifeless body, Bree thought. Katie had always been very perceptive about things like that. Looked like the shooter had pulled up to the front and shot Eleanor from his car. An easy distance, and she'd been standing in a lit room.

"She went someplace else," she told her sister.

"I don't want her to go someplace else."

"Me, neither," she said and blinked back tears. "Do you want to turn on the TV?" She wanted to give her sister something else to think about. Katie wasn't good with emotions. Grief was hard for her to grapple with. It would take a long time and a lot of talking, a lot of getting used to.

"We don't watch TV now."

No. Their favorite shows weren't on until later. "Maybe we'll catch a rerun. Something good."

"Okay."

She turned on the TV and found a repeat episode of *Bones*. Katie liked that. Bree wanted to hug her sister, wanted to be hugged in return. She'd almost run into

Jamie's arms earlier, would have done it, but he'd held himself so obviously aloof.

She'd been the one to push him away.

And yet, the fact that he didn't pull her into his arms still hurt. The exact kind of unreasonable female logic she always hated. She wasn't a drama queen. She was a deputy sheriff. She was strong and capable. Because she'd always had to be strong and capable for her sister.

But just now, some emotional support would have been great.

A small part of her honestly regretted pushing Jamie away.

Maybe Eleanor had been right and she saw things too much in black-and-white, at least when it came to her private life. Just because her life wasn't optimal for a long-term relationship, maybe it didn't mean that she couldn't have anything.

Except it did. Because she wasn't the one-night-stand type. When she fell for someone, she fell completely, which always ended up in heartbreak.

She'd accepted that. Accepted that she would give relationships up.

But it hadn't hurt so much until today.

Jamie popped his head in, address book in hand. He handed it over. "Why don't you go take care of what you need to. I'm beat. I wouldn't mind sitting for a sec." He glanced at the TV. "Hey, that's my favorite show," he told Katie. "Mind if I watch?"

Katie shook her head seriously, and Jamie dropped to the floor in the middle of the room. He was alpha male, a warrior, a doer, the kind of man who would always be first in the line of fire and liked it that way. Yet he understood what she needed, that she needed to be there to handle this. And he pulled back so she could have it.

She moved toward the door. "Thanks." And then she left, secure in the knowledge that whatever she found downstairs, whatever else happened, nothing would get through Jamie to get to her sister.

Chapter Ten

Agent Herrera was waiting in her office when Bree walked in on Monday after she'd dropped Katie off at work.

"Heard you had trouble at home. Let me know if there's anything I can do to help," the agent said.

"I appreciate it. Get anything out of Garret about the fake twenty?"

He shrugged. "He got the money at a gas station. It checks out." He scratched his jaw. "But Angel Rivera will be a decent lead, it looks like. He's actually involved, as opposed to coming into connection with the bills unwittingly."

"Did the hospital release him yet?"

"He'll be released in an hour or so. I'm taking him into custody and back to Washington."

"Hope he'll be more forthcoming with you than he was with me."

"He'll talk. If nothing else than for a deal. We got enough on him to put him away for a while. Found a couple of dozen counterfeit bills at his place this morning. Search warrant came through, finally."

"So are the bills from an old print run, just turning up now?"

He shook his head. "New. High-tech paper and ink. We'll definitely be tracking that. I expect we'll find a serious operation."

"Any clues so far? Are bills showing up anyplace else?" She really didn't want any of this connected to her town. The last thing she needed was the CIA descending in large numbers.

"I just got a call about similar bills showing up in Arizona and New York. That's why I'm heading back to the main office. I'll be putting together a task force and widening the investigation."

"Did you find out how Angel Rivera is connected?"

"Not yet. But Rivera works in transportation. He drives a truck for a produce distributor that brings up truckloads of fruit from Mexico. His routes are all over the South and up the Eastern seaboard."

"So the origin of the money could be south of the border?" Honestly, as long as it wasn't her county, she'd be happy.

But the agent shook his head. "Could be, but unlikely. The technology on these notes is pretty amazing. It's not some handmade printing machine some Mexican farmer threw together from spare parts in his shed."

"There's a paper mill south of the border, not far from here," she told him.

"We'll investigate that to be on the safe side, but this looks like something we usually see from even farther south."

"You mean South America?"

He gave a brief nod. "I'm looking into that. I'll be in

touch. I just wanted to come in to thank you for your help. And ask for one more favor."

She waited.

"Angel Rivera has a brother in prison down here. He went in just a few weeks ago on drug charges. He used to work for the same shipping company. Any chance you could look in on him? See if you can push him into admitting to being involved? He's locked up. He'll be more motivated to talk. Maybe in exchange for a reduced sentence. Let me know if you get anything from him."

He shoved his hands into his pockets in a frustrated gesture. "I don't want to wait around, setting up an appointment with the prison when his lawyers can be present and all that. I want to get moving with this. Putting together a task force will take time and paperwork, approvals. I need to be back at the office and set up a serious op. We need to find the source of the money and stop it."

She could certainly understand that. "No problem."

"Even if the younger Rivera doesn't talk, we might be able to use him to soften Angel up a little. Maybe the older brother will give us something in exchange for a promise to make his little brother's life behind bars easier. Prison is a risky place for gangbangers. Not all who go in come out."

She nodded, thinking of the prison hit Jamie was investigating.

"I appreciate the help. We'll keep in touch." Agent Herrera walked to the door of her office, but then turned back before opening it. He watched her for a second before he said, "The other day, I was leaving here when a man was coming in. Is it possible he was Jamie Cassidy?"

Okay, she hadn't expected that question. "You know Jamie?"

"What's he doing here?"

"Consulting for CBP. How do you know him?"

"I was involved in one of his other consulting gigs," he said after a couple of thoughtful seconds.

She had a fair idea what that might have been. "At a time you can't specify, at an undisclosed location, on a mission of indeterminate nature?"

A smile hovered over the agent's lips. "Something like that."

"Was that where he lost his legs?"

The agent shook his head. "He had them there, and put them to good use. It's good to see him back in action. He was the hero of the day."

"Hero, how?"

"I'm sorry. That's confidential information."

"In generalities? I'm assisting his team with something. He's my liaison. I'd like to know what kind of man he is."

He still hesitated for a long second. "Without any specifics… There were bad guys and they land mined a whole village. Jamie's team moved in, at night…." He shook his head. "He was the rear guard. When his teammates were blown up, he rushed in, under heavy gunfire, and dragged them out one by one. He kept going back and getting hit. He didn't stop until he bled out to the point of falling unconscious in the middle of the village. But he got everyone out who could be saved."

She wondered who had saved him. Maybe reinforcements came. She wanted to ask more, but the agent lifted his hand to cut her off.

"This stays between the two of us."

And Bree nodded. "So you don't know how he lost his legs?"

"Not a clue," the agent said. "But I wouldn't be surprised if he threw himself on a grenade." And then he left to go about his business.

She sat behind her desk, thinking for a while about Jamie, about the kind of work he did. Then she set that aside and made a note to figure out what prison the younger Rivera was vacationing at presently. She was going to call his lawyer and see about an appointment to visit later. But first she needed to find Jason Tanner.

Eleanor was dead. Jason couldn't be allowed to hurt anyone else ever again.

She hadn't taken him as seriously as she should have. Her mistake. But she wasn't going to make another with the man. She was going to use every tool at her disposal, call in every favor, track every lead until she found him and put him away.

JAMIE LOOKED THROUGH the database of images he'd been granted temporary access to that morning. Bree had an APB out on Jason Tanner and his red pickup truck, but Jamie had something better: access to military satellites.

No way in hell was he going to let the bastard get within striking distance of Bree again. Jamie needed to track him to his lair.

Jason would be staying somewhere close enough to swing by to see Bree, but not in town where Bree could run into him. Jamie made the whole south part of the county his target. The satellite identified ninety-six images of pickups the color, make and model Tanner was driving, information Eleanor had given the police after the vandalism on the front lawn.

Jason would be holed up in a motel, most likely, so Jamie went after those. He identified seven matching vehicles in motel parking lots and printed the list of addresses.

"I'm off to check on something," he called out to the office in general as he stood from his desk.

Keith and Mo were on office duty, the rest of the team out on the border or following leads.

Mo looked up. "For the deputy?"

Jamie nodded.

"Let us know if we can help," Keith put in, no teasing this time.

They'd all sworn to protect and serve, and the hit on defenseless women didn't sit well with them.

"I appreciate it." He walked out and made his way to his car. He had hours before he had to go back on duty again. Plenty of time to check the addresses on his list.

He first went to the nearest motel he had marked, drove around it, found a red pickup like the one he wanted in the back, but it wasn't Tanner's. This one didn't have a scratch on it.

He was looking for one that had a smashed-in front grill, at least. Those unicorn statues had to have left their mark.

The next address didn't pan out, either. The next after that didn't have a red pickup. Whoever had it might have moved on already.

Jamie made note of that. He would come back if none of the others panned out. For now, he just wanted to do a quick rundown on his list.

He found what he was looking for at the Singing Sombreros Lodge half an hour later. Grill busted, hood dusty, the pickup was hidden in a narrow place between the lodge's two main buildings, parked with its back to the road so the damage in the front wouldn't be easily seen.

Jamie walked around it, tested the door, found it locked. He looked through the window. Nothing incriminating in sight. He could see nothing on the seats beyond fast-food bags and empty beer cans. He left the pickup and walked into the lobby of the main building, flashed his CBP badge.

"Do you have a Jason Tanner registered?"

The clerk, an older man, bald with a Santa Claus beard, scanned the computer screen. He had an antique banjo hanging on the wall behind him. "I'm sorry. I don't see anyone with that name listed."

"Do you know who has the red pickup?"

He frowned. "Some young guy." He looked at his log. "Wait a minute. John Tansey. Here it is. I keep telling him to park that pickup in the lot where it should go. He doesn't listen."

"Room number?"

"Is he in trouble?"

"Yes, he is."

"The guy's having a bad week, I guess. He hit a deer day before yesterday. Banged that nice truck right up. Didn't even save the deer. He's traveling, I suppose. Still, other people would have been happy to take all that venison off his hands. Don't like no waste." He shook his head mournfully. "Room sixty-eight."

"Appreciate it." Jamie looked down the hallway. "Place is full?" He didn't think so, judging by the handful of cars in the lot, but better to double-check. He didn't want anyone getting hurt. It'd be easier for him if the lodge was mostly deserted.

The old man shook his head. "Rodeo crowd cleared out yesterday."

Jamie thanked him again then walked down the hallway toward room sixty-eight. He checked his weapon before he knocked. No response came, but he did hear movement in there, a chair scraping.

"Open up. Customs and Border Protection."

He heard the window open inside. "Put your hands in the air! I'm coming in." Gun in hand, he kicked the door in and caught a flash of a man's back as he jumped out the window.

Jamie dashed across the room and jumped after him. He landed in some landscaping done with stones and cacti, his prosthetics unable to balance on the uneven ground with gravel rolling under his boots. He went down, but was up the next second.

Still, the time wasted added to Jason's lead. He'd already made his way to his pickup and was behind the wheel and driving away, nearly running over Jamie as he ran in front of the car instead of taking a shot at it. He wanted this done without a fatality if he could help it. He and his team were supposed to keep a low profile.

He dove out of the way, rolled and jumped up and ran for his own car. He'd left it unlocked and the keys in the ignition just in case, which came in handy now. He was behind the wheel and after the man within a minute.

The lodge was on the edge of one of the dozens of small towns north of Hullett, the traffic sparse, a straight country road ahead of them. Tanner would have nowhere to go to get out of sight, nowhere to hide. It didn't stop him from running.

The red pickup sped up, sixty-five, seventy, seventy-five, eighty. Jamie kept pace. They were up to ninety-five in another few minutes, Jason running cars that were in his way off the road.

Okay, he was putting other people's lives at risk now. Jamie pulled out his weapon, but didn't aim it at the back of Jason's head.

Even if he wasn't trying to keep a low profile, he only killed if it was an absolute necessity. Tanner wasn't a trained soldier; he wasn't a terrorist. He was a stalker with a mental disability. Catching him would take more work than simply taking him out, but Jamie wanted to give that a go first.

He waited until they came to a stretch of highway that was for the moment deserted save the two of them, then shot out the pickup's back tire.

The vehicle spun almost immediately, went off the road, swerved all around, kicking up a dust cloud as it ran one wheel up a sizable rock that helped to flip it on its side, the tires still spinning as the pickup stopped at last.

Jamie ran his own SUV off the road and circled back, stopped a hundred feet or so from the wreck and got out, keeping his car between him and Jason until he measured up the situation. Jason had to be considered armed and dangerous.

"Come out with your hands in the air!" he called out.

Nothing happened.

"Customs and Border Protection. Come out with your hands in the air, Jason."

But once again, Jason didn't stir. As the dust settled, Jamie moved forward carefully, keeping his weapon aimed at the pickup, watching the cab and the driver's-side door that now pointed skyward, the only possible exit point.

He went around until he could look in the front window. Jason lay flopped over, blood on his forehead. The smell of gasoline filled the air.

The ignition had to be shut off and fast.

Jamie rushed forward, but climbing up the pickup wasn't easy. A long minute passed before he made it up on top. Then he needed both hands to pull the heavy door open, against gravity, seconds passing by during which the both of them could have been sent sky-high by an explosion.

He reached in and turned off the engine first before grabbing for the man. He got hold of an arm and started hauling him up. This was where legs that felt could have come in handy. Finding leverage was difficult like this, on a surface that was uneven, unstable and slippery.

"Come on. Wake up and push, dammit." He gritted his teeth and pulled as hard as he could.

He'd had to decide at one point, after the depression, after he'd fought his demons, that he wasn't going to let anything stop him, and he wouldn't now. Not even when Jason's shirt ripped and Jamie lost balance and fell back off the pickup, the fall rattling his tall frame and knocking the air right out of him.

He got back up and climbed again, this time making sure he got a better hold on the man. He got Jason out halfway, then all the way, lowered him to the ground, slipped down next to him then dragged him a safe distance from the gasoline fumes. On a hot day like this, the sun alone could be enough to ignite something.

"Hey, wake up." He pulled up the guy's eyelid to check his pupils.

And then the man was coming to at last, moaning as Jamie searched him.

No weapon.

"Where is your gun?"

Another moan came in response. Not altogether helpful.

Jamie swore. They were going to need the murder weapon. He wanted a conviction. He wanted to make sure the guy could never come after Bree again. So he ran back to the pickup, climbed back up again, down into the cab and looked for a gun.

Nothing.

Maybe Jason's weapon was still at the hotel. Maybe in his rush to escape he didn't have time to grab it. Or maybe he'd discarded it after the hit, thinking it'd served its purpose.

Did he even know that he'd hit the wrong woman?

Jamie scampered out of the overturned vehicle and went for Jason, who was sitting now and holding his head, still moaning. "Help."

"Stay down." He called Bree. "I got Tanner." He gave

his location and a brief explanation. Then he called 911 and asked for paramedics.

GRIEF AND ANGER swirled inside Bree as she watched from behind the two-way mirror as Delancy and another officer questioned Jason Tanner. He'd changed since she'd last seen him. He'd grown taller and filled out, and a five-o'clock shadow covered his face. He fidgeted on his chair, his eyes darting around the room. He was definitely off his meds. When he was taking them, he had an eerie sort of vacant look.

Since she was personally involved in the case, she couldn't go in there. Conflict of interest. At least they had him. And she had Jamie Cassidy to thank for that. She could have kissed him when she'd caught up with him by the side of the road.

The paramedics had already been checking Jason out when she'd arrived. He was scraped up and shaken but hadn't sustained any serious injuries. They'd pronounced him well enough to be taken in.

And now here they all were. Delancy didn't pull her punches as she questioned him.

"I had nothing to do with that," he whined. "My head's hurting."

Jason had admitted to the stalking and photos, even to the vandalism, within minutes. But he denied the shooting. Of course he would. He might have had some mental issues, but he wasn't stupid. He wasn't going to admit to murder.

Bree itched to march in there and confront him. Eleanor was gone, dammit. For what? A decade-old obsession? If she was the crying type, she would have cried over the unfairness of it.

She pushed to her feet and might have barged in on the interrogation if Lena hadn't opened the door and whispered, "We've got a problem."

Bree hurried out to the hallway. "What is it?"

"Bank alarm just went off. Got a cell-phone call, too. There's someone at the new bank with explosives."

Explosives. Bree stared at her. *Seriously? Now?* "A bank robbery?" She wanted to stay and watch the interrogation unfold.

"Don't know. Sounds like it."

Mercury must have been in retrograde. She glanced around the office, trying to pick who to take with her. There was nobody around. Brian and Delancy were with Jason. The others were out on calls. She couldn't take Lena. Somebody had to stay and man the station.

The insanity never stopped. Welcome to a cop's life. Well, she couldn't complain. She was the one who'd chosen it. And she did love it. On most days.

Chapter Eleven

Her gaze landed on Jamie, who was coming out of the break room with a cup of steaming coffee, watching her.

He'd come in with Jason Tanner. She didn't think he would have waited, but he had, apparently. And he'd heard everything Lena had said. He was walking straight toward them.

"Who's your bomb expert?" he wanted to know.

"Pebble Creek is too small to have its own SWAT team or bomb squad. We call in the pros." Bree nodded to Lena to do just that, then took off running for her car.

If she had to go alone, she had to go alone. Crime didn't stop just because they were at full capacity.

But Jamie was running behind her. "Hang on, I'm coming."

"Not your jurisdiction." She should have stopped him, but she didn't want to spend time arguing. She jumped into her car and took off for the bank, leaving him to do what he wished.

A cruiser was already waiting in front of the bank by the time she reached the building. Mike Mulligan's. Then she saw him, a thirty-year veteran of the force, pushing bystanders back and making sure everyone was safe. Bree parked her own cruiser strategically, so the two would begin forming a barricade to take cover behind.

Jamie, pulling in behind her, did the same. He jumped out and ran toward her. "I can help if you need someone. I know something about explosives."

Of course he did.

"Start evacuating the adjoining buildings," she told Mike, then turned to Jamie. "All right. Fine. Stay back here. I might have to call for you." Then she rushed forward in a low crouch toward the bank's entrance.

She ducked down outside the front door, opened it a crack, held her badge up so whoever was inside could see.

"I'm Bree Tridle, deputy sheriff. I'm here to give you whatever it is you need."

"Too late," came the response from inside—an older male, judging by the tone. He sounded raspy, maybe a smoker.

She didn't recognize the voice, and couldn't see inside very well through the UV-protection film that covered the glass. All she could make out were shapes.

"How about I come in so we can talk about this?"

"No."

"I can help."

"Can you help me get justice?"

Oh, damn. One of those. Why couldn't it have been over something easy, like money? Justice was a very subjective thing.

"Is killing innocent people justice? Women and children in there?" She could make out two smaller shapes, she thought. Might be kids clinging to their mother.

A moment of silence passed. "Why should I care about them? Nobody cares about me."

"I do. I wouldn't be here if I didn't. Let them go. We'll trade. Me and whatever I can do to help, for them. I'm a cop. I signed up for this. Those people in there didn't. One injustice won't erase another." Whatever it was he thought had been done to him.

More silence stretched between them.

"Those people can't do anything. They can't order anyone to do anything. They have no contacts. No power. I do. I'm the deputy sheriff."

"No trade." His voice shook a little this time. He was getting frustrated.

Okay, no time to waste.

"Then just let me come in. You'll have one more hostage."

And, after an interminable moment, the man said, "Fine." He cleared his throat. "You come in, hands in the air. Leave your gun outside. I see a weapon and we all go to Jesus today."

"Forget her," Jamie called out a foot behind her, scaring the living daylights out of her. How on earth had he snuck up on her? "You don't want a woman in there who'll faint in panic at the first thing that goes wrong. I'm coming in to help. Unarmed."

She shot him a death glare and whispered, "Go away." She could have killed him. They were in the middle of a hostage situation. This was no time for meddling.

"Who the hell are you?" the man inside wanted to know.

"Jamie Cassidy. I work for the United States Government. I can get you things you'll never get from a small-town deputy."

Oh, no, he didn't. Did he just disparage both her sex and her position within the space of a minute? She sent him a Texas death glare.

"Both of you, inside!" the man ordered. "Hands high above your heads."

She turned back to the bank, pulled her weapon from the holster and dropped it on the ground, pushed the door open wide enough to step inside and tried to kick Jamie backward but missed. "We're so going to talk about this," she said under her breath, in a hiss.

He pushed in after her anyway.

In the middle of the main area of the bank, in front of the teller booths, an old man sat in a wheelchair, holding a panicked woman in her twenties in front of him, a handgun pointed at her.

Her eyes wide, her face pale, she looked to Jamie instead of Bree. "Help me!" Her high-pitched voice echoed under the extrahigh, ornately decorated ceiling.

The old man shook her to quiet her. "Untuck your shirts, pull them up and turn around in a slow circle," he ordered in his raspy voice.

Behind him, about a dozen civilians lay face down on the pink marble floor, hands over their heads. Bree sincerely hoped none of them carried concealed weapons and had a mind to start trouble. An amateur shootout was the last thing she needed.

Then again, if someone did have a weapon, they would have probably done something by now.

"Everything is going to be okay," she said to the man

with the gun, as much to as the hostages, as she reached for the hem of her shirt.

Jamie did the same, showing off the fact that he'd come in unarmed.

"You should let these people go," Bree said as she tugged her shirt back down. "Whatever complaint you have, I'm sure it has nothing to do with anybody here."

The man watched her for a long moment, exhaustion and desperation in his eyes. He might have thought about what he was going to do here today, but reality was always different. She hoped he was beginning to see at last that this wasn't his best idea.

"Listen. Why don't we just end this now, peacefully, before anybody makes any mistakes? Everybody's scared and tense. But honestly, nobody's hurt." She flashed an encouraging smile. "This is a damn good place to quit."

"You go over there." The man gestured toward the corner with his head, appearing not the least touched by her plea and sound reasoning.

She did as she was asked, and so did Jamie. They slid to the floor next to each other, kept their backs to the wall. The old man in the middle swung the gun to point it at Bree, but he still hung on to the young woman with his other hand, ignoring her whimpering.

Bree stayed as relaxed as she could under the circumstances and prayed that Jamie would put aside his macho commando instincts for a minute, stay still and not do anything stupid.

Don't escalate. She glanced at him, trying to send him the telepathic message, hoping he got something from the look in her eyes before she turned back to the man in the wheelchair.

"I'm Bree Tridle, as I said, and this is Jamie Cassidy," she added, very nicely. "Would you mind if I asked your name?"

"Antonio Rivera."

She drew a slow breath. Like Angel Rivera? What were the chances it was a coincidence? Very slim.

"You took my son away from me," he yelled at her weakly. "You shot him."

Connection confirmed. Now what? How could she use this to her advantage?

"Only just barely," she said. "Flesh wound. And he shot at me first. He'll be fine." She widened her smile and did her level best to look positive.

"He'll be in jail. His brother is already in jail. What do I have left?"

She had no idea. No wife, she guessed, and scrambled to come up with something.

"Bank's taking the house," the man went on, his face darkening. He adjusted his grip on the gun.

"I'm sorry. Maybe I can work something out with the manager. Do you know Cindy Myers? She sure has a lot of pull at this place. She's very nice, actually. She has two boys, too. Younger than yours. We went to high school together. She'll help you if she can. She's very good that way."

The old man spat on the polished marble floor. "You're just saying that so I let everyone go. I ain't stupid."

"You're holding an entire bank hostage. I know you

can figure things out," she said to placate him, while she tried to see what kind of bomb he had.

She spied half a dozen sticks of dynamite. They weren't difficult to come by, unfortunately. Ranchers used them for all kinds of things, including clearing large boulders from their fields.

However, she couldn't see what kind of setup he had under the duct tape that ran around his chest, holding everything in place. She had no idea what he was using for the trigger mechanism, and no idea what to do even if she could spot it, honestly.

She glanced at Jamie, hoping he was catching more than she was, maybe even working on a plan. They sure could have used one of those. She had no idea whether the SWAT team had arrived yet or when they were coming.

The young woman Antonio held was trembling.

"And what's your name?" Bree asked. Making Antonio realize that she was a real person with a name, somebody's daughter, might help somewhat.

"Melanie."

"Do you have anybody from your family here?" Bree pushed further.

Melanie shook her head and began to cry.

"Shut up," Antonio barked at them.

She couldn't do that, Bree thought, so she took a gamble. "What happened to your legs?"

He might get mad, or he might start talking. Either way, it would gain her time until reinforcements got there.

"What's it to you?" He glared at her, but then he said, "Wire mill."

"I'm sorry. That must have been difficult." She acknowledged him and his troubles. "But you came through it. You'll come through this. Your sons will get out of prison. I'll help you find housing if we can't talk sense into the bank. There's always help available."

"I don't want help," he said darkly. "I just want this to be over with."

The way he said that, the tone of his voice, the bleak look in his eyes, troubled her. Because she knew he meant it. His coming here had never been about getting the bank to change their minds. This was suicide, pure and simple. He just didn't want to go alone.

She drew a slow breath, trying desperately to think of a way out of this, something, anything she could say or do so the standoff didn't end with a bunch of mangled bodies.

"Do you want to speak to Angel? I could probably get him on the phone." She had Agent Herrera's number. "You tell him to cooperate. I'll do anything I can so that he gets a fair deal. Maybe even a reduced sentence."

"Too late." His voice was cold with determination, as bleak as his face.

Melanie sobbed out loud. Some of the hostages squeezed their eyes shut; others stared wide-eyed. A middle-age man was hyperventilating. There was a new kind of tension in the air and they all knew it.

At least there weren't any kids in the bank. She'd been mistaken about that, thank heavens.

But they were out of time.

Jamie shifted next to her.

No, no, no. Her gaze went to him.

He probably had a hidden backup weapon somewhere on him. He would go for it, then Antonio would set off the bomb, for sure, and they would all die.

EVERYTHING HE WAS pushed him to attack. He'd been trained to charge forward and take down the enemy. He was a warrior. He'd been trained to fight with guns and explosives. His brain and body were weapons.

Jamie shifted again, looking for an angle, a split-second opportunity.

But if he tackled Antonio, the man would set off the bomb. Bree and Jamie were sitting the closest. They'd be toast, for sure. He wasn't as worried about himself, especially if he thought a move like that might save the hostages, but he wasn't willing to risk harm coming to Bree.

"Let me tell you something," he began, and couldn't believe he was talking. It didn't feel even half-right. He was a soldier. He'd been rough and tough pretty much from the beginning and, all right, fine, he might even have been overcompensating a little since he'd been cleared for active duty again.

He didn't have a softer side. For him, to show softness meant to show weakness, which was the dead-last thing he wanted to show, wanted to be.

And yet when Bree's life was at stake…

His usual M.O. of pushing harder wasn't going to work here.

"None of us are here because we want to be," he said. "I'm guessing you'd be doing something a little more fun if you had other choices."

The man glared at him.

Not exactly progress but, hey, they were still alive.

"Between the three of us, we should be able to figure a way out of this," he said, even as part of him was still looking for the man's weak spot, a way to rush him.

SHE SAW HOW he was looking at Antonio Rivera. Bree was pretty sure Jamie would attack, and soon. She wanted to warn him not to, but he wouldn't look at her, and she couldn't say anything out loud for fear of setting off Antonio.

But instead of making his move, Jamie kept talking, his voice low and calm. "I know what you mean. I've been where you are now. Hell of a place."

Other than his words, there was dead silence in the bank, the hostages pretty much knowing this was a Hail Mary effort.

Antonio shot him an angry look. "You haven't. So shut up."

"All right. I'll shut up." He raised his hands into the air, then pushed to his feet slowly. "But let me show you something."

She held her breath, along with the rest of the hostages.

Antonio moved his gun to point at Jamie's chest.

Slowly, carefully, Jamie reached to his belt, unbuckled it, then unbuttoned and unzipped his pants and let them drop to his ankles.

Antonio stared, along with pretty much everybody.

Jamie's shirt came down to the edge of his boxer shorts, but left the end of his stumps in open view, the skin puckered, white and red scars crisscrossing his skin. For the first time, she got a good look at the straps that held his prosthetics in place.

A couple of women gasped.

She very nearly did, too. Seeing both the living parts and the metal somehow made the sight starker than when she'd rolled up his pant legs before and had seen only the prosthetics. Those were somehow sterile, removed, cold metal. But his scars, the terrible destruction of his living flesh… She swallowed the lump in her throat.

"I didn't want to live," Jamie said in a low voice. "At the field hospital, I begged them to let me die. When they didn't, I promised myself I'd take care of it as soon as I recovered enough and had the strength."

Antonio listened.

"You get to this dark place," Jamie went on. "And it's bad. When you're there, it doesn't seem possible that things will ever get better again. It's like the life outside, the things other people do and see, that's not real. You almost don't even see it."

The hostages watched him silently, barely daring even to breathe.

"Like when you're over there, in the mountains for years on end, people shooting at you, you killing, blood every day. Every day one of your buddies gets blown to pieces. And it seems like that's the only world. Like back here, this was just a dream, the houses and the family and the rain, the banks and the malls and teenagers who go shopping. It's a dream or a fantasy. It doesn't exist. Not to you."

Antonio still pointed the gun at him, but his arm sagged a little.

"Thing is—" Jamie bent slowly and pulled his pants

up, buckled his belt "—the other world…it's there. It's real. And the people in it hurt when you leave them."

"Ain't nobody will hurt for me," Antonio said, but his voice wasn't as hard as before.

"Your sons will," Bree put in, talking around the lump in her throat, thinking about Jamie's seven brothers and the sister he would have left behind if he'd been a weaker man and taken the easy way out. "They cared enough about you to take care of you. They'll hurt."

She drew a slow breath. "And all the families of all the people in here. They are going to hurt and they are going to grieve. People in here have fathers and mothers and kids. They didn't get to say goodbye. Don't make them go through this."

Then everything happened at the same time. Antonio shoved the young woman away from him so he had use of both hands.

Jamie dove for him, but he was too late.

Chapter Twelve

The man blew his own head off a split second before Jamie reached him. As the hostages screamed, all he could do was secure the bomb.

He ignored the blood and gore and the crying and focused on the mechanism. No timer. He looked over the manual control with a flip switch—clearly a home-made job, but with enough of a punch to take out most of the building.

Thing was, as primitively as it was put together, he couldn't guarantee that it wouldn't go off if someone tried to move Antonio. Or if the man's lifeless body slid out of the wheelchair. So he kept working on it as a SWAT team rushed in and spread through the bank, a dozen men dressed in black, holding assault rifles, shouting.

"Everybody down! Everybody down!"

Some of the hostages had leaped to their feet when Antonio had discharged his gun but now flattened themselves to the marble floor once again.

Bree stayed where she was, her hands in the air. "It's okay. Everything's under control. I'm the deputy sher-iff. My badge is in my left back pocket."

One of the men checked it for her. "She's okay."

She lowered her hands. "This is Jamie Cassidy. CBP consultant, explosives specialist. He came in with me."

"Status?" the team leader asked.

"One perpetrator. Antonio Rivera. Self-terminated."

"The bomb is still active," Jamie put in as one of the SWAT members rushed over to him, probably their bomb expert. "Simple trigger mechanism. It's a pretty shoddy job. You need to get these people out of here."

The guy checked out the sticks of dynamite and twisted jumble of wires as the rest of his team jumped into action, helping the hostages up and rushing them toward the exit.

"Want to take over?" Jamie offered.

The guy shook his head. "You've got your hand on the wire. Go ahead."

That was pretty much standard operating procedure. The chances of success went up exponentially if the man who started a disarming op was the one who finished it. It wasn't something easily handed over midrace.

He focused on the wires, tracing each to their connections, careful not to set off the trigger. The SWAT guy held Antonio in place, making sure the body wouldn't flop.

"All right. Okay. Almost there."

Then, finally, the last wire was detached.

By that time, there were only three people inside: Bree, Jamie and the man helping him. The SWAT team had cleared the building.

"Well done," the bomb expert said, putting the explosives into the safe box someone had dropped off at some point. "I'll take it from here." He walked away with his precarious charge in his arms.

For the moment, until someone came for the body, Jamie and Bree were alone. They walked away from Antonio, but didn't step outside. Press waited out there, cameras flashing, the news team recording everything. The last thing he needed was his picture on TV. He was an undercover operative.

Bree's eyes were haunted, her face grim as she glanced back at the prone body. "He didn't have to die."

Dead bodies didn't bother Jamie. He was used to the carnage of battle. But for her... Two violent deaths in the space of days were probably way more than the small town of Pebble Creek was used to seeing. She'd had a pretty tough week.

While he was comfortable with death, he wasn't comfortable in the role of comforter. Yet something inside him pushed him to be just that, for Bree. He filled his lungs and waded into unfamiliar territory.

"We did what we could. It could have been worse. The bomb didn't go off. You kept him distracted for a good long time," he said. He really was impressed with her. "What you did gave the SWAT team a chance to get here."

Her head dipped in a tentative nod. "I thought for sure you were going to rush him, right at the beginning. I thought for sure we'd be toast if you did."

"I thought about it. Then I thought maybe I should try your technique of sweet-talking him. You must be rubbing off on me. I hope there's a cure for that," he teased, hoping it would lift her spirits a little.

"Wouldn't exactly call what you did sweet talk," she said, but gave a tremulous smile.

He reached for her, gratified when she went willingly into his arms. He brushed his lips over hers, relieved beyond words that they were both alive. He had no idea how Mitch Mendoza, his brother-in-law, handled going on joint missions with Megan before she'd taken some time off for the baby. Seeing Bree in danger had been nearly more than Jamie could handle. He would definitely not want to be in a situation like this ever again.

Her fresh, subtle scent, soap mixed with a light perfume, was in his nose, her curves pressed against the hard planes of his body. She was one of those good things he'd given up on at one point in his life. It seemed surreal that here he was, with the woman of his dreams in his arms.

But she was real in every way. And for now, she was with him, lifting her face to his. So he kissed her lightly. Because he really needed to feel her warmth and life and the reality of her being.

Antonio Rivera hadn't been able to let go.

Jamie rested his forehead against hers. He had let go of some things, but not everything, he thought. What if he could let it all go: the past, the pain, the idea that he was a fighting machine and only that?

She made him want to reexamine his assumptions and the way he lived these days. He didn't know if he could, if he should. But he wanted to, for the first time ever.

He dipped back for another taste of her lips.

She tasted so sweet, so right. She was infuriating. He'd nearly had a heart attack when she'd run up to the bank's door to offer herself in exchange for the hostages. Yet, in hindsight, he should have seen it coming. She was no coward. She did whatever she thought had to be done.

She took care of her town; she took care of her sister. He admired her, he realized.

The kiss deepened, yet it still wasn't nearly enough. What would be enough? Would anything ever be enough where Bree was concerned?

He had no idea, he admitted to himself as he pulled away. He had so much darkness around him. In some ways, his past still bound him. She was all light and smiles. He was a surly bastard. He didn't want his darkness to touch her. Temporary slip of willpower or not, he simply wasn't the right guy for her.

He would have told her that, but people were filing in through the door. Some of the SWAT team were coming back to finish their business.

A BOMB IN a bank, with a fatality added, required enough paperwork to make her head spin. She would have more follow-up work the next day, but she had to set that aside and go get Katie, so Bree powered off her computer and locked up her office.

Jason Tanner was in holding, his parents notified. They retained a lawyer for him. He'd confessed to the photos and the unicorn massacre, but he would not budge on the shooting. Maybe tomorrow, Bree thought. Tomorrow was another day.

The station was buzzing; some of the bank hostages were still there, giving statements, something Lena and Mike were more than capable of handling.

"Tell Katie I said hi," Lena called over as Bree told them she was leaving for the day.

The events at the bank crowded into her head as she drove, as she went over what she could have done to achieve a better ending to the standoff. She was the one who'd caught Angel Rivera. Angel had made bad choices. So had Antonio, in the end. Could she have done anything differently?

She was deputy sheriff, but she couldn't say she was happy when someone went to jail or died, even if they were criminals. First and foremost, she was a peace officer. She wanted peace for her people. Which was why she made sure crime prevention was a very real program in the county, not just a political hobbyhorse to be dragged out at sheriff elections.

She looked in the mirror to make sure she looked okay before she picked up Katie. She drew a deep breath and forced a smile on her face. *No bringing the job home.* The only fast and hard rule she never broke.

She pulled over in front of the big yellow building where her sister worked, and Katie jumped into the car and started talking about her day immediately. Katie lived in the here and now, always. It was an amazing way to live, one that Bree sometimes envied. No worries, no regrets, no self-blame.

"Mrs. Springer brought cupcakes today," she was saying. "They were chocolate with chocolate frosting. They had chocolate sprinkles."

Bree pulled into traffic. "You can never have too much chocolate."

"That's what she said. Except when you're a dog,

because chocolate kills dogs. Then even a little is too much."

"Very true."

"We don't have a dog."

"No, we don't. We have unicorns."

"Scott said once they had a burglar and their dog chased it away."

Bree glanced at Katie then back at the road. They'd had some scary vandalism, then a fatal shooting at the house within the space of a week. Just because Katie lived in the now didn't mean she didn't have logic. She did, and plenty of it. And maybe logic said that if bad things could happen at their house as they had, they could happen again.

"You know the bad guy we talked about?"

Katie nodded.

"We caught him today. Jamie did, this morning. The bad guy is going to jail. All locked up."

"And can't get out."

"That's right."

"Scott was in a car accident once," Katie said. It was a non sequitur, and they talked about that next.

She saw Jamie's SUV in front of her house as soon as she turned onto her street. He'd gone into work after they parted at the bank. He only had half a shift, as Mo had to do something with his stepson and they'd traded time.

His seat was tilted back, she saw as she came closer. He seemed to be asleep. Good. He deserved some rest.

Katie got out and went straight to the front door with the keys. She loved locking and unlocking things, and any kind of lock mechanism. She could play with a combination lock for hours when she'd been younger.

She had a whole collection she'd accumulated over the years. Some she'd picked up with their mother on garage-sale outings—their standing Saturday morning mother-daughter date that had since been replaced by hanging out with Sharon. Many other locks since, even antique ones, had been given as gifts by friends— several by Eleanor. Katie could remember the combination to every single one of them.

Bree walked over to Jamie's car. He had all the windows rolled down, probably to catch a breeze.

His eyes were open by the time she reached him. "Hey."

Her gaze caught on a bundle of yellow police tape on his backseat. He'd gathered that up from around her property. So Katie wouldn't have to see it and remember.

Her heart turned over in her chest. "Hey."

"Thought I'd stop by to make sure everything was okay."

"Jason's in jail. Thanks to you. I think we're done with trouble for a while. Hopefully."

He nodded, looking tired and rumpled with bristles covering his cheeks; he was so incredibly sexy, he took her breath away.

"What are you going to do about that busted living room window?" he wanted to know. "It doesn't look too safe the way it is."

She glanced at the empty frame. The contractor who worked with the police station, people who cleaned up crime scenes, had taken away the broken glass when they'd come to clean up the blood inside. She'd recommended them to families of victims many times in the past. They did excellent work. But they didn't do repairs.

"I called it in. Should be fixed tomorrow. It's a standard-size window, so at least I didn't have to do special order." That would have taken forever.

"How about I hang out on your couch tonight?"

He was asking and not telling her. Definite progress from Jamie Cassidy.

"It's not exactly a high-crime area. And I'm well-armed. I'm kind of the deputy sheriff."

The corner of his mouth lifted a little. "For my peace of mind, then."

Because he cared?

There went that funny feeling around her heart again.

"You're just here for the triple-winner breakfast," she joked. "Nobody can resist my salsa egg scramble."

His lips tilted into an almost smile. "Maybe." And then he got out, unfolding his long frame, and followed her in.

Katie was already going through her predinner routine.

"Jamie is having dinner with us." Bree took off her gun harness and hung it in its place, out of reach, although she didn't have to worry about Katie. Her sister was excellent with remembering and following rules to a T.

"Hi, Katie."

"Hi, Jamie." She glanced through the hole in the window at her unicorns, and seemed to have no problem with Jamie being there. She skipped to the kitchen cabinet and grabbed another plate.

Bree went upstairs and changed into a pair of jeans and a tank top, then padded back down to start dinner. Fried chicken steak, an old Texas staple, was one of Katie's favorites.

"What can I do to help?"

She stopped for a moment to look at him. "When was the last time you slept?" He worked long hours for his team, then he was helping her in between.

"I'm good."

"I have a well-oiled dinner routine with Katie. How about you lie down on the couch for a minute?"

He raised an eyebrow. "So because I'm a man, you assume I'd be no good in the kitchen and you're telling me to stay out of the way? Very sexist."

"Deal with it." But she was smiling as she shook her head. "You'll get to do manly things later," she said, without really thinking about how that sounded until his face livened up.

"Not what I meant." She tried to backpedal, laughing.

He looked skeptical, one dark eyebrow rising slowly. "What did you mean, exactly?"

"Like chopping wood out back." Or something like that.

He didn't look convinced.

So she turned to the stove while he walked off to take a predinner nap.

She didn't think anyone could sleep through the pots banging and Katie's chatter, but he did. He must have been truly exhausted. But he rolled right to his feet when she finally finished the gravy and called him to dinner.

She could barely concentrate on the food. She was too distracted by the man at her table. He had a presence that filled up her kitchen. But while he filled Bree with awareness that tingled across her skin, Katie was acting as if he was a member of the family and his eating dinner with them happened every day. For some reason, maybe because of the great unicorn rescue, she had accepted him fully and unconditionally.

"Excellent dinner. I appreciate the invitation," he said over his plate. And ate like he meant every word.

He probably didn't get many home-cooked meals, she supposed, liking that he appreciated her cooking.

"He's making the happy face," Katie put in.

"Yes, he is." Bree put a happy face of her own into play.

Her awareness passed after a while, and she began enjoying their dinner together. There was such a warm, homey feeling, such a normalcy to them sharing a meal. Maybe because of his nap, maybe because of the meal, the harsh lines on Jamie's face relaxed for once and stayed that way.

She liked this. She liked it a lot.

Not smart. She sighed. *Heartbreak ahead.* Her head sounded the warning.

Too late. She was enough of a realist to know that there was nothing she could do to stop herself from falling for him.

WHAT THE HELL was he doing here? Jamie thought as he lay on the couch in Bree's living room in the middle of the night, staring at the ceiling.

She didn't need him. She was a good cop. She could

take care of herself. Jason Tanner was in jail. And as she'd said, she lived in a pretty good neighborhood.

He hadn't been lying when he'd asked to stay for his own piece of mind. Bree mattered. And so did Katie. She was a sweet kid. Quick, too. She'd put together a puzzle of Klimt's *The Kiss* before he finished a small corner.

Of course, the painting the puzzle created put kissing into his mind. And Bree. And he hadn't been able to clear those images out of his head since. His emotions and thoughts were in a jumble. He didn't like that. He was used to always having a clear battle plan.

Except, this was no battle.

So why was he fighting his own feelings?

He rolled to his feet. He hadn't taken his prosthetics off. While it was unlikely that anyone would break in, he wanted to be ready if there was trouble.

He walked across the room then stopped, thought some more about what he was doing. He was very likely making a mistake. He walked up the stairs, anyway.

He knocked as quietly as he could, prepared to go back down if there was no answer.

"Come in."

He pushed the door in slowly, not entirely sure he should.

She sat up in bed, the worn police academy T-shirt she wore as a nightgown covering most of her, except for her amazing legs. He could have stood there staring at her forever.

She swung her feet to the ground as if to stand up, but then she didn't.

He moved to her without words and sank to his knees

in front of her, pulled her closer, her legs on either side of him as he rested his forehead against her collarbone.

"I couldn't sleep," he said against her T-shirt, breathing in her soapy scent. He liked the way she smelled, the way she felt, the way she fit against him.

Her head lowered, her lips coming to rest in his hair. "Me, neither."

He looked up into her face, which was illuminated by the moonlight. Time for the naked truth. "I want you."

For a nerve-racking moment, she didn't say anything, but then she smiled.

Oh, man. Maybe it would have been better if she sent him away. "I don't know how it's going to work."

Her smile turned into a wicked grin. "A virgin? Don't worry. I'll be gentle."

And he couldn't help but smile back. She could make him smile like nobody else. It was a miracle. He really had been a grouchy bastard over the past couple of years.

To be honest, he almost did feel like a virgin. She was like no other. He didn't want to mess this up. He didn't want to repulse her.

"Step one would be to lock the door," she advised him.

And he got up to do that. When he came back to her, he sat next to her on the bed.

"Okay, so the first part is called foreplay." She shifted onto his lap. "Tell me if I'm going too fast and you don't understand something. We'll go back and repeat whatever step you're having trouble with."

"You're a good instructor," he said as his arms went around her.

"I train rookies at the station all the time."

He threw her a questioning look.

She smothered a laugh. "Not in this!"

"I hope not," he said with a sudden shot of jealousy, as he pulled her head down to his for a kiss.

She was in his arms, her lips pressed against his, her arms wound around his shoulders. His entire body was alive and hardening with desire within seconds.

He deepened the kiss and took what he needed. She didn't protest. When she dug her fingers into the short hair at his nape, desire rippled down his spine.

He wanted her. She was the only woman he'd wanted in a very long time. This was not something spur of the moment; this was not trivial. The two of them in this room meant something, something he wasn't sure he was ready for.

But he couldn't walk away from her.

He shifted them until they were lying side by side on the bed.

Okay, that was smoother, so far, than he'd expected. He was up on one elbow next to her, their lips still connected. He had a free hand. He was a soldier, trained to take advantage of every tactical advantage.

"I don't know what you're doing. Here with me. You're perfect. I'm…" He was going to say messed up, but she cut him off.

"Stubborn?"

"No way."

"Surly?"

"When warranted."

Then he forgot what they were talking about as he tugged up her T-shirt and put his hand, fingers stretched out, on her flat stomach. Her skin was warm and smooth and begged to be explored. He moved his fingers upward.

She gave a soft groan and lifted her chest.

He wanted to be inside her so badly it hurt.

His hand cupped her breast; there was no bra, just warm skin and a pebbled nipple that he was ready to taste. He pulled up the soft material and lowered his lips to the tight bud.

Her hands kneaded his shoulders, her head tilted back.

"Take it back. I'm not perfect," she said in a whisper.

"What?" His mind was in a haze. He lifted his head. She shifted to look at him. "I'm not perfect."

"A whole state begs to differ. You were Miss Texas. Don't you miss the beauty-queen days?"

She looked away.

"What is it?"

"My mom wanted that." She turned back to him. "She wanted me to be extraperfect, maybe because Katie wasn't…. I didn't really like the beauty-pageant thing."

He watched her, the emotions crossing her face.

"When my parents died in the fire, I was devastated. Then a few days later, when we were picking through the ashes, I came across some of my pageant wardrobe, all charred. And I thought, with Mom gone, I'd never have to go up on stage again. And I had never before felt such relief in my life." Her voice broke.

He held her closer. "And you felt guilty."

"I wasn't relieved that my mother was dead."

He kissed her. "You were relieved that you didn't

have to live a life you never chose. It's not like you shirk responsibility. You take care of Katie."

"That's different. I want to. I love being with her."

He kissed her again, amazed that she would share this with him, that she trusted him enough to open up. This was about more than sex, a warning voice said in his head. For the both of them.

He ignored the voice. His body wanted what it wanted. He went back to kissing her soft skin.

His mouth made the trip back to hers, lingering on her delicious neck in between, then back down to the other nipple. He wanted to keep kissing her for hours, but the urgency building in his body pushed him to take things to the next level.

He rolled her under him, pulled up her knees, one then the other on either side of him, pressed his hardness against her soft core and groaned with the sharp pleasure of the contact. He rocked into her, kissed her over and over, and that was enough for a few more minutes. Then it wasn't.

He shifted them again and pulled her shirt over her head, while she did the same with his, their arms tangling. She was down to her skimpy underwear, her soft skin glowing in the moonlight, bared for him.

She reached for his belt buckle. Because there was no hesitation in her, he didn't feel any, either. He helped her.

She tugged down his pants. He reached for his prosthetic leg on one side. She watched what he did and helped him on the other side, her fingers frenetic and impatient.

Because she wanted him.

With everything he was and he wasn't.

Then the metal was gone, then her underwear, then his. She whisked out a foil wrapper from her nightstand and helped him with that, too.

He loved the feel of her hands on him.

He moved to cover her amazing body with his. Then his erection was poised at her opening for a second before he sank into her moist, tight heat. His mind exploded first, then his heart.

The distance, the walls he'd built, the darkness he'd carried, they all fell away.

There was only Bree.

Chapter Thirteen

Bree woke alone, and after a second, she could vaguely remember Jamie kissing her goodbye before he went into work at dawn.

Her body felt like…cotton candy—a big fluff of happiness. She couldn't stop grinning. Even the toothpaste ran down her chin while she brushed her teeth.

She dropped Katie off at work, went into the office and did some more paperwork regarding the incident at the bank the day before. She wanted to talk to Jason Tanner, still in lockup, but thought better of it. She didn't want to mess up this case. She didn't want him to get off on a technicality.

He needed to be held responsible for what he'd done, be locked up and get help for his mental problems. As he was now, he was a danger to society.

Instead of going back to his holding cell with her questions, she called around to see when she could go over to the prison to talk to Angel Rivera's younger brother. She wasn't looking forward to having to tell him about his father's death at the bank. Angel would have to be told, too, so she sent off a quick email to Agent Herrera about that.

Since she couldn't talk to the younger Rivera without his lawyer present, she tracked that information down first.

"You gotta be kidding me," she murmured as she took in the screen. Steven Swenson. Or Slimeball Swenson, as he was known in law-enforcement circles.

He had very little regard for the law, and none whatsoever for the police. He'd sued probably every police department in the county at one point or another. Everything the cops did was an "overreach of power" in his book, and he was happy to cause as much trouble as humanly possible.

He was famous for his utter lack of cooperation. She so did not look forward to having to talk to him. She made the call, anyway. When he didn't pick up, she was almost relieved, even if she knew she'd have to try again. She left him a message.

She went through some more paperwork, handled some walk-ins then braced herself and called Swenson again. Still nothing. The guy didn't call her back, either. He wouldn't. The word "helpful" was completely missing from his dictionary.

The next time her phone rang, it was Jamie on the other end.

"Hi. Sorry I left so early."

Her heart leaped at the sound of his voice, images from the night before flashing across her brain. Parts that had no business tingling when she was on duty came awake. "You had work."

"I just don't want you to think I was doing the 'guy runs away in the morning' thing. I wanted to stay."

The quiet admission made her heart swell. "I can't

see you running away from anything. You're not the type."

"Neither are you."

"No," she agreed.

He hesitated for a moment. "So what are we going to do about this?"

"We figure it out as we go," she said tentatively, expecting him to come up with ten reasons why a relationship between them couldn't work. Heck, she could have come up with twenty on her own.

But instead, he said, "Okay." Then he said, "Lunch? I can probably get away for half an hour. I'm on office duty today."

"I'm going to take a working lunch. I need to see a guy's lawyer."

"Have fun."

"Not with this one. It's Slimeball Swenson." She was going to drive by and see if she could catch him in person.

"Hostages are suing already?"

"No. Nothing to do with the bank. It's about the counterfeiting case. I'm tying up a loose end for the CIA agent in charge."

"I'll see you tonight?"

Her heart leaped again. "Like you ever asked permission before for barging into my life without notice?"

He chuckled on the other end.

She'd wondered once what it would take to see him smile. And now that she'd seen him smile... She was rapidly falling for him.

Don't get ahead of yourself. Don't get your heart broken. It was one night. Neither of them wanted anything permanent. They both had their lives set up in a way that worked for them.

"I'll see you tonight, then," he said. "Especially if you have leftover chicken steaks."

And even if it was something temporary, whatever they had between them, she felt a thrill at the prospect of spending another night with him. "You only like me for my cooking."

"I pretty much like everything about you, Bree."

Her heart gave a hard thud. "Now you're just angling for dessert." She made a joke of it, even though she was ridiculously pleased.

After they hung up, she called Swenson again. Maybe he was with a client and that was why he wasn't answering. She left him another message, telling him she was coming over.

But before she could get away, a couple of teenagers were brought in: a drug bust. She handled that; one set of parents was belligerent, blaming everyone but their offspring, the other apologetic.

A full hour passed before she could drive off to see Swenson over in Hullett, her mind wandering to how incredibly good Jamie and she had been together and what she was going to do about that. A complicated question, so she drove the back roads, giving herself a few extra minutes to think.

She was so preoccupied that she was at the reservoir by the time she noticed that a dark van was following her. All the windows were tinted, so she couldn't make out the faces in the front, only two menacing dark shapes.

They were the only two vehicles on the abandoned

road. She sped up. So did the van. It kept gathering speed, closing the distance between them.

"JUST WANTED TO see how you were doing," Jamie told his sister, Megan, over the phone as he sat behind his desk at the office. "How is baby Bella?"

"As grouchy as you are. She's teething." His sister made some nonsensical baby noises on the other end.

You couldn't tell now that she was a tough under-cover operative. In fact, she'd met her husband on a South American op where they'd nearly killed each other before they'd fallen in love.

"Oh," she said. "You should see her. You wouldn't believe how fast she's growing. She's a little cham-pion at breastfeeding. Aren't you, my little moochy-woochy?" She cooed.

He winced.

He'd only seen the baby once, in the middle of a screaming fest. He had no idea why people had babies. Forget mortal combat, babies were scarier.

"Are you calling to volunteer to babysit?" his sister wanted to know.

Right. Maybe in an alternate universe. "Sorry, too busy saving civilization as we know it."

"Sure, use that old excuse," Megan said in a droll tone, but then she laughed. "How are you? Is working stateside strange? How are the guys? God, they're hot. Don't tell Mitch I said that. How is the job?"

"Good."

She waited.

"Everything's okay."

"Well, no sense singing a whole ode about it. You

know how I hate when you talk my ear off. Sheesh, what are we, like girlfriends?"

"Very funny."

"I'm known for my sense of humor. And loved for it." She cooed to the baby again before returning to him. "So you're calling to tell me what, exactly?"

"Just to see how you all are doing."

A moment of silence passed. "Is there a woman?"

"What? On earth? Over three billion and counting. Some of them are pretty annoying."

"I know for sure you're not talking about me." She paused for a second. "I think there's a woman. You're softening. Is she the type to babysit?"

Probably. "There's no woman."

"Well, she's obviously good for you," Megan went on, ignoring his declaration. "When do we get to meet her?"

Family. A synonym for people who stick their noses into your business and enjoy it. "Oh, look. I better go. Terrorists are attacking. They're coming out from all over the jungle—"

"Yeah, whatever. You're calling from your office phone. I can see the number on my display and—" The baby cried in the background. "All right. But we'll talk about this mystery woman later. Take care of yourself. We all love you, Jamie."

His throat closed up suddenly. "I love you, sis. Give a kiss to my favorite niece for me."

He hung up and thought about his family, the rest of them. He really should be in touch more often. He thought about the baby. He should send her a gift. He would have to ask Bree what would be appropriate.

She would know. She was good with family. She was good with pretty much everything. He would ask her for some advice tonight.

With that resolution made, he turned back to his computer, to the task he'd interrupted to make the spur-of-the-moment call.

He so wasn't the spur-of-the-moment, check-on-family kind of guy. Maybe Megan was right and he *was* softening. Great. Just what he didn't need.

He looked through the secondary list from the prison where Jimenez had been recently incarcerated, scanned pages the warden's office had emailed him and checked the list of attorneys visiting clients on the day the kill order had been passed to Jimenez. A name jumped out at him: Steven Swenson. Might be Slimeball Swenson, the attorney Bree had just mentioned on the phone.

He tapped his finger on his desk as he stared at the screen, bad premonitions sneaking up on him.

So the same lawyer was representing the guy she was investigating for counterfeit money, and the guy Jamie was investigating for doing a hit for the Coyote. If Slimeball Swenson was the one who'd carried the hit order to Jimenez from the Coyote, then he was one of the Coyote's men, too. From what they knew about him, the Coyote worked with some of the most ruthless killers in the business.

And Bree was on her way to Swenson.

He dialed her number, a thousand fears cutting through him while he waited for her to pick up.

"Jamie!"

The sickening crunch of metal that followed the single word had him on his feet. "Where are you?"

"On the old mining road by the reservoir. There's a van behind me."

"Steven Swenson," he called to Shep as he ran for the door. "Local attorney. Find him. He's the Coyote's man. Send someone to pick him up." Then he was through the door, clutching the cell phone to his ear. "Are you okay?" he asked Bree.

"They're trying to push me into the water. I don't think—"

Another sickening crunch came.

"Bree?" He ran for his car and shot out of the parking lot, heading for her.

She didn't respond. Maybe she'd dropped the phone. She probably needed both hands on the steering wheel.

The way he was driving, so did he, so he switched to Bluetooth and tossed the phone onto the passenger seat. He could hear her yelling on the other end, car tires squealing.

His heart pounded.

"I'm coming," he said, in case she could somehow hear him. "Hang in there. I'm on my way."

Thank God the back roads were clear. He made the half-hour drive in fifteen minutes, the longest fifteen minutes of his life. He got there just in time to see Bree's cruiser tumble into the dark water of the reservoir, pushed by the van behind her.

He rolled down his window and shot at the van with his left hand. He had no hope of hitting anyone, but if he could scare them off, it would be enough.

He kept shooting, emptying his clip, slammed a second one into place and shattered the van's back window at last. He could see two men in the front, hunched over the dashboard to avoid his bullets. One of them shot back, but then they finally decided they wanted to stay alive and the van sped away.

Then he was at the water's edge, jumping from his car, kicking off his pants, taking off the metal that would have dragged him down, and dove in, sinking.

He'd learned how to swim without legs, but not well enough. He'd focused too much on the other aspects of his physical therapy, like regaining his balance on dry land and how to adjust his hand-to-hand combat skills so his moves would still work with the new reality of his body.

Now he wished he'd spent more time in the pool.

He used his arms to maneuver himself forward in the murky water toward the spot where he'd seen Bree's cruiser sink. If all he could do was help her out of her car and somehow push her up, even if he stayed on the bottom, he'd be happy.

BREE FREED HERSELF from the car just to get tangled in a giant ball of wire someone had dumped into the reservoir. Probably illegal dumping from the wire mill. She was so going to issue a ticket for that. If she lived.

She struggled to swim, dragging the heavy ball of metal behind her. She bumped up to the surface for one quick gulp of air before the weight dragged her back down.

She doubled her efforts and made it up to the air again. But with the tangle of metal hanging from her left foot, she couldn't stay afloat. She went back down again.

She could go up a few times, she realized, but when

she got tired, the wire would permanently anchor her to the bottom. She gritted her teeth and went down instead of up this time, trying to untangle herself from her anchor.

The inch-wide wire was slimy with rust and algae. Her fingers kept slipping without being able to find a good grip.

When her lungs began to burn, she abandoned her efforts and swam up for another gulp of air, dragging the weight with her. She could only stay up for seconds before the wire pulled her down again. Her arms and legs were tiring.

How many times could she do this? One more time? Twice? Certainly no more than that.

Desperation squeezed her chest.

The wire cut into her ankle, into her fingers as she tore at it. This time, when she went up for air, she had to struggle harder to make it.

Chances were she was going to die here, she thought on her way down again. There were only two things she regretted. That she would leave Katie alone, and that she hadn't told Jamie Cassidy that she cared about him.

But even as she thought about Jamie, he appeared in the murky water next to her. He scared her half to death for a split second before she recognized him and sharp relief washed through her.

He helped her with the wire, shoved her up even as he sank a little. She got hold of his arm, then kicked away toward the surface.

Then she could breathe again, and he was right there, the two of them dragging, pushing each other toward shore like some weird, desperate tag team. When they finally made it out, they could do little more than lie in the mud on their backs and gasp for air.

"I didn't get them." He coughed up water. "I let them get away."

Her lungs burned. She was ridiculously grateful just to be alive. "I'm so glad you showed up. I was running out of steam fast. You saved my life."

"It's not enough. I want to know who's after you, dammit. I should have caught those men."

She brushed the wet hair out of her face. "Oh, well… As long as you're playing God, maybe you can do something about the drought. I'm sure a lot of Texas farmers would be grateful."

He turned his head from her.

A moment passed before she realized he was looking at his prosthetics, a few hundred feet away. He got up and maneuvered himself that way, supporting his weight on his hands.

Her gaze caught on the way his wet shirt stuck to his back and upper arms, outlining his muscles. Those were the arms that had saved her. He had an incredible body. She didn't think she could ever get tired of looking at him.

He strapped his legs on then pulled up his pants.

"You know, we do have a public-indecency ordinance in place. You seem to have a habit of going pantless in public," she remarked as she stood and squeezed water out of her hair and clothes.

He glanced back as he got to his feet. "You going to arrest me for that?"

She sighed. "I kind of like it. Does that make me shallow?"

Surprise crossed his face, then a half smile formed. "You're not what I expected."

"Is that good or bad?" she asked as she caught up with him.

But instead of answering her question, he said. "Don't drown again. It makes me feel..." He shrugged.

She watched him for the rest, but he didn't finish.

"Were you scared for me? Is this a mucho-macho thing? Not admitting to being scared? For the record, I was terrified."

He reached for her, caught her arm and pulled her close. He dipped his head to hers and brushed his mouth over her lips. "I was scared for you. I don't think I've ever been this scared."

"I'm a tough Texas deputy."

He gave a rare full smile at that. "I know. And the stupid thing is..." He glanced down then back up to hold her gaze. "I feel like I don't want to let you out of my sight. Ever."

Oh. Warmth spread through her chest. It quickly turned to full-on heat when he kissed her.

They were wet and dirty from lying in the mud. There was a van with armed men out there somewhere who wanted her dead. Since she figured the chances of catching up with them at this stage were ridiculously slim, she gave herself over to the kiss.

Live in the moment. She'd learned that from her sister.

And after a few seconds, she could barely remember where they were or how they'd gotten here. The thing about Jamie was he could transport her in an instant to some place where she could barely remember reality.

He was a seriously good kisser. He kissed her as if she was the most important thing in the universe to him, the only thing.

That kind of stuff could go to a woman's head.

They fit together perfectly. They moved in unison, each knowing what the other wanted without a word having to be said. She'd never felt like this with anyone before.

"You're not what I expected, either," she told him when they finally pulled away.

He looked her over. "I'll take you home. You need to change."

"Will I see you tonight?"

He nodded.

"I'll have dinner ready." God, they sounded like an old married couple. It pleased her to no end.

But he didn't show up that evening. He was called in to deal with some smugglers on the border, so she spent the night alone, having to be content with only dreaming about him.

Chapter Fourteen

The following morning, Jamie sat in his SUV outside Steven Swenson's house, Bree next to him. Swenson worked out of his converted garage, which served as his home office. He was a one-man law firm. Maybe nobody wanted to work with him. According to Bree, he was pretty much a jerk.

Jamie's team, as well as Bree's, had searched the house and office the day before, but the man had been gone.

Taped to Jamie's dashboard were printouts of half a dozen versions of what he might look like if he came back wearing a disguise. With a beard, with a bald head and so on. Bree's idea. She had some computer program at the station.

Swenson had small, close eyes, a crooked nose and a cruel mouth topped with a mustache that was yellow from smoking. Tall and skinny with a slightly bent back, he even looked like a weasel.

"He'll be back," she was saying, watching the house. "It doesn't look like he took much. He left in a hurry."

They hadn't found anything incriminating either in the house or in the office. Then again, Swenson had passed the bar exam, presumably, at one point. He was probably smart enough not to keep a log of his illegal business with the Coyote.

Because life was never easy.

"You called to let him know that you were coming over," Jamie said. "He probably thought you were onto some of his dirty dealings. He panicked, ordered a hit then took off until the dust settles."

"I'm betting he's connected to the counterfeit money."

"And to the Coyote, too. Should have figured those two were linked." Why not? The Coyote ran human smuggling, guns and drugs. It made sense that he would have a hand in everything that was illegal and big business. He controlled a large area and a veritable army of criminals.

Not for long; Jamie's team always got their men.

"What if Swenson doesn't come back?" Bree asked.

The bastard had tried to have Bree killed, Jamie thought as he looked at her. He could never look at her without being a little dazzled. "Then I'm going to track him to the ends of the earth."

She shook her head at him. "You know, from anyone else that would sound like fake action-movie dialogue, but when you say it, I know you actually mean it."

He smiled at her. She got him. He liked that. He liked way too many things about her.

"He didn't go south," she said as she glanced at the abandoned house once again. "Border agents are watching for him. I put out an APB yesterday. He could be holed up somewhere else."

"He owns no other properties beyond this place. He

has no siblings. Mother and father dead. Never been married." Jamie had run the guy through the system as soon as he'd gotten back to the office the day before.

"He could be with friends," she said, then thought for a second before continuing. "Who does he trust?"

"A guy like that? Probably nobody. I wouldn't if I was in his place." If he was caught, the law was the least of his problems. He knew very well that the Coyote could reach people in prison, have them killed.

"He's lying low somewhere. We have a state-wide APB out on him and his car. Every cop in Texas is looking for him. I'm betting he knows that."

Jamie drummed his fingers on the steering wheel as he ran a couple of possibilities through his brain. "He represents criminals. Most of them are in prison. Which one of his clients has a place that stands empty?"

He pulled out his phone and called that in, talked to Mo on the other end. Mo and Keith were in the office, with access to information a regular sheriff's office could only dream of.

"I'll run some queries," Mo said. "I'll call you back when I have something."

"Thanks." Jamie put the phone down, trying to think what else they could be doing.

Bree shifted in her seat, turning to him. "When your top-secret mission is done here, will you all be leaving?"

"The office has been made permanent. The border needs to be monitored. CBP is set up for illegal immigration. Terror threats are a whole different level, and the problem is not going to go away in the foreseeable future. It needs different people with different training."

"I'm glad," she said. "That you and your team are

here. I wasn't at the beginning when I first found out about it."

They talked a little more about that, how times were changing. They kept watching the house, seeing no suspicious movement. Half an hour passed before Mo called back.

"I have an address for you. I found a couple of things, but I think our best chance is a remote farmhouse. One of Swenson's clients inherited it from his parents recently. The guy's sitting in federal prison. Swenson is trying to sell the place for him to cover legal expenses for an appeal."

"Thanks. We're heading over. I'll call in to let you know what we find when we get to the place." Jamie punched the address into the GPS and took off.

"You need backup?"

"Let's wait and see if he's even there. And I've got Bree."

"Thanks," she said as he hung up.

"For what?"

"For treating me as an equal partner."

He wasn't sure what to say as he flew down the road, heading for the highway.

"This way." She pointed in a different direction. "I know a dirt-road shortcut."

Which was why he looked at her as a partner. She knew what she was doing. Still, as much as he trusted and admired her skills, he did feel a sense of protectiveness at the thought of her going into danger.

Maybe he should have asked for that backup. "What if he's not alone? What if the men who pushed you off the road are with him?"

"I really hope so," she said as she checked her weapon, flashing the first scary smile he'd seen on her.

In another five minutes he reached the dirt road and turned onto it. His SUV bounced over the gravel. In a little while, they could see the abandoned farmhouse in the distance, surrounded by outbuildings. A red-and-blue For Sale sign greeted them from one of the front windows.

"Swenson's last stand," Bree said.

He scanned the ranch. "No cars."

"He'd be smart enough to pull his car into the barn. He knows we're looking for him. How close do we pull up?"

He could see tire tracks in the gravel driveway in front of them. Somebody had definitely been out this way lately. Of course, it could be anybody, even people who were looking to buy the place.

"We'll pull up all the way. I don't think he'd start shooting right away. He'll hope we think the place is abandoned and drive away. He's a lawyer, not a sharpshooter. He hires out his dirty business. He'll try to avoid a shootout with law enforcement if he can. He knows the odds are not on his side."

"So what's the plan?"

"We pull up, keeping in the cover of the car as we get out. If there's no attack, we'll walk around the outbuildings first." He slowed the car as they reached the end of the driveway, the gravel crunching under the tires.

"We'll make our way to the shed," she said. "That's closest to the end of the house. He might only have a small bathroom window there, or none. I'll stay somewhere visible from the front windows to distract him. You sneak up to the side."

"Exactly." Man, it was easy to work with her. She had a quick mind.

"How do I know when to come after you?"

You don't. You stay where it's safe, he wanted to tell her, but he knew her well enough to know that she wouldn't accept that. And he did trust her to handle herself.

"If things go well, if he's in there, I'll bring him out through the front door. If things go badly, you'll hear the shots." They were both wearing Kevlar vests.

"All right. Let's get him."

He stopped the car and pulled his weapon out, waited. Nobody shot at them. So far, so good. He opened his door. No movement in the house. He stepped to the ground but stayed behind the open door for a second as he scanned his surroundings. Still nothing. Then he stepped to the side and closed the car door.

He was out in the open.

If Swenson was in there and he was going to do something stupid, this was the time to do it. But nothing happened. Jamie nodded to Bree. She got out on the other side.

They both had their weapons ready as they moved forward, walking a few paces apart, ready to provide cover for each other. But all remained quiet as they passed by the house, checking it from the outside only, from a dozen or so yards away. The curtains didn't move, and there was no sign that anybody was watching them from inside, yet Jamie's instincts prickled.

They walked to the barn. Bree covered for him as he

stepped inside into dusty darkness. They listened. No sound or movement anywhere in the dim interior. They turned on their flashlights to see better and panned the cavernous area in front of them. The stalls stood abandoned, farm tools and moldy hay taking up most of the space.

The old, wooden ladder to the hayloft looked promising, but rickety, to say the least, leaning more than a little. Bree tested it then shimmied up, keeping her gun out. She weighed less than he did. Still, he stood ready to catch her should the ladder break under her.

She disappeared over the edge of the hayloft. The wooden floor creaked under her as she walked around, checking every corner, sending dust sifting down between the cracks of the floorboards.

"Nothing up here," she called down before reappearing at the edge and climbing back down with care.

They left the barn and checked out the rest of the outbuildings. No sign of cars, although the grain silo was definitely big enough to hold a vehicle. Or more than one. It had no windows to look inside, and the door stood padlocked.

They moved on to the shed, according to plan. This they found unlocked. They went inside together.

The light coming through the open door and small window was enough; they didn't need their flashlights here as they looked around. Old, rusty equipment took up most of the space; things were piled randomly and perilously on top of each other. Jamie popped open the small window in the back and climbed through. Bree walked back out to distract whoever was watching them.

Keeping low, Jamie rushed over to the side of the house—no windows on this side, so nobody would see him—then moved around to the back. He stopped under the first window there and inched up. He saw a sparsely furnished bedroom, but there no sign of anybody and nothing was out of place.

Disappointment tightened his jaw. Maybe they were wrong about the old farmhouse. Maybe Swenson had gone someplace else.

He snuck over to the next window—open a crack— and popped up to eye level. This bedroom was just as deserted as the first one, but clothes lay scattered on the bed here.

Bingo.

He wedged his fingers into the opening and pushed the window up inch by slow inch, then climbed inside without making a sound, careful with his boots on the old, hardwood floor. He registered the clothes: faded jeans and a light shirt. Could definitely be Swenson's.

A duffel bag had been half kicked under the bed. He edged it open with his gun carefully and found more clothes, a box of ammo, some pill bottles and a stack of twenties held together by a rubber band, several thousand dollars' worth.

Things were looking pretty good.

He left the bag where he found it and moved to the closed door. Voices filtered in from the other side, at least two men talking.

Okay. They had Swenson, but the man wasn't alone.

Jamie pulled out his cell phone and sent a quick text to Mo, asking for backup. A month ago, he would have gone in, waiting for nobody. But he no longer needed to push the envelope every single time just to prove something to himself.

Now he had Bree, and that changed things, too. And Bree had Katie. So, no, he didn't always have to do everything the hard way. The smart way was better.

He put his phone away and turned the knob silently, hoping to hear what the men were talking about while he waited for reinforcements. Whatever intel he gained would come in handy later, and could be used against the men in interrogation.

"Nobody saw our faces," someone said. "And we had the license plate covered with mud. Ain't nobody gonna recognize us, no way. I'm telling you, man."

There was a long pause, and then a different voice said, "I can't take any chances. I'm sorry."

Then a gunshot, and Jamie had to sprint forward, because he knew the gunshot would bring Bree running.

He burst into the living room to find Steven Swenson holding a gun while a man lay bleeding on the floor, looking pretty much dead.

As Jamie burst in, Swenson swung the gun toward him, his face startled, eyes wide. "Who the hell are you?"

"Put your weapon down! Customs and Border Protection," Jamie ordered.

Swenson's gaze darted back and forth, calculating. "Hey, man. I've been ambushed by a burglar. Clear case of self-defense. I'm an attorney. I'm not illegal."

"Put down your weapon."

Swenson hesitated, swallowing, measuring Jamie up, almost as if he was waiting for something.

What the hell was he waiting for? "Put down your weapon!"

Then the door banged open and another man came through, looking a lot like the one on the ground. They could have been brothers. The newcomer had Bree, one hand around her midsection, another holding a gun to her head.

As he took in the body on the floor, rage contorted his face. He yelled in Spanish, cursing Jamie and all his ancestors, assuming he'd been the one who'd fired the fatal shot.

"Calm down," Swenson advised, probably still thinking he could somehow come out of this clean if he only played his cards right. "Everybody calm down!" But he didn't sound too calm himself.

The guy with Bree didn't seem to be listening. His weapon hand was shaking as he swore at them all in Spanish.

The tension was escalating out of control, seconds from where it would hit conflict point.

And Jamie froze.

The bastard had Bree.

For a second, all he could think of was that family in the Afghan mountains. He couldn't save them. People on his team had called him a hero, but he hadn't been able to do anything heroic back with that family. He'd let them die. His fault.

And he blamed himself even more because nobody else wanted to blame him.

The only thing worse than being called a hero and put on a pedestal was being a failed hero.

And here he was again. The old darkness came back

all at once and hit him hard. The thought of another failure paralyzed him. Bree meant more to him than he'd admitted, even to himself. And she was a split second from a bullet.

She looked at him with nothing but trust in her eyes. And at long last, in her eyes, he found himself. Not the overly tough guy he played to avoid pity, not the scarred mess he hid from others, but something truer and better.

His mind cleared.

"Hey." He lifted his hands into the air, but hung on to his weapon. "Nobody needs to die here."

The man holding Bree kept swearing, crying now, but Swenson looked interested. He shifted his weapon to his buddy. "You let her go."

As soon as Bree was free, he would shoot the guy, Jamie was pretty sure. Then there'd be no one to point a finger at him. Jimenez was gone, either lying low someplace or dead. Swenson would have nobody to testify against him.

"Everybody, put down your weapon," Jamie said in his best field-commander voice. "Let the deputy sheriff go." He shifted so he'd have a better angle on the guy who held Bree. She was not going to get hurt here, dammit.

"I have the right to defend myself in a home invasion," Swenson yelled.

His goon flashed a confused look at him. Swenson tightened his finger on the trigger.

He was going to go for it. And since he wasn't a professional, chances were pretty good he'd hit Bree by accident.

Jamie had to act first.

If he shot Swenson, the other guy would be startled and might pull the trigger on Bree. Which meant Jamie had to take him out now.

Straight in the middle of the forehead was his only option, or he might twitch and squeeze the trigger before he died.

One, two, three. He held his breath, so even that wouldn't interfere with his aim, brought his hand and weapon down and shot at the bastard.

Unfortunately, Bree, having correctly read Swenson's intentions to make a move, did some self-defense maneuver at the same moment. She jerked forward with a sharp cry then dropped herself to the ground, which jostled the man as he grabbed for her, so Jamie's shot went into his shoulder.

The man shot at him as Bree rolled away behind the cover of an ancient recliner, even as Swenson shot at his own guy.

Jamie ducked behind the couch, hitting the lawyer in the arm on his way down. He couldn't go for a kill shot. They needed information from the bastard, dammit. He pulled his backup weapon from his boot and popped up long enough to throw it toward Bree, then flattened to the floor as a hail of bullets came at him.

Bree must have caught the gun because the next thing he heard was her yelling, "Freeze! Pebble Creek P.D. Drop your weapons!"

Jamie came up for another shot at Swenson just as the young gangbanger squeezed a shot off at Bree. Dammit, it was like the O.K. Corral in there. She shot back, springing up, but got hit, the bullet knocking her on her back.

Something snapped inside Jamie.

"Drop your weapons! Drop your weapons!" He rushed forward, yelling at Swenson. He was ready to put a hole in his head if he threatened Bree in any way.

The gangbanger was dead, he registered, lying in blood next to the other one. Bree had gotten him even as he'd gotten her.

Swenson shot at Jamie, missed, and then Jamie was vaulting on top of him, bringing him down, smacking him hard to make him go still.

"Bree?" he called back as he disarmed the man, flipped him, then handcuffed him.

"Bree?" He could turn back at last.

She was still on her back. His heart stopped.

But then she moved and sat up slowly. "That hurts."

And he could breathe again.

She was shaking her head and rubbing her chest through the Kevlar that had protected her.

"Man, I hate this part. It's going to leave a bruise, I know it."

He went over to her and helped her up. "Are you okay?"

"I'm fine. Let's finish this." She strode straight to Swenson.

"You have the right to remain silent." She read him his rights while Jamie went to check on the bodies, checking pulses to make sure the men were as dead as they appeared.

Bree was back in cop mode, calm and matter-of-fact, pulling the lawyer to his feet, efficient as always while Swenson whined about the bullet that had gone through his arm, tossing out words like "police brutality" and "liability" and "legal protection."

She didn't let him rattle her one bit.

Man, she was hot in action.

Jamie wanted her. And it wasn't just the adrenaline rush.

He wanted her forever.

"All right," she said. "Let's take him back to the station."

He straightened. "Sorry. My team will want to talk to him first."

She narrowed her beautiful eyes at him, then relaxed her stance and gave a blinding smile that had his heart beating double. "I'm sure you agree—"

"Don't even try the sweet-talk thing. It's a matter of national security." Four SUVs tore down the driveway as he said that, all belonging to his team. He hoped they impressed his point on her.

"Fine." She didn't look happy, but she handed Swenson over. "I can be reasonable. How about we share him?"

"Make you a deal. You can have him when we're done with him."

She was still smiling at him. "We make a good team."

Yes, they did. They were good together in every way. He needed to think about that instead of running away from it. But not now.

Mo, Ryder, Keith and Shep were jumping out of their cars and came running.

Chapter Fifteen

"I want the Coyote," Jamie told the man in the interrogation room.

The small space was hot, the air-conditioning cutting out from time to time. Swenson was sweating.

He had been protesting up a storm, demanding his rights and barely taking a breath. "I'm injured. I need more first aid than your idiot buddies handed out. This is the United States of America, not a third-world country. Who the hell are you, anyway? I'm going to be suing every single one of you for this unbelievable treatment. Count on it. You're going to answer for this."

He claimed he didn't know the two hit men at the farm. They were intruders, he'd said. He insisted that any shots fired by him had been fired in self-defense. If any bullets had come near Bree or Jamie from his gun, that was by accident. He was scared and he wasn't good with weapons.

"When are you going to let me go?" he demanded.

Jamie shook his head. "This is how it goes. I'm asking the questions here." He said the words slowly so Swenson would understand. "We'll stay right here, in this room, until you give me what I need. It's as simple as that."

"I have rights. I know the law. I want a lawyer." Swenson shot him another outraged look. He had quite a repertoire. He could have made a career on the stage. His acting ability had probably come in handy in the courtroom in the past, but was gaining him nothing here. He stomped his feet as he said, "I have the right to know what I'm being charged with."

Jamie drew his lungs full and let him have it. "Aiding and abetting terrorists."

That shut the idiot up.

He paled a shade. A moment passed before he fully recovered. "You're all crazy. I want my lawyer. I demand legal representation. That is my right as an American citizen."

"You'll find the procedures are different for a terror suspect. What do you know about the Coyote? When was the last time you saw him?"

Swenson shot to his feet. "We live under the rule of law in this country. I have rights." Apparently, he still didn't understand the kind of trouble he was in.

"Too bad you didn't remember those laws when you were breaking them."

"Do you understand who I am? I'm a prominent attorney in this county. I have friends who are judges and politicians."

Jamie stood, too, running out of patience. "Do you understand how little I care? Do you know how many good men I've seen ripped to pieces overseas by our foreign enemies? And then here you are, an American, and you're betraying your country? Want to know how I feel about that?"

He braced his hands on the table and leaned forward, his voice cold as he said, "I'm not a great fan of traitors. So here are your choices. Do you want to leave here alive or in a body bag?"

That got through to the man at last. His shoulders dipped, his words losing that tone of outraged superiority as he dropped back onto his chair. "I have no idea what you're talking about. I don't know anything about terrorists. I swear."

"Yet you work for a man who's setting up an operation to smuggle terrorists into the country. How far are you involved with the Coyote?"

More sweat beaded on Swenson's forehead.

"Look," Jamie told him. "This is about the last chance you have to be smart here. You don't want to further align yourself with him by protecting him."

The man swallowed hard and wiped his forehead with the back of his hand. The indignation on his face was replaced by worry lines and fear.

"All I know about is the counterfeit money. I swear. I didn't have a choice. When someone like that sends you a message that he wants your help, you help," he rushed to say, eager to speak now. "I want a plea bargain. I tell you about the money, you drop any charges that have to do with terrorism. There's no way you're going to pin that on me. No way."

He jumped up, but immediately sat back down again. "I want to cut a deal."

Jamie flashed him a dispassionate look. "I think you're under the mistaken impression that we're negotiating here. I want to know everything you know about the Coyote. Let's start with his real name."

"I don't know. I really don't."

"Where does he live?"

"I don't know."

"Here is a hint. You'll fare a lot better if you prove yourself useful to us. So let's try again. What do you know about the Coyote?"

The man stared at him, his entire body tight with tension, desperation in his eyes. "He tells me what he needs through messengers who come then disappear."

Jamie waited. "Solitary confinement," he said after a minute.

"What?"

"You give me that bastard and I'll arrange that you don't go into the general prison population." Meaning he might have a chance to survive the first week.

Swenson stared at him. Shook his head, but then almost immediately said, "Okay. Solitary confinement." He drew a deep breath. "I know where he'll be Monday morning. He needed to have something done. Medical. I hooked him up with a doctor friend who doesn't always keep patient records."

Somebody who was willing to take bullets out of criminals and gangbangers, most likely. What did the Coyote want with him? With the kind of money he had, he could have afforded the most expensive Swiss clinics. But the *why* wasn't as important as the fact that they finally had a straight link to the bastard.

Two days from now.

With enough information, they could set up an op to

grab him. They would have enough time to make him talk, enough time to set up a trap for those terrorists.

For the first time in a long time, Jamie relaxed a little. The lack of progress over the past couple of weeks had gotten to them all. But now they had some actionable intelligence, finally. "Start talking."

This was it. They'd finally caught a break, and they were ready for it.

BREE LOOKED UP as Jamie walked through the door at dinnertime. He looked about as happy as she'd ever seen him. He wore blue jeans, a black T-shirt and his ever-present combat boots that she'd learned were fitted to his prosthetics to provide him with extra stability. He'd left his cowboy hat in his car. He was carrying a shoe-box full of cookies.

"You bake?"

"Very funny. It was a gift."

"From a woman?" She hated the jealousy that bit right into her.

"I sent a young couple into the witness protection program today. She was grateful, that's all."

Just as long as they weren't going to see each other again. She took the box he offered and set it on the counter. They looked great—a bunch of different Mexican fiesta sweets.

"Any progress with Swenson?" she asked. "I want him when you're done with him."

"That won't be for a while yet. He's talking." He watched her for a second as if wanting to say more, but then he didn't.

Fine. She knew what kind of work he did. He'd never

be able to share everything with her. She was okay with that. She understood it.

"We found the van that pushed your car into the reservoir," he said. "DNA evidence will link it to the two goons Swenson had at the farmhouse with him, I'm pretty sure. Ballistics already linked one of their guns to the bullet that killed Eleanor. Jason Tanner wasn't lying about not being the one who shot through your window."

She stared at him, various emotions mixing inside her. Jason's parents were in town and had made an appointment with her for tomorrow. At least she didn't have to tell them that their son was a killer. The family had suffered enough already, so she was happy for that.

Jason needed meds and to be in a facility where his movements were monitored. Mental illness wasn't a crime. He needed the kind of help he wouldn't be able to get in prison.

"So the men who shot Eleanor are dead. How do you feel about that?" Jamie asked, watching her.

"Good." While Jason had her sympathy, those two killers definitely didn't. They'd known what they were doing. They'd gone after her to stop her from investigating the counterfeit money business.

Jamie nodded, then looked around, up the stairs. "Where's Katie?"

"Over at Sharon's house for a sleepover. It's Sharon's birthday. Katie is not big on sleepovers, but she wanted to try. If I get a call in the middle of the night, so be it. I want her to have as many normal experiences as possible."

"She'll do fine. She's a sweet girl," he said. "How was your day?"

"All party and cakes. Mike had his retirement shindig."

"Liked his fishing pole?"

"You bet. I thought he might sneak out of the party to go and try it. It'll keep him out of Bertha's hair." Bertha was nearly as excited about the pole as Mike. She grinned.

Talking to Jamie like this felt nice: sharing their day, just being together without being in mortal danger.

He was standing in front of the living room window, which had finally been fixed, the late-day sunlight outlining his body—tall and wide shouldered. The man was pretty impressive, prosthetics or no prosthetics.

"A hero returning from the day's business." She said out loud the words she was thinking.

But instead of taking the compliment in the spirit in which it was offered, he frowned. "What are you talking about? I'm nobody's hero."

"You're mine. And I'm sure there are plenty of other people who feel the same."

"You don't know anything about my past."

"I know you've seen hard times. I know you risked your life for others."

"People died because of me."

"They shouldn't have plotted to attack our country."

He shook his head, a haunted expression coming over his face. "Innocent people."

"It wasn't your fault." She believed that with everything she was. He was good to the core, and honest and honorable.

"A whole family," he said. And then he told her a story that made her heart bleed and had her blinking back tears.

"The bastards went slow, made them scream. For days. And they would stop, they told me, if I gave them the location of my unit."

"They wouldn't have," she told him.

"I know. They meant to kill them from the beginning, to teach the rest of the village a lesson. And yet, I—"

"You couldn't have done anything to make a difference. If you'd given up information, more people would have died."

He rubbed a thumb over his eyebrow. "Sure, that sounds all reasonable and logical. Except in the middle of the night when I'm startled awake because I'm hearing their screams." He shoved his hands into his pockets. "I never told that to anyone before, not even the shrink at Walter Reed," he finished, and stood aloof, as if not sure how she would react.

She wanted to rush into his arms, but she wasn't sure if he would want it. Last time they talked about things between them, each had been adamant that there could be no relationship, nothing beyond the professional. Yet it was too late. They were friends, at the very least.

And more. If she said she felt nothing beyond friendship, she would be lying. "I wasn't sure you'd come."

He raised an eyebrow.

"Tanner is in jail. You have Swenson. His goons are dead. I no longer need a bodyguard."

"You never really needed one. I know you can handle pretty much everything yourself."

She narrowed her eyes. "Who are you, and what have you done with the real Jamie?"

He smiled. "I kept coming because I like being here with you."

Her heart rate picked up.

He looked at her, turning stone serious in a split second. "Do you want me to leave?"

Her heart sank. "Do you want to leave?" Then she laughed out loud. "I can't believe I just asked that. Could I sound more like a high school girl?"

The smile came back onto his handsome face. "I definitely don't want to leave."

"Good." She drew a deep breath. "Not that I have the faintest idea what we're doing here."

"We're having a relationship."

They were? "I didn't want a relationship."

"Me, neither. But I stand my ground even when I'm scared. Not that I'm scared. I'm just saying, in case you are."

"Really? You're going to play the 'who's chicken' card? Now who sounds like a high school kid? Where's the mucho-macho stuff?"

He came closer, caught her by the waist. He wiggled his eyebrows. "I can show you my manly ways. If you'd like."

"So you want me to ask for it? You think you're so hot you can make me beg? That's what you really want, isn't it?" she teased him, giddy with happiness that he was here and she was in his arms, that they had a whole night in front of them.

His gaze focused on her mouth. "I just want to stop

you talking so I can kiss you," he said as his lips descended on hers.

He kissed so good. So unfair. How was she supposed to think and come back with some snappy response? Her knees were going weak; her brain was getting rapidly scrambled as he tasted the seam of her lips then teased his way inside, claiming her mouth fully.

She melted into his arms. There were times to be tough deputy chick, but this wasn't it. Her entire body tingled. She felt so incredibly good. Giddy, happy. She wanted this. She wanted him. She wanted more with every passing second.

When she was past all reason, he pulled back. Just enough to look into her face. He kept his strong arms around her waist.

His intense gaze held hers. "Why don't you want a relationship?"

"Oh, sure," she said weakly. "Ask questions when I can't think."

"I thought about it on the way over. I don't want this just to be a casual thing."

Nothing about Jamie Cassidy was casual.

"It's that..." she started to say, then stopped to figure out how to word it. "I'm pretty busy with work on the average day. And now we have sheriff's elections. Katie doesn't like change. If I ever got seriously involved with someone, I picture it as someone with a steady schedule and a stable job." She drew a deep breath. "Someone who might take care of Katie if something happens to me in the line of duty."

His arms tightened around her, his voice rough as

he said, "Nothing's going to happen to you. That's an order. Do you understand?"

"You're not the boss of me."

His eyes narrowed.

She narrowed her own right back. "Your job is more dangerous than mine. As little as I know about it, I figured that much out. So if I can put up worrying about you all day, you can put up with worrying about me."

"Fine," he said, not looking the least bit pleased. "I care for Katie. I don't think she minds me. I would do anything to protect her. You know that."

She supposed she did, but hearing the words still made her feel better. "I've never seen her warm to someone as fast as she warmed to you. She has this sixth sense to know instinctually who's a good person. That's a big point in your favor. Among others."

He brightened at that. "There are others? What are they?"

She tried to pull away. He wouldn't let her.

Oh, for heaven's sake. "You do a fair job at kissing," she admitted reluctantly.

He pulled himself to full height. "Fair?" And then he dipped his head to hers and stole her breath away.

By the time he pulled back again, she would have admitted to being the tooth fairy, let alone that he was a good kisser. She probably looked fairly bamboozled, because he had a pretty proud look on his face.

"You're not bad yourself." He winked at her. "We'll figure the relationship thing out. I would do anything for you and Katie. You know that, right?"

This was the man who'd carried wounded teammates

out of a war zone until he bled out to the point where he could no longer stand. Yeah, she believed him.

"Why?" she asked anyway.

"Because I'm falling for you." He held her gaze. "And I play for keeps. So let that be a warning."

Okay, he'd certainly laid his cards on the table. Warmth spread through her. Her heart seemed to swell in her chest.

"My life is never easy. Katie will always have to come first. I'm all she has. I'm responsible for her. You might not realize what you're taking on."

"I'll be around. I can promise that much. I'm permanently stationed on the border. But life is never a cakewalk. Mine has its own glitches."

Yes, it did. She so didn't care. She wanted him. So she reached up and, bold as you please, pulled his head back down to hers.

This kiss was softer, deeper, even more spine-tingling than the last, a confirmation of what they were feeling for each other.

He picked her up and her legs wrapped around his waist, his hardness pressing into her. He carried her toward the stairs, but she ran her hands up under his shirt as she hung on to him and they didn't make it.

He ended up pressing her against the wall in the hallway.

Heat suffused her as he rocked against her.

"Take off your shirt," he demanded.

She did.

He trailed kisses down her neck, to her collarbone, down into the valley of her breasts.

A moan escaped her throat.

"Yeah," he said, and brought up his hands to push her bra down, holding her against the wall with his pelvis.

Then his lips were on her nipple that was so hard, it ached. For him. And he did this thing with the tip of his tongue, a rapid back and forth movement that took her breath away. That was before he suddenly enveloped the nipple in the wet heat of his mouth and sucked gently. Pleasure exploded through her body.

She hung on to his shoulders for dear life.

Her entire body begged for him. She ground against him and he ground back, the need at her core intensifying to an unbearable level.

"We're not going to make it to the bedroom," he said in an apologetic, raspy whisper as he switched to the other nipple.

By that time, she could barely even remember that the house had another floor.

He teased her and suckled her until she was cross-eyed with need, tearing impatiently at his shirt, then at his belt buckle.

He slid her to the ground, but only until they had both stripped out of their clothing—in frenetic, jerky movements, working zippers with one hand, still reaching to touch each other with the other, their lips barely separating. Sweet mackerels, he was gorgeous.

He produced a small foil wrapper from somewhere and stumbled with it as he opened it without looking.

His body was carved from granite, every muscle perfect, and he had a lot of them. She wanted to touch him and never stop, her hands moving from his chest to his rock-solid abdomen and buttocks.

She couldn't help herself. Fine, she didn't *want* to help herself. She squeezed.

He groaned and lifted her again, up against the wall. She wrapped her legs around his waist, his hardness pushing deep inside her, stretching her, caressing her from the inside, filling her completely.

"Oh, wow," she said, barely able to catch her breath.

"You can say that again."

She simply moaned, because he began to move inside her and she was suddenly beyond speech.

The sex was amazing. He was amazing. Pleasure raked her body. She wanted to touch every inch of his skin and she wanted him to touch hers. She wanted his lips on hers and she wanted to never stop kissing.

Oh.

The man knew how to move.

Wave after wave of pleasure began where they were joined, then rippled through her body. Then the pleasure reached a crest and washed over her completely, her body contracting around him as she called out his name.

He stilled, held her, kissed her, caressed her.

She'd barely come back down to earth when he started up again, a steady rhythm at first, then gathering speed.

She was utterly spent. "Jamie?" She couldn't take more of this.

Or could she?

Okay, she could, she realized as delicious tension coiled inside her all over again.

Then she remembered how long he'd been holding her up like this, how long he'd been supporting her weight. Did that feel uncomfortable for him? Was it hurting him?

"Do you need a—" Her breath caught and she couldn't finish.

But he somehow knew what she'd been about to say. "My legs never get tired," he said, and grinned. Then he pushed deeper into her, sending her body soaring all over again.

Later, when they were spent and both still breathing hard, she slipped her feet to the ground, and they leaned against each other, supporting each other, holding each other up.

"I want to say something."

"Okay." She pulled back so she could look into his eyes.

"You're the light of my life." He gathered her close against him. "I love you, Bree Tridle."

"I love you, too. But don't let it go to your head and get all protective. I'll still be deputy sheriff, even if I'm your girlfriend. So no putting on bossypants."

He laughed out loud before he kissed her. "No, ma'am."

* * * * *

Don't miss the exciting conclusion of HQ: TEXAS,
by award-winning author Dana Marton,
when SPY IN THE SADDLE
goes on sale next month.
Look for it wherever Mills & Boon® Intrigue books
are sold!

A sneaky peek at next month...

INTRIGUE...

BREATHTAKING ROMANTIC SUSPENSE

My wish list for next month's titles...

In stores from 18th October 2013:

❑ Christmas at Cardwell Ranch – BJ Daniels

& Would-Be Christmas Wedding – Debra Webb

❑ Renegade Guardian – Delores Fossen

& Catch, Release – Carol Ericson

❑ Scene of the Crime: Return to Bachelor Moon
   – Carla Cassidy

& Spy in the Saddle – Dana Marton

Romantic Suspense

❑ The Colton Heir – Colleen Thompson

Available at WHSmith, Tesco, Asda, Eason, Amazon and Apple

Just can't wait?

Special Offers

Every month we put together collections and longer reads written by your favourite authors.

Here are some of next month's highlights— and don't miss our fabulous discount online!

On sale 1st November   On sale 1st November   On sale 18th October

Save 20%
on all Special Releases